Let The Truth Be Told

A Novel by Sonny Hudson

authorHOUSE®

AuthorHouse™
1663 Liberty Drive, Suite 200
Bloomington, IN 47403
www.authorhouse.com
Phone: 1-800-839-8640

© 2008 Sonny Hudson. All rights reserved.

No part of this book may be reproduced, stored in a retrieval system, or transmitted by any means without the written permission of the author.

First published by AuthorHouse 1/17/2008

ISBN: 978-1-4343-5339-9 (sc)
ISBN: 978-1-4343-5340-5 (hc)

Library of Congress Control Number: 2007909981

Printed in the United States of America
Bloomington, Indiana

This book is printed on acid-free paper.

In a time of universal deceit, telling the truth becomes a revolutionary act.
George Orwell

Prologue

October 25, 2001

FRED ABRAHAM WAS TROUBLED. As the CFO for Daniels Robotics Corporation (DRC), a defense contractor based in Arlington, VA, it was his job to ensure that all of the financial reports were in order. He'd gone over all of the paperwork several times and things just weren't adding up. In all of his years as CFO he had never had any problems reconciling all of the company's accounts and receivables, but this time he couldn't account for $25 million dollars. While $25 million was barely a rounding error to a company with annual revenues of $15 billion, it was his job to make sure that everything was balanced to the penny as he did the end of the year reports. Like many government contractors, DRC followed the federal government's fiscal year schedule, so fiscal year 2001 had just ended as of September 30. Even though DRC was a privately held company, they still produced an annual report that was certified by the President and CEO, Richard Newcomb, and forwarded to their Board of Directors. Newcomb had founded DRC and built it into a defense contracting juggernaut, and as the majority stockholder he had enormous wealth and power. *Forbes* had estimated his net worth at upwards of $15 billion dollars in their most recent list of America's wealthiest people. While that was a reasonable estimation of his financial worth, it mattered little to Richard Newcomb and men like him. In the hyper-competitive world of Washington, DC, and in defense contracting in particular, what really matters is power, influence, access, and political connections. Judged by these measures, Richard Newcomb was without peer.

Abraham called Newcomb and asked to meet with him regarding some anomalies in the financials. Newcomb agreed to meet at 4:30pm after he was finished with some other meetings and calls. At precisely 4:30 Abraham stuck his head into Newcomb's office. "Richard, you clear to meet now?"

"Sure, come on in. What's on your mind? You mentioned some anomalies while you were working on the end of year statements?" Newcomb didn't seem overly concerned. Even this late in the day he still looked calm, cool, and collected despite his hectic schedule. He was usually seen in expensive, custom-made Italian suits and shoes, custom-made shirts with French cuffs, and impeccably groomed. Today was no exception. The guy had the brains of a successful CEO and the looks of a gracefully aging movie star. Twice married and divorced, he was considered one of the most eligible bachelors in DC and was never lacking for female companionship.

"Yeah, I guess you could call it an anomaly. Everything is in order, all the revenues and expenses are matched, all of the bank statements and investment accounts, everything. I'm actually ahead of schedule in getting the final 2001 statement together, except I can't figure out where we're missing $25 million. One of our accounts, based in the Caymans, is coming up short. I know that we sometimes use some of the offshore accounts for payments to PAC's that we support, or for payments to subcontractors in other countries when they have to pay a little extra 'gratuity' to have the so-called government officials act more cooperatively, but I'm not finding any paper trail to support any of the usual expenditures." Abraham knew that these types of payments were often outside of the letter or spirit of US laws, but sometimes that was just the cost of doing business in our global economy. He didn't care for doing business that way, but he knew how the game was played, and if that's how Newcomb chose to run his company he didn't have a real issue with it. After all, Newcomb and DRC had been very, very good to him over the past 10 years.

"Only $25 million? Oh, thank God, I thought maybe we had a serious problem on our hands," Newcomb said as he flashed a big smile. "That sounds familiar. Hold on one second, I think I have some information on that transaction here in one of my files."

"That would be great if you do, sir."

Newcomb fumbled through a file in his desk drawer for a moment and then produced a document from the folder. "We're in luck. Last April, I had the Caymans bank transfer $25 million to establish a new account with a bank in Yemen. Some of our contractors over in the Middle East were complaining about pressure from some of the locals because DRC wasn't making any 'investments' in their economy. By establishing that investment account there it's allowing us to show our goodwill towards some of the local tribes, and their bank has additional cash readily available that they can loan to some less than creditworthy individuals. At interest rates that would make an American loan shark blush, I might add." Newcomb had concocted this little story more than six months ago, and now he watched Abraham's reaction to see if he accepted it.

Abraham took just a few seconds to process what he'd heard. "That's great. I figured there was a simple explanation. If I can have a copy of that transfer I can close this little chapter out and have the 2001 financials on your desk for signature by the close of business this week." He didn't really care at this point about the legality or morality of the money transfer, just so he had the documented paper trail to allow him to complete his work. Abraham stood up and extended his hand to Newcomb. "I appreciate you taking the time to fit me in on short notice."

"No problem at all. I appreciate your thoroughness and eye towards detail." Newcomb shook his hand and walked Abraham to the door. "You have a nice evening, and I'm sure we'll be talking over the next few days. Let me know if anything else pops up that you have questions about."

Newcomb knew that this day was inevitable. Fortunately, he had documentation that could pass muster with any CFO or outside auditor. Still, he'd rather not have any of this made public or shared with the board; even though they were a privately held company and not subject to all of the rules and oversight of public corporations, he couldn't afford to take any chances. Particularly since virtually 100% of their business was done with the federal government. No, you could never be sure that some future event wouldn't have you opening your books in front of some congressional committee. Much better, he thought, to make sure that no record of this wire transfer ever makes its way into the 2001 financial statements.

Newcomb closed his door and sat back down at his desk. He reached into the third drawer on the right hand side and lifted a false bottom to retrieve a cell phone. The phone was specially modified to carry encrypted voice traffic; nobody trying to monitor would be able to hear anything but white noise.

Only people with similarly modified phones would be able to converse with Newcomb, and in this case there were fewer than a dozen of these phones in existence. He punched in a private number from memory.

A voice on the other end answered. "Foster."

"This is Newcomb. Are you secure and able to talk?"

"Yes, I'm in my car on the Dulles Toll Road heading towards Reston."

"We have a situation. The $25 million problem has finally come up."

"As we expected it would. Is it time to implement the contingency plan?"

"Yes, I'm afraid so. I'll have my CFO finish the 2001 statements with the paperwork your team provided, and after he and I both sign off on the report I'll simply substitute some forged documentation from the Caymans bank showing that the money is still there."

Foster said, "Then we'll need to take steps to eliminate your CFO immediately after that to close the loop."

"Unfortunately, yes," replied Newcomb. "Not something that I want to do, but it's definitely a necessary step. We can't afford the loose end, especially since he'll be using that 2001 report throughout the next year when briefing analysts, the board, etc. I need your team to take care of him, but please make sure that it looks like natural causes, or maybe a simple accident. We don't need to have any cause for an investigation, plus I want to be able to ensure that his wife and family are well taken care of without any bureaucratic delays."

"Not to worry. We can certainly accommodate you on that. I'll have one of my men ready to move as soon as you give the word. I assume that will be within the next week or so?"

"Yes, probably anytime after close of business this Friday. Actually, the sooner the better after he and I sign off on these reports. Sorry to have to ask you to do this so soon after launching the new company."

Foster spoke. "Not a problem. I still have many of my old resources from my days at NSA. Consider it done. I'll just wait for your call." With that, Foster hung up.

By Friday night, as expected, the 2001 financial statements were concluded and signed off. Newcomb invited Abraham out for a celebratory drink and dinner at one of his favorite area restaurants just a few miles down Shirley Highway/I-395 in the Shirlington section of Arlington. They enjoyed a great meal of Chateaubriand accompanied by a stellar bottle of 2003 Plumpjack Cabernet, and Newcomb realized that he was really going to miss Abraham. He genuinely liked him and enjoyed his company. As they were finishing their meal Newcomb excused himself to use the restroom while the waitress came to clear their plates. He asked the waitress to bring them each one more glass of wine.

As the glasses of wine were delivered Newcomb handed the waitress his credit card for the meal. When she returned with his card and the receipt he filled it out, leaving her a very generous tip. He always did for the especially attractive ones, and this girl was way beyond attractive. She had to be nearly six feet tall, with blonde hair, deep emerald colored eyes, and a body that made his mouth water. For someone like her a $250 tip really didn't seem excessive, especially if there was any chance that flashing his money around might get him her phone number. As he and Abraham stood to leave he saw a look of growing panic and fear in the CFO's eyes. His face was red and he was starting to sweat profusely. Before Abraham could utter a word, and before Newcomb could do anything to try to help him, Abraham fell to the floor, taking the table and everything on it down with him. He clutched his chest and fought to catch his breath, the look on his face betraying the terror he was feeling as a massive heart attack quickly, and painfully, drained the life from his body. Newcomb tried loosening his tie, tried talking to him to keep him calm. He yelled for someone to call 911, even as he looked down at his friend and saw his eyes grow wide and his body go limp. If the paramedics had been sitting at the next table they wouldn't have been able to save him from such a severe heart attack. As it was, with the ambulance taking more than ten minutes to reach the restaurant in the heavy DC-area traffic on this Friday evening, Abraham didn't have a prayer.

Newcomb was shocked beyond belief. He knew that Foster's people had planned to silence Abraham, but he'd had no idea where or when, only that it would be soon. This couldn't be coincidence; it had to be the work of Foster's operatives. When the ambulance finally took Abraham away the EMT's knew that there was no need to hurry. Their passenger was dead at the scene. The coroner would perform an autopsy since the death occurred outside of a hospital or a doctor's care, but there was no need to rush. It would be several days before he'd get to it since this was a weekend and, to all appearances, not much of a mystery.

With no reason to suspect foul play, the coroner would not begin to look beyond a simple heart attack, never even consider the possibility of poisoning. Foster was a master of spy craft, and he'd had a hand in many assassinations over the years, though never as the actual assassin. Always as the planner, the man behind the curtain pulling the strings. The drug that was used to induce Abraham's heart attack, a powerful paralyzing drug called Succynocholine, was virtually undetectable, especially if the autopsy was more than 12-24 hours after the person died. When the coroner took a look at the body before him he would see a man that could be a poster child for all of the risk factors for a major myocardial infarction. Abraham was fifty-two years old, at least seventy-five pounds overweight, cholesterol and triglycerides that were off the charts, and he was a serious Type A personality in a stress-filled job. Lucky he lived as long as he did. Case closed.

All of which worked perfectly into Foster's plan, which, as always, had worked flawlessly. His operative would be leaving the country tomorrow for a well-deserved vacation, her career as a waitress beginning and ending on the same day. Jennifer had proven herself once again to be an indispensable member of his team, and whether she was introducing herself as Samantha, Heidi, Angela, or one of her other many aliases, she always got the job done. Men see her and think only of her beauty and her sexuality, never perceiving her as a threat. Mistake. *Big mistake.*

March 23, 2004

DR. LARRY M. SILVERSTEIN, A PhD in Economics, was a tenured professor at the College of William and Mary. 36 years old, single, with few friends, he lived alone in an apartment not far from campus, just a block from the restored historic area of Colonial Williamsburg. Even in the heady atmosphere of academia Larry Silverstein was a bit of a misfit. While brilliant in the eyes of both his students and his faculty peers, he was utterly lacking in social skills, whether in a one-on-one meeting or a group interaction. And as one would expect, his lack of social skills, coupled with his dry demeanor and even drier sense of humor, made his classes far from popular on campus.

While considered a bit wacky or eccentric by those who knew him, he was not the type of person to go around espousing crazy conspiracy theories. He was a serious academic and a man with very refined taste in literature, art, and music. His apartment, though modest, had an enviable collection of rare and first edition books, original oil paintings by some of the masters of the 20th century, and a CD collection that would be the envy of many opera, classical, and jazz buffs. Yet, he had found himself becoming more and more consumed by the conspiracy theories surrounding 9/11. He was a voracious reader and spent hours, every day, poring through document after document, website after website, trying to unravel the mysteries behind that unconscionable event. Fully aware that others considered him a bit odd and that the wrong kind of attention could cause embarrassment to the school, to say nothing of endangering his own standing and reputation there -- tenure be damned -- Dr. Silverstein was not about to add to that reputation by voicing his concerns in public, at least not until there was concrete proof to back up his theories. He only wished that he had one true friend, one close confidant, that he could share his thoughts and theories with, someone to listen to him and challenge him and make him consider other points of view. That's what friends do. That's what spouses do. He had neither, and the realization had lately left him feeling lonelier than he could ever recall.

His research led him down many alleys, mostly with dead ends. Then in early 2004 he stumbled on some information that unnerved him, but he wasn't exactly sure why. It was more of a feeling than anything concrete, but the more he tried to ignore his uneasiness the more he was drawn back to it. He had decided to try to correlate the revenue and earnings of the top defense industry contractors with their involvement in Afghanistan and Iraq, and then track that back against any unusual events at those companies that may have occurred within a two year period before and after 9/11. As expected, there were tons of companies in the defense industry that were seeing huge jumps in revenue and earnings since the onset of the Afghanistan and Iraq invasions. Nothing really unusual there; obviously defense contractors sell more weapons and make more money when the country is either at war or gearing up for war. What caught his eye were the deaths of a few executives within months of 9/11, including the CFO from Daniels Robotics, the President of Banning Technologies, and the VP of Advanced Technologies for Adams & Scott. Two men and one woman, all between the ages of 45-52. All dead from massive heart attacks. All dead within three months of 9/11. Silverstein felt a chill every time he went back over these documents. Is there a statistical probability that this could happen, or is this more than a coincidence? Sure, three middle-aged people in high-powered, high-stress positions dying is not that unusual, but in that short a period of time? And all of them executives with large defense contractors that are making billions of dollars off of the War on Terror, and, by extension, the events of 9/11? That required just too much of a leap of faith for him, and one thing he wasn't was a man of faith.

Silverstein was a careful and methodical researcher and wasn't about to call any attention to his theory without checking things out a lot more thoroughly. He spent virtually every night for the next two weeks checking and rechecking every site, every document, every blog that he could find. He still didn't feel that he had things 100% corroborated and verified, but he was growing increasingly excited and anxious about his theory. He certainly had not found anything that made him think that he was on the *wrong* track, and after all the rigorous investigation he had done, to say nothing of the high standards to which he held himself when performing research, that was significant.

At the end of a particularly long week, what with his class schedule and long hours spent doing research, Larry decided to take a break from working on Friday night and get back to his usual weekly routine. He did a little bit of laundry while watching the 6 o'clock news, then he headed down to the Green Leafe Café, a long-time locals hangout across the street from the William & Mary campus and stadium. He liked their food and their huge selection of regional and microbrew beers. More than anything, though, he liked hanging out here because it gave him a sense of belonging, a sense that he wasn't alone. Not that any of the staff or the patrons paid him much mind beyond the usual pleasantries, but to him it was the closest he usually got to human contact outside of his classes. He ordered a mug of Boddington's Pub Ale from England while he looked over the menu. When the waitress came he decided to stay with the English theme and ordered fish & chips and a side salad. As was his habit, he brought a paperback book with him and spent his time going back and forth between the book and the TV over the bar. The place was pretty full, and as he looked around he recognized many of the regulars. Sitting at the bar was someone that was decidedly *not* a regular; no way would he, or any man, have missed her. Tall, with flowing red hair. Incredibly long, gorgeous legs that totally captivated him, even more so because of the long side slit and the 4" heels. Once she even caught him looking, practically staring, and she just gave a smile. Her beautiful green eyes sparkled, and if he hadn't been so absolutely petrified of women, he would have tried to strike up a conversation with her. It was an understatement to say that he'd never had a lot of luck with the ladies, but who was he kidding? This girl was miles out of his league, and, for that matter, out of the league of every guy in the place. Still, he could certainly enjoy the view while it lasted.

While Larry was sitting at the Green Leafe, eating his food, drinking his beer, and absolutely gawking at the unattainable, two of Foster's operatives were inside Larry's apartment retrieving any and all documents that were related to his 9/11 research. They went through his computer and made copies of all of his files and documents, and then deleted anything and everything related to 9/11 from the hard disk. They were thorough and professional, even cleaning the history files and 'cookies' from his web browser to ensure that no trace of these sites or documents was left behind. Nothing was missed, nothing was left to chance. When they were done, Larry's apartment looked just like it had when he'd left, and nothing about what would be found here by the police, his family, or anyone affiliated with the college would raise any suspicion. The stage was set. Not for Larry, since he would be dead before the night was out. This stage was being set for the people that would come to collect Larry's things or to learn about his miserable life after he was gone. It took less than an hour, then the operatives were heading back towards DC.

Around 10pm Larry signaled his waitress that he was ready for his check. Thank God, she thought. Why did she always seem to get stuck with this loser almost every Friday night? This guy had been camping at her table for more than two hours and hadn't ordered anything but a small dinner and a couple of beers. While he paid the bill and hit the men's room, the beautiful redhead that had been sitting at the bar left. Alone. When Larry came back through the bar and saw that she was gone he was disheartened. God, for just one more glimpse. Stepping out to the sidewalk he gave a quick look around the streets, but she was nowhere to be seen. After a few seconds of scanning the area he resigned himself, reluctantly, to never seeing her again. Turning left and walking up Scotland Street, he saw few people out and about on this cold, early spring night. When he was about a half block from his apartment he was walking in the shadows from the nearby houses and the trees and shrubs. Williamsburg was an extremely safe town, at least this part close to the college campus and the restored area of Colonial Williamsburg.

Nothing to be scared of, virtually no crime in this neighborhood, he assured himself....

That was Larry Silverstein's last thought. He didn't feel the bullet hit him in the back of the head, nor did he feel it exit just above his right eye. There was no sound, no loud bang, save for a little spitting sound from the silenced Smith & Wesson handgun. No screaming witnesses, no barking dogs. It was just the same peaceful neighborhood, though for the first time in decades, a neighborhood where a man lay dead in a pool of blood. Larry had hoped to see her one last time, and ironically, had he simply turned around a few seconds before the bullet smashed into his brain he could have had his dying wish. She smiled at the thought of seeing the excitement on his face when he recognized her, hoping against hope, at least momentarily, that he was about to get lucky. Then the excitement and the lust would be replaced by terror when he saw the deadly weapon in her hand, realizing that his life was about to end. She always enjoyed the moment when men came to the realization that this woman, this object of their lust, was about to take their life. The rush, the high, was almost indescribable.

Tonight she'd introduced herself to people as Samantha from Dallas, Texas, just one of many aliases used by this highly prolific, highly professional assassin. Satisfied with her mission, she walked the few yards back to her rental car and drove off towards Interstate 64. Along the dark roads she removed her red wig and shook out her beautiful, natural blonde hair. God, she hated wearing wigs, but she had to admit that it was one of the few downsides to her job. Her chosen occupation had made her a very wealthy woman and had afforded her travel and adventure in many of the world's most exciting and exotic locales. She was the epitome of the smart, successful entrepreneur, and she flourished in a field that was, by all accounts, a man's world. Business was brisk, but for now, business could take a break. She would be leaving first thing tomorrow morning from Dulles Airport for a two week bareboat charter sailing the Greek Isles, courtesy of the man that had contracted her for this hit. It was a three hour drive to get to her hotel near Dulles, and she couldn't help but reflect on her great fortune and successful career. *I am truly blessed*, she concluded with a smile.

Chapter 1

September, 2007

KEITH BRYANT, PHD, WAS IN that twilight state of half-awake/half-asleep, and he really didn't want to wake up. He was vaguely aware of light butterfly kisses on his chest, his stomach, his shoulders, and his right ear. His brain may still be half-asleep, but another part of him was definitely waking up; he could feel himself getting more and more aroused with each touch and kiss. He finally gave in to the sensation and allowed his brain to catch up with his penis and fully awaken. Reaching over to stroke her hair, she just gave him a little smile and a light kiss on the lips.

"Morning sunshine," said his bedmate in a deep, sultry voice. "I don't suppose a girl could entice you into a continuation of last night's fun and games this Sunday morning, could she?"

Keith smiled, remembering the incredible night of lovemaking they'd had last night. Actually, they'd had many nights of incredible lovemaking over the last four and half months they'd been together, but every day seemed to be even better than the last, at least for Keith. He felt pretty confident that Loren felt the same. If her behavior, both in and out of bed, was any indication, she definitely felt the same. "I'm surprised you have the energy for another go this morning after last night's marathon."

"Don't worry about me old man," she giggled. "I think I've proven that I can take all you've got to give, and then some. But if I need to, I'll be glad to prove that to you one more time." She rolled over on top of him and kissed him deeply, their naked bodies twisting and writhing. She took his wrists and held them tightly over his head as she ground her body against his, knowing that he loved having her on top just as much as he loved it the other way around. Keith was by far the best lover she'd ever had.

Keith gave himself over to her completely. Whatever she wanted was fine by him. Loren was the first girl in his life he could honestly say that he cared more about being there for her, pleasing her, than he did about himself. He couldn't even begin to remember how many women he'd been with over the years, but he knew that the number was considerable. He'd never had any complaints, to be sure, but he had to admit that, with very few exceptions, he didn't care as much about his partner's feelings or pleasure nearly as much as he did his own. That had all changed since Loren came into his life. While he may have loved some of the women in his past, he had never fallen as hard as he had for her.

Their lovemaking was hot, passionate, and intense. Their bodies were covered in sweat and the bed was, to put it mildly, a wreck. They didn't care. They laid there exhausted, still holding each other like they were clinging to the last life-jacket on a sinking ship. Keith stroked her lower back lightly, lovingly, and whispered, "Have I mentioned lately how much I love you?"

Loren looked at him through half-closed, glazed eyes and gave a little smile. "Actually, it has been a while since you told me. Funny how you always seem to want to say that after having hot, passionate sex. Is there a correlation?"

Keith laughed. God, she had the greatest, if at times bawdiest, sense of humor of any girl he'd ever known. Probably just one more reason that he loved her, as if he needed any more reasons. "There might be. But I think I'd still love you even if you withheld sex from me for a whole 24 hours. If you could."

"Oh, right, Mr. Stud Muffin," she laughed. "Who could ever possibly stand to forego your great sexual prowess for a whole 24 hours?" With that, she took a pillow and covered his face and pretended to smother him. They both laughed and rolled around the bed, tickling each other, smacking each other on the ass, and just loving being together. It wasn't long before all of that touching, tickling, and naked body rubbing had them ready for Round 2 on this Sunday morning.

Keith finally made his way out of bed around 9:15, and he let Loren doze for a few minutes while he got up to feed the dogs. She always slept great after their lovemaking, and he loved to just sit there and watch her sleep. She was so beautiful, just lying there with that look of pure pleasure and contentment on her face. It was all he could do most times to refrain from touching her, groping her, trying to arouse her all over again.

He finally made his way downstairs and found the dogs waiting to head outside to do their early morning business before breakfast. Most days he was up and feeding them by 7:00am, but on most weekend days he managed to sleep in a little later, particularly since Loren moved in. Fortunately, Bo, the black Lab, and Winston, the yellow Lab, were good sports about it. He was worried about them being jealous when Loren first moved in, especially since both dogs were used to sleeping in bed with him. With both dogs weighing just over 100 pounds, even a king-size bed wasn't big enough for him, Loren, and the dogs, so he made them start sleeping downstairs.

"Come on guys, let's get breakfast and then you can go upstairs and wake Mom up." They were huge dogs, and they ate enough to feed a small town. He remembered something that one of his old friends had told him once when he was first considering getting a dog: "Big dogs make big shits." It always made him smile, the thought that he should choose the type of dog he would get based on how big their dog shit piles were. Still, he had to admit, it was true. When he cleans up behind Bo and Winston you would think it was a couple of Clydesdales. It didn't matter though. He wouldn't trade them for anything in the world.

The dogs gobbled down their food, and, as was their habit, they went back outside to go to the bathroom one more time before coming in to settle down for their early morning nap. When they came back in, Keith told them, "Go on guys. Go get Mom out of bed." That's all the encouragement they needed. They went bolting up the stairs, sounding like something between an earthquake and the launching of the space shuttle, and leapt onto the bed. The fact that the bed didn't collapse was a testament to the fine craftsmanship of the Amish people in Lancaster County, PA that built it, because there is no way that furniture is built with the thought of two lovable but rambunctious, knucklehead Labrador Retrievers jumping on it from clear across the room. Loren tried to cover herself as best she could when she heard the 'Labrador freight train', as she affectionately called them when they were excited, running up the stairs. Bo and Winston simply bathed her in licks and kisses. She tossed and squirmed and squealed in mock protest, as she always did, but she loved it when the guys came up to wake her like this. Like she always joked, if it weren't for the occasional internal injury when a 100 pound dog plants his bear-sized paw on her stomach or crotch or boob, this would be one of her favorite parts of the day.

"OK, OK, I'm awake. Bo, *please* get your nose out of my crotch. I love you, but I'm not *in love* with you." She tried pulling the sheet over her head but Winston kept pawing at it so he could lick her face. "Owww. Damn it, Winston, your claws feel like Gentle Ben! We have got to take you in for a pedicure this week. And get your tongue out of my ear. God knows where that tongue of yours has been". With that, Winston managed to get his snout totally under the sheet and gave her a big, sloppy-wet kiss on the mouth. "Bleeehhh. That was the wettest kiss I've had since the sixth grade." She reached out and petted and rubbed on both guys, and they finally settled down and snuggled up next to her. Loren loved these morning wake-up calls, especially on weekends when she had time to relax and enjoy it and didn't have to rush to get ready for work.

Keith finally spoke from the door. "So, cheating on me in my own bed, huh? And a *ménage a trois*, no less!"

"What's a girl to do when she finds two such handsome men in her bed?" Loren smiled back at Keith. "Why don't I lay here and entertain my two gentleman callers while you get in the shower? Then when you're done I'll get cleaned up and we can maybe head out to the Boar's Head Inn for brunch. Sound like a plan?"

"Sounds like a great plan, actually. Unless you want to join me in the shower so we can save a little time and a little water…"

"Yeah, I got your number, mister. We get in that shower together and we'll probably run the well dry before we get out of there. Besides, weren't you the one saying just a half hour or so ago that you probably wouldn't be able to walk today after the loving I put on you last night and this morning?"

"Was that me? I must have been delirious at the time. Fortunately, the recuperative powers of youth, or at least the recuperative powers of not-quite-middle-age, can be pretty incredible with the right, um, ……stimulus."

Loren laughed and flung a pillow across the room at Keith. "Well, the 'stimulus', as you so romantically put it, needs to wait until later. I need some good coffee, some good food, and some good wine, and lots of it. And not necessarily in that order, either. Plus, it looks like a gorgeous day outside.

Maybe later today we can get back and go for a horseback ride and let the dogs get a little exercise, too."

"That sounds great. I'll go downstairs and start the coffee for you and bring the paper in, and you can relax for a bit on the porch while I'm in the shower and getting ready. I'll yell up when the coffee is done, OK?"

"Thanks, sweetie." She had never felt so taken care of or so loved.

About 15 minutes later Keith came to the bottom of the stairs and yelled up to tell her that the coffee was ready. Loren put on her robe, with absolutely nothing on under it, and came downstairs. Keith had brewed a pot of her favorite Kona coffee and placed it on the table on the porch, right next to the Sunday *Washington Post*, a hot croissant with sides of butter and orange marmalade, and a small vase with a single red rose. "Madam, may I please seat you?" Keith asked in his worst French accent.

"But of course," replied Loren, sounding more like Pepi Le Peu, the cartoon character, than Catherine Deneuve, the sultry French actress. She sounded so bad she even made herself laugh.

"I thought you might want a little something to tide you over until we get to the Boar's Head so I made you one of the croissants I got yesterday at the bakery. Can I get you anything else before I head upstairs to take a shower?"

"Yes, just one thing," she said, as she pulled him gently to her for a kiss. "I love you."

Keith gave her another light kiss and said, "I love you, too." Keith smiled at her. "Now go on and drink your coffee before it gets cold. I'll be back in a bit, looking a lot cleaner and smelling a lot better, hopefully worthy of taking the most beautiful girl in Charlottesville out on the town for Sunday brunch." He gave her a quick kiss on the forehead and turned back into the house to shower and dress.

Loren kicked back in the rattan chair and enjoyed the scenery and the solitude. Keith had bought the property, known as Rainmaker Farm, about five years ago. It was just outside of Charlottesville in a town called Ivy, and while less than fifteen minutes away from the UVA campus where he was a professor of International Relations at the Woodrow Wilson Department of Politics, it felt like a whole different world. The farm was about 270 acres, and while small by Texas standards, it was pretty impressive for this part of Virginia. Keith was the quintessential gentleman farmer. He had a herd of about 30 cattle and three horses, and while he enjoyed doing some of the chores around the farm himself, most of the real work was done by a middle-aged couple that lived in a caretaker's house on the property. The farm was also a great place for Bo and Winston to run and explore. They usually spent hours each day running around the fields, chasing the abundant wildlife, and playing in the creek that ran through the farm. Loren's thoughts drifted; she daydreamed about living on the farm with Keith as his wife, about having kids and raising them in such a wonderful place. If this wasn't heaven, it was pretty darn close.

She relaxed with her coffee and croissant, and took her time reading the newspaper. The *Washington Post* was a real treat on Sundays. During the week she never found time to do more than glance at the local Charlottesville paper, the *Daily Progress*. But Sundays, that was a whole different story. If she was just lounging and lazing around, she could think of no better way to wile away the hours than reading the *Post* and catching up on the news of the world.

When Loren graduated high school back in Alexandria, VA she knew that she wanted to study government and political science. An exceptional student in high school, she was accepted at UVA and began her studies there in September of 1994. UVA challenged her intellectually, perhaps for the first time. She studied hard her first year and avoided many of the trappings of college life, including the parties, sorority rush, most of the football and basketball games, spring break, even boys. Finally, in her second year, she started to come out of her shell a little bit and dabble in some of the more fun things that college had to offer, courtesy of her roommates who were, quite frankly, tired of her being such a downer. Loren started to dress a little bit nicer, take a little bit more care and pride in her makeup and appearance, and involved herself in things other than studying – like parties, sorority rush, most of the football and basketball games, spring break, and even boys. She even had her first serious boyfriend during second year. Though she'd had a few dates in high school she'd never been serious with any one guy, and until Kyle came along she was still a virgin. That finally changed one Saturday night about halfway through second year after a night of frat parties and drinking. In that grand tradition of lost virginity during the college years, it happened back in his dorm room, complete with the sock on the doorknob as a signal for his roommate, and it was dreadful. Like most college guys, Kyle talked a good game about his sexual experience and prowess, but he was fumbling around and as nervous as she was. Thankfully, that first dreadful experience didn't sour her on men or sex, at least not for long.

Loren graduated from UVA *magna cum laude* after 4 years. Many of her professors encouraged her to continue her studies and work towards her Masters, but Loren wanted to go out into the 'real world' and try to apply what she'd learned to real world problems. She also wanted to have some experience under her belt before moving on to graduate school, her logic being that having the work experience in a government-related field would only make her application to grad school that much stronger. Finding work in DC for the World Bank, Loren spent the next few years working on projects that provided electricity and clean drinking water for several impoverished African nations. For the first time in her life she was able to see real poverty and hopelessness firsthand. She saw people dying for lack of basic human needs, like clean water and sanitation, or lack of food. Worse, she saw the political corruption of many nations firsthand, as the leaders of some countries lived in opulence and pocketed foreign aid dollars while turning a blind eye to the suffering and death of their people. This only steeled her resolve to make a difference in the world.

After three years with the World Bank, Loren applied to and was accepted at the John F. Kennedy School of Government at Harvard, earning her Master's in Public Administration and International Development. Upon completion of her time in Cambridge, she took a job at UVA as a research and teaching assistant in the political science department. This was the perfect fit for Loren; UVA still felt like home to her, and she could start the research towards her PhD while working at the university. It was after a few weeks back in Charlottesville that she met Keith at a departmental cocktail reception. She was standing around talking with her new faculty advisor, drink in hand, when Keith brushed past her. She didn't get a great look at him, but from what she saw he certainly didn't look like some stuffy old professor. Far from it. She tried to be discreet but couldn't stop herself from practically staring at him. Thankfully, he didn't seem to notice since he was constantly engaged in conversation with other faculty and staff members. She took it as a very good sign that he seemed to be popular and friendly with so many people at the party, and he seemed very much at ease in this type of social setting. Probably a professor that had been around for a few years, she thought.

When Loren saw Keith move towards the bar to order another drink she casually sidled over in that direction. She heard him order a glass of Cabernet from the bartender. Hoping that this might be her chance to strike up a conversation – something that the geeky Loren would have never considered back in her early college days – she sauntered up to the bar. Seeing the bartender hand Keith his glass of wine, Loren opened with, "I was thinking about ordering a glass of the Cabernet. Is it any good?" Pretty lame, she knew, but hopefully he'd appreciate that she'd made the effort to start a conversation. Better something subtle than trying to use a corny pickup line the way guys usually do, but still she was so nervous trying to make the first move that her palms were sweaty.

"If it were any worse I probably wouldn't even use it for a meat marinade, to tell you the truth. I figured that it's so bad that I won't have any problem keeping myself from overindulging tonight and driving home under the influence." He gave her a friendly smile and continued. "May I order a glass for you or would you rather have something that's actually drinkable?"

"Well, after that ringing endorsement I guess I should skip the Cabernet and just have another Cosmopolitan. Since it will be my third I guess I can always take a cab home." She tried to give her most playful smile and giggle, but whether it was her nerves or the fact that she actually had already had two Cosmos she wasn't sure if she was coming across cute and flirty or drunk and pathetic.

"Bartender, a Cosmo for the lady, please." Then he turned to Loren and offered his hand. "Hi, I'm Keith Bryant. You must be new here at the School. I haven't seen you around here before."

"Hi, I'm Loren Davis," she said while shaking his hand. "And yes, I am new here. I just started as a teaching and research assistant this semester. It's a pleasure to meet you." She noticed that he held her hand just a little longer than was necessary, but she definitely did not mind. In fact, she was already letting all kinds of sexy thoughts enter her mind and she had only met him moments ago. My, how she'd come out of her shell over the last ten years or so.

They spent the rest of the night talking and laughing. Loren was still amazed at how natural and easy it was that first night that they met; they talked like long lost friends and found that they had many common interests. Keith was very polite and very gracious, always making it a point to introduce her to everyone that came up to speak with him and always making sure that she was a part of the conversation. He was interesting, he was funny, and though he didn't try to show it, he was obviously brilliant, to say nothing of drop-dead gorgeous. He was about 6'1" and 185 pounds, with wavy, dark black hair and green eyes. If there was an ounce of fat on him she sure as heck couldn't see it. She assumed, correctly, that he had been an athlete because she'd never seen too many men in their late 30's (Keith was 38) that hadn't started to get that middle-aged spread or, at least, some serious love handles. After talking together for over two hours she realized that he had talked little about himself, instead steering most of the conversation towards getting to know her. Most guys she'd dated spent the first date, if not all dates, trying to impress her by talking about themselves, their careers, their money, their toys, their lives. Not Keith. He made her feel like the only person in the room. As the reception was winding down, Keith offered her a ride home since, as she'd said, she had had several drinks. Normally Loren would not have accepted a ride from a virtual stranger, but tonight she didn't hesitate. When they got to Loren's apartment, Keith walked her to the door, shook her hand goodnight, and told her how much he had enjoyed meeting her and talking with her. No clumsy moment trying to kiss her, no lunging at her or trying to grope her, just a handshake and a complement on how much he'd enjoyed their time together. Was this guy for real?

As he turned to go, Loren decided to once again seize the moment. "Keith, I really enjoyed being with you tonight. If you're not busy next weekend, would you be interested in having dinner with me?"

Keith flashed that killer smile again. "Actually, I'd like that very much. I wanted to ask you, but I didn't want you to say 'yes' tonight after having a few drinks and then maybe regret it, or even forget it, in the light of day."

"I don't think there's much chance of that. In fact, come here and let me show you how unlikely I am to change my mind." She took his hand and pulled him to her. She kissed him, lightly at first, and then more passionately. It was, as they say, the start of something big. They had their first date the next weekend and been together ever since. They dated for several months and then Loren moved into his place over spring break.

Keith finally came downstairs after showering and dressing. She had to admit, he did clean up nicely, and seeing him dressed in his nice slacks,

Brooks Brothers oxford shirt, Johnston & Murphy shoes, and Armani sports jacket still made her weak in the knees.

"God, you look so good I could just eat you up. Maybe I need to take you back upstairs for Round 3 and just skip brunch." Loren giggled as she said it.

"Sorry, hon, but this body needs nourishment. You've about worn me out, but I'd love a rain check."

"Party pooper. Well then, if you can't be enticed to join me in the shower I guess I'll just have to go get cleaned up all by my lonesome self." With that, she slowly walked away, all the while slowly letting her silky robe slink off of her shoulders and onto the floor. She loved the teasing and the playful times they enjoyed together. By the look of the tightness in the front of his pants, he was enjoying the teasing just as much as she was.

Keith grabbed a glass of orange juice and went out on the porch to relax while Loren got ready. He knew from experience that he was in for at least an hour wait, if not more, but she was well worth the wait. She was a great looking girl when she was just hanging out around the farm with her hair pulled back in a ponytail and little or no makeup, but when she got dressed for work or for dinner out, she was an absolute knockout. At 28 years of age she still had a body that girls 10 years younger would envy, and with her wavy blonde hair and gorgeous green eyes she turned heads everywhere she went. At 5'8' and about 140 pounds she had curves in all the right places and, in his mind, was definitely built the way a woman should be built.

He kicked back in the chair and took a long look at the beautiful surroundings and trappings of the farm. Dr. Keith Bryant was feeling happy and content for the first time in years. It had taken him a long time to bounce back from the deaths of his parents, having lost his father to pancreatic cancer in 1997 and then his mother to ovarian cancer in 1998. The only immediate family he had left was his sister Julia, and she lived 3,000 miles away in Carmel, CA. Growing up they weren't the richest family in town, but they were certainly comfortably ensconced in the upper-middle class and had a beautiful home in Great Falls, VA, and both Keith and Julia attended the top private schools in the area. Keith's parents always taught them that with a life of privilege comes a life of responsibility, a responsibility to make the world a better place for themselves, their families, their community, and their country.

Keith had always promised his parents that he'd make something of his life. They actually had no doubt, as he was a top student and a gifted athlete. An all-state wide receiver for his high school, he was recruited by many of the top schools in the country, including Notre Dame, Miami, Texas, and Florida State. Keith never gave any of them any serious consideration. His heart had always been set on attending the United States Navel Academy in Annapolis, MD, and the Naval Academy was glad to have him. His grades alone would have probably gotten him consideration, but with his athletic career, his family connections, and the reputation of his private school, St. Albans, he was exactly the type of cadet the Academy wanted.

It was at the Academy that Keith first fell in love with government, political science, and international relations. He dove into the material with a love that he'd never felt for any other subject, even though he had been one of those rare students that had loved school and loved learning for as long as he could remember. By the middle of his sophomore year he knew that he'd found his calling in life; he would pursue his Masters, and perhaps even his PhD, in government/political science. First, though, he had a commitment to fulfill, namely, a commission in the US Navy upon graduation from the Academy.

The Navy offered him many opportunities to travel, including trips to a number of exotic locales like Pearl Harbor, Tokyo, Bahrain, and Saudi Arabia. His favorite assignment, though, was the six months he spent at the Naval Postgraduate School in Monterey, CA. The fact that Monterey and the surrounding areas of California are some of the most beautiful places in America certainly didn't hurt. The best part, however, was that he had a chance to spend some real quality time with Julia since she lived just a few minutes away in Carmel. Always close, they grew even closer during that time. Keith helped her out at the small art gallery that she owned in Carmel, and he managed to drag her out to Pebble Beach to play golf, a game she hadn't played in almost ten years. Keith teased her that it seemed incomprehensible that she lived just minutes away from some of the preeminent golf courses in the country – Pebble Beach, Spyglass, and Spanish Bay – and not play golf. Even if you were a hacker, it was worth the exorbitant greens fees just to take in the beauty of these courses along the Pacific Ocean.

After his Navy hitch Keith moved to Charlottesville and completed his Masters in Government and International Relations at UVA. While working towards his PhD he decided to get some practical experience and spent about two years at a small consulting company in Washington, DC that focused on the political considerations of oil exploration in remote corners of the globe. Keith flourished in this environment and was fast-tracked to become a partner, but he had already chosen a different path. Deciding that he had enough contacts, enough experience, and enough money to hang out his own shingle, Keith started his own company, Bryant International. He based the company out of a small but comfortable office in Charlottesville. There was no need for anything too expensive or too ostentatious, at least not as he was starting out, since the nature of his business would take him to DC, New York, and other international cities to meet with clients.

Being his own boss suited him well. He was able to take on only the clients and projects he wanted, and to a large degree he was able to control the amount of travel so as not to interfere with his studies at UVA and the completion of his doctoral dissertation. From both a financial and quality of life perspective, Bryant International had been very good to Keith in the ensuing years. Though he was a full professor at UVA, his salary could have never paid for the farm, the cars, the boat, and other toys that he loved so much. Those were all paid for courtesy of Bryant International, not to mention the three books on international politics that he had written and published after earning his doctorate degree. As Keith soon found, having those three little letters 'PhD' behind your name carried a lot of extra weight when it came to billable rates and hours, opening doors to new client and project opportunities, and when pitching a book to the publishing houses. His consulting business had picked up dramatically since 9/11 as company after company wanted to use his knowledge of the international political scene and his knowledge of Muslim culture, in particular, to learn how to operate in the Middle East, Indonesia, and other parts of the world. Keith had expanded Bryant International by bringing on twenty-two new associates and a General Manager over the past few years, and annual billings had grown to over $40 million. If Keith were willing to give up his life as a professor of Government and Political Science at UVA and really focus on Bryant International he could probably grow the business to $75-$100 million in revenue, but he was very happy with the balance in his life. As it is, he teaches a few classes, he does some consulting, and he writes a book every now and again. Now, with Loren in his life, things are close to perfect.

⌘

KEITH WAS EXCITED, AS ALWAYS, that the new school year was finally here. He was teaching two classes this semester. Both were undergraduate classes: Comparative Political Systems 401, which he'd taught for several years, and The Politics of Conspiracy, a new 400-level course that he had designed, written, and 'sold' to the Dean of the School. He was especially excited about the new course. He was smart enough to know two things. First, that not every event in the world is the result of a conspiracy, and second, that sometimes there is more to the story behind events than the official version. He hoped to work with his students to explore the impact that the modern press and modern communications have on conspiracies, how the internet and the rise of blogs, YouTube, and similar communities of interest keep the conspiracies alive, and how our government feeds the conspiracy frenzy through lies, half-lies, and cover-ups. The course called for studying conspiracies throughout history, including the murder of Julius Caesar, Lincoln's assassination, Pearl Harbor, the Kennedy assassination, and 9/11.

Keith knew that his students would love this course. Many of those registered for the class he had taught in other courses, and he knew them all to be extremely bright, extremely inquisitive, and extremely tenacious in the search for information. The fact that Keith could continue to conduct his own research into the 9/11 tragedy right alongside his students was just icing on the cake. He was not by nature a conspiracy nut, but when it came to 9/11 he made no secret, at least to his closest friends, that he didn't believe the official version any more than he believed in Big Foot or the Loch Ness Monster. Maybe less. He fully believed that the hijackers were Al Qaeda, but not for one minute did he think that the story was that simple. Somebody had to finance and plan the operation, and while he considered it plausible that Osama bin Laden could plan the operation he believed strongly that there had to be considerable outside help with the financing and the day to day logistics of getting the hijackers into the country, trained for their mission, and kept under our government's radar for the months prior to 9/11. For that, he believed that two things were needed: someone with extremely deep pockets for the financing, and someone with the connections within our government. It didn't escape him that both of these requirements could be met by a single, well-connected individual or group of individuals. He was determined to find out the true story of 9/11; in fact, it was the subject of his next book. The book was already taking shape; he just needed to continue digging to uncover The Truth. Keith was determined to find information that had so far eluded others, and through sheer force of will and tenacity he usually accomplished whatever he put his mind to. He was not naïve enough to believe that it would be easy. Far from it. He knew that there were some very powerful people hell-bent on keeping The Truth from being discovered.

On one point, though, Keith was *very* naïve: in thinking that his actions were going to go unnoticed by those very same people.

Chapter 2

PATRICK ROCKWELL IS THE FOUNDING partner of a small but extremely influential and well-connected law firm in Charleston, SC and the leader of Let the Truth Be Told (LTBT), a group of researchers and academics that fervently believe that there is more to the 9/11 story than our government has told us. Only 39 years old, Patrick has already made a comfortable life for himself, though, admittedly, he came from a privileged background and upbringing. Born and raised in Charleston, his family has long, deep roots in the low country area of South Carolina. And, as anyone from Charleston can tell you, coming from the right family is everything. Having money, and plenty of it, certainly helps, but only so long as it's *old money*. Those *nuveau riche* newcomers, especially from up north, are tolerated, at best. Tolerated, but never truly accepted, into polite society. No such problems for Patrick. His family was worth millions, both sides of the family were well respected, and they were true patrons of the arts and other civic and charitable organizations in the area. Educated in the best private schools, followed by undergraduate studies at Princeton and law school at Duke, Patrick was destined for success. It didn't hurt that, having come from a wealthy family, he left law school and entered into the working world without a penny of student debt. That enabled him to take on work supporting important social causes on a pro bono basis when he thought that the little guy was getting wronged by the government or others powerful forces. After having seen one too many instances of government agencies and big businesses twisting the truth, if not outright lying, he felt drawn to the cause of defending the powerless and downtrodden.

Unlike many of the groups and individuals out there raising wild theories and accusations against any and everybody associated, however tentatively, with 9/11, LTBT maintains a high-level of objectivity and professionalism. Patrick insists on having all LTBT members provide well-researched, well-written, and well-documented submissions for their website. No rambling, no half-baked accusations, no personal attacks. Different from many other conspiracy groups, LTBT membership isn't made up only of liberals out to smear George W. Bush and his minions. In fact, many of the members would even identify themselves as Republicans, though, to be fair, they are all embarrassed by what their party had become over the past 10+ years with the growing influence of the religious right and so-called conservatives. LTBT has only five core members, that is, members that have a say in reviewing, editing, and approving their official statements and postings. Scattered across the US, they are the epitome of the virtual and connected team: video conference calls, reviewing and editing documents via web conference, and staying in frequent communication via mobile phone, e-mail, and instant messaging. The core team of LTBT meets every Tuesday night at 8:00pm Eastern time to discuss the latest research projects that they, as well as the 20 or so associate members, are working on. The core team members are spread across the country, across all time zones. Still, they wouldn't miss these meetings for anything short of World War III. It's much more than a hobby for them, it's their mission.

"Let's get this meeting started with an update on current projects," said Patrick, kicking things off promptly at 8:00pm. "Tony, why don't we start with you." Patrick liked to start on schedule and keep to the agenda and time allotted. That wasn't just because he's a stickler for punctuality – punctuality is expected in polite society, after all – but partly it's his desire to get things done, spend time with his family, and get to bed at a decent hour. After all, though he often thinks of the LTBT as his life's calling, it's the law firm that pays the bills and keeps him driving his cherished Aston-Martin, fishing on his 56' Viking convertible, and his family in their lovely Victorian home near the harbor.

Tony moved his chair around until he was satisfied that he was well-positioned for the video camera. No matter how many of these video and web conferences he did, both with the LTBT and at work, he never got used to the technology. The quintessential absent-minded professor, Tony was a brilliant mathematician at the University of Colorado in Boulder but not the most functional human being out in the real world. A lifelong bachelor, as much by choice as by the fact that he's not most women's idea of Mr. Right, or even

Mr. Desperation, Tony is truly married to his work. Even he can understand why he's somewhat less than a chick magnet.

"OK, here's what I've got since the last meeting. I've received a really good report from my guy up in Boston concerning the collapse of the World Trade Center towers. He's never been a real believer in the theory that the towers were brought down by explosives, but he's approached the problem with an open mind. Whereas some of the lunatic fringe is convinced that there was a second group of terrorists on the ground that supported the hijackers by planting thermite explosives in the sub-basement areas, he doesn't find any evidence to support that theory. He's gone through all of the official documents and testing, of course, not that we would rely on those exclusively, if at all, but he's also done his own analysis. Bottom line, his position, and I submit that it should be ours, is that the towers were brought down by a combination of the impact, the sloshing around of tons of jet fuel, and the resulting fires that weakened the structural beams to a point that the floors pancaked down on each other. Not glamorous, not sexy, and to a large degree, pretty much in line with what our government has told us."

"Damn, I hate it when that happens." This was spoken, only half in jest, from Terrell Jackson, PhD of Engineering at Georgia Tech. "But speaking from an engineering perspective, I can concur that, as much as I may not like it personally, the government's explanation about the collapse is plausible."

Tony continued, "I'm with you on that. I'd like to take this report, do some edits and tweaks over the next few days, then submit it to the rest of you for final review. If we're all then aligned, I vote that we post it on our site and make this the official position of the LTBT."

There were nods of agreement all around. Patrick said, "Alright then, let's make it so. Thanks, Tony, for the update. And our thanks to your team for their hard work on this research. I know it's taken them several months of effort to pull this together, so please let them know how much we appreciate it."

"I'll be sure to."

"Alright, then. Who's next?" asked Patrick.

"I'll be glad to jump in," said Jeff Anders. Unlike Tony, Jeff Anders was very comfortable in front of the camera and with the technology; in fact, he'd designed and engineered the technology solution that LTBT used for their calls and collaboration. A computer and internet guru, Jeff made several fortunes during the dot-com boom years and was one of those rare individuals that still had his money years after the bottom fell out of the market due to savvy investing. Nowadays he's primarily a venture capitalist interested in funding technology startups committed to finding creative solutions for harnessing technology to improve the lives of people around the world by bringing them improved communications, education, or agriculture. His primary motivation for joining LTBT was the loss of several close friends on 9/11 that worked at the World Trade Center. He made a promise to their families, and to himself, that he would use every possible resource at his disposal to make sure that they had the real answers to what happened that dreadful day.

Jeff continued, "I've been working with my team on digesting and making sense of all of the thousands of pages of documents, both from official government sources, so-called 'expert' sources, and the lunatic fringe, regarding the level of US government involvement in 9/11. As you know, the conspiracy theorists generally break down into two camps, the "Made It Happen On Purpose" or MIHOP group and the "Let It Happen On Purpose" or LIHOP group. Of course, I guess we have to concede that there's a third group, those that believe that things went down exactly as George W. and the government boys claim it did, but since we agree that there are relatively few of them, and their collective intelligence is probably too low to measure, we can probably throw that view out the window right from the start." Everyone got a good laugh out of that little joke; they may try to keep an open mind, but every once in a while they do enjoy taking a little jab at the 'true believers'.

"Basically, it comes down to this," said Jeff. "It's going to take a lot more work and a lot more time to ever prove to ourselves, much less the world, that the MIHOP view is true. As much as we joke and poke fun at the incompetence of George and his Beltway boys, it's a whole 'nother stretch to say that they intentionally caused the deaths of 3,000 people on 9/11. I'm not saying that I can't be convinced, I'm just saying that, so far, I find it much easier to believe that they knew that the attacks were coming, somewhere and at some point in the near future, and failed to stop it. I think we're much closer to being able to put together enough proof to convince the world that we're right. Maybe not beyond all doubt, but certainly beyond most reasonable doubt."

"So you're saying that our government most likely knew of the plans ahead of time and failed to take any action to prevent it? To what end?" Patrick spoke the words, but the thought was on everyone's mind.

"Simply stated, our government did it for political gain. The Bush administration thought that this catastrophe would galvanize the country and give him a virtual blank check to prosecute the war on terrorism while totally ignoring the domestic agenda, or at least any domestic agenda beyond what his fat-cat band of rich Republican friends demanded. You know, forget raising minimum wage for the lowest-paid workers, but make sure to lower the income tax rate and capital gains taxes of the bazillionaires. Forget about health care for every American, but make sure that the oil companies get every possible tax break and obscene profits as they drive up the price of a gallon of gas to $3. And, for all practical purposes, it worked, at least for a while. Bush had huge support for going after the Taliban in Afghanistan, both domestically and internationally. I think there were two major mistakes in their judgment, though. First, they totally underestimated the carnage that would result from 9/11 by not foreseeing that the World Trade Center towers would collapse, killing thousands. Second, Bush and his cronies forgot the most important lesson from our military skirmishes and police actions of the past few decades: Americans talk a good game, but they don't have the stomach for dead soldiers. When our planes are raining down laser-guided bombs on our enemies we're all glued to CNN watching and waiting for the big explosion and everyone is all smiles, but as soon as we have to put boots on the ground, and as soon as those soldiers start dying, the American public is ready to bring our boys home."

"And he made a serious miscalculation about invading Iraq. Not just militarily, but in his estimation of the American public's willingness to believe in him and his pretzel logic for the military action," stated Karen Richardson, the lone female among the LTBT leadership team.

"There's an understatement if I've ever heard one. Here's the thing: when people voted for Georgie-boy in 2000 they had to know, unless they were just incredibly stupid, that he was going to find an excuse or fabricate an excuse to invade Iraq. He had to. Saddam tried to kill his daddy. And you know what? I could have respected the hell out of him if he had been a man and maybe walked up to old Saddam and slapped him across the face and challenged him to a shootout at high noon. Hell, I would not have even minded if he'd just sent in a SEAL team or DELTA team to kill Saddam. Nothing wrong with that, but NO, he's got to involve the entire US military in this to settle his little score, and now thousands of Americans are dead or injured, to say nothing of tens of thousands of Iraqis that had nothing to do with 9/11. WMD my ass."

Terrell Jackson piped in, "And to say nothing of the really big lie about Iraq being involved in 9/11. If anything, Saddam hated Bin Laden as much or more than we do, and vice versa. Now all our war has accomplished, other than wasting tens of billions of dollars and thousands of lives on both sides, is the creation of the biggest breeding ground and training camp for terrorists the world has ever known."

"Right," said Jeff, "and the situation seems to be devolving by the minute. Anyway, let me wrap up my status report with one other key piece of information that we're trying hard to dig deeper into. The problem is, this piece could be interpreted as ammunition for both the MIHOP'ers and the LIHOP'ers, so we want to be certain that we have our facts, and our analysis, beyond question."

"Sounds intriguing", said Patrick.

"It is. It's nothing that you probably haven't heard or read about before, it's just that you get a whole new perspective when you put it in the context of a timeline. Or, maybe more accurately, when it's viewed through the prism of 5-plus years of world events since 9/11. So here goes. We all know that Dubya and his rich oil baron friends from Texas, including Bush Sr., met with members of the Taliban regime in Texas before Jr. ever got into the White House, right? All the oil folks tried to convince the Taliban, at that time the rulers of Afghanistan, to allow American oil companies to build an oil and gas pipeline across Afghanistan. In case you're not aware, one of the largest, most promising oil reserves left on Earth is under the Caspian Sea, and everybody, and I do mean everybody, wants to get their hands on that oil and control the pipeline. The route is planned to go from the Caspian, across Turkmenistan, into Afghanistan, cross the border into Pakistan, and then finally terminate in the Arabian Sea. The last thing that the American oil companies, to say nothing of our government, want to see happen is to have someone else control that route, especially if the route instead goes through Iran and into the Persian Gulf. That route, to put it mildly, is actually shorter and more direct than the route through Afghanistan, but you can imagine how much our people want to keep this oil from flowing through Iran and having America even more susceptible to their economic blackmail. At any rate, even with the promise of huge bucks from the Americans, the Taliban turned them down flat. OK, so far so good?"

Getting nods all around, he continued. "Alright then, so now we fast forward a couple of years. George W is elected king – at least in his mind – and 8 months after taking office we have 9/11. Al Qaeda is quickly identified as the terrorist organization that carried out this plot; I don't think anybody disagrees on that point. And guess where Al Qaeda happens to have their base of operations, and guess who provides them with protection and support? Afghanistan, and our old friends the Taliban as their benevolent hosts. Obviously, the American people are screaming for vengeance and the government and military are more than ready to provide it. We invade Afghanistan, bomb them to hell and back, and then send in some ground troops to mop up the place. The Taliban runs and we hand-pick a new government led by Hamid Karzai, a guy that seems pretty sharp and aboveboard but is inevitably seen as a puppet of the US government by most of the Muslim world. So, any guesses to what one of the first major moves Mr. Karzai does upon being placed on his new high and mighty throne?"

"Let me guess" said Tony. "He pushed through the oil pipeline deal that George and all of his rich oil robber-barons wanted?"

"Bingo! Give the prize to that cynical old number cruncher from the Rocky Mountain State. What it boils down to is this: we've fought wars in the past that, once you cut away all the patriotic prattle and all of the bullshit, were all about the money. It may have been taxes, like in the Revolutionary War, or it may have been about oil, like in the Persian Gulf War, but make no mistake – it was about money. In this case, one could argue, it's taken things a step further and we're looking at a war that was fought not just to go after Al Qaeda and the Taliban but to ensure *future* oil revenues for Dubya and his friends. If American companies build and control that pipeline they'll recognize billions in future profits. In a nutshell, I think of this as 'war as investment strategy,' our government acting as a Wall Street bank, only with lots of guns and bombs."

"And he says that I'm cynical!" chuckled Tony. This drew more smiles and laughter by the others.

Patrick spoke. "Jeff, excellent work by you and your team. Your arguments are clear and insightful. And, may I add, damn entertaining even if they prove not to be true". This last part said with a smile and a laugh. "Let's see if we can wrap up your team's investigation and have something ready for the rest of us to review and post within the next 30 days. Think that's reasonable?"

"I don't think that will be a problem. If anything develops that changes the timeline I'll send a message to the leadership team or raise it on one of our weekly conferences."

"Great. OK, let's move on so we can try to end at a reasonable hour for those of us on the East Coast, just in case we want to try to pretend that we have some semblance of a home life. Karen, how about you?"

"Glad to, guys." Karen Richardson was the only female and the only African-American on the leadership team for LTBT. Patrick didn't choose her as a member to try some great diversity experiment; rather, he chose her because she was brilliant in her field. While only in her mid-30's, Karen had already proven herself to be one of the best and most sought-after telecommunications consultants in America. Having worked for Accenture directly out of Wharton Business School, she helped to build and expand their telecom consulting practice by 300% during her tenure there and was always in demand as a speaker and presenter at every major industry conference and trade show. Though she was treated well at Accenture and became the youngest partner, male or female, in company history, she decided that she'd be happier following her entrepreneurial desires. She established her own consulting firm and was quickly in demand by dozens of major corporations and government agencies that were contemplating the migration to newer Internet Protocol (IP) technologies for their voice, data, and video needs. Many of those companies and agencies became her clients for the long-term, and it wasn't an exaggeration to say that most of them wouldn't consider making any type of move or technology investment without first discussing it with her and having her bless it.

Karen continued. "As you know, my motto is 'follow the money'. Without question, money is the root of all evil. For that matter, the more we investigate supposed terrorist incidents the more we find that ideology is often used as nothing more than a cover story for kidnappings, extortion, and even bombings and destruction of property. I've spent time since our last meeting studying the financials surrounding two key conspiracy theories that continue to gain momentum. Namely, the theories that Larry Silverstein, the owner of the World Trade Center, participated in the plot to destroy the buildings to get the $2B+ insurance payment, and second, the theory that some individuals and large investment houses had foreknowledge of the terrorist plot and used that knowledge to make a killing, if you'll excuse the pun, in the financial markets."

"I've heard and read about those theories, but honestly, I've never put much credence in them," said Jeff. "It would take some seriously cold, callous bastards to allow their country to be attacked and thousands of people to be killed just to make a few dollars."

"Well, I agree with you that it would take some cold and callous bastards to do this, but keep in mind that we're not talking about 'a few dollars.' We're talking about billions of dollars, and God knows that we see people killed every day for the change in their pockets. Still, like you, I've never put a lot of credibility in these theories and now the evidence bares this out. Rather than bore you with lots of spreadsheets and accounting mumbo-jumbo let me just cut to the chase: the numbers don't support either of these theories. First, Larry Silverstein already has more money than God, and while getting another $2 billion dollars is nothing to sneeze at, he actually stands to make much more than that during the expected usable life of the WTC. Plus, should he decide to sell the buildings, and there is absolutely nothing to support rumors that he'd been trying to sell them for years, there are dozens of companies that are both capable of paying for and managing the property and have an interest in owning premier, high-profile properties in and around Manhattan. This includes everyone from Donald Trump to companies based in Hong Kong, Beijing, Tokyo, Zurich, Dubai, and other financial capitals. Bottom line, I don't find any evidence, nor do I find any motive, that implicates Larry Silverstein. I'll be glad to forward you all my detailed findings for review, but my recommendation is that the LTBT post our findings on this theory and shoot it down once and for all."

Patrick asked for a quick voice vote on Karen's recommendation, and, as expected, the agreement was unanimous. "Seems like we're more of a conspiracy theory group that shoots down conspiracies and ends up supporting our government's position more often than not. We should be ashamed to show our faces," Patrick said with a smile.

There were smiles all around, but they all knew that he was right. While every one of them believed that there was more to 9/11 than the government was willing to share, they also recognized that reckless and outlandish theories only served to shield the government by making the real truth harder to find, or, when it's actually uncovered, to be recognized and accepted as the truth. In many ways, their greatest service to the conspiracy community was debunking many of the more outlandish claims and getting more people to focus on discovering the real reasons and the real culprits behind the greatest American tragedy in generations.

Patrick continued, "Since we're all aligned let's get the posting done this week regarding Mr. Silverstein. Karen, you said that you also had some more information to share relative to the investments and profits made by some companies?"

"Yes, and on that subject I can be brief. There were allegations made in various internet postings and in front of the 9/11 commission that certain institutional investors made a bundle of money trading options for United and American Airlines. The SEC and the FBI both investigated and found no impropriety, but I decided to have my team dig a little deeper. We even went straight to the horse's mouth in a couple of cases, actually meeting with the head person at the investment funds. Bottom line, there is plenty of evidence that points to the fact that these investments were made on the basis of legitimate market trends and conditions in place in advance of 9/11. There was even one investor newsletter for options traders mailed out two days prior to 9/11 recommending this very strategy. So, basically, no conspiracy, no deep dark secrets. We're not even talking a large chunk of money, either, to be truthful. Certainly not when compared to the money we were looking at for the insurance payout on the WTC. I say we put this little half-baked conspiracy to bed for good."

"Any objections from the group?" This from Patrick. "No? OK then, let's consider the matter closed and update the posting on our website. That should put an end to that crazy little 'theory', and I use the word cautiously." Then he added more lightly, "Let's just hope that everybody doesn't start thinking of us as part of the big conspiracy, or a government apologist, since we seem to find more reasons to discount all of these theories rather than jumping on the bandwagon! OK, last but not least, let's hear from Terrell before we move on to new business."

"Great, thanks Patrick," said Terrell. "I'm getting ready to shoot holes in probably the craziest conspiracy theory of all, the crash of the American Airlines plane into the Pentagon. Or, if you want to believe the whack-jobs out there, maybe the plane that didn't hit the Pentagon and maybe just disappeared into thin air like it was part of a David Copperfield magic trick."

Terrell Jackson grew up in the Atlanta area and had never really left. A child prodigy, he excelled at math and cognitive reasoning problems. He could have easily graduated from high school at age twelve and entered college, but his parents held him back to try to give him something closer to a normal life. Still, when your IQ is off of the charts it's hard to be normal, especially around kids your own age. Terrell stayed in high school and graduated at fourteen, by that time having taken virtually every course, including every college prep and AP course, offered by his school. He had full-ride scholarship offers from every top engineering school in the country, including MIT, Rensselaer, and Cal Poly, but in the end he decided to stay close to home and close to his parents. Fortunately, Georgia Tech, one of the other top engineering schools, was right in his backyard. He had his undergraduate and Masters degree in his hands by the time he turned 19, and by the time he finished his doctoral thesis at age 23 he was already being recognized as one of the preeminent structural engineers in the world. His 'day' job was Adjunct Professor of Engineering at his alma mater where he taught classes to students barely younger than himself. His passions, though, were consulting on large construction projects and exploring the many conspiracy theories surrounding 9/11. As with everything he did, he approached his work with LTBT with a very scientific, very methodical, and very disciplined approach. Once Terrell set his mind to solving a problem or researching some obscure or inane aspects of one of the many conspiracy theories there really was no stopping him until he was absolutely sure that every angle, every permutation of the problem had been studied, documented, and either proven true or false. With Terrell there was rarely, if ever, a situation that ended up in the gray area.

Terrell continued his explanation of the conspiracy theory involving American Airlines Flight 77 that hit the Pentagon. "What we've got out there is a bunch of yahoos contending that the Pentagon wasn't damaged by this massive Boeing 757, rather that the Pentagon was actually bombed or hit by a cruise missile 5 minutes earlier than the official time of impact."

"And what, pray tell, do these rocket-scientists base their theory on?" asked Tony.

"They base it on four things, really. Probably in case someone can ever disprove one point they can fall back on one or more of the others. Point one: These people claim that the clocks inside the damaged area of the Pentagon actually stopped five minutes before the supposed impact time of the American Airlines flight. Point two: There are no videos or high-quality still pictures of the plane hitting the building. They reason that the Pentagon, supposedly one of the most secure buildings in the world, must be ringed by hundreds, if not thousands, of security cameras, so surely one of them would have had to see the impact if it truly happened. Point three: The impact point on the building is not nearly the size of a Boeing 757, instead being much closer in size to the expected impact damage that would be caused by a cruise missile or other projectile. No word from these nut jobs, by the way, about who supposedly fired the missile, where they fired it from, and how they acquired it. And finally, Point four: When all else fails, try some logic. That is, many of the conspiracy theorists hold that it would be impossible for a plane — essentially, a big, slow-flying metal projectile — to penetrate the defenses of the Pentagon to hit the building. In other words, they don't know what defenses the Pentagon has, but they just know that the world's most important military facility, home to the world's most awesome military, simply *must* be protected from all possible invasions, whether by land, by sea, or by air. They cannot believe that our government would leave the Pentagon defenseless against a simple passenger plane, especially when planes routinely take off and land hundreds of times a day at Reagan National Airport just a mile or two away. For what it's worth, I can't say I totally disagree with that particular point. Seems pretty stupid to me, too."

"So I assume you're prepared to shoot holes in their theory?" asked Patrick with a smirk, knowing that Terrell loves poking holes in other groups' conspiracy theories almost as much as he likes developing his own.

"Oh, gladly, though I am disappointed that this wasn't as much of an intellectual challenge as I'd hoped. It was rather more like shooting fish in a barrel. Regardless, here goes. On Point one, the clocks stopping minutes before the plane was to have crashed, we could not find one witness that reported any type of power interruption that would account for the clocks stopping. If anything, every single witness testified that they were going about their business as usual until the impact, and in fact, data that was recovered from several computers showed that they were being used up until the time of impact. As far as the supposedly stopped clock, we did find several witnesses, including someone on the building maintenance staff, who concurred that the clock had been broken for several days prior to 9/11 and was on the maintenance list for repair or replacement. On Point two, it's true that there are no high-quality videos. I would have expected any number of state-of-the-art digital video camera to be placed around the Pentagon, but if that's the case, and we haven't been able to confirm or deny that, none of them seem to have captured the impact. Keep in mind, of course, that the plane would be traveling probably 200-plus miles per hour, so fixed cameras would be lucky to get one or two frames probably, at best. There are several amateur videos and a handful of surveillance videos, none of which are especially conclusive on their own. Official channels are working to enhance some of these videos, reportedly more than 75 of them from area businesses, tourists, etc. to try to get more detail. Still, we were able to interview dozens of eye witnesses that saw the plane hit the building and, without exception, they were able to positively identify it as an American Airlines jet. Any questions so far?"

"No, you're on a roll. Keep on," said Karen, hoping to get through Terrell's part of the presentation so that she could take a much-needed bathroom break. She may have had to go to the bathroom, but like the others she was too fascinated to risk missing a moment of this.

"OK, then, on to Point three. I've studied the photographs from the Pentagon. I consulted on the damage to the building and the plan for reconstruction. I have the measurements, and I have the blueprints. On top of that, and at the risk of sounding immodest, my background gives me an expertise that these conspiracy cretins don't have when it comes to studying the point of impact. In the first place, the damage to the building is going to be caused primarily by the fuselage, not the wings, and the fuselage is basically a 12-foot aluminum tube. You don't expect a 12-foot aluminum tube, especially one that is going to squish in on itself like an accordion when it impacts at 200 mph, to do the damage that these people assume. It's been said that some of the conspiracy theorists expected a hole all the way through the building, or at least a hole that is the size of the plane's wingspan and the height of the plane's highest point, the tail. That's almost 125 feet for the wingspan and 44.5 feet for the tail height. Obviously, that didn't happen for one very simple reason: the Pentagon is a very big, very well-built, heavily reinforced building. It's certainly not indestructible, but it does offer significant resistance to that giant flying tube that's crashing into it. Essentially, the plane was disintegrating before the wings and the tail could penetrate the building. That also accounts for the relative sparseness of debris, though, contrary to some reports, there was a significant amount found."

"As sick as some people are today I'm surprised that some of it didn't show up on eBay," said Karen, only half in jest.

"True enough," replied Terrell. "OK, last item. Why was the Pentagon defenseless against a civilian airliner crashing into it? Where were the surface-to-air missiles or the shoulder-fired missiles that we've all imagined? For that matter, where was any type of defensive response, even something as small as an MP firing off a few rounds from his Glock sidearm? The honest answer at this point is that we simply don't know. What I'd like to suggest to the leadership team is that I keep heads-down on this one area for the next couple of weeks to see if we can flesh it out a bit. I think we're OK to publish and post the other findings, but I'd really like to probe a lot more into this question of Pentagon protection. Not that it will necessarily turn out to be some huge deal or any kind of smoking gun that unites all of the conspiracy theorists, but it just bugs me."

Patrick asked, "How do you plan to go about investigating the military's protection plan for the Pentagon? Think that some general is just going to share that with you?"

"Puhhleeease," replied Terrell. "No, I think it's time for me and my team to start poking around a bit in the Pentagon's computer systems to see what information might be stored there. Maybe Jeff would be interested in lending a hand, just to make sure that we don't set off any bells and whistles or leave any tracks?"

"Sounds like a fun little challenge to me," said Jeff. "Count me in. I always find the DoD computers and network firewalls to be a way to keep my skills honed. I'm there for ya man, just let me know when."

"Alright then, it's agreed," said Patrick. "We'll post our position on Terrell's first three conspiracy pieces and we'll defer a final decision on the Pentagon protection issue until after he and his team, assisted by Jeff, gather more information and bring it back to us for further discussion. You guys be careful – we don't need to set off any alarms that will bring LTBT to the attention of the government. So far we've managed to fly pretty much under the radar, and I think we'd all agree it's best to try to keep it that way."

Everyone concurred with the plan, so Patrick moved the group on to new business and the discussion of the next conspiracy theory that needed to be researched, namely, the assertion by some people that United Flight 93 was shot down by an American fighter jet instead of crashing into the Pennsylvania countryside when the hostages tried to take back the plane from the terrorists. He knew that all of the leaders in LTBT wanted nothing more than to confirm that there was, in fact, a big fat conspiracy at the very top of our government. It's something they all believed, although they all believed slightly different versions of the conspiracy. Whether it was the government, Big Oil, the military industrial complex, or one of God knows how many different bad guys out there in the world, they knew beyond a shadow of a doubt that there was more to 9/11 than our government was telling us. Now they just had to keep lining up the conspiracies and knocking them down one at a time until, one day, only The Truth was left standing. Patrick had no illusions that the United Flight 93 conspiracy would crumble under close scrutiny and research. That's OK, though. That will be one more misguided theory shot down, one less distraction for all of the conspiracy theorists out there. One step closer to The Truth.

Chapter 3

THE US GOVERNMENT HAS HUNDREDS of buildings in the greater Washington, DC metropolitan area. Some are awe-inspiring examples of period architecture; grand monuments that take up entire city blocks. A few, though massive in scale, are about as awe-inspiring as your average 1960's elementary school. It doesn't mean that important work doesn't go on in there. Important decisions of state being made. Bureaucrats bureaucrating. Decisions being made, or not made, that could impact the American public, if not the world. Many buildings are open to the public for tours, like the White House, the National Archives, and the Smithsonian. Most are well marked on city maps and even the worst cab drivers can usually find them, even if they can't pronounce them. Even many of the buildings that house our "secret" spy agencies sit right out in the open with signs pointing the way from all of the major roads, such as the CIA in Langley, VA and the NSA at Fort Meade, MD. There are some lesser-known agencies, such as the National Geospatial Intelligence Agency, that sit outside of DC in the suburbs, and while they don't exactly welcome the public their locations are certainly far from well-kept secrets. Of course, this being DC, there are a few groups or agencies whose very existence, to say nothing of their purpose, their employees, and their locations, are totally hidden from public view. Most of these agencies, if that's what you want to call them, are known to only a handful of people within the government. In the best traditions of our government there is usually an attempt to have some checks and balances lest the Administrative Branch run amok, or at least that's how the Legislative Branch spins it. There may be some oversight from the Senate Select Committee on Intelligence, the supposed crème de la crème of our elected representatives that swear, 'with God as my witness' that they can keep the most important secrets of our nation secret, 'cross my heart and hope to die.' Even if it will bring them more power. Even if it will get them re-elected. Even if their wife – or mistress – begs them to share the secrets. America can rest easy knowing that we've only shared our most sensitive intelligence secrets with fifteen partisan politicians, their staffs, the people that prepare the briefs and budgets for the Senators, and, well, ... Maybe we *shouldn't* be resting so easily.....

Destiny Communications Group LLC, or DCG, is a different type of government agency with a very simple and very narrowly focused mission: they are charged with monitoring all forms of communications traffic, both domestically and internationally, to see what the conspiracy groups are saying and thinking. See what kind of crazy fantasies they're thinking up. And more importantly, make sure that they can never say or prove anything that is, simply, The Truth. No one had to tell Colonel Edward J. Foster, the founder of DCG, how important this mission is or how critical it is to his country. Unlike the 300 million Americans that he had sworn to protect, he knows The Truth about 9/11. Every detail, every conspirator, every dollar -- he knows. Less than ten other people in the world know what he knows. Other people *think* they know, but much of their 'inside knowledge' is misinformation, misdirection, and false flags. Domestic monitoring is, of course, illegal under virtually every statute and every agency directive ever written in the US. Foster didn't consider that an issue. One, because he simply didn't care. In his view, you do what needs to be done to keep America safe from its enemies, both foreign and domestic, and the law be damned. Second, he was operating under a Presidential Directive signed by The Man himself within days of the 9/11 tragedy. For all practical purposes, should the shit ever hit the proverbial fan, he had a 'get out of jail free' card tucked safely away. That scenario never bothered him in the least. He was a soldier, a patriot, and he would damn well do what his Commander in Chief told him to do, especially in this instance when he absolutely agreed with the mission. If that put him in harm's way, whether on the battlefield – which he'd never had the privilege of seeing – or before a congressional committee and federal prison, then so be it.

DCG was set up as a front company based in Reston, VA, and outside of Foster and a handful of others, none of the 200-odd employees have any idea that they are a part of one of the most secretive government agencies in the world. They are totally off the books; no record of them as a government agency, no government budget, no oversight committees in Congress, nothing.

Ostensibly, DCG is a company that sells telecommunications equipment, computers, and Microsoft software to large government and commercial customers, and total revenues have grown to more than $250 million per year. In one of the biggest ironies, DCG has grown to become one of the top suppliers of technology and professional services to the federal government; the government paying a secret government agency with taxpayer dollars to provide other government agencies with state of the art technology, which keeps the secret government agency in business. The irony was not lost on those very, very few that were in the know.

DCG was founded by Colonel Ed Foster on October 1, 2001 upon his 'retirement' from the United States Army after a distinguished twenty-five year career. His expertise in military intelligence, satellite imagery, and cryptography had led him to the NSA during the past seven years, and that same background proved invaluable for DCG's real mission. Actually, his retirement was a ruse; he'd been hand-picked for this assignment by the Director of the NSA. Technically, he was still a full-bird colonel, but to the world, including his family, he was officially retired. All of his salary and benefits came directly from DCG, and he had deferred receiving his monthly pension checks until he was older. He could hardly complain. His salary and bonus from DCG far surpassed the income that he could ever have hoped to achieve with the military. For that matter, the company had become so successful that nobody in the government, not even the President, could match his income. And what a perfect cover company he had built! Admittedly, he did have some advantages over the typical startup company, like a $12,000,000 line of credit or slush fund from the government to get things started. To keep the veil of legitimacy Foster made his monthly payments to the 'bank' just as he would if the funding had come from Chase Manhattan. Though he had fielded several offers to sell the company or take it public that was obviously something he couldn't and wouldn't do. God, he can't imagine anything possibly being a bigger pain in the ass than being a public company in today's corporate world and having to deal with all of the requirements of the Sarbanes-Oxley rules. Fucking Enron and MCI. Because of their stupidity and greed American companies were now drowning in rules and paperwork and audits. He didn't know which would be worse, having his company discovered as a front for the US government or being forced to become a public company and having to comply with Sarbanes-Oxley.

There was another advantage to the way he set up DCG, and on this point he really felt justified in giving himself a pat on the back. He almost wished he could share the secret so he could brag about it to his family and friends. When he founded DCG as a telecommunications and networking company it gave him the perfect cover. He had a company that sold and serviced all of the high-tech equipment, both hardware and software, that virtually all companies use. It also justified him hiring a dozen or more Cisco, Microsoft, and computer networking engineers, and these folks usually had unfettered access into end-user customers' networks. And, perhaps best of all, it gave him cover for having an incredible amount of dedicated bandwidth for the really powerful servers and massive storage devices that were dedicated to the mission. The handful of employees that did know about DCG's real mission, all former operatives with the CIA or NSA with Special Forces backgrounds, took care of the monitoring responsibilities from a purpose-built, shielded command complex below DCG headquarters. While the Bunker, as it is less than affectionately known, is not luxurious, it's an internet and computer geek's dream. There is more bandwidth coming into the monitoring room than most of the office buildings in New York City. There are walls of plasma screen monitors, and a server farm that would be the envy of many small Internet Service Providers. The amount of storage for the massive amounts of data that are routinely accessed from the internet, the communications grid, and all other sources is mind-boggling: twenty petabytes, more than all but a few of the Fortune 100 have at their fingertips.

Most important, and in Foster's view, the most impressive, is the custom software that his team had written. They had created a data mining program that was so sophisticated, so powerful, that it was capable of sorting through every word of monitored communications worldwide. Running on a massive, purpose-built supercomputer, Electra, as the system had been dubbed, could find relationships between people, words, expressions, pictures, languages, internet addresses – hell, probably even thoughts – for every communication that was posted to the internet, spoken across any wired or wireless network, broadcast on TV or radio, or printed in a newspaper every single day of every single year. Foster's measure for how valuable Electra is to his work is based on what she *doesn't* give you. That is, with the huge quantity of data being fed into her, you would expect to get overwhelmed with thousands, if not millions, of hits to follow up on. That doesn't happen with Electra. The team sees about thirty to fifty hits per week, and in the four years that Electra's been on line they've seen less than a dozen false positive hits. With Electra's power, Foster's spooks don't have to do the heavy thinking. They have only two tasks, to keep Electra happy and operating at optimal efficiency, or as they refer to it, 'her daily care and feeding', and second, follow-up on any leads she generates. What Electra does would take a team of thousands of engineers to accomplish. If that were even possible, from a manpower standpoint, you could throw secrecy right out the window. With a tool as powerful as Electra, Foster is able to run his operation with just five hand-picked men, and even then he never has more than two or three working at any given time. The wonders of modern machines. And unlimited budgets.

⌘

Foster was down in the Bunker meeting with his team, something it seems he gets to do less and less these days since the time demands on the CEO of a $250 million company, even one that has a much more important mission hidden from public view, is considerable. While he tries to leave most of the day to day operations to his second in command, Bob Manning, he still insists on daily briefings with Manning and once a week sit-downs with the whole team to discuss the latest developments. Everything that his team does is focused on one thing and one thing only: keeping the world from learning The Truth about 9/11. His team doesn't even know The Truth; they *think* they do, but in fact they only know snippets mixed in with a few credible lies. Foster hated that he couldn't share the entire truth with his team. They were good men, and good, patriotic Americans doing what was asked of them by their government. Still, the need for security is paramount and trumps all other feelings of friendship, loyalty, or fairness. They say that information is power. Foster has a different spin: information is power, but information is also isolating when you can't share it with anyone else, not even your closest friends or family. But, as he always reminded himself, this is the path he'd chosen for himself a long time ago, and there's no turning back now. There are a lot of bad people in the world that would gladly kill him and everyone he knows to get what's in his head.

Foster started things off. "OK guys, what's the latest chatter out there in whacko-land? Aliens came to Earth and kidnapped George W. and replaced him with a body-double? The WTC collapsed from faulty steel and concrete in a plot perpetrated by the trade unions to get more work? Give me your best shots – I could use a little humor today."

Warren Adams was the first to speak. "Nothing quite so fun and exciting as that, but still a little bit of juicy gossip. First thing we've been seeing is a lot of chatter from Europe, mostly France, about a possible link between Osama and the Russian mafia. It's turning up on several chat rooms and a handful of conspiracy sites, but we haven't seen the rumors jump to the mainstream press yet. The prevailing theory seems to be that the Russian bad guys paid Osama and his merry band of terrorists to attack the US for one of two reasons. First, to keep the Feds from investigating the Russian mob in the theft of nuclear material that's reportedly now on the black market. And second, in a conspiracy theory obviously inspired by *Die Hard 3*, the Russian mob used the cover of the terrorist attack to rob the Federal Reserve and/or to steal information from networks left undefended by the disaster. Things like credit card data, business data, consumer information for identity theft, and so on." Like all members of the team, Adams was former Special Forces and had 15 years at NSA. Unlike the others, he actually had a degree in engineering from MIT and a Masters degree in mathematics from the University of Maryland. He was one of the driving forces behind the development of Electra and had, in fact, developed many of the statistical algorithms that she used to find relationships within the data.

Foster asked, "So why did Electra send a warning on this? Sounds like the typical ramblings of a thousand other conspiracy sites."

"That's the fun, juicy gossip part," continued Adams. "It seems that a certain French arms dealer, Pierre LeClerc, is trying to sell some low-grade nuclear material, reportedly stolen from a Russian reprocessing plant a few years back, to some bad guys from the Middle East. Not enough material for a decent nuclear bomb, but certainly enough to make a dirty bomb that could cause some deaths and a lot of panic. LeClerc has started to come under investigation by any number of agencies and he's trying to use these rumors to shift the focus on others. So far it actually appears to be working. He's lying low and acting like Mr. Upstanding Citizen, hanging out at Cannes and in Monte Carlo, and the investigation is starting to focus on the Russians."

"OK, then, here's how I want us to proceed," said Foster. "Let's help to keep this conspiracy theory active for as long as we can. It's not the most credible theory we've heard lately, but we should be able to get some mileage out of it. Join in the chats and postings, and if things start to wane let's post a few false-flags to keep the interest up. The whole robbery scenario probably won't have any legs, but the Russian mafia angle probably will. And Warren, when you get a chance, insert some chatter into the mix that will get the NSA and other agencies back on the trail of LeClerc. I don't want him moving that material to the bad guys." Foster knew that this last part was really outside of their charter, but he wasn't about to let nuclear material get anywhere near the hands of Muslim extremists if he could stop it. But since the NSA, outside of the Director himself, didn't even know that DCG existed, he had to find creative ways to share intelligence.

"What else we got on the radar?" asked Foster.

Bob Manning spoke. "The biggest thing we've been tracking this week is all of the activity by members of Let the Truth Be Told, the conspiracy group headed up by that attorney in Charleston. Electra has raised a few flags because of the sheer volume of communication going on between the members."

"How many members do they have"? This from Colonel Foster.

"They have five core team leaders spread across the country, and each leader has their own extended team that provides research and information. The actual number of members seems to fluctuate, but during this past week we've seen communications between twenty different people in addition to the core team leaders. These guys are good; you don't see them coming up with a bunch of whacko shit. In fact, over the last couple of months they seem to be concentrating more on punching holes in some of the other theories out there than in trying to establish their own credible theory."

"And what is Electra's take on why they're doing that?" Foster wasn't sure that he saw a logical reason for a group of conspiracy theorists to be spending time shooting down 9/11 theories, no matter how outlandish, instead of focusing attention on the government or promoting their own version of The Truth.

"Electra believes, and all of us concur, that Let the Truth Be Told is intent on disproving any and all conspiracy theories that don't align with their interpretation of the 9/11 conspiracy. And, by the way, they're damn good at what they do; we've read the research and postings that they've put together crushing some of the popular sacred cow theories, like the one that says that the WTC was taken down by hidden explosives, not by the force of the airliner crash and the resulting fire. The only thing that we're not clear on at this point, nor is Electra, is what they really believe to be The Truth. They've played their cards very close to the vest since the group was first formed when it comes to their conspiracy theory."

Foster thought for a minute before he spoke. "I think we need to keep an eye on this Let the Truth Be Told group. We don't want them shooting down too many conspiracy theories that are useful for keeping the nutcases occupied and moving down the wrong path. Plus, if these guys are that good, if and when they start shouting their own conspiracy theory from the mountaintops people just might listen – and they may be too close to the real Truth. Bob, see what you can dig up on these guys and fill me in on it next time we meet. If there's anything that warrants more drastic measures we'll address it then."

"Yes sir," said Manning. He looked around the room at his team. In addition to Warren Adams he had three other top-notch engineers and clandestine operatives on his team: Eric Torres, Brad Hanover, and Les Mattox. "Alright, guys. You heard the man. Let's do some background searches on these guys, and let me know about anything and everything that Electra kicks out."

Foster asked if there were any other questions or issues to be discussed before he had to head back to his office for a meeting.

Brad Hanover spoke. "Sir, there is one thing that we're keeping our eye on after Electra raised a few flags. There's a professor down at UVA, guy by the name of Dr. Keith Bryant. In addition to teaching he runs an international relations consulting firm based in Charlottesville called Bryant International, plus he's written a few books on government issues. Kind of stuff geeky government types and diplomats like to read. Electra apparently made a connection based on two things. First, he's teaching a new course this semester at UVA called the Politics of Conspiracy, and per the course literature it proposes to look at the impact of conspiracies on world events throughout history, including, of course, 9/11. Second, he's been doing a lot of online research about 9/11, including examination of available government documents, the 9/11 Commission Report, and just about every conspiracy site and blog on the net. Electra believes that he's doing all of this in preparation for a new book on 9/11. I decided to verify this assumption; I accessed his computer remotely and found an in-progress manuscript, just as Electra suspected."

"How far along is the book, and did you see anything damaging?" This from Foster.

"Nothing damaging, in my opinion. Very well researched, very well written, but nothing new or particularly earth shattering at this point. I'd estimate that he's about halfway done, but that's only a guess. I would expect that he's got a lot more research to do before he feels that he has a credible answer or theory, especially one that some other person or group hasn't already published. Still, I wouldn't bet against this guy coming up with something. He's got the credentials, including the Naval Academy, four years in the Navy, and a Masters and PhD from UVA. He's no dummy or whacko."

"Let's do this then," said Foster. "Keep on monitoring Dr. Bryant and keep me up to date on a daily basis. If we see any reason, any reason at all, to be concerned, we'll move on this guy. Bob, start digging into his background, find out everything you can about him, particularly where he's vulnerable in case we have to discredit him. If we can get eyes and ears on him in the classroom, so much the better. From this point forward, let me know immediately if Electra comes up with any additional flags on this guy."

Foster paused to collect his thoughts, and then continued. "Gentlemen, I don't have to tell you that adversaries like Dr. Bryant are potentially more dangerous to our cause than all of the whackos out there combined. People discount the ranting of the nutcases, but this guy will have a lot of credibility if he comes up with a reasonable scenario to explain 9/11. He's already a published author, so he probably won't have any trouble getting someone to publish the book and get it on the market. All we need is someone with legitimacy publishing a best seller and telling his story on Larry King. It won't even matter if he's not 100% correct, I don't want this guy going public and getting traction with a story that is even half correct. Let's stay on top of this and be prepared to take action against the good Professor on short notice should it become necessary." Foster would not hesitate, not for even one second, to eliminate anybody that was a threat to his country. And, in his mind, having The Truth made public was as grave a threat as his country could possibly face.

"Thanks for your time gentleman. As always, it's an honor and a privilege to serve with you. Bob, after you've got the plan together and everything is locked and loaded, give me a call and we'll get together so you can bring me up to speed. Maybe we'll grab some dinner afterwards if you don't have to rush home."

Foster left the room wishing that he could spend more time with his men, more time down in the Bunker doing the real work, the work he loved. Unfortunately, the rest of his day was going to be consumed in meetings and briefings for Destiny Communications Group. He'd rather take a beating than have to sit there pretending to give a shit, but this is the mission he'd chosen. He made his way back over to DCG and wondered what new fresh Hell waited for him today.

Chapter 4

By October the University was back into the regular fall semester routine. The UVA football season was well underway, and, to everyone's surprise, they were having their best season in years. The students were back to their usual lives of a little studying and a lot of debauchery, the fact that fully 75% of the students were below the legal minimum age for drinking having little or no negative effect on their partying ways. And, of course, the faculty was ready for a vacation getaway. Keith was no exception. He was having a hard time juggling the demands of teaching his courses, keeping his consulting business focused and moving forward, and finding the time to research and write his book. Luckily, things with Loren continued to be fantastic. She had her own undergraduate class to teach as well as the research she was doing towards her doctoral degree. Still, she always found time to help him out when things were starting to spin out of control, whether it was helping him read through student papers, prepare for his next lecture, or helping him prepare reports for Bryant International. She'd also proven herself to be a top-notch researcher when he needed help working on his book. With her computer skills and her incredibly sharp, analytical mind, there never seemed to be anything that she couldn't find, study, and condense into its most important and salient points.

As Keith had expected, his new course on the Politics of Conspiracy was a big hit with the students. His classes were always popular and quickly filled up each semester, but this one was even more popular, with several students even adding the class during the second week as word of mouth spread around the School. The Dean had even talked to him about adding additional sessions for this course next semester. As much as Keith enjoyed teaching the course he was reluctant to commit, not even for the Dean. He didn't want to have too much of his time taken up with teaching and little time left for the consulting business or writing his book. He was already feeling stretched and stressed, and they weren't even two months into the new semester. Why subject himself to the same, or worse, during the spring semester?

Today was a light day for him, relatively speaking. He had a Conspiracy class for an hour and a half in the morning, then he was off to Bryant International for a couple of meetings around mid-day. If everything went as planned he should be home early enough to cook Loren a nice dinner. Maybe something special like beef short ribs braised in a cabernet reduction, some risotto with Fontina and Parmesan-Reggiano, and sautéed *haricot verts*. And since it's Friday night, maybe a bottle or two of Napa's finest from his well-stocked cellar, a collection that many 5-star restaurants would envy. As Keith pulled into the school parking lot in his new BMW 750Li, even the jaded students of UVA, many of whom drive very expensive, top of the line cars -- courtesy of Mommy and Daddy -- took notice. While he'd really rather be driving a hot sports car like a Ferrari or Lamborghini, he thought that the 750Li was a pretty good road car for a big, comfortable four-door sedan. He liked to run it hard on the winding, twisting back country roads outside of Charlottesville, especially Route 250 between Ivy and Crozet. He always felt in control, and so long as he was the one behind the wheel speed never scared him. Put him in the passenger seat though, ceding control to someone else, and he was usually a nervous wreck.

Class began at 9:00 and Keith was pleased, as always, to see that the students were there on time and ready to go. He'd like to think it was because he was a great professor, but he knew that it was the subject matter. His Conspiracy class had become the talk of the School of Politics and one could often hear students talking about this theory or that theory in the hallways or around the grounds. Unlike many professors, Keith didn't spend the entire class time lecturing the students. Instead, he encouraged interaction and the exchange of ideas, reasoning, correctly, that the students learned much more from hearing alternative ideas and points of view than they did by having a professor blather at them for the whole semester. Besides, Keith learned a lot from the students as well, and it often opened his mind to new ways of thinking about a problem. There were 35 students registered for the class, mostly third and fourth year undergraduates. To Keith's way of thinking, this class size was optimal. It fostered friendships and class interaction, plus it allowed the professor to know his students. At many schools, including UVA, many popular and/or required courses, particular first year core courses, are taught in classrooms that resemble small concert halls and have up to several hundred students. The professor – or, more often, a graduate assistant – stands before the multitudes and lectures. Lecture: a one-way communication of information. How is that learning?

Keith sat his things on his desk and addressed the class. "Good morning everyone. Is everybody ready to pick up where we left off last time?" Seeing nods all around, he continued. "So, last time we met we finished our discussion about the Lincoln assassination and how conspiracy theorists pointed fingers at everyone from Lincoln's wife, to the Mason's, to disgruntled Southerners. More importantly, we took a look at how the media of the day helped fuel the fires of the conspiracy theories, even in the days long before the internet, or even TV and radio, were around to spread the word. Does anybody have any further questions about the Lincoln assassination or any further points they think we need to discuss before we move on to our next topic?" Keith looked around the room and saw that there were no questions or comments.

"I don't know if that's a good thing or a bad thing when you guys don't have any more questions or comments. Is that because we covered the subject so well or just because you're bored with Lincoln? Or maybe just because you're too tired to care today and you'd rather be somewhere else?" Keith asked with a smile. Seeing smiles and hearing a bit of laughter from the class he felt that it was OK just to move on.

"OK then, we'll keep marching forward. When I put together the syllabus for this course I wasn't sure in which order we'd study each event. At first I thought about looking at it chronologically, working our way from the days of Caesar up to the present. But, to be honest, I wanted to be able to go with the flow, see where things take us as we explore the various conspiracies. Rather than jump from Lincoln to the next chronological event, the bombing of Pearl Harbor, I'd like us to jump ahead to one of the latest world events that have stirred countless conspiracies, namely, the tragedy of 9/11. For most of you, this is probably the most relatable event we'll study this semester since it's the only one to have happened in your lifetime."

"What about the conspiracy that placed that dude in the stands at the Chicago Cubs playoff game to interfere with the ball and cost the Cubs a shot at the World Series back in 2003? What are the chances that the guy,

Let The Truth Be Told

purely by chance, was in the right place at the right time to cost them the game?" Everyone laughed at this comment from a student named Barry, including Keith. Barry was, to no one's surprise, from Chicago. Most avid sports fans, especially Cubs fans, will probably never forget the incident since it was probably the most egregious case of fan interference ever, and like most modern conspiracy theories, it was caught on tape and rerun millions of times on every newscast in America.

"Well, that world changing event notwithstanding," said Keith with a smile, "I think you'll all find that the events of 9/11 were even more likely to foster many conspiracy theories. Some of the theories we'll look at are, in most people's opinions, nothing more than the wild imaginations of the lunatic fringe. Others, though, have been put forth by some pretty smart, well-educated and well-connected people. It doesn't necessarily mean that they're right, it just means that their positions *might* warrant a little more digging. During our discussion on 9/11, which we'll probably be studying for the next four to five weeks, we'll look at a variety of sources for our information. Some will be traditional readings, including the 9/11 Commission Report. In addition, you're going to be doing a lot of research on your own. I'll be providing you with a list of conspiracy theory sites and blogs, but I encourage you to explore and surf on your own. Be prepared to come to class and share what you've found with the rest of the class; I'd suggest book marking the best sites or saving the best documents, then we'll let you share your findings with the class. And remember, this isn't a competition. This is an opportunity to learn, both for you and for others. I want you to keep an open mind as you do your research, but I also want you to be a bit of a skeptic. Shoot holes in the theories you and your classmates uncover, but do it with facts, not conjecture or opinion. Everybody with me so far?"

The excitement in the room was palpable. Keith was challenging his students to dig for the truth about something that was one of the defining moments in their lives. Like their parents or grandparents before them, who could tell you without question where they were when they heard the news about John F. Kennedy being shot, these young men and women could tell you exactly where they were, what they were doing, even what they were thinking, when they saw or heard the news about the planes hitting the World Trade Center and the Pentagon. It was classes like this, filled with the best and brightest students who were eager to learn, not just be taught, that made Keith want to be a college professor in the first place.

"Alright, a couple of more things. We're not here to debate politics or bash Bush, or Cheney, or Rumsfeld, or Clinton, or any other politician. Trust me, you'll find that there's more than enough blame to go around when you start digging into 9/11, but let's try to keep it civil. We're also not here to pass judgment on Islam or the people that practice that religion, or any religion for that matter. It doesn't matter if you're a Democrat, a Republican, an Independent, or a communist, you deserve to be shown respect while you're sharing ideas in this classroom." Keith couldn't believe that there were actually a good number of students in the class that identified themselves as Republicans – something virtually unheard of when he was a student – but he had to keep reminding himself that most of these young people came of age during a time of Republican majorities in the House and Senate, as well as many years with a Republican president. Arrogance, corruption, lying, and hypocrisy were all they'd ever known, at least in his more liberal view. He'd just have to keep that little thought to himself.....

"Next, I have a little surprise for you guys, and I hope you'll take this in the spirit that it's intended. Let me start by saying that there is absolutely nothing in what I'm about to tell you that is meant to be self-serving. I'm *not* looking for free labor, and I'm not looking for anybody in here to be a suck-up." You could have heard a pin drop in the room. "I've been working with my publisher on a new book about the 9/11 tragedy. The basic premise is simple: I'm trying to determine the truth, the whole truth, and nothing but the truth about what happened that day, including who planned it and who financed it. That's where you have the opportunity to help. You guys are as smart, if not smarter, than any of the so-called experts out there posting conspiracy theories about 9/11. As you do your research for this class I want you to keep your eyes, and your minds, open to anything that could be useful in our search for answers. Develop your own theories if you're so inclined, just be prepared to defend your position with proof and documentation. Be prepared to present your theory to me and your classmates, and expect a critical audience. We owe it to you to be critical, because once you take that next step, telling the world that you have a conspiracy theory, people will say hurtful things about you. Maybe even do hurtful things to you. It can affect your ability to get hired by many employers. It can affect your ability to get government clearances. Many people will assume that you have a mental illness or are, at the very least, 'a little off in the head'. Study this thing long enough and you might just be a little nuts," Keith said, trying to lighten the mood a bit. "I will promise you this: any ideas that you bring to the table that get referenced in the book will be attributed to you, including any quotes taken from papers you prepare for this class. In addition, I plan to pick the top student, the one that contributes the most towards our understanding of the 9/11 conspiracy, to write the Foreword for the book – and that includes having your name on the cover." Keith paused and took a breath. "So, whaddaya think?"

The whole room erupted in hoots and hollers and applause. Dr. Keith Bryant was already a virtual rock star around the School of Politics, but this was just going to push his star factor even higher. His offer was unconventional, to say the least, but the class was definitely excited and inspired by the idea. Most of the students, if not all of them, had aspirations of earning their Masters and PhD's, and they were aware of the pressure to have articles published in academic journals. To get a shot at having their words, their research, used in an important non-fiction book by Dr. Keith Bryant was more than most undergraduates could ever hope for.

"Alright, before we get started I want to leave you with one thought. You guys know that I don't try and wax philosophical up here very often, right? But I want to share something with you, something that has a lot of meaning for me, and I hope it will have a lot of meaning for you as well. It's something that a boss once told me when I was working one of my first 'real' jobs. I won't date myself or embarrass myself by saying what the job was, but to be truthful, it really doesn't matter. I don't think I learned anything of value from my boss or from the job other than this one thing, and for some reason it's stuck with me for years. It goes like this: '3% of the people think, 7% of the people *think* they think, and 90% of the people would rather *die* than think'."

Keith paused and surveyed the room, seeing the inquisitive looks on the students' faces.

"To tell you the truth, I don't know if he made that quote up or if some famous philosopher like Confucius or Gandhi or Nietzsche said it first. All I know is, it's always resonated with me. So many people in the world go through their life without ever really thinking. They just read what someone has written, decide that it aligns with their own views or biases of the world, and then adopt it as their own without giving the first second of critical analysis. It's probably always been this way, but the problem has been exacerbated in our world of instant communications. It's been exacerbated by our MTV society, our sound bite politics, our ADHD-obsessed country. It's been exacerbated by CNN, MSNBC, and Fox News. But you guys are better than that. You don't just hear the news, you *listen*. Two totally different things. You don't take for granted that just because Fox News expresses an opinion that it's necessarily correct, right? 'Fair and balanced' notwithstanding, they still have an agenda, just like they accuse CNN or the *New York Times* of having their own agenda. You're not just smart, you're capable of *thinking*, and that's what I need from you. Approach this 9/11 project by thinking critically. Don't get caught up in all of the political dogma. Everybody with a political axe to grind has a conspiracy theory. Don't get caught up in your zeal to prove something that may not be there, something that may be intentionally misleading. Think. Dig. Research. Discuss. Analyze. Verify. Collaborate. Work within your study groups, and I'll set up a schedule to meet for an hour every week with each group to review your progress and discuss your findings. Bottom line, strive to be one of the 3% that actually *thinks*. Use the brains that God gave you for something besides parroting the words and so-called thoughts of others."

Keith looked around the room and saw that everyone in the class was glued, absolutely hanging on his words. "At the risk of sounding corny or trite, you guys are the future leaders of our country. You're here at UVA because you want to be among the best. You want to learn and grow and network and be ready to make your mark on the world. Well, this is your chance. Your chance to make your mark years earlier than you'd ever hoped, and at the same time find the truth about one of the most heinous crimes in the history of mankind. You'll be opening old wounds when the truth is uncovered, but you'll be providing one of the greatest services that you can ever give your fellow countrymen: the chance to know the truth about what happened to their husbands, their wives, their children, their friends. The chance to bring the guilty to justice. The chance to bring closure to a country that desperately needs it. Don't just take this on because you want a good grade in my class, and don't do it just because you want to see your name in print. Do it because it's something good for your fellow man. Do it because it's something good for your soul. Do it because it's something that cries out to be done, and you're one of the few, *one of the 3%*, that's capable of thinking this through to its conclusion." Keith stopped and waited to see what the reaction would be from the room. He didn't know what to expect, but he hoped that they accepted his sincerity and the truth of his words and didn't think it was just some older guy giving a sermon.

Someone in the room, Keith didn't know who, started to clap. Then others joined in, and just like that the entire class was clapping and cheering. Keith was taken aback. He hadn't meant for his little speech to be so passionate or inspiring. He couldn't stop himself from blushing from embarrassment, but he was happy that his words had been so well received. "Thanks, all of you. I'm glad that you feel as passionately about this as I do. I'm inspired by you guys; you give me hope for the future. Thank God that there are people like you that your generation can look to as our future leaders." Keith smiled. "Alright, then, let's spend the rest of our time today putting together a plan for how we're going to proceed going forward. I'm open to your ideas and suggestions – just don't try to suggest that we skip the final exam. Everything else is on the table."

The class was eager to get started. They were all engrossed for the rest of the session, offering suggestions and taking notes on what they could and should do. One student was particularly engrossed; in fact, he didn't just take notes, he had a miniature video recorder hidden in his backpack to make sure to capture every word, every nuance of Dr. Keith Bryant and his class. He was one of the students that didn't come in until the end of the second week of classes, but nobody gave that a second thought. Students were always changing classes during the Drop/Add period, and about a dozen students had added Keith's Conspiracy class after they heard the buzz around campus. The new student's name was Mathew Hilton, or at least that was the name on his student ID, his transcripts, his UVA application, and his driver's license. He'd been provided a totally new identity and an apartment near campus, and he had a fabricated back story or history created for him that the university would never suspect. As a supposed transferee from Georgetown University, all of his paperwork was in order and his grades were stellar. Hilton was, in reality, a contractor hired by Bob Manning of Destiny Communications Group, and he'd been brought in to monitor and report on Keith's Politics of Conspiracy class. And what he'd witnessed today definitely required making an immediate report to Foster and Manning. While his job was only to monitor and report, he was more than willing to do the dirtier jobs if it became necessary. He actually preferred it versus sitting in a class full of spoiled rich kids that wanted to play junior detective. Like all of the contractors that Manning turned to, Hilton was a former soldier with Special Forces training. Now he was totally freelance and worked for anyone, anywhere, for any side or cause, if the money was right. The hallowed halls of Mr. Jefferson's university had seen many things over the centuries since it was founded, but this had to be the first time that it had seen a mercenary and stone-cold killer sitting in its midst ready, willing, and able to kill one of the school's top professors.

⌘

Loren was enjoying her semester. She was working with a colleague of Keith's, Dr. Donald G. Gibson, that she liked and respected. Her research towards her doctoral dissertation was going well, and if everything continued on schedule she hoped to have it completed within the next 18 months. Things with Keith couldn't be better. They both worked hard, especially Keith with his teaching, his consulting, and his research and writing, but they always made time for each other. Their weekends were magical, whether just lazing around the farm, visiting the many vineyards around Albemarle county and the surrounding areas, or cruising on Keith's beautiful 78' Marlow Explorer, *Kismet*, on the York River and Chesapeake Bay. They'd now been living together a little over five months, and she felt totally comfortable and at home. At the same time, their relationship seemed fresh, new, and exciting. Every day brought them closer as they learned new things about the other and as they spent time together. She was really hoping that he'd pop the question over the Christmas holidays and ask her to marry him. Loren smiled to herself, thinking that if he didn't she might just have to step up and take the initiative again like she did the night they met. She'd taken a chance then and look how well things had worked out!

It was late in the afternoon and Loren was sitting out on the porch enjoying a beautiful early fall day. Thanks to the wireless LAN access that Keith had installed she had access to everything she needed when working from home, even if that meant sitting out on the porch enjoying the afternoon with Bo and Winston while she did it. Thank God for modern technology.

What Loren didn't know – what Loren couldn't know – is that every word she typed on her computer, every word she spoke on her cell phone or the home phone, and every word that she spoke in the house was being monitored by operatives for DCG and analyzed by Electra. Bob Manning and his team had hacked into her PC, as well as Keith's, and dropped in a software worm that allowed every keystroke to be captured. Even though both Loren and Keith kept their anti-virus software up to date, and both their home network and university network were protected by firewalls against computer hacking and intrusion, getting access was child's play for Manning's team. The same for the monitoring on their home and cellular phones. Planting listening devices in the house was a little trickier. First there was the unpredictability of Loren and Keith's schedule, then there were the comings and goings of the caretakers, and finally, there was Bo and Winston. Still, these were only minor inconveniences for the DCG operatives. They got access to the house and were in and out in less than thirty minutes. The listening devices were placed in the bedroom, kitchen, living room, and on the porch. Manning's team hadn't really learned anything yet from the bugs, but they had been able to listen in on some pretty passionate talk and lovemaking. A nice little perk for guys with little or no social lives, to be sure.

Even though the listening devices weren't yielding anything substantive yet didn't mean that the DCG team hadn't dug up any information. Far from it. When Colonel Foster gave Manning and his team orders to dig in to Keith's and Loren's lives they didn't waste any time. Within a couple of days the team had assembled volumes of information on both of them. To say that DCG now knows more about Keith and Loren than they know about each other, or even more than they know about themselves, is an understatement. They had copies of their transcripts from every school they'd ever attended. Copies of every tax return. Copies of every resume, every job performance review, and every job application they'd ever had. Copies of their credit card statements going back over ten years, and the same for their bank statements. Copies of Keith's lecture notes and copies of his masters thesis and doctoral dissertation, and the same for Loren. Copies of things that aren't supposed to be made public, like both of their medical records from every doctor and hospital they'd ever used. They had even managed to get their hands on the records from a Planned Parenthood clinic where Loren had gone seeking an abortion when she was barely twenty-two; Loren had never even shared this with Keith, and only one other person in the world besides Loren even knew about it. DCG knew what they ate, where they ate, and how much they paid to eat. They knew where Keith and Loren traveled and what they did when they got there. Manning's team fed all of this information to Electra and asked her to find something, anything, that could be used as leverage should the need arise. Other than the abortion in Loren's past, something that wouldn't even begin to raise an eyebrow if made public, Electra couldn't find anything to use as dirt. That was merely an inconvenience to Colonel Foster. Just because there's no dirt doesn't mean that he can't have his people create the dirt and insert it into someone's history in such a way that it becomes part of the official record. Should the situation ever necessitate such action, Colonel Foster and his team would have no compunction whatsoever about doing just that.

Chapter 5

Keith's class was barely two weeks into the project and already they had done an incredible amount of research. If he'd had to do it all himself it would have taken at least six months to accomplish the same, even assuming that his research would have driven him in the same directions. He learned long ago that research was a very personal, very individual endeavor. Even if two people started at the same place and were told what the end result should be, it's a virtual certainty that they'd take vastly different routes getting there. The class had, inevitably, used many of the same resources that Keith had used, so while the information gained from those sources didn't put them any closer to the Holy Grail, as the class had come to call it, it did provide them a great learning experience since much of it was new to them. Plus, Keith and the class all benefited from hearing the interpretation and perspective on the data from other students. Already the class was starting to 'think'. Keith was pleased.

As he had promised, Keith had been meeting with each of the five study groups every week to see how they were progressing and to provide them guidance. It was amazing the discipline these students displayed, both individually and within the study groups. They assigned tasks among the team members and had a rigorous peer review system in place. Before they would bring something to Keith or the larger class, at least two members of the study group had to review the information. The peer review was part interrogation, part support group, and part devils-advocate. As with top students everywhere, these guys were supportive of the team or group but still very competitive individually. The last thing they wanted was to look bad in front of their peers, so they really did their homework before sharing anything with the group. Likewise, Keith didn't want to let his class down, so he was also working hard reviewing and critiquing their submissions while also doing his own research.

As the class settled down Keith opened his notes. His plan was to spend part of their time together today talking about the collective finding of the study groups and the rest of the time talking about their plans for the coming week. "Good morning everyone. Let me start off today's session by thanking you guys for all of the great work and research I've seen from you over the past couple of weeks. The volume of research, and, more importantly, the quality of research, that you've shared with me has been incredible. What do you guys think, has this been a worthwhile project so far?" The class seemed unanimous in their enthusiastic responses, so Keith continued. "I want to talk to you today about some of what I've found through my research over the past twelve-plus months, and also debrief you on what you guys have provided me. Then we'll talk a bit about next steps."

"First, let me talk to you a little bit about two of the main schools of thought concerning 9/11. Two of the study groups are already working these angles, so for them this may be more of a review, but for the rest of you this will perhaps be new. The first theory is that the government, or some parts of our government, knew about the plans for 9/11 and did nothing to stop it from happening. This is known in the conspiracy communities as LIHOP, which stands for 'let it happen on purpose'. The concept of LIHOP isn't new; in fact, in the past 100 years we've seen the same concept raised for the bombing of Pearl Harbor, the JFK assassination, and other world events. Basically, the reasoning behind LIHOP, as it applies to 9/11, is that the government knew that Al Qaeda was going to do something big and that they were going to do it sometime around September of 2001. The government may not have known the details, but regardless, they didn't act proactively to find out the details or prevent anything from happening because the attacks served some purpose in our government's eyes. We'll talk more about that in a minute. First let's look at the other conspiracy school of thought, called MIHOP. MIHOP stands for 'made it happen on purpose' and theorizes that factions within our government caused the actions of 9/11 to take place, whether through funding of the operation, planning of the operation, or maybe both."

"May I ask a question please, Professor Bryant?"

"Sure, Sandra. Go ahead." Sandra Goodwin was a fourth year student majoring in Government and Political Science and hoped to go on to pursue her Masters degree, and like all of the students in his class she was very bright and very inquisitive. Students like her often made Keith wonder if he'd be able to get into a top college like UVA or the Naval Academy if he were just coming along now. The level of competition was definitely higher than when he was first starting college, that's for sure.

"Obviously, there are always a lot of whackos out there that come up with all sorts of crazy conspiracy theories, but has your research turned up any credible proponents of either LIHOP or MIHOP? It seems to be a real leap to presume that our government would allow the killing of thousands of our citizens if there had been any foreknowledge of the events or any way to prevent them."

"That's a good point, but I'd take it a step further to say that there is even a huge leap between subscribing to LIHOP versus MIHOP. Not that it's not still a major breach of trust for a government to allow something like 9/11 to happen if they *could* have prevented it, but think how much worse it would be to learn that your government actually *caused* it to happen for some sort of political and/or financial gain. But to answer your question, yes, there are some very credible people in both the United States and around the world that are proponents of both LIHOP and MIHOP. What we don't have, in either case, is the smoking gun that proves them true. This is actually a very similar situation to the JFK assassination: a very high percentage of Americans disbelieve the official Warren Commission report and the follow-up investigations into that tragedy, but without hard proof the theories just languish. It's been over forty years since Kennedy was shot, and we're no closer now to having everyone believe the official story than we were when it happened. Maybe less so."

"What kind of proof would be required, in your mind, to rise to the level of a smoking gun?" This from a third year student named Travis.

"At least one or more of several things. First, a paper trail of communications between conspirators, such as e-mails, memos, etc. Second, one or more unimpeachable witnesses or participants to the conspiracy. And third, and often most important, is the money trail. In today's world, forensic accounting is one of the most important crime-fighting tools that the authorities have."

"So, Professor Bryant, you're not a believer in LIHOP or MIHOP are you?" This from Ward, a fourth year student from Hampton, VA with aspirations of going into politics.

Keith thought for a minute to formulate an answer. He always tried to keep his beliefs and prejudices just below the surface so as not to unduly influence the students. He wanted them to form their own educated opinions about the world, not latch on blindly to what he, or any other professor, believed. Keith sighed, and then took a deep breath before speaking. "I've always been careful not to go too far in sharing my beliefs with you, feeling that it's more important to help guide you, help you learn to think critically and form your own opinions regardless of the subject matter. I'd be a liar if I didn't say that I like it when others agree with me or respect my opinions. We all do; I guess it's that little narcissistic trait in all of us. But as your professor, I'm in a slightly more influential position than the average guy on the street, right? I mean, you might agree with what I say because you want a good grade in my class, or because I'm helping to advise you on your thesis or writing a recommendation for you for graduate school. I also may have more influence because you see the letters 'PhD' behind my name, or because you know I've written some books on government and international relations. My point is, I'm happy if you hear what I have to say and you use it as one more data point as you come to your own conclusions – we're back to that *thinking* thing again – but don't listen to my opinion and automatically assume I'm right and make it yours." Keith paused and scanned the faces in the room, hoping that what he said would satisfy their curiosity and allow him to move on to something else. No such luck. They were hanging on his every word. "That being said, do you still want to know what I think?"

Everyone seemed to be of the same mind and affirming what he was most afraid of.

"I was afraid this day would come. Damn." Keith smiled and tried to laugh it off. He knew that there was no easy way out of this. "OK, here goes. Sorry to shock or disappoint you all, but actually, I am definitely a proponent of the MIHOP theory." To a person, you could see the shock on their faces. "In other conspiracies, like JFK and Pearl Harbor, I'm not a MIHOP, or even a LIHOP. But when it comes to 9/11 I am firmly and unapologetically in the MIHOP camp. I've not asked you guys to believe that theory or even try to prove that theory for me with your research, but I believe that if the research is done and the paper and money trails are followed, we are going to find that someone within our government had direct involvement with planning and financing 9/11. If that is in fact the case, I think the evidence will show, incontrovertibly, that certain government officials, certain highly influential members of the so-called 'military-industrial complex' and certain financial organizations intentionally caused 9/11 to happen. Al Qaeda flew the planes into the building and killed the people, but they were merely the people carrying out the contract. In all likelihood Al Qaeda doesn't even know that they were our patsy. As far as they know they carried out their mission against the Great Satan. Imagine their shock if they found out that they did it at the *request* of the Great Satan."

Conrad Fox, one of the leaders of the UVA chapter of the College Republicans, was already becoming agitated and angry. "Are you suggesting, for even one moment, that President Bush is complicit in the tragedy of 9/11? That is a very serious allegation for anyone to make."

"No, I'm not alleging that at all. What I *believe* is that some members of the US government are directly involved. Who those people might be – White House insiders, the Pentagon, certain members of Congress, members of the intelligence community – I don't know. I do know that the number of people having direct knowledge of the conspiracy has to be extremely small. Regardless of the current administration's attempts to stamp "Secret" on every document that's printed, including the menu for state dinners, there is no way that this could remain secret if the conspiracy was broad-based."

"Or, the fact that the secrets have never leaked out could be because you're totally off-base and there are no such secrets to be revealed," continued Fox.

"You're absolutely right, and that's a very important point relative to what I stated earlier. I have my beliefs, but they should not automatically become your beliefs *especially* when I cannot back up my beliefs with proof. If you are provided incontrovertible evidence that any theory or statement is true and you choose to ignore it, then you're not holding onto your own theory, you're just being ignorant. However, in the absence of such proof, and to Mr. Fox's point, I don't have such proof to provide you, you owe it to yourself to view my opinions with the same skepticism that you would show any other researcher. We can respect each other's opinions and a person's right to have that opinion without accepting their opinion as truth. Mr. Fox, thank you for helping me make that point"

"Professor Bryant, why don't you believe that George Bush could be complicit in 9/11?" This from Alex, a former homecoming queen and head cheerleader at her high school in Rockville, MD. She was a fourth year Government/Political Science major and hoped to work in the White House or Capitol Hill upon graduation.

Keith hesitated once again, collecting his thoughts. He really didn't want to go there, but he didn't really see a good way out of answering the question. "I was hoping not to have to go down this rat hole with you guys, but I guess there's no going back now. Look, it's really pretty simple: just as I don't want to influence you're thinking about the 9/11 conspiracy, I don't want to burden you with my political philosophy. My politics really aren't germane to our discussions within this class, at least inasmuch as I don't let my personal feelings intrude on what I'm trying to teach. You know, politics used to be a bit more private, but those days seem to be long gone. People used to say that the two things you never wanted to discuss at a dinner party were religion and politics, because no matter what you believe, no matter how sincerely you believe it, and no matter how much you try to show respect for other people's opinions, you'll still end up alienating someone in the room. I'll share a bit of my political thoughts with you here, but again, form your own thoughts. Agree or disagree with me as you like, because that's your right. But if I have to go out on a limb to answer Alex's question, I'm going to try to give you the whole unvarnished truth, because my perspective – what I truly believe, politically – does impact and influence how I approach my research and my writing. So you guys are sure you want to hear this, right? You're not going to decide you dislike me and this class based on my political leanings, are you?"

Without exception, the members of the class agreed that they could and would respect his views. Still, Keith wasn't so sure, but at this point he felt committed. "OK, here's where I'm coming from. I don't think Bush was directly involved in the events of 9/11 for a few reasons. First, I don't think that George W. Bush has it in him to be that evil. Don't get me wrong, I don't think he's a good man. Far from it. I think he's a 'Christian of convenience' when it's useful to rally the troops from the conservative base to his cause *du jour*, and I think he's the worst thing to happen to this country, politically, in at least one or two generations. Nobody in history has gone to such great lengths to try to divide this country along political lines: blue states versus red states, rich versus poor, black versus white, American citizens versus immigrants, 'stay the course in Iraq' patriots versus 'cut and run' terrorist lovers, and the list goes on and on. Second, I don't think George Bush is smart enough to have had any hand in this kind of complex plot, and even if he were he'd keep far away from any involvement in order to maintain some plausible deniability. If recent history has proven anything, it's that somebody will leak information to the press and there will be the inevitable paper trail. No, Bush may not be the sharpest knife in the drawer, but he's smart enough politically to keep something this big as far away from him as possible."

One of the students had a question. "Professor, what makes you think that President Bush is dumb? He's got credentials that are pretty impressive, and isn't he the only President to have a Harvard MBA?" Carter St. John was another of the College Republicans. He was a good student and someone that was destined to go far. He came from old money in Houston and his family was very active in the Texas Republican party. In fact, they had been big campaign and financial supporters of George W. Bush, as well as his father.

"That's very true, Carter. As we all know, he graduated from Yale. Excellent school, without a doubt. Of course, and pardon me for digressing, because I really don't want this to be a Bush-bashing party, all of us know, even if we're ardent Bush supporters, that the only reason he got into Yale was because of his daddy. Left to rely on his own grades, test scores, etc., he probably would have gotten turned down for his local community college." That statement elicited a lot of laughter from most members of the class. "But in fairness, he did make it through Yale, and he did later go on to earn his MBA. From that point on, through all of the trials and tribulations that you guys have heard about – his National Guard service, his forays into the oil business, the baseball teams, etc. – he's basically had daddy there to bail him out time after time. He really is an anomaly to me. He seems utterly incapable of doing anything on his own, but he parlays his family and business connections into becoming the Governor of Texas and then the President of the United States. It's like he's 'Forest Gumped' his way through life, but without the charm and the bad haircut." Once again the class was laughing at his statements. Maybe if he got fired from UVA for talking this way in front of his students he could go on the comedy club circuit, he reasoned. "So let me reiterate: I don't think Bush was complicit in 9/11 because I don't think he's smart enough and I don't think he's evil enough. That doesn't mean, by the way, that I don't believe that there are some people within Bush's administration, perhaps some very senior members, that are evil enough to have been involved."

"Care to name names on that point?" asked Jennifer Ellis, with a smile.

Keith laughed. "No, I don't think I'll touch that one at this point, but let me say this: I hope that George W., for all of his many faults, stays healthy and remains as our president until the end of his term, because as much as I dislike him, as bad as I think he is for this country, the line of succession is much, much scarier."

Carter St. John had another question, this time getting even more personal. "From all that we've heard you say today, as well as things you've said in other classes, things you've written in your books, and so on, it seems pretty obvious that you're a far left-leaning liberal Democrat, so by definition you would hate George Bush and his administration."

Keith didn't take the bait and try to make this into an ideological argument, especially not in front of the entire class. "I can see why you might think that, in light of the so-called 'evidence' that you sited. But actually, you'd be wrong. While I'm certainly more liberal than Mr. St. John, I actually consider myself more of a middle-of-the-road guy. Where I stand depends more on a particular issue than on any party or ideological allegiance. For example, I'm very much in favor of a strong national defense – typically associated with conservatives – but I'm also completely pro-choice when it comes to the issue of abortion and family planning. Obviously, that's a more liberal stance. In my mind, people throw around these political labels to pigeonhole others, often using one or two issues as litmus tests to decide if someone is conservative versus liberal, Democrat versus Republican, or God-fearing Christian versus secular humanist. I don't subscribe to that, and one thing I hope that my students take away from all of my classes is to look beyond the generalities, the stereotypes. Again, it gets right back to that notion of *thinking*. While we're on the subject of my political leanings, let me share another thing with you. Listen up, because I think this may be one of the most important points you can take away from this whole semester. Mr. St. John believes that I'm a liberal Democrat. I'm OK with him thinking that, because I can think of worse things to be called – although he probably can't," Keith said with a smile. Luckily it had the desired affect, because Carter St. John smiled, too. "But to be truthful, for many years I supported and voted Republican. In fact, as a kid I worked on the local campaign committee in support of Ronald Reagan in both of his presidential bids, and then, when I was old enough, I actually voted for George H.W. Bush once. During that period, the Democrats were in control of both houses of Congress and I was livid with their actions and their uncooperativeness with the administration. I once suggested, only half-jokingly, that they should lock the doors of the House and Senate, even if that meant putting Congress under sort of a 'house arrest', to allow the administration's policies to move forward. So how's that for pretty radical thinking?"

"Professor, you said that you voted for Bush Sr. once. I assume that means that you voted for him the first time he won election in 1988 but then voted against him in 1992 in favor of Bill Clinton?" This question came from Jason Highsmith, a fourth year student from Connecticut.

"Jason is right on the money. I voted for Bush Sr. for his first term but then voted to throw him out on his ear after one term in favor of Bill Clinton, a Democrat. That's a pretty dramatic shift, is it not? That brings me to the point that I wanted to make: Sometimes there is a right man, or a right woman, for the times. If we look back to 1980, we were still in the Cold War era, the Soviet Union was starting to spin out of control after their debacle in Afghanistan, and it was just a dangerous time in the world. Along comes a cowboy, Ronald Reagan, who was just the man for this period in history. He talked tough and stood tough against the Soviet Union, or as he called it, the 'evil empire'. Because of his presidency we saw the fall of the Soviet Union, and soon after, the fall of the Berlin Wall. Reagan was no Mensa candidate himself, to be sure, but he was the right man for the job. Jimmy Carter, God bless him, was probably one of the smartest men to ever occupy the Oval Office, but he could have never done what Reagan did. In fact, for all of his brains he was probably one of the least effective Presidents of the twentieth century. Good man, but wrong man for the times. George Bush Sr. won election not so much because he was the right man for the times but because he could continue in the steps of Reagan. That period of time needed another Reagan, and Bush Sr. performed admirably, for the most part. However, here's where it starts to get interesting, where we see a shift in Washington. Most of you were not even yet in kindergarten, but one of the most important social changes of the late 20th century was taking place and we're still living with the repercussions today. Anybody have a guess to what I'm talking about?"

Amber Kervin spoke up. "Are you referring to the Republicans taking control of the House and the Senate?"

"Exactly. After about forty years in control of both houses of Congress, the Democrats are thrown out. Now here come the Republicans promising to save the day, led by Newt Gingrich and his minions. They have their 'Contract With America' and they're bringing in the religious right to help lead our country out of its supposed moral decay. Then we witness the spawning and growing influence of groups like the Moral Majority, led by the Reverend Jerry Falwell. We see people like Pat Robertson gaining new political influence and, magically, building a new university and broadcasting network a few hours down the road from here in Chesapeake. Every conservative cause suddenly has a new audience and a new group of champions promising to shepherd legislation through Congress. So, in a nutshell, when I witnessed the growing influence of the religious right and the conservative, Republican majority in Congress, I no longer felt comfortable having a Republican president. I'm afraid of what will happen to the social fabric of America if we start having rubber-stamped legislation coming down the pike courtesy of the Republican party, especially when it comes to major social issues such as separation of church and state."

Amber followed-up with another question. "So your disaffection with the Republican party had more to do with their shift towards the Christian right than with George Bush Sr.?"

"Absolutely. Again, keep in mind the concept that I spoke about a few minutes ago, that sometimes there is the right man or right woman for the times. I like to expand that thought to include groups of people as well, in this case political parties. Simply stated, my thoughts and beliefs haven't changed that much over the past twenty years, *but the political party that represents those beliefs has changed.* For the past ten to fifteen years, the Democratic party has been more centrist and the Republicans have been more radical and conservative, at least in their rhetoric. In addition, think about some of the stereotypes of the political parties and see how they've changed. Republicans are supposed to be fiscally conservative, yet under this administration they've gone from a budget surplus – courtesy of eight years of a Democratic president – to being trillions of dollars in debt. Does that sound like the party of the balanced budget and fiscal conservatism? How about this one: the Republican party has always claimed to be the party of 'small government'. They said that Democrats were for big government and were only around to 'tax and spend'. But here we are today, almost eight years into the reign of George W. Bush and, for many of those years, with a Republican majority in the House and Senate, and what's happened? The government has grown bigger than ever, and not just because of the creation of the Department of Homeland Security. Recent figures have shown that the number of government employees is at the highest levels in history. We could site more examples of party changes, like all of the Republican ethics scandals after coming to power promising to clean up Washington, or the fact that Republicans are now gung-ho for military action, yet if you look at the party in years past, say during World War II, Korea, and Viet Nam, they tried to block the Democrats from taking military action. I apologize for being long-winded, but all of this is just to say, look beyond the party affiliation, beyond the stereotypes, and beyond the hype. Look at what your leaders stand for, what kind of character they have, and hold them accountable for fulfilling the promises they made to get elected. And be sure that you recognize when the times are changing and be sure that you're looking to leaders that are the right person for those times."

Keith looked around the room to see how his message was being received. Generally, his message was resonating with most of the class. You could see them deep in thought, giving thoughtful consideration to what he had said. A few, like Conrad Fox, were less than thrilled with his views, but even those people were smart and respectful enough to consider viewpoints different than their own.

If Conrad Fox and some of his College Republican brethren – or, as many on campus referred to them, the "Hitler Youth" – were a little annoyed at Keith's views, one person was absolutely seething with anger. Mathew Hilton, the operative for Colonel Foster and Bob Manning, was ready to explode. If he were allowed to, he'd gladly kill Dr. Keith Bryant right here, right now. Even though he didn't carry a weapon while attending classes, on specific orders from Foster and Manning, he would gladly snap the neck of 'that liberal little cocksucker', as he usually referred to him, if he could get him alone. He knew that Keith was a former athlete and former military, but that didn't concern Hilton at all; he was a trained killer.

Hilton kept his opinions to himself, as he always did in Keith's class. He'd made it a point to always sit near the back of the class, change seats each session, and avoid interaction with the other students as much as possible. Better to remain a mystery to others, someone that they would have a hard time describing to authorities should the situation ever arise. Of course, it's a little hard to blend in when you're 6'2" and 220 pounds of solid muscle, but Hilton did what he could to play that down, including wearing loose-fitting clothes, covering up the tattoo on his upper right bicep, and growing his hair a little longer than the standard military cut. He knew that Foster would never give his approval to kill Keith, at least not for the supposed sin of expressing liberal views, but he was going to make sure to report everything that was said as soon as he got to his secure mobile phone in his car.

For the next twenty minutes Keith fielded questions from the class about his thoughts, their thoughts, their similarities and differences. He was sure that, had he allowed it, this discussion would have gone on for the rest of the day. "One last thing for you guys before we start getting into the real points of discussion for today's session, not that it hasn't been a blast so far," said Keith with a smile. "I've asked my research assistant, Lowell Westbrook, to create a website on the university intranet for all of our information to get posted. I'm not ready to share this information with the outside world, and I'll ask you to please not share anything created within this class with anyone outside of here. We don't want to embarrass the University by posting our theories, especially half-baked ones, on any of these conspiracy theory blogs or websites. All of you will have secure access to the site; for now, it's read-only, and all postings get approved by me and posted by Lowell. Consider this another tool for your research. Read and learn from your peers, see where they're going with their research, what conclusions they've reached. Remember, we're approaching this is a team, not as competitors."

⌘

LOWELL, HIS GRADUATE RESEARCH ASSISTANT, was certainly more than capable of building and maintaining the website. He had a BS and MS degree in Computer Science, as well as an MS in Government and Political Science, from UC Berkley. Though incredibly bright, Keith didn't consider Lowell among his favorite graduate assistants he'd ever had. He was a little bit cocky, thought he was just a little bit better than everybody else because he'd graduated from Berkley. He tended to talk down to the students in Keith's undergraduate classes when he was leading a session. Rather than engaging them in the class and sharing ideas he preferred to stand up and lecture. Keith had told Loren on several occasions that he thought Lowell was in love with the sound of his own voice. When Keith tried to provide Lowell with constructive feedback about his research, his teaching style, or his dissertation, he got very defensive and argumentative.

What Keith didn't know, couldn't have known, is that Lowell was a friend and colleague of Jeff Anders, the Silicon Valley guru and core team member of Let the Truth Be Told. Lowell and Jeff had connected during Lowell's time at Berkley, though this was before Jeff Anders and the LTBT group had really formed. Lowell worked for one of Jeff's companies and had caught his eye because of his incredible computer and programming skills. Lowell became one of Jeff's key people and was instrumental in identifying and helping run several of the startup companies that Jeff invested in as a venture capitalist. They remained friends to this day, even as Lowell chose to cash out and return to school to pursue his PhD at UVA. Lowell knew about Jeff's current involvement with Let the Truth Be Told; in fact, he had assisted Jeff and his extended team with research on several occasions over the past year or two. He would definitely have to share some of the more important postings from Keith's class with Jeff. Lowell didn't want to hurt Keith or anyone in his class, but he felt that the work that Jeff and LTBT were doing was important for America, much more so than Keith's book or class project. If he'd only known the chain of events he was unleashing by his simple act of betrayal, perhaps he would have reconsidered. On the other hand, perhaps not. Sometimes you just can't save the true believers.

Chapter 6

Mathew Hilton pulled out of Charlottesville early Friday afternoon and headed to Northern Virginia to meet with Colonel Foster and Bob Manning regarding the week's developments, or, more accurately, his reaction to minor developments. He had called Foster as soon as he was back in his car after class. He was using a DCG-provided mobile phone with NSA-level encryption, so there was no need to worry about someone monitoring his calls, but Hilton was still too much of a professional to risk using the phone until he was safely in his car and heading away from the UVA campus. Hilton had tried his best to be accurate in his assessment of the week's events, particularly in his review of today's class, but his deep disdain for Keith and his liberal bullshit politics was definitely skewing his thinking and causing him to embellish things. Foster was an astute judge of character, particularly when it came to hired professionals like Hilton, so he was not overly alarmed by what he'd heard. Still, Foster was not about to take any chances. He ordered Hilton to pack a bag and get himself up to DCG headquarters as quickly as possible. Ever the good soldier, especially when he was being paid this kind of money, Hilton rushed back to his apartment, threw a few things in a duffel bag, including his weapon and spare ammunition, and headed north on Route 29. The trip to Reston should take a little over two hours on a good day – assuming that the DC area ever *had* a good day for traffic. Today it took Hilton nearly three hours, so by the time he reached the DCG office he was about to explode with anger.

Colonel Foster, Bob Manning, and Mathew Hilton met in the conference room in the Bunker. Not that Foster ever allowed any of the Bunker specialists or hired operatives to show up at the real DCG headquarters, but there was no way that he was going to let a hothead like Hilton in there. The Bunker was totally soundproof, so if they needed to let Hilton blow-off some steam there was nothing to worry about as far as being seen or overheard. Or, Foster smiled to himself, if they needed to blow Hilton's head off instead, they could also do that in complete privacy. Hopefully it wouldn't have to come to that…good operatives are so hard to find.

"What can I get you gentleman to drink?" asked Foster. "Surely it must be after 5 o'clock somewhere on this Friday afternoon."

"Scotch rocks for me, since you're pouring" said Bob Manning.

"And how about you, Mr. Hilton?" Even though Foster knew Hilton's real name he would never use it, not even in private. Better to always be in the habit of using the alias.

"Jack Daniels rocks. Make mine a double, if you don't mind. It's been a helluva week, especially with the Friday afternoon drive up here. I'm glad I don't live around here full-time anymore and have to put up with this fucking traffic everyday."

"I'm sure. We really appreciate the fine work you're doing, and especially your willingness to drop everything on a Friday and come up to DC at the last minute." This from Foster.

"No problem, especially since you guys are being more than generous with the compensation. Plus, I have to admit, as irritating as this professor and his class can be, it is a more pleasant environment than I often have to work in. Least I'm not slogging through some nasty-ass jungle in the Congo or something."

Foster eyed Hilton and had to work hard to veil the contempt that he felt for him. Dealing with cretins like him was a part of the game in the intelligence business. It took a certain type of cold, detached bastard to be able to operate in this world. Hilton was certainly that, though Foster wondered if perhaps he'd crossed the line from trained professional to sociopath somewhere along the way. "True enough. UVA and Charlottesville certainly don't qualify as a hardship duty location. Let's talk about what you've observed there so far, where you see Dr. Bryant and his class heading. I've seen your daily reports and your videos from the various classes and study groups, and they've been excellent, but I want to get your perspective. You're there with the subjects, so you know better than anyone what's happening." Foster knew that operatives like Hilton had serious egos, especially when you appealed to their brains rather than just their brawn, and a little stroking might help things along.

"OK, here's what I see happening. Dr. Bryant is a seriously smart dude, but he's ate up with his liberal bullshit. He believes, and he's hell-bent on proving, that some members of our government are complicit in the events and cover-up of 9/11."

"Has he made direct reference to any particular member of the administration being complicit?" asked Bob Manning.

"No, to be fair, he's actually come right out and said that he doesn't know who is complicit. He's even made it a point to say that he doesn't believe that Bush was directly involved, though he did it by damning him with faint praise when he said that Bush was too stupid to have come up with a plot this secret and this sophisticated."

Foster knew that this was a gross oversimplification of what was said, but he let it pass. "So no references to any particular people or agency then? Nothing to indicate that he had evidence, or supposed evidence, implicating members of the administration, the intelligence or defense community, or private citizens?"

"No, nothing like that. At least not yet. As you know, he's enlisted his students to help with the research, including dangling a major carrot in their face when he told them that they would get their words and reference material cited in the book and a chance to write the Foreword. For these geeks that was almost as good as dangling the winning lottery ticket in front of their faces."

Bob Manning also found Hilton to be a boor, at best. Still, he kept up the façade. "Where do you think he's trying to go with his research?"

"He's made no secret that he's a firm believer in the MIHOP theory, so he's definitely steering things in that direction. My impression is that he's a straight arrow and won't fabricate and publish a theory based on speculation. He's already a published author, a successful businessman, and has shitloads of money. He's the type to be more worried about his reputation as both an author and an academic. In a nutshell, this guy is going to keep on digging until he finds evidence to support his theory, assuming that such evidence exists. He's enlisted the help of 30-plus students as virtual research assistants, and even though these are undergraduates, mostly third and fourth year, we shouldn't take their abilities lightly. They're a bunch of arrogant little fuckers, but they are unquestionably bright, capable, and focused"

Colonel Foster had a question. "What do you make of Dr. Bryant's move to have the class' information posted on an internal website? Should that be a cause for concern for us at this point?"

"To be honest, I'm not sure. It's obviously something that we're going to have to watch closely as the situation develops over the next few days or the next week, but right now I don't think they have anything to post that doesn't already exist in dozens of other places on the internet. He's trying to go to great lengths to make sure that information is not shared with the outside world at this point. He wants to make sure that if and when they have something worth talking about it's done in such a way that no harm or embarrassment will come to the university, or to him and his students, for that matter. I think he's smart enough to realize that posting a conspiracy theory, regardless of whether it's about 9/11, UFO's, or Bigfoot, makes you about as welcome at a place like UVA as an AIDS patient in a sex club." Hilton had to smile at his little attempt at humor. Foster and Manning seemed less amused; must have a stick up their asses, he thought to himself.

"Makes sense," said Foster. The more he talked to Hilton the more he knew that he really, really, didn't like him. This would be the last time that DCG used his services. For that matter, Foster wasn't sure if he'd even be left alive when this thing was over. "Anything else we should be watching? Perhaps his girlfriend, his assistant, or some other student or faculty member?"

"I've been keeping tabs on his girlfriend, Loren. Not that that's hardship duty – though it may be a little 'hardship', if you get my drift. She is one major league peace of ass." Hilton thought that was hysterical. Foster and Manning merely smiled, though he didn't realize that behind those smiles they were both ready to cut his heart out and feed it to him. "She spends a lot of time doing her own research for her dissertation, as well as quite a bit of time helping Dr. Bryant with his research and his classes. Off hours those two are joined at the hip; you rarely see one without the other. True love, I guess. I don't have too much on the research assistant, Lowell Westbrook. Apparently a pretty smart guy, double Masters, working on his PhD. Reportedly made a bunch of money working in Silicon Valley and doesn't have to worry much about getting a real job while he's here working on the doctorate. I've only seen him a handful of times, comes across as kind of snotty to most people, in my opinion. If you think he's worth watching I can step things up a bit, maybe drop in a listening device in his office, that kind of thing."

"Actually, we may need you to take things a bit further than that with Mr. Westbrook," said Foster. "Let me fill you in a bit where he's concerned. As you're aware, in this business information is on a need to know basis. In this case, we think you need to know the following: Lowell Westbrook could be a threat to us due to his connections with some of the more highly educated and highly regarded people in the conspiracy community."

Hilton interrupted, smirking. "Did you say highly educated and highly regarded? Isn't that a bit of an oxymoron when you're talking about these conspiracy nuts?"

Foster fought to keep himself under control. "In many cases, the members of the conspiracy community are quite intelligent and they often have a large following. Some, of course, are just whackos, but in the case of Lowell Westbrook we are very decidedly not talking about those kinds of people. We're talking about people that are highly educated, extremely thorough, and extremely professional. We don't take them lightly, and neither should you."

"OK, gotcha. Has he already crossed the line with you, or are we still just in the wait-and-see mode?"

Manning picked up for Foster. "He's kept in touch with an old friend named Jeff Anders pretty regularly over the past year or so, based on his phone records and e-mail records. Anders is one of the principals of a research group called Let the Truth Be Told, and they are an incredibly strong player in the conspiracy theory world. We originally looked at Westbrook just because he was Dr. Bryant's research assistant, but we soon found the link between him and Anders." Manning didn't add that it had taken Electra only a few minutes of data crunching to find that connection. "As soon as Dr. Bryant kicked off this Politics of Conspiracy class this semester the chatter between Westbrook and Anders picked up, though, to be honest, Westbrook hasn't really had anything worthwhile to share to this point. That seemed to change earlier this afternoon, however, coincident with the events from today's class. Westbrook wasted no time in communicating with Anders and telling him about the new intranet site and the information that he expected to be posting on it."

"Looks like our Mr. Lowell Westbrook is a sneaky little shit, doesn't it?" asked Hilton.

"Yes, it seems that he is," answered Foster. "He even went a step beyond simply informing Anders about the intranet site. Mr. Westbrook actually created a backdoor into the university's intranet site to allow Anders and his cohorts *carte blanche* access. For all practical purposes, Anders is going to have access to every single word that gets posted on that site, and that is *not* a good thing for us."

"Why is that an issue for you? You said that Anders and his conspiracy group already have their own website and their own theories posted out there. What's it matter if he reads the information posted by a bunch of college kids for a class project?"

Foster crafted his words carefully so as to convey the seriousness of the situation without betraying too much confidential information. "Keep in mind that the postings aren't just from the students, though we should never downplay their capabilities. They are a very bright bunch, otherwise they wouldn't be sitting at UVA. Plus, they have the power of collaboration, and you never know where the collective thinking of a large group of people is going to lead. It could easily lead them to places that we don't want them to go. In addition, remember that Dr. Bryant will also be posting information on that site, information that he will use in his book. He's already stated, in his class, that he is targeting his research at information that can prove his theory that factions within the American government were directly responsible for 9/11. Even though no such proof exists – can't exist, since it's not true – having well-respected people like Dr. Bryant poking their nose around where it doesn't belong can cause a lot of embarrassment for some highly placed people."

Hilton didn't totally believe Foster's statement about no proof of government involvement, but at this point he didn't really care. He wasn't being paid to care. He was being paid to keep an eye on people that could cause harm to our government, and whether or not those people were making shit up or had proof from God himself was of no concern to Hilton. He would do whatever was needed to meet the goals of his employer, especially if that meant the opportunity to work for this obviously well-funded outfit again. "So how do you want me to proceed? Do I need to make Mr. Westbrook disappear?"

"Not quite yet," said Foster. "Let's keep an eye on things over the next few days. Hopefully it won't come to that, but, to be honest, I'm not optimistic about Mr. Westbrook's future. Be thinking about a way to handle this situation, and make sure that it can never be traced back to you. You're too valuable of an asset and we need to keep you in the mix there with Dr. Bryant and his class. Report back to me by Monday noon to discuss your plans for terminating Westbrook if it should come to that. Speak to nobody but me and Manning. Nobody. Got it?"

"Definitely. What about Dr. Bryant and his girlfriend? Are you considering action for them as well?" Hilton really hoped so. He wanted to be able to handle those jobs personally.

"Not yet. I am sending a team down to talk to Dr. Bryant, though, and I want you to be aware so that you can plan appropriately. That is, make sure not to have any contact with these people, never be seen talking to them, sitting near them, etc."

"What are you going to say to Bryant?"

"I'm going to have someone, ostensibly from the intelligence community, visit Dr. Bryant. We're going to tell him that we have been able to foil attempts to enter restricted government sites, and we believe that members of his class are trying to circumvent our safeguards to gain access to Secret and Top Secret documents in violation of the law. We're still working through the scenarios, but we might, if necessary, even suggest that one of his students is involved in something subversive, possibly a sleeper cell for a terrorist organization."

"You think he'll buy either one and back off?"

"Probably not, but for his sake I sincerely hope so. Dr. Bryant is not a bad man, and we are *not*, contrary to what you may believe, anxious to eliminate average American citizens for exercising their constitutionally protected rights. But make no mistake: if Bryant becomes a problem, and if he can't take the subtle hint that we're about to give him, we will not hesitate to escalate things." Foster let the thought hang in the air for a bit then continued. "Our team will visit Dr. Bryant early next week, probably on Tuesday. As I said, we're still reviewing potential scripts and scenarios, and then we have to create the paper trail that substantiates what we're telling him. In the interim, we need you to continue with your inside surveillance, and don't hesitate to contact us if something noteworthy happens. Err on the side of caution and over-communicating. This situation is developing rapidly and we have to stay ahead of it."

"I hear ya. I'll definitely stay in touch, and you just let me know if and when you need to kick the pressure up a few notches."

"Good," said Foster. "Then we're done for now. We've taken the liberty of booking you a room for tonight and tomorrow night at the Hyatt at

Reston Town Center just down the road if you don't need to get back to Charlottesville. We realized that you rushed out so quickly today that you probably didn't have a chance to get a hotel."

"That's mighty nice of you. I appreciate it."

"Oh, and one more thing," added Manning. "You have dinner reservations at Morton's for 8:00pm tonight, if you'd like to keep them. I know that there are many good restaurants in Charlottesville, but since you're playing the 'starving student' role I doubt you've been able to enjoy any of them. By the way, the reservations are for two."

"Which one of you is joining me?" asked Hilton.

"Actually, neither one of us," said Foster. "A young lady named Heidi will be calling for you at your hotel around 7:45pm and joining you for dinner. Or for the whole night, if you wish. Think of it as a small reward for a job well done, plus we know you've had to be totally hands-off with the coeds in order to maintain some semblance of anonymity. We figured that you could use a little female companionship about now." Foster smiled. What he wasn't telling Hilton was that Heidi had many names and many different looks, and she was as deadly as she was beautiful. Foster had hired Jennifer - her real name, at least as far as Foster was concerned - on many occasions to deal with problems both large and small. Hilton wasn't yet a big problem, but he felt certain that at some point he would be.

"Wow. I don't know what to say. This is definitely an unexpected pleasure. Thanks for taking such good care of me. I really mean that." This was the first time that Foster or Manning had seen Hilton speechless. That was thanks enough for them.

With that, they all stood and shook hands. Hilton left to enjoy his good fortune, while Manning and Foster went back to their discussions. Once Hilton had left the Bunker, Foster turned to Manning. "Get with Jennifer tomorrow and debrief her, see what kind of pillow talk our Mr. Hilton shared with her. She's not wearing a wire, right?"

Manning answered, "No, we didn't want to risk it. Hilton's a pro and he might get suspicious and check. We'll rely on her memory, the old fashioned way. She's done that before for us and it's never been a problem. I think we ought to kick her a few thousand dollar bonus for having to deal with this asshole for an entire night, don't you?" He was only half joking.

"Yeah, I think you're right. I'd like to kill the cocksucker myself, personally. Let's give Jennifer a little something extra after you debrief her. Let me know what was said. If Hilton blabs about this mission to her, at all, then I want him dead. Even if he's like a vault and doesn't say a word to her, we're going to have to deal with him as soon as he's done his part down in Charlottesville. He's a loose cannon, and the last thing we need is someone like him left around to bring us down. Put together a few contingencies for his disappearance and we'll decide on a plan and timeline within the next few days. Agreed?"

"Agreed. I wish we didn't still need him, 'cause I'd love to see him disappear tonight."

⌘

HILTON CHECKED INTO HIS HOTEL and took a shower. He was looking forward to tonight. He wasn't stupid; he knew full well that this Heidi, or whatever her name really was, was being sent in by Foster and Manning as a test. That's OK. He'll play the role and won't even come close to revealing anything about himself or his mission. At the very least, he'll get a decent meal and a good lay out of this trip. Fucking jerks, he thought to himself. Think they're so much smarter and so superior to him since he was just the muscle. That's OK. He knew better. He'd do exactly what was asked of him, and if and when the time came for him to take out Westbrook or Bryant or anybody else, he'd do it with a smile. For him, it was all about the money. His plan was to work until he'd socked away a few million dollars and then retire to some faraway, exotic island in the sun. With a little luck he hoped to make that dream a reality by the time he was 35.

Hilton put the finishing touches on his hair, brushed his teeth, and finished getting dressed. He actually cleaned up pretty well and had never had a problem getting with the ladies, though many times his missions weren't exactly conducive to romance. At promptly 7:45 there was a knock at his door. Punctual, he thought. A prostitute with some class. Hilton tucked his pistol into the back of his pants and headed for the door. He wasn't expecting anything to happen; if Foster and Manning had wanted him dead they could have taken him out down in the Bunker and easily disposed of his body. Here at the Hyatt there was less to worry about, but better safe than sorry. He checked the peep-hole quickly and then opened the door. Before him stood one of the most beautiful women he'd ever seen, and God knows he'd seen, and had, many. She was tall, almost as tall as him with her 3" heels, and he was 6'2". Natural blonde hair, deep emerald eyes, and a body that was the equal of any that had ever graced the centerfold of Playboy and other men's magazines. For the second time that day he was rendered speechless. Heidi just smiled, apparently used to having this affect on men.

"Hi, Mathew, I'm Heidi. It's nice to meet you," she said, offering her hand.

Hilton reached out and gently shook her hand, nervous almost to the point of stammering. "Nice to meet you, too. I understand that we have reservations for 8:00pm at Morton's here in the Town Center."

"That right. I hope Morton's is OK with you? If not, there are several other great restaurants right here, like Clyde's, Paolo's, and McCormick & Schmick's."

"No, Morton's is fine. I've actually been craving a nice steak. Would you like a drink before we go? There's a mini-bar here in the room."

"Maybe I'll take you up on that later. We have all night…or maybe even all weekend, if you're up for that. For now why don't we head on over and we can have a drink or bottle of wine with dinner?" Heidi gave him a smile that could have melted the polar ice caps.

"That sounds good." God, he was as nervous as a kid on his first date. His palms were sweaty, and his dick was threatening to burst right out of his pants. Hopefully she won't notice that…. He reached for his sports jacket, and while slipping it on said, "And I'd love it if you are able to stay the whole weekend. It would be nice to have the company, someone to hang out with, see the sights with. If you're able." He was starting to babble again. Real smooth.

"I think that can be arranged," she said, and reached over and kissed him lightly on the lips. Men were so easy, she thought to herself.

⌘

JEFF ANDERS WAS ON THE phone with Patrick Rockwell late on Friday afternoon filling him in on the earlier conversation and e-mail exchange that he'd had with Lowell Westbrook, though, following their usual protocol, only Jeff knew Lowell's identity since he was on his extended team. Both Jeff and

Patrick were excited; they knew of Dr. Keith Bryant and both of them had, in fact, read one of his earlier books. Though they knew about his Politics of Conspiracy class from Lowell's report, they had never held out particularly high hopes that anything would come of it. They thought it was just another class project. Upon hearing that Keith was targeting his personal research towards MIHOP, they thought that he might be a kindred spirit. They also believed that, as a serious scholar and researcher, Keith would shoot holes in many of the more outlandish theories, just as Let the Truth Be Told did.

"This can't be anything but good new for us," said Patrick. "I don't think I can see any downside. Can you?"

"No, I don't see any either," responded Jeff. "Dr. Bryant is allowing his students to focus their own research on any and all possibilities, but he's acting much like LTBT does in having peer review sessions to sort out the good from the bad, the truth from the bullshit. And with Dr. Bryant personally reviewing everything before it gets posted, we know that he is going the extra mile. My guy agrees that Bryant won't put out any outlandish claims or anything that is not 100% supported by the evidence. He's essentially acting just like LTBT."

"My first inclination is to trumpet his findings and postings as further proof of the accuracy of our work. Then later, if he's amenable, maybe we can even approach him about collaborating on some of our research. From what we've seen and what we've heard, this guy might just be good enough and tenacious enough to finally ferret out The Truth." This from Patrick.

Jeff Anders thought this through. "You're definitely right on that last point. I don't care who nails the bastards that financed and controlled 9/11, just so it gets done. As far as working with Dr. Bryant, that could probably work. Of course, there is going to be speculation about how we got access to their site in the first place. I don't want my resource to get burned. Maybe we can just put it off on an overzealous LTBT associate that hacked his way in?"

"Maybe I have an even better idea, if we don't mind a little white lie. We leak it to another conspiracy site first, albeit very surreptitiously, and let them take the credit for finding the UVA info. We'll then just pick up on it from there. Your source is protected, and Dr. Bryant doesn't have to be any the wiser. He can hardly hold it against us or other groups for simply repeating what we'd found posted on other web sites."

"That's brilliant," responded Anders. "What he doesn't know won't hurt him, plus it will definitely serve the greater good for everyone concerned."

"Exactly," said Patrick. "Can I leave it to you and your team to set this up for next week? Work with your guy on the first postings and then let's get the word out there. For now there's really nothing compelling to report, but just putting out the word that an eminent researcher like Dr. Keith Bryant has an entire class at UVA focused on conspiracy theories, and that he's personally focused on MIHOP research, is very powerful. It will re-energize many of the researchers out there and add substantial legitimacy to the MIHOP movement."

"I can make that happen. Just one more thing I think we should touch on before we jump off this call."

"What's that?" asked Patrick.

"Security, or rather, the need to be increasingly vigilant where our personal security and the security of our data is concerned. I know you guys always joke that I'm a little too paranoid, but we all know that LTBT is on the government's radar. It occurred to me that Dr. Keith Bryant may also be on their radar, or if he's not, he soon will be once this information starts hitting the internet. I think I want to start putting some extra precautions and layers of protection in place to try to keep Big Brother at bay, at least for a while. For that matter, if we're hoping to be collaborating with Dr. Bryant somewhere down the road, perhaps it would be in our best interest to share our concerns with him, as well. The worst thing that can happen is to have his work destroyed or discredited by the government before it has time to do some good."

"You're right, of course." Patrick thought for a minute and then continued. "I, for one, really appreciate your paranoia and keeping us safe. Maybe you can reach out to Dr. Bryant via your source immediately after his postings get made public and offer to help secure his data. He'll probably refuse your assistance, but he's a smart man. He'll take steps to be more secure."

Conversation complete, Patrick and Jeff said their goodbyes and went back to their respective worlds. As soon as they hung up, a record of the call was created in the Bunker at DCG headquarters in Reston, VA. Electra added that call record to the incredibly huge volume of daily data that she processed. Lucky for Treadwell and Anders that Electra was only noting the time and duration of the call; Foster and Manning were already putting steps in motion to start recording all calls made by, to, and between LTBT members, just as they had for Keith and Loren. The operatives at DCG were familiar with the work that Jeff Anders did, so they knew that he would have taken some formidable steps to secure both the voice and data for LTBT. They expected to find much more than basic firewall protection, instead expecting multiple layers of intrusion prevention and detection. They expected phone calls to be routed to multiple servers and destinations, certainly domestically but possibly even internationally. Monitoring any communications that LTBT wanted to keep private, whether voice, data, or video, was not going to be easy. Yes, LTBT would be a worthy adversary, and the DCG operatives, with the exception of Foster and Manning, took it as a bit of a challenge to be able to face-off against one of the best and brightest that Silicon Valley had ever produced.

Foster, on the other hand, didn't think of it as a game or a challenge at all. He considered it a matter of survival, both his and others. Foster was like a chess Grand Master: he always thought and planned several moves ahead. He was so good that many that worked with him or for him swore that he could read minds. In this case, he could see the possibility that Dr. Keith Bryant and members of LTBT could join forces and work towards a common goal – to find The Truth and put him, and others just like him, on death row for murder and treason. That alliance could never be allowed to happen, regardless of who had to be eliminated. They would never care, never understand, about the greater good that came out of 9/11, like the War on Terror. The greater good that continues to this day, and will continue in the days to come, if we're going to stop our country from being held hostage by the Middle East oil producers, by radical Islam, and by upstart little fucks like President Hugo Chavez in Venezuela. The greater good that comes from having conservative politicians in power rather than a bunch of bleeding heart liberals that want to raise taxes and slow our economic growth, or leave our borders unsecured while rewarding illegal immigrants with amnesty.

Most of all, they would never understand the most important part of The Truth: Foster and the other conspirators were already putting plans in motion for the next 9/11.

Chapter 7

IT WAS A LAZY WEEKEND for Keith and Loren, and they both loved it. The weather outside was lousy, with cool temperatures, gusty winds, and even an occasional sprinkling of rain, but that was fine with them. While they loved being outdoors and active, every once in a while it was great to just lie around the house and take it easy. With the skies gray and overcast, it was the perfect excuse for sleeping late and just being lazy. Keith even took a nap on Saturday afternoon, something he rarely had time for. Both he and Loren spent some time on their computers, doing a little bit of work here and there but mostly just web surfing. They finally set the PC's aside long enough to watch the UVA football game on ESPN. UVA continued their winning ways, this time against Miami. That would make the students and faculty a little bit happier, at least for a few days. Later in the afternoon Keith decided to whip up a pot of chili, figuring that that would be just the ticket on such a cold, wet, miserable day. Loren came in the kitchen and watched him cook; something about watching her man in the kitchen always seemed to bring about her most lustful thoughts. Maybe it was the way he handled the knives as he chopped up the onions and peppers. Maybe it was the wonderful smell as the vegetables sautéed. Hell, maybe it was just the fact that she was on her third glass of wine and Keith looked so damn good in his old Levi's and golf shirt. Whatever the reason, she had to have him. Now.

"Hey, Chef, why don't you take me upstairs and handle me like you handle those knives?" she cooed in his ear. She kissed his neck lightly and nibbled on his ear.

Her kisses were giving him chills. Not a great thing to happen while you have a razor-sharp knife in your hand. "Well I could take you upstairs, but you have to decide if you're hungrier for what I'm cooking or hungrier for me," he said, turning to face her and kissing her lightly on the lips.

"Actually, I want both. But first, I think I'm hungrier for this," she said breathily, all the while grinding herself on his thigh. She reached down and ran her hand over the growing bulge in his jeans. Her kisses grew more passionate, her desire getting even hotter. "Why don't you shut that burner off before you burn down the house, and then you can take care of this fire first."

Keith didn't have to be asked twice. With one hand on Loren's ass, his lips locked with hers, he managed to use his other hand to shut off the stove and move the heavy Le Creuset pot off to the side. His hands now totally free, Keith was practically tearing Loren's blouse off in his rush to get her undressed. She had this affect on him all the time, but God knows it never got old. They never made it upstairs, finally falling onto the couch in front of the fireplace and making love with an intensity that neither had ever known with any other partner. It was an intensity that few people ever experienced in their entire lives regardless of how many partners they have. Their words, their moans, their sounds were so intense that even Bo and Winston left the room, seemingly in embarrassment, as if they were voyeurs and not welcome in this private moment. Keith and Loren didn't come up for air for almost an hour, and by then it was practically dark outside and the fire in the fireplace was starting to fade. Keith smiled to himself; there couldn't be a better way to spend a lazy Saturday afternoon.

Due to Loren's little interruption of Keith's cooking, dinner was a little later than planned. No matter. The chili still got to simmer and have the flavors meld together for a couple of hours, and the crusty rolls that Keith had picked up from Lagniappe Bakery on Friday afternoon were the perfect complement to this simple, warm, filling dinner. She loved the fact that he cooked for her. It was one of his passions. She could cook, at least enough to stay alive, but she'd never enjoyed it or found a passion for it the way that Keith did. They ate dinner in the family room while watching some of their favorite shows that they'd recorded on DVR during the week, and it was after midnight when they finally went to bed, both grateful for the fact that they'd had a day totally to themselves without having to run any errands or even leave the house. It made Keith realize the profound changes since Loren came into his life; in the past he never could have sat in the house on a weekend day, regardless of the weather. His weekends, pre-Loren, were always taken up with sports, or boating, or whoring around with the girl *du jour*. Now, it didn't matter so much what he did or if he did nothing at all. The only thing that mattered was that he spent his time with Loren. When he talked to his friends they all joked that he was now seriously pussy-whipped. That's OK. He knew the truth. For that matter, so did his friends. He was just truly, madly, deeply in love. He'd finally, after all of his years dating around and sleeping around, found his soul mate. He wasn't about to let her get away.

Keith slept great that night, Loren snuggled close and resting her head on his shoulder. He finally woke up about 8 o'clock Sunday morning and went down to get some orange juice and start the coffee for Loren. While he let the dogs out, he picked up the Sunday paper from the driveway and brought it back to the house. Maybe he'd finally get a chance to look through it before they got dressed to head out to brunch later this morning. Keith made coffee for Loren; he never drank the stuff, but she could go through a couple of pots per day if she wanted. She claimed it was a throwback to her undergraduate days of pulling all-nighters writing papers or studying for exams. Keith had done the same late nights when he was in college, he just used Coke or Pepsi for his stimulant. He'd just never acquired a taste for coffee. Most mornings he made a small pot of Kona coffee for her, and she'd usually have one big mug at the house and the rest in a stainless travel mug for the car. With the coffee started he sat down to have his orange juice and an apple turnover that he'd gotten from the bakery. He relaxed and took his time reading the front page and world news sections of the *Washington Post*.

He was just about to put the paper away and head up to wake Loren when the front page of the Business section caught his eye. The heading of the article read, *"Daniels Robotics Corp Wins $2.4B Award to Develop Remote Bomb Detection Technology"*. Keith knew of Daniels Robotics Corporation, or DRC. He had done a little bit of consulting work for them a few years back, helping them develop an action plan for building better working relationships with the military and government of Afghanistan and Pakistan. DRC developed drone technology for the military and had been one of the first to prove the viability of remote controlled, pilotless aircraft in armed conflicts. The drones were able to capture incredibly sharp, detailed pictures of the battlefield or target and transmit them back to commanders positioned a safe distance away. Later, DRC and their partners managed to modify the drones to support combat missions in addition to their passive aerial reconnaissance. This was accomplished by adding the capability to fire missiles at ground-based objects such as enemy bunkers, tanks, or personnel. Now it appeared that DRC was expanding into other parts of the military and security market. The article went on to say that DRC was already developing, and close to deploying, advanced robotics to detect and defuse Improvised Explosive Devices, or IED's. IED's were the single biggest hazard facing our troops in Iraq, and Keith feared, as did many others, that their use was going to spread to other conflicts, particularly urban and guerilla conflicts. It only made sense; they were very inexpensive, generally easy to conceal, could be made by anybody with the least bit of bomb-making skills, and they exacted a heavy price in deaths, injuries, and psychological damage. DRC had won a contract worth hundreds of millions of dollars to build the anti-IED robots and stood to make millions more as they were sold to military groups around the world, to say nothing of law enforcement organizations in cities both large and small. With this latest contract, DRC was also expanding into the realm of airport security by creating better machines for detecting both liquid and solid explosives, as well as 3-D imaging technology to improve the TSA's ability to detect banned items from luggage and passengers, including firearms. Apparently DRC had acquired another company, Security Imaging Concepts, to be able to gain a foothold in this market segment.

Something about this article was making Keith uneasy, almost giving him chills, but he couldn't quite put his finger on it. He had come across references to DRC in some of his 9/11 research but he hadn't really paid it much mind. It seemed that there were a few references to them being one of the companies that had made a lot of money in the defense and security industries since 9/11. That point certainly couldn't be argued; just within this article there was reference to several billion dollars, and that's without digging into their earnings reports, stock prices, etc. over the past five years. That old saying of 'follow the money' kept spinning in his head. Is it possible that DRC, or others like them, could have been involved in 9/11, actually working with others to cause this terrorist act to happen? Are there actually people out there sick enough to cause 3,000 of their fellow citizens to be killed just for the money? People that care so little about their fellow man that they'd set this type of plan in motion knowing that more people would die when America retaliates against…whoever? Keith tried to stay detached and think this through, not react from emotion. *He needed to be one of the 3%*

that think, he told himself. He paced the floor as he thought, finally moving outside to the porch.

He kicked back in his favorite rocker and closed his eyes to think. Bo and Winston lay down by his feet, one on each side of his chair. His mind raced. Of course there were people and companies cold and callous enough to do this. Hadn't there always been people that profited from war? Yes, but profiting from war and causing war, or at least terrorist attacks, are two very different things. Or is it? Hadn't some people always tried to instigate wars for their own purposes, whether to conquer lands or acquire the riches of others? Hadn't some tried to stir the pot for purely monetary gain, like William Randolph Hearst when he reportedly told one of his photographers, "*You provide the pictures and I'll provide the war*" during the run-up to the Spanish American War? If some individuals in the US government were, in fact, complicit in the 9/11 plot, isn't it a virtual certainty that some members of the military-industrial complex were involved to provide off-the-record financing? Wouldn't those same companies be rewarded by the government later and stand to make obscene amounts of money from the defense and security buildup that was guaranteed to happen in the wake of 9/11? Keith could envision someone at DRC, if not others, sitting there with an Excel worksheet in front of them as they calculated the Return on Investment from their 'contribution' to the conspiracy. The thought almost made him nauseous.

There was something else bugging him, too, but he wasn't sure what. He needed to go back to some of his earlier research and see if something triggers it. Keith decided that the best thing he could do right now is simply step back for a while and clear his mind. He could follow this up later today or early this week. The trail might lead nowhere but he knew to trust his instincts. They had never let him down before. Right now his instincts were telling him that if he and Loren had any shot of making their brunch reservations at noon he better get upstairs and rustle her out of bed. As usual, he decided to enlist the assistance of a couple of big Labs that were the perfect wake-up call. Well, not as perfect as wake-up sex, but today it would have to do. He told Bo and Winston to go wake her up and they tore off through the house and up the stairs. Keith decided that he'd bounce his thoughts about DRC off of Loren during brunch. Her instincts were almost always right on the money.

⌘

Keith and Loren had brunch at one of their favorite places in the area. The restaurant was called Palladio and it was located about 20 miles north of Charlottesville at the Barboursville Vineyards. It was a beautiful setting. It reminded him of dinner at Auberge du Soleil in Napa, or one of the beautiful villas in Tuscany. In fact, the menu at Palladio was very reminiscent of Italy, and the quality of the food could go toe-to-toe with many of Italy's best. Keith had a salad of roasted early fall vegetables, risotto with wild mushrooms and butternut squash, and a roasted garlic marinated Guinea Hen. Loren shared his appetizer of roasted fall vegetables and had the oyster and fennel stew and the seared Ahi tuna served atop a salad of fingerling potatoes, wild mushrooms, zucchini, olives, and cipollini onions. Since neither were white wine drinkers, they skipped the offered wine pairing and went straight for a bottle of the Barboursville 2004 Sangiovese. Loren said she was too full to order dessert, so in the tradition of women the world over, she said, "I'll just have a bite of yours." Usually that 'bite' turned out to be at least half, but that was OK with Keith. They shared the tiramisu.

As they finished up the last of their dessert and wine, Keith told Loren about the article he'd seen that morning about DRC, including his thoughts about their huge profits after 9/11. He also told her that something was nagging at him about the whole DRC thing and that he was considering backtracking through his research. Loren listened, without interruption, and then said, "I think you have to follow your line of reasoning. It might lead nowhere, but it's certainly a plausible thought. I mean, you've been approaching this all along as a MIHOP type of conspiracy. If that approach is true, and I'm 100% in agreement that MIHOP is at least possible, if not probable, then there is every reason to at least follow through with research on DRC to see if they could be a player in the conspiracy. Even if you don't find anything incriminating about DRC, who's to say that your research down that path won't lead you to someone or some company that is involved? Your research will lead you to others that do the same kind of work, the same type of defense and/or security contractors, as DRC. Maybe one or more of them will turn out to be the bad guys, but you may never find them if you don't start with DRC."

Once again Loren had taken a lot of information and boiled it down to its essence. And as always, her reasoning and logic were spot-on. Keith absolutely needed to follow this thread, however slim it might be. He'd start by reviewing all of the research that he'd done on defense contractors to see where that might take him, and then search through the public financial records of DRC to see if anything jumped out at him. He knew that he could always enlist the help of the CFO at Bryant International to help sort through the accounting if things got too deep for him. This was good, he thought to himself. He felt like a detective that had just uncovered a new lead in a cold case, and now he was really energized by the idea of digging in. He'd get started tomorrow morning, but for now, and for the rest of the day, he was going to put this on the back burner and enjoy Loren's company. She had mentioned wanting to take a drive up to Skyline Drive to see the fall foliage. Not exactly his idea of a good time – couldn't you see plenty of leaves, both on the trees and on the ground, right there on the farm? – but he was more than happy to accommodate her. Today was actually a beautiful fall day, albeit a little bit breezy. Yesterday's rain and cold had finally given way to clearing skies. Keith wondered if there'd even be any leaves left on the trees after yesterday, but what the heck. It was Sunday, he was spending time with the woman that he loved, and he'd just had an exquisite meal. He should count his blessings once again, he mused, for he was truly a lucky guy.

Actually, Keith was a very lucky guy and this was his *very* lucky day. He should be playing the lottery or hitting the craps tables in Vegas, he was so lucky. If the conversation he'd just had with Loren had happened at home, or over the phone, he would be dead by morning. They both would. For that matter, if they had sat at an outside table today rather than an inside table, the parabolic microphone being used by Foster's men would have picked up their whole conversation. Dead. Thankfully, with the noise being generated by the kitchen and the other restaurant patrons, as well as the jazz combo playing just off of the main dining room, the listening device was of virtually no use. The surveillance van was positioned near the back of the parking lot at Palladio, and fortunately for the people inside the van they had raised no suspicion. Still, they had no way of knowing what Keith and Loren had talked about over lunch, and that was very disconcerting to them, to put it mildly. Nothing to be done about it now. Better to leave shortly after Keith and Loren pull out and reposition themselves back near the farm. One of the other teams could follow them if they went somewhere else before going home, but this vehicle and crew couldn't risk being noticed. The men in the van cursed their bad luck, and really cursed the decision made a few weeks back by Foster's advance team, under the direction of Mathew Hilton, not to place listening devices in Keith's and Loren's cars. Such devices weren't expected to be needed since they didn't usually commute together, plus the potential risk of trying to place the devices when the cars are parked right outside of the School, or in their garage, wasn't deemed worth it. With their phones bugged, their house and offices bugged, and their computers and network compromised both at home and at the School, virtually every base was covered. Still, 'virtually' wasn't the same as 100% covered, and DCG wasn't in the business of doing anything with less than 100% certainty. Somebody's head was going to roll for that lapse in judgment.

⌘

WHILE KEITH AND LOREN WERE finishing their meal and heading towards Skyline Drive, Mathew Hilton was driving back to Charlottesville on Route 29. He had spent almost the entire weekend with Heidi and it had been 36 hours of good food, great wine, and lots of hot sex. It was probably the best weekend of his life, if he was honest with himself. Sure, she was obviously a pro and was being well compensated for her time, but that just made it that much better. No strings attached, no emotions. He had no doubt that she was probably briefing Foster and Manning on every aspect of their weekend together. That's OK, too. He hadn't said a word about his work or his mission. Lucky for him; he had no way of knowing that Heidi was under specific orders to kill him, and was quite capable of doing so, had he opened his mouth about DCG or his work in Charlottesville.

While he drove down Route 29 he gave some thought to how he might eliminate Lowell Westbrook if and when the orders came, and he fully expected to get those orders within a few days. Obviously, the usual tools of the trade were out, like a gun, knife, or garrote. That was too bad; at least with these scenarios he could choose the time and the place and minimize the variables, but he could not afford for there to be any type of official investigation. Murders always raised way too many questions. No, it had to look like an accident or natural causes. Since Westbrook was young and healthy the choices for simulated natural causes are pretty limited. Plus, once again, it would likely generate an investigation as to how a seemingly healthy young man dropped dead so suddenly. The truth is, most poisons are detectable if the person doing the autopsy has a reason to look, which, in this case, they would. After considering his options, Hilton concluded that the only real answer was to stage some sort of accident, preferably in a relatively controlled environment like Westbrook's home. His cell phone rang and snapped him back to reality. "Hilton here."

"Hilton, it's Foster. We need to talk. Are you secure and free to talk?"

"Yes, all secure, sir."

"We have decided on a timeline for taking action against Lowell Westbrook. You need to be prepared to move on him sometime Tuesday late afternoon or early evening. Is that doable?"

"Yes, sir. I don't see any problem with that timeline. I've given some thought as to how to eliminate him, and I think it's best if I just help him have a little accident at home or work. Unless, of course, you have other ideas."

"No, what you're proposing sounds perfect. One other thing: we have a two man team posing as FBI agents that are going to drop in on Dr. Bryant and his girlfriend early Tuesday evening. We'll give them this one warning, and unless I miss my guess, Bryant will hang tough. That's why Mr. Westbrook needs to have his accident the same night. I assume that Dr. Bryant will be suspicious when he hears of Westbrook's accident, and hopefully he'll be spooked enough to start to be amenable to our position."

"And if not?" asked Hilton, relishing the thought of the huge bonus he would earn by taking Keith and Loren out.

"We're only giving him one chance to do the right thing. If he's still pursuing his research and creating possible problems for us, we will move against him, and his girlfriend, by mid-week. We may not have the luxury of being subtle with their elimination. It would probably be best to eliminate them at their farm, perhaps a staged home invasion. You have other resources there in Charlottesville to assist you if it comes to that."

"Sounds good, sir. You just give me the word and I'll make it happen. Oh, and sir? I wanted to thank you again for taking such good care of me while I was in DC. I had a great time this weekend spending time with Heidi and hanging out around the city. I appreciate it."

"No problem. Maybe after you finish this assignment I can arrange for you and Heidi to get away for a few weeks to some exotic location, like maybe Aruba, or Fiji, or the Maldives." Foster didn't add that the next time Heidi saw Hilton it would be to put a bullet in his head.

"Wow, that would be fantastic. Thanks, sir."

"We'll be in touch. And keep us posted on developments on your end." With that Foster hung up the phone. He had already spent an hour debriefing Jennifer/Heidi earlier, and she reported that Hilton never broached any information about his work. He didn't know whether to be happy or sad about that fact; he was so looking forward to the day when Hilton had outlived his usefulness and could be eliminated.

On his way back into town Hilton decided to do a little reconnaissance work to get prepared for Lowell Westbrook's impending accident. He started at the School, taking time to view the stairs from all angles, scope out possible hiding places for an ambush, identify the location of all security cameras, and look for potential spots where events could be witnessed. It certainly wouldn't be easy, and he came to the immediate conclusion that there was no way to pull this off during the average school day. Too many variables, too many chances for something to go wrong. Better to look for a Plan B, he surmised.

After Hilton left the university he made his way over to Westbrook's townhouse. It was about 6:30pm when he pulled up just down the street. He sat in his car for almost 30 minutes watching the place. There were no lights, no signs of life. Was it possible that he wasn't home this Sunday evening? He had an idea. Picking up his cell phone he called Directory Assistance and got connected to the local Domino's Pizza. After placing his order and giving Lowell Westbrook's name, address, and phone number, he sat back and waited. Just over 30 minutes later the Domino's delivery driver pulled up in front. He sprinted to the door and knocked. No response. He knocked a little bit louder and announced himself. Still no answer. Hilton could see the driver cursing and muttering to himself as he walked back to his car. Finally the driver took off, squealing his tires in anger.

Hilton figured this was his one chance to check things out. No guarantee that Westbrook wouldn't come home at any minute, but that's a chance that he had to take. Hilton casually walked up to the door, then pretended to be fumbling for his key. Actually, he was picking the lock with his pick gun, a favorite tool of locksmiths and burglars alike, and he was inside within twenty seconds. He wasn't about to turn on any lights, but he closed the curtains as a precaution so that his flashlight beam couldn't be seen. He knew that Westbrook lived alone, so that was certainly something in favor of killing him here. He went to the top of the stairs and looked down. Pretty steep, and since this was a townhouse with a very modern design, it had ten foot ceilings on the first floor. That was a big plus in Hilton's expert opinion, since that meant that there were even more steps between floors. The more he looked around and considered his options the better he liked his plan. There was a guest bedroom directly across from the master, and it was less than three steps from the top of the stairs. That would be a perfect hiding place. Or the bathroom directly across from the top of the stairs offered another alternative. This could definitely work. All he had to do was break into the townhouse and wait for Westbrook to come home. He'd then wait for his chance to either push, or if necessary, throw him down the steps. If the fall didn't kill him, and you never can tell about those things, Hilton would just have to help things along a little bit with a quick snap of the neck. Either way, Lowell Westbrook would not be a problem for Colonel Foster and his group any longer. Hilton was satisfied with what he'd seen and the plan he'd come up with. Simple, quiet, relatively little chance of something going wrong. He'd let Foster know his plan during his next update and would prepare himself to carry out this part of the mission. If things continued on the timeline that Foster had planned, he'd be back here dealing with Mr. Westbrook in less than 48 hours. Just thinking about it gave him a rush of adrenaline. God, he loved his work.

Chapter 8

Sometimes it's the little things in life that separate the lucky ones from the unlucky ones. A car goes flying through an intersection and you realize that, had you been going even one mile per hour faster, you would have been broadsided and likely killed. You're walking into a convenience store and you hold the door for the little old lady that's approaching, and she ends up buying the winning lottery ticket – the ticket that would have been yours if you hadn't been so damn polite. Keith and Loren had been lucky on Sunday at Palladio. If the weather would have been a few degrees warmer, or if it hadn't been so windy, they would have sat out on the terrace to enjoy the day. If they had, Foster's men would have heard their conversation with their high-tech listening devices. That would have been very unlucky, indeed. Keith and Loren would have been dead by the next morning.

Sometimes what seems to be bad luck is really just good luck in disguise. The problem is, most people stay so caught up in their own little world that they don't notice or can't tell the difference. Keith's good luck and fortune continued on Monday, though he was feeling anything but lucky. He'd hoped to get started on his research into the financial world of DRC, but instead he was getting ready to head to the airport for a hastily called meeting with one of his top clients in New York City. What a time to have to run a business, Keith thought. Just when he felt like he was onto something big, something meaty, in his research into 9/11. His client, DALCAL Oil Company, had called Sunday night because they were having problems with the Nigerian government, or, more accurately, their Nigerian workers, and production was coming to a virtual standstill. They wanted to talk to Keith to get a better understanding of the political situation in Nigeria and the surrounding countries, and, they hoped, entice Keith to act as their intermediary in-country. Keith was not about to get roped into that kind of commitment, though he was not against putting his Africa-focused team on the project. He'd have to explore that with DALCAL. The contract could be worth several hundred thousand dollars over the next few months, but he was just too stretched with the commitments he already had to take this on personally.

Keith's flight was at 7:00am on Monday morning out of the Charlottesville airport, but before he left he called Lowell Westbrook and, apologizing profusely for calling him so early, arranged for him to cover his classes for the day. Fortunately, Keith only lived about 20 minutes from the Charlottesville-Albemarle airport, and, thank God, it was a small enough airport that you can park, go through security, and be at your gate in a fairly short time. At least his US Airways flight up to New York's La Guardia airport put him in there around 8:45am. DALCAL was arranging for a limo service to pick him up when he landed and to return him in the evening for his flight home, so at least he didn't have to hassle with rental cars, traffic, and parking. The more time he spent in the Charlottesville area and away from major cities the less he cared for them, especially New York. Keith made it to the airport and to his gate with only about five minutes to spare before they started boarding the plane. Like virtually every flight in and out of Charlottesville, Keith's flight was on a small regional jet that seated only 36 people, and, like virtually every flight in and out of there, it was completely filled. Keith had no illusions of being able to work on the flight that morning. The seats were so small that a toddler would feel cramped. With work out of the question, Keith did his best to get comfortable. He cranked up his iPod as soon as the flight attendant announced that it was OK for passengers to use laptops and other portable electronics, and he tried to put everything, including the stiffness already creeping into his legs and back from these tortuous seats, out of his mind for the next hour.

The meeting with DALCAL went well. Keith was able to offer them some valuable advice, and the CEO agreed to contract with Bryant International for three months with an option for an additional three months. Keith committed to having his Africa team work directly with DALCAL's management in New York and their engineering and management group in Nigeria. Things went so well that, even with a nearly two-hour lunch at Le Cirque 2000, Keith was ready to fly home a few hours early. The return flight that he'd booked was scheduled to leave at 7:30pm, and it was the last flight leaving La Guardia that could get him back to Charlottesville. He didn't ever like booking the last flight out at night, particularly since he was flying to a small airport. Those last flights seem to mysteriously cancel a lot more often than others; he couldn't count how many times he had been stranded somewhere overnight trying to get back home. Keith went online before leaving DALCAL's office to see if there were any seats left on the earlier flights. As he expected, all of the earlier flights were sold out. He would have to keep his 7:30pm flight. Worst of all, that flight wasn't even direct, requiring an almost two hour layover in Charlotte, NC. He wouldn't arrive in Charlottesville until almost 11:30pm.

Keith called Loren to give her the news on his schedule. "Sorry, honey. I tried to get out on an earlier flight, but as usual, there's just nothing available. Everything is full. I can't understand how all of the airlines can be losing money and crying poverty when there's not an empty goddamn seat on any flight. They pack people in like fucking sardines, don't provide any food any more, and then charge you out the ass for the privilege of flying with them."

Keith didn't often curse like this, so Loren knew that he was upset. "I'm sorry, sweetie. I know you have to be exhausted after getting up so early this morning. Maybe you can sleep in a little later tomorrow morning?" asked Loren.

"Probably not," answered Keith. "I have a lot I need to do before my first class tomorrow. Anyway, enough of my complaining. How was your day?"

"It was fine, uneventful. I came home and took the dogs out for some exercise, threw the ball to them for a while. I'm just going to stay in tonight and get caught up on some of my research, probably just heat up some soup and make a grilled cheese sandwich for an early dinner. Very *haute cuisine*."

"Yeah, Rachel Ray better watch out or you'll be taking over her empire." That at least made Keith smile. "I'm glad you got to play with the dogs for a while. I know they loved having some attention."

"Yeah, they had a big old time. It was good for me, too. God knows I could use some exercise after sitting around on my big old butt all day working for a living."

"You don't have a 'big old butt', and if you know what's good for you, you never will," he said with a smile. "You know that your ass is a '10', just like the rest of you."

"Ah, aren't you sweet. You think my ass is a '10'. That's about the most romantic thing I've ever heard any man say." She teased him about it, but she loved the complement anyway. What girl of her age wouldn't be thrilled to hear a man say that her butt was still perfect?

"Yeah, I thought it was pretty romantic, too. I wish I was there right now to rub my hands all over it and snuggle up to it instead of sitting around La Guardia waiting for my flight."

"Business travel is *soooo* glamorous, isn't it? I think you may have said that once or twice before."

"True," Keith said with a smile. "Anyway, it's about time for my limo to arrive, so I'd better go. I'll see you around midnight, assuming everything is on schedule. Give the dogs a hug for me, OK? I love you."

"I love you, too. Drive careful coming from the airport, and watch out for deer. If you're too tired to drive home call me and I'll come pick you up."

"Thanks, but that won't be necessary. I'll be fine. Get some rest and I'll see you when I get in. Bye. Love you."

Loren said goodbye and hung up the phone. She really didn't like it when he had to travel and be away. Not that she was scared to be alone – OK, the farm could be a little dark and creepy at night if you stopped to think about it, which she tried not to do – she just liked having him there. Thank goodness for the dogs. They were great company, and, she was sure, great protection should anything ever happen. Before sitting back to watch TV she went over and set the alarm system. That at least gave her a little bit more piece of mind.

Keith finally rolled in a few minutes after midnight. Bo and Winston were the first ones to greet him at the door. Loren had hoped to be, but Bo, the big lummox, had practically knocked her across the coffee table as he rushed to get by. And, Winston, all 110 pounds of him, had stepped right on her foot as he ran past. She would have sworn it was a Humvee instead of a Lab. As she half-yelled, half-laughed, Keith couldn't help but crack-up at her at she hobbled towards him. He always was the first to laugh, usually uncontrollably, when someone stubbed their toe, or tripped, or had any little instance of clumsiness. It must be a guy thing, like watching and appreciating the Three Stooges.

"Jesus Christ, did anybody get the license number of the truck that just ran me over in my own living room?" she asked, still laughing.

Keith was still laughing uncontrollably, and the dogs were jumping up on him, giving him kisses, their tails wagging so hard it would have left a bruise on his leg if they made contact. "God, that was the funniest thing I've seen in a long time!"

Loren smiled. "I'm glad that me and my pain are here for your amusement. Jesus! Somebody needs another pedicure. It felt like a freakin' bald eagle clawing my foot when Winston stepped on me."

This sent Keith into spasms of laughter again. His sides were starting to ache. "Thanks, I needed that laugh. Come here and give me a kiss."

"Gee, thanks a lot. I get sloppy seconds." With that Loren reached for him and hugged his neck and then kissed him on the lips. "Ooh, gross. Is there anyplace on your face that the dogs haven't slobbered on you?"

Keith was laughing again. "Not so much. Guess they were happy to see me."

"Yeah, well, I'm happy to see you, too, but I'd like to have a dry spot to kiss you. That was just nasty!"

"Tell you what, why don't I drop my stuff here and then run up and take a shower. Then you can show me just how happy you are that I'm back home with you."

"Ummm, that sounds like a plan. Yeah, definitely take that shower. I just put on fresh sheets this morning and you smell like dog slobber mixed with New York. And for my money, the dog slobber is the better of the two smells." Loren started to pick up Keith's laptop bag and move it out of the doorway. "You want me to fix you something to eat or did you have dinner at the airport?"

"I had almost two hours between flights so I grabbed some Chinese food at Charlotte airport. It was awesome, as always."

"You're unbelievable. You go from Le Cirque 2000 at lunch, easily one of the top restaurants in the country, to Chinese take-out from the airport food court. I'm surprised your stomach can take it."

"True. I guess I'm just an equal opportunity eater." Keith smiled at her and gave her a little kiss on the cheek. "Why don't you go ahead and lock up down here and I'll be ready for bed in about 10 minutes."

"I'll be in bed, but I'll probably be asleep. After the way you laughed at me when I got hurt, and after I had to settle for sloppy seconds on the kiss, you'll just have to do without the pleasure of my company tonight," Loren said with a little fake, flirty pout.

Keith took a nice long, hot shower and felt so much better when he got out. Nothing makes you feel dirtier than traveling, especially when you're packed into a tiny little plane with too many people and too little ventilation. He tried to be quiet as he slipped into bed. It was almost 1:30am, and it had been a long day for both of them. He would understand if she were asleep. She had dozed off, but as Keith slid his arm around her waist and kissed her lightly on the neck she stirred. She rolled over slowly and smiled up at him, then slid her arms around his neck. "I'm really glad you made it home. I don't like it when we have to be apart for the night." With that she gave him a long, deep, lingering kiss. That whole idea about withholding 'the pleasure of her company', well, that went right out the window.

⌘

It was Tuesday morning, and up in Reston Colonel Foster was growing concerned about the situation that was developing with Dr. Keith Bryant and Lowell Westbrook. Bryant had been pretty quiet over the past few days, if for no other reason that he'd been spending time with his girlfriend and then traveling for business. Not so Lowell Westbrook. He'd been burning up the phone lines and the e-mails to Jeff Anders. Nothing he'd shared to this point was of any significance so far as the secrets of 9/11, but the fact that he was so willing to provide any and all information to Anders and his cohorts at Let the Truth Be Told was a concern. It was a certainty that Westbrook was going to leak Bryant's research as well as the research of the entire class, and there was no way Foster could risk that. Bryant had to be dissuaded from his current line of research, and idle threats were not likely to work. He had to be lead down a different path, or rather, he had to have the research lead him down a different path. It was up to Foster to provide that different path. He'd have his team start working on insertion of some false flags and dead-ends that they could scatter around the web. They'd planned years ago for contingencies like this. He just hoped that Bryant was smart enough to follow the trail and not be so bull-headed as to try to stick to his current way of thinking. As a researcher and academic he should know that he has to let the evidence take him where it leads whether it fits nicely into his theory or not. If he refused to follow the new evidence and his current path took him anywhere remotely close to The Truth, Foster would not hesitate to have him, and everyone close to him, eliminated.

Lowell Westbrook was another problem altogether. Regardless of where Foster and his team led Dr. Bryant, Westbrook was going to continue to leak that information to Anders. On the surface that didn't seem so bad; keep Anders and the LTBT busy researching and shooting down more bullshit theories meant less time for them to stumble onto The Truth themselves. But Foster's mind was already working several steps ahead, considering all variables, working through a lot of what-if scenarios, and considering the pros and cons of every possible move. What worried Foster more than anything is that LTBT, with all of their experience investigating the events of 9/11 and poring over thousands of documents and looking at dozens, if not hundreds, of different conspiracy theories, might quickly realize that the path they're leading Bryant down is a ruse. They might realize that everything that Bryant is researching, every document, every link, every name or reference, didn't even exist a few weeks ago. No, Foster couldn't allow Westbrook to continue sharing information with Anders. He had to be eliminated, and quickly. Time for Mathew Hilton to earn his bonus.

Foster called Bob Manning and arranged for them to meet in the Bunker conference room in thirty minutes. While he was never reluctant to make a decision, even when it involved taking someone's life, he wanted to consult with Manning to make sure that he hadn't overlooked some other idea or input. He also wanted to get the latest readout from Manning's team and Electra, see if any late-breaking news might sway him to delay action on Westbrook or to take more drastic action on Bryant.

At 9am Foster walked into the Bunker conference room and found Bob Manning already there, poring over reports. "So what's the latest, Bob? Anything much changed since we spoke yesterday evening?"

"No, not really," answered Manning. "Nothing that you're not already aware of. Are we still a 'go' on Westbrook for tonight?"

"Since you say that nothing has changed then I think we still have to move on him. Can you see any reason to hold, or do you see any potential fallout that I may not have considered?"

"I still see Westbrook as the biggest threat here. Even though Dr. Bryant is the principal, it's Westbrook's link to Anders and the LTBT that is our biggest concern. We need to eliminate that link. After that, we can probably control Bryant without any more bloodshed."

Foster sat silently for a few moments, pondering what Manning had said. "Obviously we'd like to minimize the bloodshed and any possible fallout from the killings. The more people that die, the more people that start to ask questions. Let me ask you this: what do you think the chances are that Anders will reach out to Dr. Bryant after Westbrook is killed? Do you think that Anders will assume that his 'accident' is another link in the conspiracy?"

"I'd thought of that. When anybody even remotely affiliated with a conspiracy dies people always assume the worst. Doesn't matter if the person that dies is 100 years old and has had five heart attacks, somebody will still assume that it was related to the conspiracy. I don't see any way around that. We can do our best to make it look like an accident, and I trust Mr. Hilton will do an adequate job, but there will always be suspicions. What we have to do is ensure that Anders and Dr. Bryant are not able to communicate. Remember, Bryant has no idea that Anders even exists; he won't go looking for him. We just have to control the communications flow from the outside world to Dr. Bryant. Not easy, but it can be done. We can trap all calls coming from Anders or anyone even remotely associated with the LTBT, same for e-mail and other communications."

"How long do you think we can keep that up? It only takes one communication to get through and sink your whole plan." replied Foster.

"Long enough for us to know what we're dealing with. If things start to spiral out of control we can always move on Anders and/or Dr. Bryant at that time. Everything being equal, I'd rather move on Bryant. If we move on Anders that will definitely be like fuel on a fire to the conspiracy nuts."

"Agreed. What about the plans to send someone to visit Dr. Bryant and Loren Davis to try to dissuade him about his class research? Is that still on for this evening?"

"Yes. I've got two of our operatives scheduled to show up at their house early this evening. They'll be carrying FBI credentials and the plan is to tell Bryant that some of his students, we don't exactly know which ones since they're using computers in the university library, have attempted to hack into restricted government and military computers trying to access information. We'll threaten to bring charges against the perpetrators, etc. and we'll appeal to his sense of decency to try to control it. Our hope is that he'll throttle the student's aggressiveness a little bit and keep them from going places, by design or by accident, that we don't want them to go. Not sure that this is going to do much good, but I think it's at least worth a try. If for no other reason, it gives us a little bit more time to get more of our fake paper trails and internet trails in place and tested."

"Alright, keep me posted on progress, and I want to know tonight the second that Mr. Hilton completes his mission. I'll also be monitoring the audio surveillance when your people go in to meet with Dr. Bryant." With that, Foster stood up and gathered his things.

⌘

KEITH HAD A PRETTY PACKED day on Tuesday, particularly since he'd been gone all day on Monday. With one class in the morning and another in the early afternoon, followed by a 3:00pm meeting with his management staff at Bryant International to discuss the negotiations with DALCAL, he would barely have time to grab lunch. Loren's day wasn't much better. She spent most of the day sequestered in the library doing research for her dissertation, then in the mid-afternoon she had a meeting with Dr. Gibson, her advisor for her PhD work. Both Keith and Loren finally rolled in around 5pm.

Keith was tired from the last two days. Too much travel, too much work and stress, and too little sleep. He didn't feel like cooking and suggested that they go out to dinner instead, maybe have a nice meal and a good bottle of red wine. Loren readily agreed; she knew that Keith needed to get back early and get some rest, not spend a couple of hours in the kitchen cooking dinner and cleaning up. They decided to head over to Duner's, one of their favorite restaurants in the area. Located about five miles outside of Charlottesville on Route 250, it was usually too far removed from the hustle and bustle of the town to draw a lot of tourists, and the menu was a little too upscale and expensive for the students to make it a regular hangout. Even still, the place filled up virtually every night, and they didn't take reservations. Keith and Loren decided to head out early and try to beat the crowds.

Just as they were gathering their things, Keith heard a car approaching down their drive. Bo and Winston obviously heard it, too, because they started going off. They certainly weren't expecting anybody, and the farm's caretakers rarely, if ever, used the main drive, choosing instead to use the other driveway that turned off the road about a quarter mile further down. It wasn't quite dark outside yet, but with all of the trees and shade near the house it was dark enough. Keith had already turned on the front porch lights, and as the car approached the security motion sensor lights came on as well. He wasn't able to see the car clearly until it was pulling into the circular driveway near the front porch, but when he did get a good look one thing was immediately evident: it was somebody official. Local police, state police, whoever – the big, blue, plain-Jane Ford Crown Victoria screamed 'cops'. What the hell was this?

Two men stepped from the car and started towards the front door. One white, one black. Both built like linebackers; Keith was a pretty good-sized man, and both of these guys were taller and probably 25-50 pounds heavier. Bigger and in better shape than any cop he'd ever seen, he thought. They reached the front door and knocked. That sent Bo and Winston into another fit of barks and snarls. Weird, Keith thought. They usually run to the door excited to greet visitors. "Quiet guys. Enough. Loren, can you hold them back for a minute while I open the door?"

"I'll try. Come here guys. Sit back here with me." Loren sat down on the couch and held a hand on each of their collars. Like that would do any good if they wanted to bolt for the door, she thought.

Keith opened the front door but left the glass storm door closed and locked. "Yes? Can I help you?"

The black gentleman spoke. "Dr. Keith Bryant? I'm Special Agent Dickson, and this is Special Agent Washington." Both agents held up their credentials for Keith to view through the door. "We're with the FBI, and we've been asked to come down here to talk with you. Sir, we'd like to talk to you for a few minutes about some potentially serious security breaches that have occurred on several government and DoD computers over the past few weeks."

"What does that have to do with me?" Keith asked.

"Well sir, it doesn't have to do with you directly. You're certainly not suspected of doing anything illegal. Rather, we believe that one or more of your students may be doing this while conducting research for a class project. May we come in and talk with you for a few minutes? I don't think it will take us long."

Keith was momentarily taken aback. It didn't take a lot of imagination to guess that the agents were talking about students from his Politics of Conspiracy class. That was the only group working on a project over the past few weeks. How the hell had the government linked the student, or students, with his class? If it were true that someone was trying to hack into government computers it didn't necessarily have to do with his Conspiracy class, right? They could be hacking for any reason, maybe just for the challenge; hackers always considered government computers the ultimate test of their abilities. "We were just getting ready to go out to dinner, but if you think we can clear this up in just a few minutes, please come in." As the agents walked in, Keith introduced everyone. "Agent Dickson, Agent Washington, this is Loren Davis. Loren, these guys are from the FBI and want to talk with me a few minutes about the possibility that one of my students hacked into some government computers." Loren stood up and said hello, but she held onto the dogs. She was scared to let go of them for fear that they might lunge at the agents.

"Honey, do you think you can coax Bo and Winston into the garage and block them in?" Keith asked. "They're really acting crazy." Both dogs were still making low, almost menacing growling noises. Keith had never seen them like this. Did they know something that he didn't? He trusted their instincts. The fact that they didn't seem to like these two guys was making the hair on the back of his neck stand up.

"Sure," she said. "I'll be right back, or I can wait in the kitchen to give you all some privacy."

"No, Ms. Davis, it's fine. It's OK if you join us. We just have a few questions at this point, so you're welcome to be here if you like."

"OK, then. I'll be right back." Loren opened the door that led from the kitchen to the garage and made the dogs go out. They were none too happy. Once she got them outside she joined Keith on the couch.

Special Agent Washington began. "Dr. Bryant, we're aware that you're teaching a class this semester called The Politics of Conspiracy. Sounds a lot more fun than anything I got to take in college." Washington smiled, but Keith didn't detect the least bit of warmth or friendliness in that smile. "We believe that at least one, and possibly more, of your students have been using one of the computers in the School of Politics library to try to infiltrate computers at the Pentagon, the CIA, and several other government sites."

"You're aware, of course, that all of our students have their own computers?" asked Keith.

"Sure," continued Washington. "But often, in these situations, people cover their tracks by using public computers rather than their own to make them harder to track. If they were using their own computers their unique IP address would be captured. By using a public PC it makes it a little harder on law enforcement. We have to get a warrant for that PC to check the hard drive, warrants for the Internet Service Provider's records, warrants for any surveillance video that may be available that puts the suspect in front of the public PC at the exact time of the breach… You get the idea."

"Makes sense. Let me ask you this: why does the FBI even know about my Politics of Conspiracy class? That sounds and feels a little bit like Big Brother to me, if you know what I mean." Keith did not like the fact that the government knew anything about his class, or his life, for that matter. He had always considered himself a good, patriotic American, but the more he got involved with his books, his research, and his business, the more he saw the dark side of America and understood why so many countries around the world resented us. It wasn't just because, as Bush liked to say, 'they hate us for our freedoms'. It went much deeper than that.

Dickson answered. "You're right, of course. It does sound like Big Brother, doesn't it? The reason is actually pretty simple. We're not monitoring the internet habits, the phone calls, or any other communications of the American people, per se. What we're doing is keeping an eye on certain websites and trying to detect patterns of who is visiting there. That is, if there is a website that has instructions on how to build a nuclear bomb, who is visiting that site? How often? Are they linked to any other people or groups that might mean us harm? If it's just your average John Doe visiting the site, whether because he's curious, he has a school project, or because he's a legitimate researcher, no problem. If, on the other hand, Mr. Doe tends to visit this site and lots of similar sites, say, on how to build and deliver a dirty bomb, and he shares that information with others via e-mail, then we take notice. Bottom line, we don't watch individuals without a court order, but we are allowed, as part of our work on anti-terrorism, to watch the sites and watch for patterns"

"As part of the government's expanded powers under the so-called Patriot Act, I assume?"

"Yes, that's correct" replied Dickson.

"And in the case of my Conspiracy class?"

"Well sir, to be honest, we haven't checked to see who's going where or who's checking out which site. But we have noticed a large increase in the amount of traffic emanating from the Charlottesville area that is hitting various conspiracy websites. Some of those sites, to be honest, are on the watch list. That's because, as I'm sure you can appreciate, our enemies might look to exploit some of the same methods used by Al Qaeda to do us further harm."

Keith didn't buy that explanation for one second. If anything, he believed that the government simply wanted to keep him, and others like him, from finding any link to the real reason that 9/11 happened and the real culprits behind it. He was not shocked to learn that certain sites were being watched by factions within the US government. He'd always assumed that to be true. He'd also always assumed that some of the information that's available regarding 9/11 was planted to throw investigators off the trail. The trick was in knowing what was real and what was fake. It wasn't always easy, but that's where hard, disciplined research paid off. Finally, Keith asked, "So tell me how I can help the FBI with regards to this hacking situation. Obviously, I don't tolerate, nor does the University, any illegal activities of this sort. The fact that you're reporting that this is happening from a University computer makes it even more important that we put a stop to it."

"The good news," said Washington, "is that the hacking attempts have not been successful to date. That doesn't mean that what's been done isn't a violation of the law, to say nothing of the University's Honor Code. But we're not necessarily looking to bring charges against a student at this point, we're just more interested in seeing the behavior cease and desist. If necessary we can get the necessary warrants to search the computers and try to determine who the perpetrator is, but to tell you the truth, there are bigger fish to fry out in the world. We'd rather not spend a lot of time pursuing this so long as the behavior stops and no restricted sites are hacked. We were hoping that you might talk to your class the next time you meet with them and try to warn them off of this type of action?"

"And what would you have me say? That it has come to my attention that some members of the class are being overzealous in their research methods and going to places they just shouldn't go?"

"Essentially, yes," said Dickson. "Tell them that any attempt at hacking a government site is a violation of the law and the Honor Code. If they're caught they'll be expelled and prosecuted. And I don't see any reason not to tell them that you've been visited by the FBI and asked to share this message. Maybe that puts a little bit more weight behind your request."

"It will also raise a lot of questions about the government's monitoring programs. A lot of people are already plenty suspicious of the government's motives in monitoring the phone calls and e-mails of American citizens under the pretense of the war on terrorism. Are you prepared to deal with the fallout that might be caused by what you're asking? What if the UVA campus, and God knows how many others to follow, erupts in protest marches and riots when they hear about this?" asked Keith. He threw this question out there, hoping to provoke a certain response.

"Well, that could certainly happen," said Washington. "The whole campus could look like a throwback to the 1960's with a bunch of protests and rallies, UVA people dressing like a bunch of hippies instead of a bunch of preppies." Another attempt at humor that fell flat. "But you're students have to understand, we're willing to let this go at this point without prosecution. We could have investigated this as the actions of a terrorist sleeper cell, maybe someone on campus with ties to Al Qaeda. That would have been a whole lot less pleasant."

And there it was. The exact response that Keith was hoping to provoke. These Agents – if they even really *were* Agents – had obviously planned multiple scenarios that they might use to get Keith to cooperate. They tried to soft-sell him, appeal to his desire to keep his students from expulsion or prosecution. After all, no harm/no foul at this point, or so they'd said. If Keith didn't go for that appeal, they'd go to Plan B. Go for the terrorist link. Threaten people with the Patriot Act. Basically, if Keith couldn't help control the situation, the government would find someone to throw under the bus. It might be any student in his class. Who knows what 'evidence' could be found or created. Hell, for that matter, it might be Keith. What better way to quiet him and put a clamp down on his book, his research, and the research being done by the entire class, than to have him out of the way? Prosecute him. Vilify him. Kill him. Any or all were possible. Once again he was feeling chills all the way down his spine.

Keith decided to play it cool. Agree with their logic, agree to have the talk with his class. Just get them out of the house. "I guess I can see your point. Look, I think it's probably just like you said, one or more of my students getting a little bit overzealous in their research. It's probably my fault. I told the class that the student that contributes the most to the project and does the best research would be asked to write the Foreword to my new book, plus I'd put their name on the cover. Maybe that made them a little bit too aggressive. I don't want to see anything happen to any of my students over this. They're good kids, they work hard. I'll talk with them during our next class, and I'm sure that I can put the fear of God into them and there won't be any more problems."

"I think you're probably right, Dr. Bryant," said Dickson. "And the Bureau appreciates your willingness to help out in this situation. If it's OK with you we'll check back with you periodically to let you know if we see any more hacking attempts, but I sincerely doubt we will after you talk with your students." Dickson stood up, followed by Washington. Dickson extended his hand to Keith. "We've taken enough of your time tonight, sir, and we appreciate it. Let us get out of here so you and Ms. Davis can get to your dinner plans. You guys have a nice evening."

Keith and Loren both shook their hands and opened the door for the agents to leave. "Drive carefully," said Loren.

"Thanks, Ms. Davis. We will." This from Washington.

As they started the car and started around the driveway, Keith put his arm around Loren and gave her a little nuzzle on the neck and whispered, "Don't say anything, don't react. Follow my lead and we'll talk when we leave."

Keith's words scared the hell out of Loren, but she had been with Keith long enough to know to trust his instincts. As they stepped back in and closed the door Keith said, "Well, that was an unexpected visit. It's not every day that we get a visit from the FBI. I hope to God none of my students have been dumb enough to try to hack into a restricted site, but if they have I really hope they'll listen to me when I tell them about tonight."

"They'd be crazy not to. I don't think you'll have to worry. Your students worship you, so they'll probably take what you say at face value and be thankful that they dodged a bullet." Loren realized that was probably an inappropriate choice of words, given the mood. Probably a Freudian slip, she reasoned. "So what do you want to do about dinner? Still want to try to go to Duner's? It's probably not too late."

"Yeah, that still sounds good. Let's let the dogs out real quick to go the bathroom, then we'll just leave them in the house while we're gone. We shouldn't be more than a couple of hours."

While they walked outside with Bo and Winston they talked very casually about the visit they'd just had, careful not to say anything that would be the least bit revealing about what they were thinking should someone, somehow, be listening in on them. And, of course, someone was. Foster had personally listened in to every word of the conversation between his operatives and Keith and Loren. Every word was recorded for further analysis. Even now, while Keith and Loren were outside, members of Foster's team were listening in on them using long range parabolic microphones and recording everything.

The dogs finally finished their business and everyone headed back into the house. Each of the dogs got one of their favorite treats, as usual, and then Keith and Loren headed for his car in the garage. They made the ten minute ride down to Duner's and were pleasantly surprised to only have to wait about five minutes for a table. The whole way down there in the car Keith avoided saying anything about the visit from the FBI, instead just focusing on the usual innocuous small talk that couples engage in every day. Keith tried to keep an eye out to see if anyone was following them, but how would he know? It was two lane roads all the way from the farm to Duner's, so any car that just happened to be traveling in the same direction, which is not unusual this time of night, could look like a tail. He looked around the restaurant, trying to be casual. Could there be someone in here keeping an eye on him and Loren? Again, though, how would he know? His stomach was churning from the anxiety.

When they were finally seated, Keith whispered across the table to Loren, "Thank God this place is so noisy. For once that's a blessing. I don't trust the FBI agents that came to the house tonight, and I don't believe their story about the hacking, not even for one second. For that matter, I don't even trust that those guys were FBI agents."

Now Loren felt the chills and the goose bumps. "Why? Are you sure you're not just being paranoid?"

"I might very well be paranoid, but I don't think so. Something just didn't feel right about them, or about their story. Call it my 'man's intuition'.

Even Bo and Winston seemed to sense something was wrong. I've never seen them that way; they were ready to attack those guys."

"So you're acting paranoid, not even talking in your own home or your own car, based on the intuition of two Labrador Retrievers?"

"Hey, I'd trust them over most people I know," replied Keith with a smile. "But seriously, their story seemed a little bit off to me. What good would it do my students to try to hack some government and DoD computers? Am I supposed to believe that they'd just be fishing around in there hoping to stumble on some evidence that supports our conspiracy theory? That's nuts. If they had developed any leads or found a trail that led them to a government or DoD site I think I'd know it. I'm with these students all the time, plus I'm meeting with them in their study groups to review their progress every single week."

The waitress stopped by the table and greeted them, then told them about the evening's specials. Keith ordered a bottle of 2001 Quintessa Cabernet, one of his favorite Napa Valley wines, and said that they'd like to enjoy a glass of wine before placing their dinner order. That was fine with the waitress. As soon as the waitress was off to get their wine they continued talking.

"So you think the FBI is lying about the whole thing?"

"Actually, like I said earlier, I'm not 100% convinced that those guys were FBI. I think they're working for the government, but God only knows who. CIA. NSA. SPCA – hell, pick an acronym. I know this sounds a little bit crazy, but they just didn't have that FBI 'look'. They were a little too big, a little too muscular. Even their suits couldn't hide that. Most FBI agents have law degrees or accounting degrees; that doesn't mean that they couldn't have been athletes, or that they can't be tough sons of bitches. Just something about these guys…they reminded me more of soldiers, not Feds." Keith was silent for a moment, gathering his thoughts. "I think somebody is trying to send me a little shot across the bow to warn me off. From what I'm not sure – there hasn't been a whole lot of substantive progress, at least not inasmuch as proving anything or uncovering information not already aired by any number of other people or groups."

"Was there one certain thing that set your radar off or an accumulation of things?" Loren always knew how to bring it back into focus.

"It was a lot of things, but the clincher was when I asked them about the possibility of creating protests and campus unrest if word got out about the government's monitoring of some of the student's web usage. They didn't even miss a beat, they just came right back with the statement that 'we could have investigated this as a possible terrorist sleeper cell' or some crap like that. If they were hit with the whole protest march and civil unrest thing out of the blue I would have expected them to say something along the lines that the government has to monitor certain communications to keep us safe from the terrorists, 'we either fight them over there or we have to fight them over here', and shit like that. Rationalize their actions. Probably threaten the University with some sort of punitive actions if we don't keep the students in line, like jeopardizing our access to government grants or government backed student aid. They didn't even go there. They went straight to the sleeper cell scenario. I think that was their 'Plan B'. They probably worked on two or three different scenarios before confronting me, and for whatever reason they decided to try to appeal to my fear of having one of my students arrested for hacking."

"OK, let's say that I'm willing to give you the benefit of the doubt on this one. Maybe these guys weren't FBI, and maybe the whole story about the hacking was just bullshit. Why the whole hush-hush, secret-squirrel stuff back at the house after they left?"

"I figured better safe than sorry. Look, this whole thing really caught me off guard. Two men just show up, out of the blue, and start talking to me about my class, my research, and so on. I think it's possible that someone, somewhere, is taking notice of the work that we're doing and, for whatever reason, they're starting to be concerned."

"Alright, but again, then why all of the cloak and dagger on your part?"

"Simple. And it's not just paranoia. There's actually some logic involved. Think about it: the class has been going on for about six weeks at this point, right? And of those six weeks, we're about three weeks into the 9/11 project. With me so far?" Loren nodded, and Keith continued. "They didn't just take notice a few hours ago and then suddenly decide to send our FBI friends down for a friendly visit, OK? Whoever is pulling their strings most likely took notice of the work we were doing one to two weeks ago, maybe longer. Something made them come out of the shadows now, some sort of tipping point. I don't know what that is, but if they've been paying attention for a few weeks, how do you suppose they did it? They wouldn't just be monitoring the student's internet usage, they'd probably be monitoring mine as well. And since I work from home almost as much, if not more, as I do from the office, why shouldn't we expect that they're monitoring that, too?"

Loren said nothing, but she had to admit that what he was saying made sense. She felt a tightness in her chest. "You're assuming that they're able to get past our network firewall, both at home and at the University."

"Right, I assume that there are many people for whom that would be a minor inconvenience, at most. One other thing concerns me. A lot of the work that we do is not just on our computers, it's collaboration. I talk to the students. I talk to you. I talk to the people at Bryant International. Talking and collaborating is what leads us to many of our best ideas. It's how we sift through the mountains of information and coalesce it down into something that makes sense, something that fits within our theories. Think about it. Most of the collaboration I do is either with you, sitting around the house and working through the stuff, or it's on the home phone, my mobile phone, or my office phone. The point is, if somebody were trying to monitor what I do, what I say, and what I think, the only way they can be reasonably sure of getting the information is to monitor our house and our phones, maybe even our cars. Maybe even my office, my classrooms for that matter."

The waitress came back with the wine that Keith had ordered and poured them each a full glass. With that she was off to tend to other tables, thankful for having one table that was planning to move at a slower pace.

"God, Keith. Do you know what you're saying? That everything we're saying, everything we're researching, every moment we're together in our own house, is being monitored? People are listening to us, Christ, maybe even watching us, when we're together?" She was getting more and more scared, tears starting to well up in her eyes.

"Look, try to hold yourself together. We don't know that I'm right, for starters. And even if I am, we don't know what their end-game is. Maybe they just want to monitor to make sure that I don't uncover something that they want to keep hidden, or maybe they hope to have me cancel the whole class project. All I'm saying is that, at least for now, we need to be careful and vigilant about what we say and what we do, particularly at the house, until we can figure out our next move. For all practical purposes though, we need to keep up appearances and keep to our normal routine." Keith knew that was asking a lot. Who wouldn't be freaked out at the thought of somebody listening and monitoring your every move, particularly in your own home?

"I'm scared." She was fighting hard to hold back the tears. "Do you think we should leave, just get out of the house, at least for a while, and go somewhere else?"

"It may come to that, but I hope it doesn't. Right now I don't want to raise their suspicions because it might just cause things to escalate unnecessarily. Like I said, even if I'm right about this it doesn't necessarily mean that we're in danger. Unless and until we see a reason to be concerned for our safety I think we should try to stick to as normal of a routine as possible. Still, I will start making some contingency plans, just in case. 'Course, I don't think I'll be using my computer to do that." Keith tried to inject a little bit of humor with that last statement, even giving Loren a little smile.

Obviously, humor was not working at this point. He had managed to scare the hell out of her, and she was scared now to the point of having her stomach in knots. They spent about two and a half hours at Duner's, lingering over their meals. Neither had much of an appetite, to say the least. They did, however, feel that this was a good night to drink heavily. Keith ordered a second bottle of the Quintessa. They continued talking about the events of the evening for the rest of their time in the restaurant. Once in the car, all talk relative to tonight ceased, and not a word about it was spoken at home. Keith had reminded Loren, again, that they had to try to maintain as normal a routine as possible when they were there. She just didn't think that she had it in her to be that good of an actor, but she knew that she had to make the effort. One thing she did know for sure: she had never felt so violated.

⌘

WHILE THE PSEUDO-FBI AGENTS WERE meeting with Keith and Loren at the farm, Mathew Hilton was also busy. He had waited until just after dark and then slipped into Lowell Westbrook's townhouse. He secreted himself away upstairs in the guest bedroom waiting for Westbrook to arrive home. There was no way to know what time he'd come home, if at all. Patience, he told himself. Hilton had every intention of pushing or throwing Westbrook down the steps in order to make it look like a simple household accident. In the event that things didn't go as planned, Hilton was ready with his own Plan B. He had a silenced pistol under his jacket, but he really preferred not to have to use it.

Around 7:00pm Lowell Westbrook came through the front door. Thankfully, he was alone. Another complication that Hilton didn't need, though he was more than capable of dealing with it if necessary. Westbrook puttered around downstairs for a while, making himself something to eat and watching TV. Finally, during a commercial break he headed upstairs. He went straight into his bedroom and changed clothes. Hilton heard the toilet flush in the master bath; too bad he didn't come out here and use the guest bathroom in the hall, Hilton thought. He could have taken him out right then and there as he exited since the guest bath was right across from the top of the stairs.

Hilton was coiled and ready. He expected Westbrook to head back downstairs momentarily, and that would be his chance to spring out and help this little 'accident' along. Momentarily he heard footsteps on the carpeting; Lowell was heading towards the stairs. Hilton had to time this just right, he knew. As soon as Lowell came out of his bedroom and was within a few feet of the top of the steps, Hilton sprang out of the darkened guest room. Lowell was startled and was about to scream, but before he could get a sound out Hilton clamped a hand over his mouth, then reached under his left arm and around his waist and literally threw him over his hip and down the stairs. Lowell flew so far that he hit about five steps from the top, his head making the initial contact with the step. He crashed down the stairs, rolling over awkwardly several times, his feet crashing through a few of the banister spokes. He ended up at the bottom of the steps, his body contorted in a way that God never intended.

Hilton walked slowly down the stairs, pleased with his performance. Almost too easy, he thought to himself. He bent over and checked Lowell. Goddamn! He was still alive! Plenty of broken bones, possibly even a broken back, he mused. Hilton took his time, considering his next step. Westbrook would probably be dead any minute, but he couldn't afford to wait around for nature to take its course, and he certainly couldn't risk leaving and then have the lucky bastard survive to identify him. No, he had to be dealt with now. "Sorry about this, old man. Nothing personal." With that, Hilton gave Lowell's neck a quick twist and felt it break. Ever the professional, Hilton reached down to feel for a pulse. Finding none, as expected, he knew that his work was done. He took a quick look out the windows, and seeing that all was clear, he slipped out into the darkness.

Hilton was quite pleased with himself and his performance. He was even more pleased that he would be receiving a $10,000 bonus for the kill, a bonus that put him one step closer to that coveted tropical island retirement.

Chapter 9

KEITH PULLED INTO THE SCHOOL around 8:45 on Wednesday morning. His first class wasn't until 10:00 but he wanted to have some time to check his email and messages. He also had a little 'thank you' gift for Lowell Westbrook for filling in on Monday on such short notice, especially after having called him at 6:00am. Keith had settled on a bottle of really nice wine, a 2001 Stags Leap Cask 23 cabernet. Loren thought that giving a bottle of wine worth more than $150 may have been a bit over the top, but Keith didn't mind since he had bought a whole case of it directly from the vineyards as soon as it was released. Since Lowell had lived for a number of years in Berkley, CA, not much more than an hour from Napa, he fancied himself a pretty good judge of fine wine. Keith wasn't sure if he really was as much of a wine connoisseur as he pretended to be; after all, Keith smiled to himself, he'd actually seen Lowell drinking *white* wine on more than one occasion. In Keith's view that was just a mortal sin. White wine was for cooking and making sauces, but God forbid if he actually had to *drink* the stuff.

Keith reminded himself to be as cautious here at the University as he was at home, maybe even more so. He had to go on the assumption that his phone and his e-mail were being monitored, and quite possibly his conversations within this office as well. For that matter, it was entirely possible that someone in his class was there solely to monitor him and the rest of the class and report back to....whom? He didn't know. He could only guess, and guessing and speculating were going to drive him crazy. Keith took his laptop PC out of his bag and put it into the docking station. While he was booting up his PC he tried calling Lowell's University extension. Straight to voice mail. He decided against trying his mobile phone. It was still relatively early and he didn't want Lowell to think that Keith was stalking him and harassing him by calling him so early two days in the same week. He would just wait a while and then try him again, or maybe see if Lowell was available via Instant Messaging when his PC finished booting. Deciding to go down the hall to grab a snack from the vending machine, Keith left his laptop to finish its boot sequence. By the time he got back he was being queried by the operating system to enter his password.

As the system came up it automatically logged him into his Microsoft Live Messenger IM account, but he could see that Lowell was not online. He'd keep an eye on that screen, he decided, so he'd know immediately when Lowell came online. Logging into e-mail he didn't find anything especially pressing, at least not in his university account. He kept separate e-mail accounts for Bryant International and for personal use, but he rarely checked either from the university's network. Both accounts did synch up with his Blackberry, however, so that gave him the flexibility to stay connected even while on campus. Keith quickly blew through the twenty-plus e-mails and the five voice mails from Tuesday afternoon and evening. Again, nothing especially pressing, just a few faculty meetings and social events to add to his calendar. Nothing from Lowell. It was nearly 9:30 when he finished, so since Lowell hadn't returned his call yet he decided to give his University extension one more try. Just as before, it went straight to voice mail. This time Keith decided to try Lowell's mobile phone, but it just rang four times and then went to voice mail. It was unlike Lowell not to be here by this time of morning. You could usually count on him being here no later than 8:30 every day. Keith decided to check with the department's administrative assistant to see if maybe Lowell had an appointment somewhere off campus, or maybe he had called in sick. Walking up to Debbie Walker's desk he inquired about Lowell, but she had not heard from him and had no knowledge of any appointments this morning. Just to make sure she pulled up Lowell's calendar – everyone in the department had the ability to share their calendars across the computer network – and found nothing there, either.

"Thanks for checking, Debbie. If you hear from him or see him come in will you ask him to come see me as soon as possible, please. I've got a class at 10:00 but I should be around after that."

Keith locked the bottle of wine in his file cabinet and headed to his Comparative Political Systems class. He'd get there a little early, but that was OK. The room wasn't used for an earlier class on Wednesday so he could go in and get set up before the students started arriving. He had to try to relax, put his mind at ease. On the way to the classroom several students stopped him to talk about his research and how things were going in the Politics of Conspiracy class. Were they just being curious, or was there some ulterior motive to their questions? Were they digging for information to report on him or others in the class? Keith realized that he was being a little bit too paranoid; all of the students that he was talking to in the hallways were kids that he'd known for a year or more, in some cases even four years. Not that people couldn't be turned, but if there really was somebody keeping an eye on him and the Conspiracy class wasn't it much more likely that the person was somebody unknown to him, somebody who hadn't been around campus for a long time? It only made sense. Keith jotted down a quick note to himself to follow through on this thought after class, maybe start to look a little more closely at the students in the Conspiracy class, the newer people on the faculty and staff, and anyone who just didn't seem to fit in. This might lead nowhere, but at least he felt like he was taking some action, albeit, very cautiously.

When class was over Keith circled back past Debbie Walker's desk. She saw him approaching. "I still haven't heard anything from Lowell, Dr. Bryant. Do you want me to try his home number?"

"That's probably a good idea, and if I don't have an e-mail or a return call from him on my voice mail when I get back to my office, I'll also try his mobile phone again."

"Hold on one second, if you can, Dr. Bryant. I'll try his number right now." Debbie dialed the number, but after four rings all she got was his home voice mail. "Sorry, Dr. Bryant. No answer there either."

"Thanks for trying Debbie. I'll check on my end and then let you know."

There was only one voice mail on Keith's office number but it wasn't from Lowell. He already knew that he hadn't been called on his Blackberry, because he had it in his jacket pocket during the entire class, though, out of common courtesy, he had it set to vibrate instead of ring. Next he checked his e-mail. Nothing. He checked to see if Lowell was logged into IM. He wasn't. Normally Keith wouldn't have felt a lot of concern, but after the events of last night he was a lot more on edge. He may not have particularly liked Lowell Westbrook, but he had to admit that he was usually reliable and punctual. This was totally out of character for him, being a few hours late and not calling to notify someone. Those little hairs on the back of his neck were starting to dance again, and Keith really didn't like the feeling. He didn't like the feeling, but he did *trust* it. He decided to walk back over to Debbie's desk; he definitely didn't want to have this conversation on the phone in case it was being monitored. "Debbie, I don't have any word from Lowell either, and I've checked everywhere. Frankly, I'm getting a little bit worried."

"What do you think we should do? Maybe drive over to his house?" asked Debbie.

"That might be a good idea, but I think that we should call the University Police and have them accompany us. We may need them to contact the property manager or someone else who can get us access to Lowell's place. He might be sick or hurt and need help and be unable to call 911."

"I have his address here in my files. Why don't I have the University Police meet us at Lowell's house and you and I can drive over there together." Debbie was one of the few people around the School that actually liked Lowell, so she was adamant about going with Keith. "I'll call them now and tell them we'd like to go ASAP, and they better not give me any shit about it. Luckily it's less than 10 minutes from here."

Keith wasn't sure, but she seemed to say this with such authority that he was beginning to think that perhaps she'd been to Lowell's house before. That was certainly possible, both were young and single, both relatively new to Charlottesville. Maybe they were an item, or at least had been at one time. After Debbie hung up from the University Police with assurances that they were rolling an officer right away, Keith said, "Let's head on over to Lowell's. My car is right outside."

The closer that they got to Lowell's house the more that Keith's stomach was twisted in knots. This is just silly, he thought to himself. There's no need to feel panicked about Lowell being late for work; there could be a million different reasons. It doesn't mean that something bad has happened. Then why does he have this terrible sense of dread? Is he just being paranoid, as Loren had said? Is he reading way too much into these events, events that are probably not even related?

The University Police were already parked in front of Lowell's townhouse when Keith and Debbie pulled up. He stepped out of his car as Keith pulled in. "Dr. Bryant and Ms. Walker I presume? I'm Officer Haskell."

"Thanks for coming to meet us, Officer Haskell," replied Keith. "This may very well turn out to be nothing at all, but to tell you the truth we're a little bit concerned."

"Not a problem, sir. I called ahead to the property manager's office, and we caught a break. She told me that Mr. Westbrook rents this townhouse from a local businessman and she has a key to the property in her office. The owner has her office keep a key in case someone should ever need to get in for maintenance, or maybe if the place goes back on the rental market when his lease is up."

"That's great. Do we need to slide over to her office to pick the key up?" asked Debbie.

"Nope. One step ahead of you. I already swung by on my way in here and grabbed the key. She was tied up with some other folks at the time, so I assured her that we'd just duck in real quickly, make sure everything is OK, and then lock it all back up. She was cool with that."

"That was nice of her. Well, shall we go take a look," Keith said with a lot more confidence than he really felt.

They all approached the door, and when they reached it Officer Haskell knocked loudly on the door and announced himself. Getting no response, he rapped a little bit louder, this time using his flashlight instead of his hand. They all listened but heard nothing. Keith didn't know whether that should be making him feel more relieved or more worried. Officer Haskell then said, "OK, we knocked loud enough that anybody inside would have been unable to miss. I guess that's our cue to use the key and go on in." With that, he removed the key from his pocket and slipped the key in the lock. If he had any apprehension it certainly didn't show. Having a gun on your belt must make you feel a little bit bolder, Keith reasoned.

As soon as the door was opened they saw Lowell lying at the bottom of the steps, his legs and neck twisted into grotesque positions. Debbie screamed, almost as if in pain, and burst into tears. Even Officer Haskell froze in his tracks, apparently stunned at what he was seeing. Not a lot of dead bodies to be seen working around a college campus, to be sure. This was his first in the two years that he'd been with the University force. "Oh my God, Lowell," was the first thing out of Keith's mouth. Keith, followed by Haskell, moved slowly towards Lowell. Debbie stood in the doorway, sobbing. Neither expected him to be alive, not with the way his body was contorted or the pallor of his skin.

Still, they had to check to be sure in case they needed to call for help. Officer Haskell felt for a pulse. Finding none, he took a step back and surveyed the room, seeing if there was anything obviously suspicious or out of place.

"Poor guy must have taken a spill down the stairs. Looks like his neck, and probably one or both legs, are broken. I'm going to call this in to dispatch and have them send the Charlottesville PD and the coroner. Maybe while I call this in you should check on Ms. Walker."

"Yeah, I think you're right." Keith moved back towards the door to try to calm Debbie. As he put his arm on her shoulder she turned and held him, burying her head in his shoulder and sobbing. He didn't know exactly what to say to her; he didn't really know her that well, and he certainly didn't know what relationship, if any, she had with Lowell.

"It will be OK, Debbie. I know that this was a shock, opening the door and finding him like this."

"Oh my God, I can't believe this is happening," she managed to get out between sobs. "We were just together the night before last, right here. We ordered a pizza and watched a movie on pay-per-view, and I ended up staying the night here with him."

"I didn't know that you two were close."

It was hard for her to talk between sobs. "We both agreed that it was probably best to try to keep our relationship pretty quiet, no need for rumors to get started around the School. We'd been seeing each other for a couple of months, maybe once or twice a week. Sometimes here, sometimes at my place."

"I'm so sorry. You obviously cared for him."

"I really do...did", and she started crying harder again. "We were trying to take things slowly, see where it led. To be honest, I think I was a little more into it than he was. I tried not to show how much I liked him 'cause I didn't want to scare him off. But things were definitely moving in the right direction." She tried to force a small smile as she made that last statement, but it was not easy to smile through that much pain.

"As soon as the police and coroner arrive, why don't I give you a ride home? They may have a few questions for us, but hopefully we won't need to stay here too long. We'll get you home and you try to get some rest, maybe take a few days off."

"I can't do that, Dr. Bryant," she sniffed. "There's nobody to backfill for me this week. Besides, I need to get Lowell's personnel information together so that somebody can contact his family, and somebody needs to clean out his office,…" as her voice trailed off and she started crying harder again.

"You don't need to be the one to worry about that. The University has his personnel information on file somewhere down in HR, and they can take care of contacting his family and working with them for anything they need locally. And I'll work with the Dean to make sure that his office is taken care of and his personal effects sent to his family. You just take it easy." Keith realized that he was probably saying all of the wrong things, but he didn't have a clue what the right things were. What had people said to him to try to console him after his parents had died? He couldn't really remember; maybe he'd been in such shock both times that the details just eluded him. Maybe everyone that talked to him tried saying the same tired, inane clichés that he was saying to Debbie.

Haskell came back in the room. "Charlottesville PD is on the way, and the coroner should be here within the hour." He went over and took another look at Lowell's body. "Doesn't look like much of a mystery on cause of death. My guess is that he just missed a step and took a header down the whole staircase." Haskell hadn't heard the conversation between Keith and Debbie over the past few minutes since he'd been in the kitchen calling in for help.

Keith pulled himself gently away from Debbie and then led her over to sit on the couch. She sat down and buried her head in her hands, her chest still heaving. Keith walked over to Officer Haskell and spoke quietly. "Officer, while you were in the kitchen I was talking with Debbie, trying to console her. It turns out that she and Lowell Westbrook were dating. That's why she's so emotional."

"Oh, Christ. I'm sorry, I didn't know."

"That's OK," said Keith. "She'll be OK, I'm sure. She just needs a little bit of time. Obviously, this was a helluva shock for her. For all of us."

Keith went back over to the couch and sat beside Debbie. He tried again to console her, reaching over and holding her hand and talking quietly. She was only in her early 20's, barely a few years older than most of his students. Too young to have to deal with this kind of pain…not that you were ever ready for this kind of pain regardless of your age, he reminded himself.

They sat mostly in silence, other than the occasional sounds of her crying or sniffling. Keith had at least thought to get up and get her some tissues to dry her eyes. Officer Haskell went outside and waited for the Charlottesville PD, apparently uncomfortable with the prospect of being in the same room with a crying female. Keith's mind was going a mile a minute, and he didn't like the direction it was taking. He was not a big believer in coincidence, and finding Lowell dead the morning after he'd been visited by a couple of government agents – or at least he assumed they were from the government, though certainly not from the FBI – was more coincidence than he could accept. Would someone kill Lowell just because he worked with Keith? To what end? It's not like they worked together that closely. Had something changed in their relationship, their dynamic, that could have put Lowell on their radar? The only thing that Keith could think of was the fact that Lowell recently took on the assignment of posting the Conspiracy class' information to the University intranet, but to date he hadn't really posted anything of any substance. Keith was sure of that; he had reviewed every single thing before it was posted, and there was nothing that wasn't readily available on any number of public web sites. Should he say something to the police when they got here? Maybe ask them to at least investigate Lowell's death rather than writing it off to a simple accident? How the hell can he do that without arousing suspicion or raising a lot of questions that he wasn't prepared to answer, even if he could answer the inevitable questions convincingly? He felt his chest starting to tighten again and his stomach starting to twist into knots. He really wanted to get out of here and call Loren to tell her what had happened, but there was no way he was going to risk discussing this, or anything even remotely involved with the events of the last 24 hours, on their cell or office phones. He couldn't risk one of them saying the wrong thing or bringing up the wrong subject, and possibly put them in danger. If he wasn't just being paranoid....

The sound of approaching sirens snapped Keith out of his thoughts and back to reality. Two Charlottesville PD cruisers drove up, followed within minutes by an ambulance. Of course, a small crowd had already gathered out in the parking lot, rumors already starting to spread about what was inside. Not that anybody knew anything, but in today's world lack of information didn't stop people from speculating and helping rumors, each more far-fetched than the one before, to spread like wildfire. Fortunately, the crowd was much smaller than it would have been had this been happening in the evening or on a weekend. Officer Haskell was outside briefing the arriving city police and the ambulance crew on what he'd found. Keith had no doubt that the police were going to take one look at this and rule it an accident. It wouldn't be like TV, with half a dozen CSI's combing over every inch of the place, pulling fibers from carpet, looking for evidence of an intruder, checking for DNA and blood evidence, and essentially solving the whole big mystery in just one hour. Without any obvious evidence of forced entry or of a second person inside the home, it was a virtual certainty that they'd rule this an accident and then send the body off to the coroner to let them determine the official cause of death. Maybe it was just an accident. As the doctors on TV always say, 'When you hear hooves, think horses, not zebras'. Maybe an accident is just an accident. Shit happens. Maybe there is no mystery, nothing out of the ordinary. Just bad luck. Keith tried hard to convince himself of that logic, but it just wouldn't stick. He kept coming back to one simple conclusion: he had stumbled onto something or into something, and someone in the US government wanted him kept quiet. Actually, that brought him to one other simple but inevitable conclusion: if they – whoever '*they*' are – are willing to kill Lowell Westbrook, they're probably just as willing to kill him and Loren. The chills started up and down his spine once again, and he was growing really tired of that feeling.

⌘

Keith ended up having to stay at Lowell's place for another hour and a half talking to the police. They also questioned Debbie, and they managed to do it with a high level of professionalism and empathy, a fact that both surprised him and impressed him. She managed to make it through their questions without breaking down again. After they were done Keith drove Debbie to her apartment, and on the way he managed to reach her roommate and informed her of what had happened. Thankfully, the roommate said she would leave work immediately and meet them at the apartment, and she'd be able to stay with Debbie and take care of her for as long as she needed. That definitely made Keith feel better, knowing that she wouldn't be left alone at such a difficult time.

Just after Keith dropped Debbie off at her apartment his cell phone rang. He saw from the display that it was Loren's name and number. Damn. Apparently word had already reached campus about Lowell's death. He had hoped to get her away from campus to tell her, hopefully away from any prying eyes and ears. Keith clicked his Bluetooth headset to 'on' and answered her call. "Hi, sweetie. I was just getting ready to call you. I guess you've already heard the terrible news about Lowell." He decided to preempt anything she might say about Lowell, just in case.

"Oh my God, I just heard a few minutes ago. And they told me that you're the one who found him. What were you doing there?" Loren was more than a little bit concerned.

"Debbie Walker and I decided to go over there because no one had heard from him or been able to reach him all morning. We met the campus police there. I just dropped her off at her apartment, and her roommate is there with her, thankfully. I thought I'd swing back by the School to pick up my things and head home for the day. It's not been a great day, to say the least. I also haven't eaten anything. Why don't you head out at the same time and let's go for a drink and a little bite to eat." He hoped that by saying this Loren would understand to hold off on a lot of the questions she may have.

Smart girl. She caught his drift. "That sounds like a great idea. Why don't I just meet you at your office then, say in about thirty minutes?"

"That should give me enough time to get back and pack my stuff up. See you then. Love you." With that he clicked off, the thought of somebody listening in on his conversations making him cautious.

Around 3:30 Loren walked into his office, trying to act as natural and normal as she could, at least considering the circumstances. She walked up and gave him a hug, holding him a long time. "I'm so sorry that you had to go through this today. And I feel so bad for Lowell and his family."

Keith was immediately aware that Loren remembered their conversation from last night about people possibly monitoring their conversations and their movements, and she was being very cognizant of that as she talked to him. He then said, "I know, I feel bad for them too. It looked like a terrible accident, like he just fell down the stairs and broke half the bones in his body. Tell you what, let's get out of here and go somewhere for a drink. I think I could use one." Keith didn't want to tell Loren about Debbie and Lowell being in a relationship, at least not here or anywhere that they might be overheard. He was afraid that that might put Debbie in danger. He didn't need anybody else dying around him.

They left the University and headed over to the Omni Hotel. Keith suggested that they go to the bar and have a couple of drinks and maybe an appetizer or two. He needed the drink and the food, but more than anything he wanted to be somewhere where there was little chance of them being monitored. He sat with his back to the wall, his eyes fixed on the doorway into the bar. There was no way that anybody could come in there and get anywhere close to them without him noticing. He had Loren sit so she would be able to see most of the other patrons. After ordering a Jack Daniels on the rocks for him – this was no cabernet day – and a Cosmopolitan for her, along with an order of nachos and some chicken wings, Keith started telling Loren about what they'd found at Lowell's place and about his suspicions. At first she looked at him like he'd lost his senses, maybe because she didn't want to believe that he was right. That was a much scarier alternative. They stopped to take a breath when the waitress came back with a second round of drinks and their food.

"So what you're telling me, in a nutshell, is that you think Lowell was killed by someone, probably within the Federal government, because they want to silence you and because Lowell was working closely with you? Doesn't that sound more than a little preposterous, especially considering that Lowell didn't work that closely with you, and, by your own admission, hadn't posted anything relevant to your class website?"

"It's not something I can prove, it's something I feel…"

Loren interrupted him. "And you feel this even more because the dogs didn't like the guys that came to the house last night, and you believe in their ability to judge people's character, right?" There was no attempt at humor in this statement, she was directly challenging his logic and doubting him. She could see the hurt, the confusion, and the growing anger on his face. "Look, babe, I love you and I think you're the most brilliant man I've ever met. But I'm just having a hard time seeing the big conspiracy here. Forget that the events seem to be totally unrelated, and forget that you said yourself that Lowell's death appears to be a simple accident, I just can't wrap my arms around the government being out to get you and everyone connected to you just because you're writing a book on the 9/11 conspiracy. You've said it yourself, you haven't uncovered any smoking gun or anything that should make you Public Enemy Number One on George W's hit list."

Keith thought about what she said for a few moments. Yes, it was the first time she'd ever seemed to doubt him in any way, but he didn't resent her for it. He needed her to challenge him, to make sure he was considering all possible angles. She was brilliant in her own right, and her insights were, as always, spot on. "Look, Loren," he continued in a low voice, "I hear what you're saying. I know that what I'm talking about seems a little bit out there, but it's kinda like what we talked about last night when our 'FBI agents that weren't really FBI agents' came to visit us. If something is, in fact, happening, the people that are pulling the strings didn't just take notice of this yesterday. They noticed something weeks ago. For that matter, they may have noticed something that we've overlooked, like a connection between two or more pieces of data that we haven't even noticed yet. I think there is a correlation between what the Conspiracy class is working on and the death of Lowell Westbrook, I just can't figure out what that connection is."

"OK, let's say for a moment that I buy into this Robert Ludlum scenario. Somebody sends those gorillas to see you last night to try to get you and your class to back off their 9/11 research. Then somebody, maybe even the same two gorillas, go throw Lowell down the stairs to either (a) send an even stronger message to you, or (b) to silence him. In my mind, option 'a' doesn't make any sense. They just warned you off a few hours before, and you told them – pretty convincingly, I thought – that you would have a talk with your students. Why try to send you a stronger message if you haven't even had the opportunity to talk to your class in the first place, right? There didn't appear to be any imminent threat from your class or the data, right, or else they would have come in guns blazing right from the get go."

Shit. She was absolutely correct. That wouldn't make any sense. "I think you're onto something, so long as we can assume that these people will act rationally. Being as they don't often want to call attention to themselves, I think it's in their best interests to be rational and to try to fly a bit under the radar. They wouldn't kill just for the sake of killing, in other words. Every action causes a reaction."

"Exactly. That leaves us with option 'b', that the bad guys wanted to silence Lowell. That doesn't say that they don't want to silence you, too, it just means that silencing Lowell was a higher, more immediate priority. What we don't know is why Lowell would *need* to be silenced, assuming, again, that his death really was something other than an accident." Damn, now that she had thought things out logically she could see where Keith was coming from, and she really hoped that he was wrong, for both of their sakes.

"My God, I think you're onto something there, Nancy Drew." Keith smiled at her, admiring that brilliant mind of hers once again. "Maybe you should be a detective instead of a political science guru."

"Yeah, well, remember I said 'if we assume his death was something other than an accident'. I didn't say I was ready to concede that it *was* something more." She smiled, hoping to ease the tension a bit.

"Maybe something happened to Lowell because of someone else in his life, maybe someone he was talking to, or someone that he was staying in touch with via e-mail, something. Maybe it's that person that is the key." Keith was silent for a moment, his mind going a hundred miles an hour. Loren sat silently, giving him a chance for some uninterrupted thought. She could almost see the wheels turning in his head. He ate a few of the nachos, so engrossed in his thinking that he probably never tasted the first bite. After a few minutes, Keith spoke again, a bit more tentatively than usual, as if he were still formulating his hypotheses in his head. "How about this: Lowell was set to be the gatekeeper for all of the information that our class is developing for the 9/11 project. Maybe he was arranging to share the information we developed with someone else, someone that the government had their eye on?"

"Like who, another writer? That wouldn't make sense. One writer is generally no more a threat than another writer, assuming that they both have credibility in the public eye. God knows you do. Even if another writer was racing to get their book out ahead of yours, that surely doesn't seem like a reason that would launch a government conspiracy. Maybe a little warfare between rival publishing houses," she said with a smile.

"You're right, but I can think of another possibility. What if it's not another writer, but instead another person or group that deals in 9/11 conspiracy theories? Think about it: Lowell arranges to provide our information to someone that has legitimacy in the field, or at least the government sees them as a threat. Maybe they want to sever that link between Lowell and this certain someone. That way the information we develop doesn't show up on some conspiracy site and start to cause unwanted attention on Uncle Sam."

"OK. But let me put my devil's advocate hat on for a minute. You keep saying that you and your class haven't found anything new or unique in your research, at least not to date. Why would the government be worried about taking action against Lowell and this alleged conspiracy group if there is no worthwhile or incriminating information as of yet?"

"I don't know. Maybe they're afraid of what we might find, or maybe someone in my class has stumbled on something and I don't know about it. I'm just guessing at this point." Keith stopped to consider one other point. "Or, there's one other possibility. The government doesn't want us teamed up or collaborating with this person or group. Maybe it's someone with enough resources and enough legitimacy that it worries the feds. Maybe the government fears that this conspiracy group will point to the fact that a UVA professor has an entire class focused on 9/11, thereby lending even more credibility to the whole conspiracy theory movement. For that matter," Keith said, speaking slowly as if he were having another epiphany, "maybe it's not what we're finding that's causing all of the attention. Instead, what if it's what we're proving false? We're helping to shoot down a lot of bogus information that's circulating out there in conspiracy land."

"I'm not sure I see your point."

"Think about it. The governments always claim that there are no conspiracies, that for every situation or event there's a clear-cut, easily explained version of events. Their version. They also know that many people don't believe that shit for a second, that's why a million different conspiracy theories seem to get generated every time. Obviously, the government never wants the public to know the real truth, right? We have to be protected from the truth, at least in their view. So the last thing they want is for someone to come along and prove every conspiracy wrong…"

"Because then all your left with is the truth," said Loren, having her own epiphany. "Holy shit."

"Exactly. Most conspiracy groups are out there making up half-baked shit all the time. Only a relative handful of researchers actually spend their time trying to debunk these theories, most hoping to eventually back into the truth. Since my class is doing serious, disciplined research, they are sometimes shooting down some of the conspiracy sacred cows. The government, if they really want to keep the truth about 9/11 from the public, can't afford for all the cockamamie bullshit to be revealed for what it is. They either have to silence those that are working against them or keep adding more bogus information to the mix, something to throw the researchers off of the trail."

"Then what you're saying, simply, is that Lowell wasn't working with some terrorist group and leaking them the information; after all, what would be the point? They already know how to blow things up and stir up fear. Instead, you think Lowell was sharing, or at least planning to share, your research with someone that is also working to uncover the truth about 9/11?"

"Right. Most likely to help them eliminate more of the falsehoods that are out there and enable them to sort through the chaff to find the real truth."

"Assuming you're right, what are you going to do?"

Keith took a minute to think this through before speaking. "I'm going to ask Cary in the campus telecom group to pull the phone records from Lowell's office phone, see if I can find anything there. Then I'll get hold of his cell phone when we're collecting his personal effects. I can probably at least check his call logs in the phone's memory, maybe see the last fifty or so calls that he made in and out." Keith was on a roll, his mind clicking even after all of the Jack Daniels. "I think I'll also ask a friend of mine in the IT department if he can have a look, quietly, at our class intranet site. I'm no expert, but it seems to me that the most effective way to share the information with someone is to open up some kind of secret access into our system, not just forward stuff via e-mail. Every time you send someone an e-mail it leaves a trail that somebody might find later. I wouldn't know how to find it, but Chris in IT could probably track it down in no time flat."

Loren smiled. "Now who thinks they're a detective?"

They continued their conversation until after 5:00, at which point the bar started filling with local businessmen and women coming in for happy hour. Crowds were definitely not their friend at this point. Keith paid the tab and they headed back to the farm, all talk about anything even remotely close to recent events ceasing for the evening.

⌘

FOSTER HAD HEARD ABOUT THE elimination of Lowell Westbrook within minutes of the killing. If Hilton's account was to be believed, everything went off without a hitch. Being a careful man, Foster had instructed Bob Manning to have one of the reconnaissance teams in Charlottesville trail Hilton to make sure that he was giving them an accurate picture. By all accounts Hilton was being straight-up. This was further corroborated by the news coming out of Charlottesville, both on the local TV news and the monitored police channels. There was no indication from any quarter that Westbrook's death was being viewed as anything other than an accident. Perfect.

Now Foster was hoping that Dr. Keith Bryant would take the not-so-subtle hint that he'd received the night before from his operatives. He called Bob Manning to check on the latest news from Charlottesville. "Anything new to report with Dr. Bryant?"

"No, looks like he went back to the University and gathered his things to head out for the day. He and Ms. Davis left around 3:30 and headed over to the Omni and had a few drinks. Guess the day's events had him a little bit shook up."

"Were we able to overhear what they were saying?"

"No," replied Manning. "Our guy wasn't able to get anywhere close to them. The bar was pretty empty when they first went in, so there was no way for him to follow them in and get anywhere close without being compromised. He did tell me that they left a little bit after 5 o'clock and went straight home."

"Any reason to believe he's getting suspicious?" asked Foster.

"I dunno. He's a smart guy. He probably has all kinds of shit floating around in his head at this point. Smart guy like that, he may think it's a little bit too coincidental for him to get a visit from the Feds one day and then have his research assistant turn up dead the next. The good news, at least in my estimation, is that if he does get suspicious it may only serve to have him back off of his current direction a bit. I mean, he knows that he can't be sure that the events are connected, and he knows that he can't prove anything – hell, the Director of the FBI would have bought those credentials, and no way anybody can prove that Westbrook's death was anything other than an accident – but maybe that will just put the fear of God into him even more."

"How so?" Foster wasn't quite following his logic.

"Think about it. If he gets suspicious that someone is after him and they have the wherewithal to know what he's working on, as well as the ability to send in operatives with credentials that are real enough to fool any and everybody, they must be some scary, well-connected people. Add onto that

Westbrook's accident; if he thinks it was staged, he is probably scared shitless at the prospect that someone with that much juice and that many resources has him in their sights."

"I see your point. Any chance, in your opinion, that he'll just take off out of fear for his life and that of Ms. Davis?"

Manning mulled that question over. "I don't think so, or at least not yet. I think he's still second-guessing himself, not wanting to really believe that this is happening. Trying to convince himself that he's getting a little bit too paranoid or that he's read too many spy novels. No, absent some other stimulus and/or some other outside interference, I don't think he's ready to rabbit. Not just yet."

"Agreed," said Foster. "But even if he does decide to run, that's not necessarily a bad thing for us, at least not at this point. He'll be leaving his Conspiracy class and the access that gives him to thirty-plus extra minds helping him do research. And unless he's incredibly resourceful, he won't be able to continue the research on his own since we have his computer, and Ms. Davis', monitored. If things start going downhill for Dr. Bryant -- and we, of course, may have to help them go downhill with some planted disinformation to discredit him -- his current publisher will probably kill his book deal. For that matter, the University will probably look to distance themselves as well."

"You're probably right. I suggest that we just monitor things over the next 24-48 hours to see how things play out. Hopefully Dr. Bryant will back off and save us the hassles and risks of taking things to the next level." Manning was like Foster and the rest of the team at DCG in that he preferred things to be able to work out quietly. The last thing a secret government organization needs is to risk shining the spotlight on itself.

"Let's hope," said Foster. "Keep me apprised of any developments. And good work, Bob. You and your team have done a great job in keeping this contained so far, and I appreciate it." Foster hung up the phone and swung back around to check his calendar. What he wouldn't give for a day out in the field, or even a day in the Bunker, monitoring the bad guys and plotting strategy. He imagined himself confronting Bryant by taking on the role of one of the FBI agents last night. God, what an incredible rush that would have been! Standing there, face to face, with the very subjects he has under surveillance. Maybe even the subjects of his next assassination order.

Let The Truth Be Told

Instead, he was about to spend the next two hours sitting in on a product demonstration and customer meeting that one of his account teams was hosting for the Social Security Administration. Christ. It's times like these, when he has to put on a smile and play the part of the ultra-successful CEO of a thriving telecommunications business, that he almost wishes he could order his own execution.

Chapter 10

Jeff Anders and Lowell never communicated using any of Lowell's regular e-mail or mobile phone accounts. Lowell had a mobile phone provided by Let the Truth Be Told, and should anyone ever try to trace the billing on that phone number it would just show up as a dummy California corporation. The same was true for Lowell's alternative e-mail accounts; he kept several personal and untraceable accounts from Yahoo. Jeff Anders had taught him well. Now, though, Anders was a little bit concerned. He was expecting an e-mail update from Lowell Westbrook either Tuesday night or first thing Wednesday morning, but so far he hadn't heard a peep. He had tried e-mailing and calling Lowell but got no response, and he also didn't respond to any Instant Messages or SMS messages sent to Lowell's phone. That wasn't like him. He was always reliable and punctual to a fault.

When it got to be 11:00 o'clock Anders' time, which was 2:00 o'clock in Charlottesville, and he still hadn't heard from Lowell, he decided to check things out a bit further. He didn't know exactly what he was looking for, if he was honest with himself, but something just didn't feel right. And in his business of investigating conspiracy theories, you spend way too much time feeling that something isn't right, or that someone is watching you. Anders started by pulling up a copy of the local Charlottesville paper on the web. It was dated Wednesday morning. He found nothing out of the ordinary or nothing to raise suspicion. Next he went to the site for the Charlottesville Police Department. Nothing there of any use, but on a hunch he decided to do a little digging to see if he could access any of the dispatch files or recent crime and incident reports. It took about 10 minutes of fishing around, and then he found it: the officer's report detailing the death of Lowell Westbrook. Anders was stunned, and the thoughts running through his head made his blood run cold. Lowell's dead. He started scanning the report. *'Apparent accident in the home, subject appears to have fallen down the stairs.'* He read through the rest of the report, but there wasn't much there of any importance, at least not until one particular line jumped out at him: *'Body was discovered by Dr. Keith Bryant and Ms. Debbie Walker, co-workers of the deceased at University of VA.'* Holy shit! Anders was floored. The timing and circumstances were just a little too convenient, and he was not one to put a lot of faith in coincidence. He didn't know anybody that was a committed conspiracy theorist that did. Call him paranoid, call him delusional, he didn't care. He just was not buying Lowell's death as an accident. But who would want to kill him, and for what purpose? And if somebody did kill Lowell, was Dr. Keith Bryant next on their radar?

Of one thing Jeff Anders was sure: he needed to get the leaders of LTBT together as soon as possible to bring them up to speed on this situation. They needed to know what's going on and consider the ramifications for LTBT. Especially if, God forbid, any of their lives should be in danger. He sent out a broadcast SMS message to the core team that was simple and to the point: *'911. Need to talk ASAP. Video bridge, 12 noon PST. Acknowledge'.* In less than five minutes he had responses from the four other leaders, all agreeing to the time and logistics. Every member of the core leadership team knew that a '911' message would never be sent out unless it was truly an emergency.

All five of the principals were on the video bridge at the appointed time. Patrick Treadwell kicked things off as soon as the last of them, Tony Winchester, joined the conference. No time was taken for the usual pleasantries. "Jeff, tell us what's going on and why you called us together on such short notice. I know we're all worried after receiving your emergency message."

"Sorry about the rush, guys, but it definitely meets the definition of a '911' situation. A member of my extended team, Lowell Westbrook, was found dead earlier today in Charlottesville, VA. He had contacted me recently about some research that is going on at UVA where he's working on his PhD."

"My God, Jeff, I'm sorry. I assume that Lowell was the resource we were discussing a few days back?" asked Patrick.

"Yes, that's correct. But I didn't call you all together because this was a friend of mine, I called you because I'm worried that his death had something to do with the information that he was planning to share with me, and by extension, LTBT."

"How did he die, Jeff?" asked Karen Richardson.

"According to the police report he fell down the steps and died from his injuries. They'll have to have an autopsy to determine the exact cause of death, but based on what I read it appears that his neck was broken, along with several other bones." Jeff then added, "I just don't buy it though. It's just too coincidental for me to put any stock in the official explanation. Lowell had just approached me within the last week about sharing the research that one of the UVA classes is doing on 9/11. It's called The Politics of Conspiracy. I'm afraid that he was on to something and someone took him out before he got too close."

"How was he communicating the information to you?" asked Terrell Jackson. "And had he sent you anything of any consequence yet?"

"He set up a backdoor access into the University's intranet site, and no, nothing worth much so far. Lowell was to be receiving the research that the class did on 9/11 for a class project and then collaborate with the professor, Dr. Keith Bryant, about which information would get posted. It was mainly a repository of information, a reference site if you will, for the class. He also informed me that Dr. Bryant was working on his own book about 9/11. They weren't particularly close, but Lowell did say that Dr. Bryant was a brilliant researcher and professor, and certainly one of the most popular professors on campus."

Tony Winchester asked, "Have you had a chance to consider any other possibilities yet? Like maybe Lowell was killed not for what he was going to post on the intranet site but because of his relationship with LTBT?" His words froze everyone. Winchester's mathematician's mind was going a mile a minute, thinking of every possible angle that could have led to Westbrook's murder, if in fact it even was murder. "You said yourself that he hadn't posted anything of any substance yet, right? But even if he had something that he was about to post it would have had to been reviewed and approved by Bryant, or I think that's how you explained the process. Ergo, if Lowell had information that was worth being killed for, we should expect that the killer or killers should have also killed Dr. Bryant."

"It sounds like you're making a leap in faith that someone – the CIA, NSA, or some other group in the government, I'm assuming – knew about Jeff's relationship with Lowell? Do you think that's a reasonable assumption?" asked Karen.

Tony Winchester considered her statement for a few seconds, and then said, "Absolutely. I think we've all learned that we should never underestimate the wherewithal of the intelligence community. We stay, or at least we *assume* we stay, a half-step ahead of them because of our built-in paranoia and our access to state-of-the-art technology, courtesy of Mr. Anders. That is decidedly not the case of the general public, and that includes Lowell Westbrook, Dr. Keith Bryant, and members of his class. Sure, Lowell would be careful in his communications with Jeff because he had the tools that allowed him to communicate discretely. But what about all of the day to day communications at the University? Phone calls and e-mails in and out all day and night. Web sites being accessed, documents being downloaded."

"I think you're on to something," interrupted Patrick. "If Dr. Bryant has this class, this Politics of Conspiracy class, it probably set off all kinds of flags in the intelligence community, or at least in the dark corners of the intelligence community that is keeping an eye on the conspiracy groups. It would be easy for them to monitor the communications between Dr. Bryant and Lowell, the students, the faculty, and God knows who else." Shifting gears slightly, he then asked, "Jeff, even if the government isn't able to monitor the communications between you and Lowell, isn't it likely that they at least know about your relationship with him?"

Jeff answered, "Definitely. In fact, I would expect the government to have a file on every person that has ever worked at one of my companies, been one of my suppliers, or even sat next to me in school."

Patrick continued. "Then is it much of a leap to assume that they know that he's contacted you even if they're not able to hear the actual communication because of our encryption? What I mean is, could they at least know that he called you, e-mailed you, IM'd you, sent you a smoke signal, etc. even if they don't know what was said?"

Jeff had to consider this for a moment, think about the underlying technology and its possibilities. Finally, "Yes, I feel pretty certain that they could. Think about it this way: they have thousands of communications going in and out of the University every day, and they pick and choose the ones they want to monitor based on where the message originates and/or where it terminates. As soon as they see a communication coming or going that can't be monitored, can't be identified, that by its very nature is an anomaly.

It's highly suspicious and raises flags all over spookville. Shit, they must have known that Lowell was in touch with me, with us."

Karen added, "Let me carry that thought a step further. They knew that Lowell was in touch with you, or at the very least they had every reason to assume it was with you because of your past relationship and the level of technology employed. Obviously Lowell didn't go around using encrypted communications to call for a pizza delivery, right? But if our intelligence friends knew that Lowell was contacting you they also had to know that Lowell hadn't told you anything yet, because they had to know that he didn't have anything yet worth sharing. Am I right? Didn't we just say that he hadn't provided you anything substantive, but we also determined that the government probably knows every single web site that has been visited, every document that has been downloaded or created, everything?"

"Bingo," said Terrell. "Lowell wasn't killed because of what he knew – he didn't know anything. He was killed because someone was afraid that he'd share whatever he eventually learned with you and LTBT. Maybe they were afraid that Dr. Bryant and his class were on the verge of finding something, like maybe they were heading down a particular path that could eventually uncover some incontrovertible evidence of a government conspiracy. That's not an unreasonable leap when you have an entire class focused on the research, to say nothing of Dr. Bryant's own research capabilities."

They were all quiet for a moment. Patrick finally spoke. "Shit. You know what this probably means, right? Dr. Bryant, if not his entire class, is probably in imminent danger. If he stumbles onto something that the government expects to remain forever hidden, I have a feeling that he'll be the next target."

"Are you proposing that we reach out to Dr. Bryant to try to warn him about what's happening? That exposure could be risky for us," said Tony.

"I think that's a risk we have to take, Tony. Particularly since it's very possible that Dr. Bryant could be close to finding The Truth, and if he is, it's up to all of us to help him find the answers and make the information public," Patrick answered.

The group spent the next hour and a half talking through a half-dozen different scenarios about how they might contact Dr. Keith Bryant, how they could convince them of their sincerity, and how they might work together to expose those responsible for 9/11. After the group had worked through all of the various ideas, Patrick said he was going to take one last minute on the call to summarize their plan of action and make sure that they were unanimous in their support. "OK, guys, let me net this out. Jeff and I are going to contact Dr. Bryant tomorrow, and for now we're going to try to keep Terrell, Karen, and Tony insulated from exposure. We will, however, provide you all with constant updates. We can be almost assured that his phones, computers, e-mail, mobile phones, etc. have all been compromised, so this won't be easy. He has no reason to trust us, and he may get spooked. We'll have to be at our most charming, to be sure," he added, trying to lighten the mood a bit. "Jeff will do some digging between now and tomorrow morning so we can try to learn everything we can about Bryant. About all we know at this point is what's written on the University's web site and in the jacket covers of his books. We need more than that. Finally, once we make contact with Dr. Bryant we are going to try to convince him that we're on the same side, see if we can collaborate in some way. If nothing else, we can help him narrow down the best paths of information by shooting down the bullshit. We've proven ourselves pretty adept at that lately. As always, we're going to have to be fluid and flexible. No telling how this might play out or which direction this might go, so please be ready to assist in any way you can if we need you."

Patrick had no idea just how true that last statement was.

⌘

THURSDAY WAS A NASTY DAY in Charlottesville, the kind of day that makes you want to stay warm and dry in the house, just curled up on the couch watching TV. A nor'easter was rolling up the coast and it was soaking virtually the entire Mid-Atlantic region with rain. They had already had almost 3" of rain since midnight, and coupled with the 30-40 mph winds it made driving miserable. Keith wished that he'd ridden in with Loren today. She had her Explorer, and while it tended to get pushed around a bit in the high winds it was at least of some use should there be any flooded roads when it was time to head home. Keith's BMW was a great road car, but it was not the best vehicle to be in when the roads were wet, or, God forbid, snow-covered. Still, they were lucky compared to the Virginia and North Carolina coasts, where they were being hit with gale force winds, heavy rain, and pretty significant flooding and beach erosion. On a heavy east wind water gets pushed into Chesapeake Bay and up the tidal rivers and creeks, and when the twice-daily high tides come it can wreak havoc. Low-lying areas become impassable to all but the biggest trucks, and many of the marinas and the boats that are berthed in them take a real beating. Hurricanes may get all of the press coverage, but experienced people in coastal Virginia know that they usually take a much worse beating from nor'easters than they ever do from hurricanes.

Around 11:45 that morning a Domino's delivery car pulled up in front of the Woodrow Wilson School of Politics at UVA. The driver got out of the car and hustled through the front door of the building and announced that he had a delivery for Dr. Bryant in Room 232. The receptionist directed the delivery person up the stairs to the second floor. While the pizza was real, the driver was not. He was an extended team member of LTBT based in Raleigh, NC and he usually provided paralegal and research support to Patrick Treadwell. At Patrick's request, he had driven up to Charlottesville this morning to make the contact with Keith. Pizza deliveries on the UVA campus were as common as preppy clothes and strands of pearls, so Patrick and Jeff reasoned that there was little likelihood of raising any suspicion should anybody be watching.

Arriving at Keith's office, the driver gave a knock on the door. Keith simply said, "Come in."

"Hi, Dr. Bryant, I have your pizza."

"But I didn't order any pizza."

"Oh, yes sir. I have the order right here." As he was talking the driver held up a note that Keith was able to read even from a few feet away. It said, *'Take the pizza. Follow instructions inside the box – ASAP.'* "It looks like maybe it was called in by the departmental assistant with instructions to deliver it to you."

Keith wasn't sure what to do. Part of him felt panicked, but he assumed that if this guy was here to kill him he'd already be dead. For that matter, if somebody really wanted him dead they could have done it on any number of occasions over the last few days. Trusting his instincts, Keith went along with the ruse. "That was nice of her. She knew that I was going to be buried in paperwork for much of the day and probably wouldn't get out to lunch. I'll have to get her up here to help me eat it. Here, let me pay you for that. Will $15 cover it?"

Let The Truth Be Told

"Yes sir. That will be more than enough. You have a nice day, Dr. Bryant." With that, the delivery man turned to leave and headed right back down the stairs and out to his car. He was back in Raleigh by mid-afternoon.

Keith lifted the lid on the pizza box and found an envelope taped to the inside of the lid. He decided that, on the slight chance that someone had visual surveillance in his office, he would step outside to one of the common spaces to grab the envelope and open it. Noting that the coffee room was empty he ducked quickly in there. Opening the lid he tore off the envelope and stuck it in his pocket, thinking he'd try to find somewhere private to read it. Grabbing a paper plate and a couple slices of pizza – it smelled too good to pass up, especially since he really wouldn't have time to go out for lunch – he headed back to his office. Keith grabbed a Coke from the vending machine on the way, and when he got back to his desk he sorted through the last few days of campus mail while eating his pizza. He removed the envelope from his pocket and, treating it just like any other piece of mail, used his letter opener to slice it open. What he read shook him to his core.

Dr Keith Bryant,

We are friends and associates of Lowell Westbrook and we are certain that his death was <u>not</u> an accident. Lowell was involved with our group, Let the Truth Be Told, which we assume you've heard of through your research. We believe that you and Ms. Davis are in imminent danger as well. We will provide you more detail, but for now please follow the steps below to contact us. (1) Go to the Charlottesville public library, but take precautions to ensure you are not followed. Use one of their computers to create an Instant Messaging account and a new e-mail account for yourself. DO NOT use your personal computer or any of your current e-mail addresses, particularly your UVA account; assume that all have been compromised. (2) Send an e-mail to the following address: information@chimeracom.net using your new account. We will be watching for your message and will respond immediately. (3) We will provide you a phone number to contact us via e-mail. DO NOT try to call us from your home phone, office phone, or mobile phone. Assume ALL are compromised. Same for Ms. Davis' phones. Be careful at pay phones or speaking anywhere in public – people are watching and listening, even from long distances. More instructions will follow. Go NOW.'

Dear God, thought Keith. This is just too much to absorb. Could this be real? He knew of Let the Truth Be Told; they were one of a very small handful of conspiracy groups that Keith actually respected. He didn't know any of them but he was familiar with their research and their methodology, and they were first rate. And Lowell was involved with them, at least peripherally? Is that what got him killed? If it is, then all of this, as he had feared, is related, including the visit from the supposed FBI agents. And it all comes back to one common denominator: The Politics of Conspiracy. But how the hell did the research going on in that class set all of this in motion? That was the $64,000 question that he kept circling back to. Keith knew what he had to do. He had to follow the instructions he'd just received and make contact with Let the Truth Be Told, and, most importantly, figure out how the hell he and Loren were going to stay alive if they really were in danger.

Keith had every intention of following the instructions from the letter, but before he left the campus he had to get to Loren. The last thing he wanted to do was scare her, but at this point it was better to have her scared and alert rather than oblivious and dead. Thankfully, Loren was in her office when Keith got there. "Hi, hon. How's your day going?" Keith asked as nonchalantly as possible.

"Pretty good so far. This is an unexpected pleasure," she smiled. "I see less of you most days than any couple I know, and we work in the same building." She saw something in his expression; what was it? Fear? She'd never known him to be scared of anything. Whatever she was seeing, she knew that he was here for a reason, and it was a virtual certainty that he didn't just stop by to say hello. "Mmmm, that pizza smells good. Did you save any of that for me by any chance?"

"Of course. I thought you might want to get away from your work for a few minutes and join me for a romantic little tété a tète in the break room or some other lovely little spot. Obviously, a picnic lunch seems out of the question today since it's practically a freakin' hurricane."

"I'd love to. You're such a romantic – you always take me to all of the nicest places." With that she got up and they started towards the break room. As they walked Loren whispered to him, "I take it that this isn't a purely social visit, judging by the look on your face. Is something going on."

"Yes, and I need to talk to you about it, but very quietly. Where do you think we can talk?"

Loren thought for a moment. "How about Dr. Butler's office on the first floor? He's out on sabbatical this semester, and I know that they've used it on at least a few occasions for visiting speakers or professors to have a place to work. I think it may even be left unlocked." Seeing that Keith agreed with her, Loren led the way down the stairs and to the empty office.

"This is good," said Keith, closing the door behind them. "Want a piece of pizza first?" he said, trying to lighten the mood a bit.

"That can wait. Just tell me what's wrong. You're scaring me, and the fact that I can tell that you're this concerned scares me even more."

"I'm really sorry. I don't want to scare you, but at the same time I have to bring you in on this and everything that is going on around here. For your own safety." Keith handed her the letter and let her read it for herself. Loren's face went ashen.

"Oh my God. Do you think this is for real?" she asked, starting to tremble.

"Yeah, I definitely think it's for real. We talked the other day, right after Lowell was killed, that it was possible that he was feeding information about my research and our class project to some other group, and I think this validates our assumption. I know about this conspiracy group, LTBT, or at least I know a little bit about them. If Lowell was involved with them, maybe providing them with information about the work that I am doing and my class is doing, that could explain a lot. I think they're genuinely concerned for our safety, and I think if we know what's good for us, we better be concerned, as well."

"So what are you going to do? Are you going to follow their instructions?"

"Yes, I don't see any other way. I need to make contact with them, and at this point I have to take on faith that what they said is probably right: all of our phones, PC's, e-mail accounts, everything, is probably compromised." Keith hesitated a bit before making the next statement, trying to think of the best way to deliver the message without causing her to panic. "Look, I don't know where this is going, but I definitely don't like the direction it's heading now. I think we need to start making preparations to get the hell out of here if we have to, and if we have to it could be on very short notice."

"You're scaring me," she said, tears starting to well in her eyes.

"I'm sorry, hon. This is scary for me, too. Whoever we're dealing with apparently has incredible resources and is not afraid to move against people they see as a threat. We just have to be smarter and try to stay at least one step ahead of them until we figure this thing out."

"What do you want me to do?"

"I think we need to create a diversion, some reason to be leaving town for a few days. I was thinking that maybe we should book a little romantic getaway for the two of us. Why don't you make some calls and see if you can find us a nice resort to use as a cover for a 4-day weekend? Maybe somewhere like The Greenbrier, or maybe the Inn at Perry Cabin on Eastern Shore. Then stop by the bank and withdraw a few thousand dollars from your account. Not too much, just enough to look reasonable for a short getaway. We have to assume that our accounts are being monitored, too, and it would raise too many red flags if you withdrew all of your money or closed your accounts. Then head home and start to get your clothes and my clothes together, maybe put everything you can into those big duffel bags that we have instead of suitcases. We'll need to travel as light as we can.

"Anything else?"

"Just one more thing for now. Call the kennel and see if we can drop Bo and Winston off tomorrow morning and pick them up on Tuesday, or whatever is reasonable based on the reservation dates you use for our weekend." He could see that the reality of the situation – or at least what he feared was the reality – had finally hit her as well. She hadn't been so much in denial over the events of the past few days as she had….rational. That was the only word he could think of. Loren was so smart, so analytical, so….literal, that she just couldn't accept that these types of things actually happened in the real world to good, decent people. "OK, I need to head out and try to establish contact with LTBT. Hopefully I'll be home around dinnertime, but if not I'll call you. I may lie to you about what I'm doing or where I'm going, depending on the situation, but I will call you. You take a few minutes and get yourself together, make sure you're OK before you head out. And be careful driving. It still looks terrible outside. I even saw the animals swimming past the windows two by two." Keith smiled.

Loren laughed at his stupid little Noah's Ark reference, at least lightening the mood for a few seconds. "I'll be careful. You be careful, too. Don't be doing any stupid *007* stuff. You're a college professor, not On Her Majesty's

Secret Service." She reached for him and hugged him tight. They held each other a long time, realizing that life had just thrown them a helluva curve ball. Keith kissed her and told her that he loved her, then slipped out the door. Loren sat in the office for a while longer, fighting back tears and starting to shake uncontrollably. She prayed like she had prayed as a little girl when she and her parents had attended the local Presbyterian church, before she had turned her back on the church and on God. As she prayed she remembered an old saying she'd heard many years before: *There are no atheists in a foxhole.* She definitely seemed to be living proof of the truth behind that statement.

⌘

KEITH DROVE DOWN TO THE Market Street branch of the Charlottesville Public Library, the trip taking twice as long as usual due to the lousy weather and even lousier drivers. Plus, as he had been instructed, Keith was extremely vigilant about being followed. He couldn't do anything that would make it evident that he was expecting to be followed; that would just show his hand. Instead, he let the bad weather and traffic work to his advantage by making frequent lane changes, moving through traffic lights when he normally would have stopped, and taking several different one way streets through downtown. If he was being observed he hoped that people would simply believe that he couldn't find the building that he was looking for, or maybe no on-street parking. By the time he reached the library he'd actually driven several miles beyond it and doubled back, and before getting out of the car he sat for a few minutes and observed the cars going by. He didn't see anything that looked out of the norm.

He finally parked the car in a garage a few blocks from the library, knowing it was safer to walk the rest of the way. Exiting the car, he tried to use his umbrella but the wind practically ripped it from his hands. It made little difference; the wind was blowing the rain almost horizontal, and it was hitting his skin with enough force to feel more like a shot from a BB gun. Fortunately, Keith's trench coat offered some protection, though his pants were soaked below the coat hem and his shoes, an expensive pair of Cole-Hahn's, were saturated as well.

The library was pretty empty today, or at least emptier than Keith expected. The fact that it was the middle of the day on a Thursday, coupled with the torrential downpour, probably helped account for some of the emptiness. Regardless, Keith was grateful for it. The last thing he needed was a lot of people sitting close by or walking around behind him while he was e-mailing back and forth with LTBT. Plus, with the library so empty, and with him taking a seat facing the front door, he knew that he'd be able to see anybody that walked in. If necessary, he could simply shut down his monitor or change screens. Keith knew better than to feel complacent, but he felt pretty sure that, had he been followed, he had lost them in traffic. As it turns out, he was right.

It took less than 15 minutes for Keith to set up e-mail and Instant Message accounts on the PC, and once that was accomplished he sent the following e-mail to LTBT, intentionally being somewhat short and cryptic:

Contacting you as requested from Library. E-mail and IM accounts setup. No evidence of being followed. Now what?

It was less than one minute before he received the following message:

Acknowledged. Will send you an IM momentarily.

It took only about 30 seconds before the first Instant Message came through to the library computer.

LTBT: *Dr. Bryant, thank you for coming.*

Keith: *Why am I here?*

LTBT: *You are in danger. We can help.*

Keith: *Who are you?*

LTBT: *Patrick Treadwell and Jeff Anders. Two of the principal leaders of LTBT. Jeff is an old friend of Lowell's from back in Silicon Valley.*

Keith: *Why am I in danger?*

LTBT: *Lowell was planning to send us information that you and your class developed to help us in our work here at LTBT. Somebody killed him either for what he already knows or for what he might learn, as well as his linkage to us.*

Keith: *Why does that put me in danger?*

LTBT: *Somebody apparently knows what you're working on and what you hope to publish. They obviously want to silence you.*

Keith: *But why? I haven't found or written about anything that isn't already out there on a million websites at this point. I haven't learned anything new.*

LTBT: *Our theory: because they're afraid you will, and with Lowell's link to us they're afraid that we will help trumpet the findings and bring 'them' down.*

Keith: *Something you don't know: the night before Lowell was killed we were visited by two 'agents', supposedly from the FBI. They tried to subtly warn me off of the work that I was doing and the project my class is working on.*

LTBT: *WHAT???? You're serious, right?*

Keith: *Totally.*

LTBT: *Well, that lends more credence than ever that Lowell's death was no accident. It also shows you that the people we're dealing with are willing to kill to keep their secrets!*

Keith: *Who are these people? CIA? NSA?*

LTBT: *No. Don't know exactly, but some group definitely off the books, not really accountable to anyone. Untouchable.*

Keith: *Shit. That's wonderful news.... What do I do (me & Loren)?*

LTBT: *We can help protect you, help you hide. ANYTHING you need we can provide, we just have to figure out how to keep everyone safe. For starters....*

LTBT: *Get cash, enough for at least a week but not enough to cause attention. DON'T use credit cards or ATM after today.*

LTBT: *Buy several disposable cell phones with pre-paid plans as well as some pre-paid long-distance calling cards that you can use from pay phones. Once you're on the run, turn your regular cell phone off and remove the battery – that way you can't be tracked via GPS signals.*

LTBT: *Get out of town, preferably in a borrowed car or a rental car paid in cash*

Keith: *How should I contact you? This same e-mail account?*

LTBT: *NO. We may use this same protocol, but we will change accounts every day. We'll always let you know what our account name will be. Once you get your new mobile phones and calling cards, you can also reach us by phone.*

Keith: *At what number?*

LTBT: *The number will change every time you call.*

Keith: *Christ – and Loren thinks I'm paranoid! How the fuck am I supposed to keep up with numbers that change every time I call??*

LTBT: *Simple. We own a block of 100 sequential numbers, so if you call any number within the range we give you it will ring directly to us.*

Keith: *OK, sounds easy enough. One last thing: Loren and I are planning to 'go away' for the weekend, actually using our phones and credit cards to make reservations for a little 4-day getaway. Thought it might provide cover in case we have to run.*

LTBT: *Great idea. Check in with us at least daily, & we'll watch your back. Next time you send us an e-mail, our address will be deepocean@hotmail.com. As much as you're able to, continue your research. It may be the key!*

Keith signed off from the account. Before closing Internet Explorer he spent a few minutes deleting the temporary internet files, the 'history', and all 'cookies'. This wouldn't stop someone with the resources of the group that was….what? After him? Stalking him? Planning to kill him? He wasn't sure how to refer to them. All he knew is, if they had the wherewithal to bug his phones and computers, kill Lowell, and create credentials that are that convincing for their supposed FBI agents, he didn't think his little PC cleanup was going to stop them. Still, if they should ever find out that he was in the library – and he still hoped that they wouldn't – the steps he took would at least slow them down a bit.

Keith had one more stop to make before heading home, and as before he had to ensure that he wasn't being followed. He was less concerned than he was earlier today; when he left the University anybody that may have been following him obviously knew his starting point. That should not be the case now, or at least he hoped it wasn't. He had not seen anybody suspicious come into the library during his time at the computer, nor did anybody come within 100 feet of him or the area where he was working. Still, he was cautious. He took a circuitous route back to his car, even though that just meant he was that much wetter when he got there. Oh well, he thought, better wet than dead. As he reached the area where his car was parked he looked around for anybody that may be watching, anybody that may be out of place. He saw no one, though there were very few people around to be seen. Anybody with any sense was indoors where it was dry and warm, not out here playing cat and mouse with cold-blooded killers. Finally getting into his car, he took off his wet coat and threw it in the back seat. He pulled slowly out of his space and kept his eyes peeled for any other cars starting to move with him. Seeing nothing, he accelerated quickly down the street and made a few turns. He pulled over for a moment; nothing. No other cars that seemed to be following him or going the same way. He pulled back into the lane and headed away from the area as quickly as he could without risking calling more attention to himself.

After about fifteen minutes Keith pulled into his bank's parking lot. Luckily the bank's lobby was open until 5pm, so he grabbed his briefcase and ran from the parking lot into the bank. God, what he wouldn't give for a hot shower and a warm bed right about now, he thought. Stepping into the bank lobby he was spotted by the bank manager, Patricia Faulkner. Keith had been banking there for several years for both his personal and business needs, so he was definitely one of her VIP customers.

"Hi, Keith. My gosh, you're soaked! What brings you out on such a gross day?"

"Hi, Patricia. I need to get into my safety deposit box to drop off a few things."

"Sure, that's no problem. Let's step into the vault and get you signed in." Patricia filled out the necessary forms and grabbed her master key before leading Keith back to his box. Keith inserted his key first, then she hers. She pulled the box out and handed it to Keith and then led him to a private area to conduct his business. "I'll be out here, so just let me know when you're done."

"Thanks, Patricia." Keith carried the box into the private room and closed the door. He opened the box, and then his briefcase. Inside the safe deposit box was what he'd come for, something that they really needed if they had to run. And more importantly, something that was totally off the record and untraceable. Keith felt certain that not even the government knew about the contents: $25,000 in cash, a Beretta 9mm pistol, and two boxes of ammunition. The Beretta had belonged to his father, and after his father died his mother had not felt comfortable keeping it around the house. Keith was experienced with guns, knew how to handle them, how to shoot them. He had hoped that his mother would keep the pistol for an extra measure of safety, but she insisted that his father would have wanted Keith to have it. He already had two guns at the house, rifles that could be used, or so he told himself, if he ever had bears or snakes or God knows what else on his property. Of course, they were locked in a hidden gun vault in his garage, so unless he was going to ask the bear or the snake to give him a few minutes to fetch one of his guns he wasn't sure how much good they would do him. He assumed, but wasn't 100% certain, that the government didn't know about the rifles he had at home. He'd installed the gun safe himself, and it was hidden behind a panel in the garage. It didn't appear on any blueprints of the house, and there were no building permits issued. Plus, neither gun was purchased with a credit card. Both had been gifts from his parents many years ago.

The large amount of cash was hidden in the box because of something his grandfather had instilled in him, namely, a little bit of wariness about banks and the government's reach into your personal business. A survivor of the Great Depression, he always told Keith that he should keep a little bit of money somewhere where he could get his hands on it without anybody else knowing about it. While Keith had a lot of money tied up in this bank, as well as a few others, he was always cognizant that the government only insured each account up to $100,000. Should that bank fail – rare, yes, but certainly not unheard of – you could be left holding the bag for everything over $100K in an account. That's why he spread his money out across so many banks and accounts, even though it drove his accounting group crazy. Still, he trusted his grandfather's advice, and every since he was old enough to have his own money he'd always kept some stashed away for the proverbial 'rainy day', and God knows it was pouring down rain today, both literally and figuratively. Keith loaded up his briefcase and finished his business with the bank, then headed home. Knowing that he had a decent amount of cash and a weapon with him made him feel a little bit better about his situation.

When he got home it was nearly 5 o'clock. Loren had been home for about 45 minutes after going to the bank, and she had already managed to get reservations at The Greenbrier. Luckily for them The Greenbrier had a cancellation, probably due to the lousy weather that was supposed to linger through at least part of the weekend. The kennel was also very accommodating on such short notice. Keith suggested that they go out to eat, ostensibly so they wouldn't have to go the grocery and spend time cleaning up before they had to leave on Friday morning. Before leaving, Keith said he just wanted to send a quick e-mail to his Friday and Monday classes, as well as the Dean, saying that he had to take the next couple of days off. Since each class had their own mailing list on the University's e-mail system, he only had to create one message telling the classes when they would meet next and what they should work on until then. He entered the two group e-mail aliases and the message was on its way. It couldn't get much easier than that, he thought. He sent a separate message to the Dean explaining the reason for his absence, though the reason was a lie. No need to involve the Dean in this mess.

Keith and Loren headed out earlier than normal for dinner, barely 5:30. This was getting to be a habit for them, hopping in the car and going to some public place just to give them a chance to talk and strategize without, hopefully, being observed or overheard. As was their practice, they got a table where they could try to keep an eye on the door and the patrons around them. The longer they did this the more their imagination started to run wild. Every person became suspicious, a potential enemy. After ordering their food and drinks, Keith filled Loren in on the events of the last few hours, including his stop at the bank. At first she acted a little bit angry or hurt that Keith had never shared with her that he had this money and this gun stashed away, but then she realized that they had, in fact, been together less than a year and she'd only been living with him a few months. This probably wasn't something that came up in casual conversation, and they certainly had not ever sat down to have a deep discussion about their finances or investments. Loren decided to focus on the bigger picture, namely, where they were going to go and what they were going to do. Keith gave her the big picture overview, explaining that a lot of what was going to happen in their lives for the foreseeable future was going to be very fly-by-night, seat-of-the-pants kind of stuff. Generally, though, it came down to this: stay alive, run like hell, rendezvous with members of the LTBT if they needed help, and find a way to continue his research. His research, he said, was very possibly the key to this whole thing. Either he was onto something or on the verge of stumbling onto something, and whatever 'it' was had already cost one man his life and had likely put their lives at risk as well.

⌘

MATHEW HILTON WAS ON THE phone to Colonel Ed Foster and Bob Manning the second he received the e-mail about Keith canceling classes on Friday and Monday. "Something's doesn't feel right down here. Bryant disappeared today for a while, and now he's taking a few days off. I don't like it."

Foster answered. "The reality is that Dr. Bryant, after having lunch with Ms Davis, left the University grounds. Where he went we're not sure. Our surveillance teams lost him due to the heavy traffic and bad weather."

"I thought these guys were supposed to be fucking professionals, and they can't keep tabs on a goddamn college professor?" Hilton practically shouted. Apparently he was forgetting that whole boss/employee dynamic.

Foster bit his tongue. "I assure you, they are quite capable and professional, Mr. Hilton. Just like you. However, sometimes things don't work out perfectly in the real world. Traffic causes delays. Weather hinders surveillance. Shit happens, as they say. Now, as far as Dr. Bryant canceling classes tomorrow and Monday, here's what we have observed: Ms. Davis has made reservations, using her credit card to guarantee payment, at The Greenbrier resort in West Virginia for Friday, Saturday, and Sunday nights. She has also booked massages and spa treatments while they're there. In addition, she has been to her bank and withdrawn $4,000 from her savings account, and she's made reservations for their two dogs at the local kennel that they use. All in all, sounds like a romantic getaway for the happy couple."

"It doesn't seem suspicious to you that he's missing classes for two days though?" asked Hilton.

"In our business, everything and everybody is suspicious. Nature of the beast. Considering, however, that Dr. Bryant stumbled upon the dead body of his research assistant just a day ago, perhaps they thought that a getaway might be in order to forget about the tragedy."

"Alright then, sir, what are your instructions?" Hilton thought that Foster was not taking this development seriously enough, but hey, he was paying the bills. If he wanted to put his whole little secret world and existence at risk, that's his business.

"Obviously, we can't risk you being seen at The Greenbrier. If Bryant sees you anywhere other than on the UVA campus it will arouse suspicion. I want you to work with the surveillance team, but you are to stay completely out of sight. Is that clear? Do not, under any circumstances, approach Dr. Bryant or Ms. Davis."

"Yes sir, I understand. I'll stay in the surveillance vehicle and help track the subjects and report in to you per our schedule."

"That is exactly what we need, Mr. Hilton. We appreciate your professionalism and willingness to be flexible as things evolve. We'll talk to you tomorrow." With that, Foster clicked off. Turning to Bob Manning, he said, "Mr. Hilton is getting rather tiresome. After this weekend, if we don't have any compelling reason for keeping him around, I think it's time to eliminate him."

Manning smiled. "Sounds good. I don't think you'll find anybody around here that is going to cry when he's gone, least of all me."

Chapter 11

On Friday morning, Keith and Loren were ready to start their life on the run. They didn't know which was more disconcerting, having to be on the run from people that were prepared to kill them, or not knowing where to go and how long to stay there. What about friends and family? What about their dogs, their home, their careers? Will the government decide to smear their names and reputations, or label them criminals or, worse yet, terrorists on the run, if they fail to catch them quickly? At what point do you just give up running, and what happens if and when you do? Do you simply change identities and try to live life below the radar, like they do in Mob movies? Keith's response to that question, when posed by Loren, was direct and to the point: "fuck that!" He could be stubborn when pushed too far, and he had an unerring sense of right versus wrong. He knew that what he was doing was the right thing for both him and his country, and if people thought that they could silence him – silence The Truth – they were sadly mistaken. He might start life on the run today in order to keep them safe and to find a way to continue his research, but he would be damned if he would end his life that way. If it came down to it, he would stand and fight for what he believed in. He may die either way, but he would die fighting.

As if the thoughts running through his mind weren't ominous enough, he had to contend with another day of absolutely dreadful weather. The rains continued, as did the heavy winds. Some areas of Virginia, particularly along the coast, had experienced upwards of 8" of rain in the last 24 hours, and quite a few low lying areas were getting hammered by rising tides and localized flooding. Even in Charlottesville the heavy rains had caused a number of streams and small creeks and rivers to overflow their banks.

They knew that they had a lot of things to take care of today before getting on the road, and the first order of business was finding a car that they could use while in hiding. Neither of them knew what to believe when it came to the capabilities of the people that were after them. Like most people, most of what they know, or, probably more accurately, what they think they know, is based on Hollywood. They assumed that their cars might have listening devices in them, to say nothing of GPS homing devices and other high-tech gadgets. In reality, Colonel Foster's team had not touched their cars. Since they rarely traveled together the thought had been that a listening device was an unnecessary risk, especially with the cars staying parked in the garage at night. No GPS tracking devices were used either, not just because of the perceived risk in planting the equipment, but because Foster knew that both of their cars were equipped with LoJack anti-theft devices. The DCG team routinely tapped into the LoJack network to pinpoint a subject's exact location. In addition, since Keith and Loren both carried cell phones, like virtually every other person in America, Foster knew that he could use the built-in GPS capability of their Verizon phones to triangulate in on them if needed. Essentially, all of the new technology that consumers demand to make their lives safer, more secure, and more convenient, is the same technology that people like Colonel Ed Foster exploit to gain access to their private lives.

They had worked well into the evening getting everything ready, a task made all the more difficult since they knew that someone was listening to every word that was said. While Loren worked on getting the clothes together, Keith sent some last minute e-mails and concentrated on saving any and all important documents to DVD's. He did this religiously at least once a week, a habit he'd learned long ago after having a PC crash the night before a major paper was due at the Naval Academy. At the University he saved everything to his hard drive, the departmental server, and, in many cases, to a USB flash drive. He had gotten Loren into the same habit. After backing up both PC's he shut them down, but instead of putting the backup disks and drives in the desk where he usually kept them, he put them all in his PC bag. He also went through all of his hard copy files and collected everything relevant to his current research. As much of that as would fit went into the same PC bag, the remainder going into a small plastic storage bin. The PC's would be left here at the house; they would never again be used, of course, but more importantly, should anyone come snooping around the house they would note that their PC's were still there instead of being taken on their weekend getaway.

Loren left around 9:45am to take Bo and Winston to the kennel in her car. Keith was visibly upset to be leaving them. He knew that they loved going to the kennel and romping and playing with all of the other dogs, but not knowing when he'd be able to see them again was tearing him up inside. In fact, it was heartbreaking for Loren, too. Before they left Keith gave both dogs big hugs and an extra treat, and he got a lot of wet, slobbery kisses in return. Neither of them knew if there were multiple surveillance teams, but at this point they had to assume that there were. That meant that Loren had to perform her role as if someone were watching her every move.

Keith left at the same time, and his car was packed with everything that they planned to take with them, including clothes, food, water, and weapons. The two rifles were hidden inside of the well-padded travel bag that he used when carrying his golf clubs on a plane, right alongside the set of Taylor Made graphite clubs that he had no intention of using anytime soon. The BMW was loaded to the gills. His first order of business for the day was to switch cars. He knew that he would be hard pressed to stay hidden so long as he was in this car. What was needed was something much more anonymous, and nothing says anonymous like a Ford Taurus. There had to be millions of them on the road, and Keith knew just where he could find one: the corporate fleet at Bryant International. He drove straight there, not trying to be evasive at all. In fact, for his plan to work he needed whoever was following him – and he was sure that somebody had to be, even if he hadn't seen them – to see him arrive at the office and then follow him for the next few hours. When he got to the office in downtown Charlottesville he pulled into his assigned spot on the first level of the parking garage. Locking his car and taking his briefcase, he walked to the main lobby entrance of the office building where Bryant International had their headquarters on the first floor. Once again his umbrella proved less than effective, but it was critical that he be seen entering the building. The receptionist was surprised to see him there on a Friday morning, knowing that he usually didn't come in until later because of his class schedule. Keith simply informed her that he was taking a few days off so that he and Loren could spend some time together. The receptionist just gave him a knowing smile, fully aware, as was everyone, that the boss had fallen really hard for this girl and was likely to end up marrying her. Maybe this will even be the weekend that he proposes, she thought to herself. With all of this rain, the weekend looked custom made for 'indoor sports' rather than outdoor activities. She smiled at the thought.

Keith walked into his office and set his stuff down, then walked down the hall a couple of offices to see his second-in-command, Michael Fitzgerald. "Morning, Michael. How's it going?"

"Hey, Keith. I'm surprised to see you here this morning. Everything OK?" asked the COO of Bryant International.

"Yeah, everything is great. Loren and I are getting ready to take off for a few days at The Greenbrier, so I just stopped in here to check on a few last things before hitting the road."

"The Greenbrier, huh? Very nice. Aren't you 'Mr. Smooth', taking her up there to the high-dollar district for a little romantic getaway," said Michael.

"Well, what can I say? Those of us with the innate charm and romantic streaks always have to show the rest of you schmucks how it's done," Keith responded with a smile. "Listen, my car is acting a little weird, running a little bit rough. Probably got something wet from splashing through all of the puddles and standing water. I thought I'd take one of the fleet cars this weekend rather than risk a breakdown out in the middle of nowhere. Hopefully The Greenbrier will let us darken their gates with a 2-year old Taurus."

Michael laughed at that. "I don't know about that. At the very least they'll probably make you show a Platinum American Express card before they let you in. Not to be nosy, but why drive a company Taurus to The Greenbrier if your car is acting up? Why not just drive Loren's Explorer?"

Keith had anticipated this question. "She's decided that she wants a new, sportier car, so she put it up for sale earlier this week and already has a buyer lined up. We decided not to risk having an accident or some other issue by driving it this weekend. You know how it is, Murphy's Law would probably jump up to bite us if we drove it up there."

"Cool. What's she thinking about buying?"

"Right now she's leaning towards either an Infinity G35 Coupe or the Lexus ES350."

"Pretty sweet rides for a grad student, don't you think?" Michael said with a smile. "Not like the old days when guys like us had to walk or ride a bike to class."

"I hear ya, Abe Lincoln. I suppose you had to walk through six miles of snow each way, too." Keith knew better. Michael came from a pretty well-to-do family from the Philadelphia area, and he doubted that Michael had ever had to walk or ride a bike anywhere that he hadn't chosen to. "Hey listen, you got time to run with me up to Rio Hill Wine and Gourmet? I thought I'd get a little food basket and bottle of wine for the owner of the kennel where we dropped Bo and Winston as a little 'thank you' for taking such good care of the guys all the time, especially on such short notice. Plus it will give us a chance to talk and let you update me on the latest with the DALCAL deal."

"Sure, sounds good. I wouldn't mind picking up a few bottles myself while we're there. We can take my car."

"While we run out how about we get the new intern to move everything from my BMW over to the company car? Is he here today?"

"Yeah, Aaron's here. I'll call him and have him bring down the blue Taurus – that's the one that's probably cleanest and has the fewest miles – and have him transfer your stuff. Why don't you leave me your keys and I'll have him do it while we're gone."

"That would be great," said Keith. "Thankfully my car and the fleet cars are parked in the garage so the poor guy doesn't drown. Two more things: I have to pack up some old papers when we get back home after the weekend, so will you ask Aaron to put as many Xerox paper boxes as he can into the Beemer after he unloads it? And ask him to leave the Taurus out by the front exit when he's got it loaded so that Loren and I can just jump in and go whenever we're ready. We probably won't be too long once she gets here from running her errands. And give him this as a little 'thank you'. I don't want him to feel like we're using him or taking advantage of him since he's the new guy," he added as he handed Michael his car keys and a $100 bill. Keith kept his house keys and other keys, just in case. He hoped that his little trick of piling his car up with boxes would be enough to fool whoever was watching when he got back; he was counting on the fact that the car would still look like it was packed for vacation to anybody that was watching from a distance. His fingers were crossed on that one.

"Damn, for $100 I'd have moved the stuff myself," laughed Michael. "How about I meet you by the exit door by the garage in about 5 minutes?"

"Perfect," said Keith as he headed back to his office to grab his briefcase, trench coat, and umbrella. He hated using Michael and Aaron in this way, but he couldn't think of a better plan. Since Michael's parking space is right next to Keith's he had to assume that whoever was following him – and somebody had to be – would see him get into Michael's car and leave. They would certainly follow.

Keith and Michael climbed into Michael's Mercedes, and as he moved out of the parking space Keith tried to casually observe if any other cars started their engines or started pulling out. He didn't see anything. Damn, he thought, were these guys that good, or is he totally off-base about this whole mess? As they pulled out of the garage and onto the street Keith continued to try to be observant. And then, suddenly, there it was. The first real indication that he wasn't just imagining things. A gray Chrysler 300 pulled out from a parking space near the entrance to his parking garage, and from where that car had been parked the occupants would have had a clear view of his car. Perfect. Now he just had to keep an eye on the Chrysler to verify that he was correct, see if it continued to follow them all of the way to the wine store, see if it was still following them as they headed back to the office later. It was about a 15 minute drive to the store, a little longer than normal because of the weather. Michael and Keith discussed business along the way, but Keith's mind was only half-engaged. Every few minutes he would scan the side-view mirror to see if the car was still following them. Invariably, it was, though whoever was doing the following was certainly skilled at their job. They managed to stay several cars back yet never got caught by any lights, nor did they make any knee-jerk reactions to lane changes or turns that Michael made. Every movement they made was fluid and natural. Had Keith not seen them pull out when he and Michael first left the garage he would have never picked this car out of the crowd.

They were in the store maybe 30 minutes, and Keith bought a nice basket with assorted cheeses, meats, salsas, a couple of baguettes, and flavored olive oil. He added a nice bottle of Tanterra Pinot Noir to the basket and then had it sealed and topped with ribbon. Although he had said that it was a gift for the kennel, in reality it would be something that he and Loren would take with them on the road. Hey, if you have to be on the run, Keith figured, may as well try to treat yourself to a few little pleasures.

As they departed the store Keith tried to take a casual look around the parking lot of the shopping center. He couldn't see the Chrysler, but he had no doubt that it was there and that the bad guys were watching him. As they headed out towards the stoplight back onto Route 29, Keith saw the Chrysler start to move towards the exit. Bingo. Keith suspected that the big Chrysler would continue to follow them at about the same distance that they had earlier. They knew that he'd eventually end up back at the office where his car was parked, but the one thing they couldn't be sure of was whether or not he would make any more stops along the way. As Keith casually checked the mirror every few minutes he saw that they were hanging back about three cars behind them, just as before. Damn, he thought, these guys are good.

Michael drove them straight back to the office and pulled the car into the garage. As Michael whipped his car into his parking space Keith was happy to see that Aaron had done as asked. His car was filled with boxes, and there was probably no way that the people following him would be able to tell from down on the street, particularly since Michael's car partially blocked their view. Even with binoculars they probably wouldn't be able to distinguish what was in the car now from what was in there earlier. Keith was smart enough to know that the ruse wouldn't last forever, but that was OK; he only needed it to work for a few hours to give him and Loren a decent head start. But first, though, he had one more trick card to play.

When he got back inside the building he ran into Aaron and stopped to thank him. "Aaron, I appreciate you helping me out. I know it falls a long way outside of your job description."

"No problem, Dr. Bryant. Glad to help. And please, you didn't need to give me the $100 for doing that. You guys treat me and pay me more than fairly here." Even as Aaron said this he was hoping that he got to keep the money. While his salary was very good for an intern he did have bills and student loans to pay.

"Nonsense," said Keith. "You keep the money; you definitely earned it, especially on such a gross and rainy day. You've saved me a lot of time and hassle, and I just want you to know that I appreciate it. You're doing a great job here at the company, and Michael and the other managers speak very highly of you. I hope you'll consider staying on with us after your internship is up."

"Gosh, Dr. Bryant, that's awesome. Thank you." Keith had just made his day, if not his whole week or month. With that they shook hands, and then Aaron gave the keys to the Taurus to Keith. "Your company car is out front, as you requested, and I made sure that it had a full tank of gas. You're good to go."

Keith thanked him again and then walked back to his office. Now it was time to start putting the second part of his plan in motion. He picked up his cell phone and called Loren. "Hi, sweetie. How are things going? You almost done with the errands?"

"Yes, just about. With the weather and the slow traffic it's taking a little longer than usual," Loren answered. She and Keith had already talked through their plan, albeit very quietly, last night. Not exactly the sexiest of pillow talk, but staying alive was starting to take precedence over sexy. "I can probably meet you at home in about 10-15 minutes if you're ready to go."

"Well, there's the rub. Something's come up here at the office with the DALCAL deal. I think it's going to take a few hours to sort things out with my team."

"So much for our romantic getaway, Prince Charming. You're not trying to weasel out of our trip are you?" Loren tried to sound just a little bit irritated, but she wasn't sure how well she was pulling it off.

"No, definitely not. I would never blow off a weekend at The Greenbrier with the most beautiful girl in Charlottesville," he said with a smile.

"Very funny. So do you just want to meet me at home and we'll leave from there?"

"I have a better idea," said Keith. "Why don't you come here to the office and we'll leave straight from here when I'm done. My car is already packed and ready to go, and you can just leave your car in the garage. Besides, I could actually use a little bit of your help and opinion on this project. Maybe with you here helping me out we can get out a little bit earlier."

"Trying to get a little free labor, huh? Let me get this straight: you screw up our plans and you want me to come and work on my day off?" Loren giggled. "You really know how to push your luck, mister."

"We'll still get out of here by mid-afternoon, so we'll get to The Greenbrier by 4 or 5 o'clock. Just in time for happy hour. It will still be a perfect weekend. Of course, any weekend that I can spend with you is already pretty perfect in my book."

"Yeah, you better keep sucking up," she said, still giggling. "I'll be there in a few minutes."

"Great, thanks. I love you," Keith said by way of saying goodbye.

"Yes, and you should. I love you, too." Loren hung up, hoping that their little ruse was going to work.

Loren reached Bryant International about 10 minutes later and took the first free parking space she saw. She knew that it wasn't so important where she parked, just so she was observed parking by whoever was following her and/or watching Keith. Leaving her car and locking it, she then entered the offices via the entrance closest to the garage. Keith was waiting for her when she reached his office. Shutting the door behind her he gave her a long hug and held her tightly. "How are you holding up?" he asked, keeping his voice as low as possible in case they were being monitored.

"So far, so good, I guess. I'm scared, though. This just seems crazy."

"It is crazy, but I know it's real. Michael and I were followed when we left the office and then all the way back here."

"You're sure?" Loren asked.

"Positive. Dark gray Chrysler 300, probably parked out on the street right now where they can see my car in the garage." Then, in a more normal voice, he added, "Let's take you around to see Michael and the DALCAL team and see if we can get things back on track. I'd like us to be out of here no later than 2 or 3pm." They then headed down the hallway, stopping to talk with Michael and a slew of others. Everyone at Bryant International knew Loren and loved her. She had, in fact, come in on several occasions and consulted with them. Where people at first expected her to be just another pretty face or the 'boss' girlfriend', they quickly came to find that she was as smart as she was attractive, if not more so. It only took her a few hours to win everyone over, and since that time she'd definitely become one of the family.

After spending about 20 minutes with the people in the office, Keith and Loren had decided that the stage had been set as well as could be expected. Now all they needed to do was make their way to the Taurus and start on their way without being observed by their shadows. Keith was counting on the fact that the car, or cars, following them had to be parked in the same general area where the Chrysler had been parked earlier, allowing the occupants to have a clear, unobstructed view of the parking garage. If that were, in fact, the case – and God knows, their lives may very well depend on it – he and Loren would not be able to be seen as they got into the company car and headed out.

"We need to leave our cell phones in my office before we roll out of here. If they're tracking us via the GPS signal in the phones that should help throw them off our track for a bit as we get on the road. That will be just one more indication to them, hopefully, that we're still here in the building," said Keith.

"But what if someone comes after us between now and the time we can get some new ones, what will we do? We won't be able to call 911 or LTBT if we're in trouble," Loren said, the tension clearly visible on her face.

"That's a chance we're just going to have to take, I'm afraid. I'm not sure what help anybody could provide, including the police, if these guys see us leaving here and get the orders to kill us. We'd probably be dead before anyone could come to our aid."

Loren looked frightened, and Keith wished he could take back that last statement. "You certainly know how to make a girl feel better," she said, smiling nervously.

After dropping off the cell phones in his office they quickly said their goodbyes and headed out the front door. Both used umbrellas, both to protect themselves from the driving rain and to help conceal their identities should somebody be watching the front of the building.

Once in the car, Loren said, "I'm going to duck down until we're well clear of this area. That way, even if they see this car leaving it will hopefully not raise any flags since it's just one guy in the car. This is one time that the weather is probably in our favor."

"Good point. Hey, and since you've got to keep your head down anyway…" Keith trailed off and just let the joke hang out there.

Loren laughed, despite the tension. "Only a man could think about sex when he's got 'Guido the Killer Pimp', or whoever the hell these guys are, following us and probably ready to kill us. You are one sick puppy."

"I'll take that as a compliment, my dear." Then more seriously, "OK, I'm pulling out and going left away from these guys. Try to keep out of sight for the next few blocks."

"Alright. Don't forget to watch your speed. All we need is to get a ticket and have your name get in the system. These guys probably have access to that kind of information."

"You're probably right. I'll keep to the speed limit, assuming that we can even drive the speed limit once we hit the interstate. I just hope that this rain eases up as we head east; the weather reports say that the storm is supposed to be moving out of the area sometime later today."

Keith followed Route 29 south for a few miles until he hit Interstate 64. Had they been heading to The Greenbrier they would have headed west. They had no intention of being anywhere along that stretch of road in case the surveillance team came looking for them. Instead, they were heading east on I-64 towards Richmond and Norfolk. Just to be safe he planned to jump off onto some parallel roads for part of the ride, like Route 250 between Charlottesville and Richmond, and Routes 60 and 143 between Richmond and Williamsburg. Before he got that far east, though, he had one important stop that needed to be made just outside of Richmond, namely a large electronics and appliance store at a mall just outside of the city.

Their shopping list was short but critical, and all of their purchases, of course, would be made in cash. All of their credit cards and ATM cards were still in their wallets should an emergency ever arise, but they knew that the government agents would be on them in no time flat should they ever use them. First on the list was a new laptop computer to enable them to continue Keith's research and to maintain e-mail contact with Patrick Treadwell and Jeff Anders. And, as Patrick and Jeff had suggested to him, Keith was going to purchase several pay-as-you-go cell phones. No signups, no contracts, nothing to trace – he hoped. The plan was for both Loren and Keith to purchase three of them, but they would shop separately and go through separate checkout lines to avoid raising any suspicion. Though they expected to be together at all times, they realized that circumstances might force them to separate. Expect the unexpected and plan accordingly, Keith had told Loren. No matter what came up, they had to be able to stay in touch. Plus, as an added bonus, they would be able to constantly swap phones as they made calls to…whom? Who would they dare call? Who would be monitored, and whose life might they endanger by calling them? Regardless, they both knew that they would have to be calling on someone, sometime, for help. Better to try to cover their tracks by using multiple phones. Their last purchase was something that Keith had thought of , something that harkened back to his military days: 2-way walkie-talkies. He could only hope that the surveillance team wouldn't be monitoring those types of frequencies, but if nothing else they may come in handy as backup communication should they get separated. They ended up purchasing a pair from Motorola that had 22 channels and a 10 mile range. Keith and Loren both thought of a few last minute items that might make things a little easier while on the move, so they picked those things up and headed off to different registers.

It took well over an hour to make their purchases, especially since it took a while for the sales person to locate the exact Hewlett-Packard laptop PC that Keith had decided on. They were anxious to get on the road, but Keith wanted to make sure they had everything they needed before they left. Once they were on the move they knew that it would be too dangerous to continue venturing out in public any more than absolutely necessary. They both breathed a collective sigh of relief when they finally got back in the car and made it to the interstate.

It was starting to get dark when Keith and Loren pulled into the Hampton Inn and Suites in Williamsburg, VA. The hotel was located right on Route 60, or, as it's known along this stretch, Richmond Road. Pulling the car around the side of the hotel, Keith walked in to register. Thankfully, the hotel had rooms available, and, best of all, they did not ask him for ID. The most confusing part of the registration process for the desk clerk was trying to deal with the fact that Keith was paying cash. The clerk stated that he'd been working at the hotel for a little more than six months and he'd never had anyone pay cash. Keith had never really considered the possibility that paying cash, in and of itself, now raised many people's suspicions since they were so used to a credit card and debit card society. Nothing to be done about that, he told himself. One use of the credit card or debit card and they'd be on his trail before he finished signing the charge slip.

"Well, it's not exactly The Greenbrier, but it's not bad," Keith said as they entered the hotel room. "At least it's clean." He carried in two small overnight bags for them, along with his briefcase. He wasn't about to let the pistol out of his sight.

"It's fine," said Loren. "I'm just glad to be out of the car and out of the rain." It had finally stopped raining about the time they got to Toano, about 12 miles west of Williamsburg. The sky was still far from clear, but at this point they were thrilled just for the rain to stop. They'd gone through countless puddles along the highways, and more than once they felt the tires on the Taurus starting to hydroplane despite their relatively conservative speed. She had noticed throughout the day that the storm had blown most of the leaves off of the trees, and everywhere you looked the ground seemed to be covered with wet and decaying leaves. Usually this part of Virginia has some leaves left on the trees until at least mid-November, but the nor'easter that had come through over the past few days had definitely done a number on them.

"It is good to be out of the car. My back is a little stiff. The Taurus, sexy chick-magnet that it is, just isn't quite as comfortable as my BMW, to put it mildly." Keith sat the bags on the far side of the king-size bed and up against the wall. "I'm getting a little bit hungry. How about you?"

"Maybe a little, but I think my stomach is just in knots from all of this. I'm not sure if I'll be able to eat."

"Well, not to sound like a mother hen, but you need to eat to keep your strength up and your mind focused. More importantly, we need to eat when we're able to. We don't know what the next few days or weeks are going to throw at us, so we have to make time to eat and rest when we're able. Remember what Jason Bourne said…"

"Who the hell is Jason Bourne?" Loren interrupted.

"Jason Bourne, the main character in several of Robert Ludlum's books. Matt Damon played Jason Bourne in *'The Bourne Identity', 'The Bourne Supremacy',* and *'The Bourne Ultimatum'*. We saw all three of them at the theatre, remember?"

"OK, I do remember seeing the movies, but I don't remember any super-wise, Confucius-like words of wisdom. So what did Jason Bourne say that was so profound?"

"In the books, at least, he often said, *'rest is a weapon'*. And I think he's right; we can't let ourselves get so tired or thirsty or hungry that our bodies start breaking down and we make stupid mistakes. We have to try and keep ourselves together to have a chance at making it through this."

"Well, I'd say that Mr. Bourne, or Mr. Ludlum, was probably right." Loren walked over and put her arms around Keith's neck, then reached up to give him a kiss. "I'll try to eat something whenever you're ready. In the meantime, why don't you run back down to the car and bring that gorgeous basket of food and wine from Rio Hill Wine up here and we'll have a little snack before heading out to dinner? I could certainly use a glass of wine, that's for sure."

"I'll run down and get the basket, and you be sure to lock the door behind me. I'll knock when I get back and you make sure it's me before unlatching the deadbolt and the security latch." When he returned from the car Keith had the basket and their little wine travel kit that they used on picnics. The kit had two wine glasses, a foil cutter, and a pretty decent wine opener. He opened the bottle of Tanterra Pinot Noir and poured them each a glass. He had also picked up a couple of small plates from the hotel's dining area. No need to be less than civilized, he reasoned, while trying to eat their cheese and other delicacies.

Keith also brought their shopping bag full of electronics back to the room and spent a few minutes unpacking the PC and the cell phones. He then plugged the electrical power strips that he'd bought into the wall and proceeded to charge all of the phones and the laptop. He knew that he couldn't count on doing it later, so he had to make sure that everything was fully charged before leaving the hotel in the morning. He'd bought two extra batteries for the laptop, explaining to the sales clerk that he often did a lot of flying and needed to make sure that he could work for at least 8-10 hours uninterrupted. While Keith expected to have access to electrical power while they were moving, you could never be too sure. Contingencies had to be planned for. That's why they had also purchased a small inverter that could be plugged into the cigarette lighter of any car, thereby allowing the computer's AC cord – or for that matter, the AC adapter for the cell phones or any other electrical device – to get powered up while driving. Finally satisfied that everything was plugged-in and charging, and, thankfully, not blowing the circuits in their room, Keith sat down to relax and have a glass of wine.

"What do you think of the wine?" Keith asked Loren. She was already on her second glass before he had even sat down and poured his.

"I love it. What made you buy this Tanterra? Had you had it before?"

"Yeah, I've had it several times when I've been traveling around Carmel and Monterey. I saw it today at the wine store and decided to try another bottle. I thought you'd probably like it."

As they enjoyed the wine and hors d' oeuvres, Loren asked, "Do you think they realize yet that we're gone?"

"Oh, yeah. Not only do they know that we've gone, I bet all hell is breaking loose right about now. Whoever is running this operation is probably about to blow a fuckin' cork over this, and he's probably about ready to see some heads roll. Ours included."

⌘

KEITH HAD NO IDEA JUST how accurate his assessment was. Colonel Ed Foster was on the verge of having a stroke. Bob Manning and the other DCG operatives in the Bunker had never seen his face so red or his temper this out of control. The words that were coming out of his mouth weren't typical for Foster, nor was the volume. Thank God this room was soundproof, Manning thought.

"Can anybody explain to me how in the hell Dr. Bryant and Ms. Davis disappeared when we had two goddamn surveillance teams following them? A couple of goddamn academics have managed to slip by professional fucking operatives?" The vein in Foster's temple looked like it was ready to burst right through his skin.

"Our people didn't get suspicious until around 3:30 or 4:00 this afternoon. Bryant and Davis were supposedly in his office with others working on a big deal. We'd overheard a conversation between the two of them where they made plans for her to come to the office to help him and his team for a few hours before leaving for The Greenbrier. Both of their cars were still in the parking lot so our guys thought nothing of it." Manning was not one to back down from anyone, including Foster, when things starting getting testy.

"And now we know that they have not yet checked in at The Greenbrier, right?" Foster asked.

"That is correct," answered Manning. "And we know that both of their cars are still at the Bryant International location, but they're gone. The lights are off and everyone has gone for the weekend."

"And did our crackerjack surveillance professionals check on their cars?" Foster wanted to know. The sarcasm and irritation in his voice was unmistakable.

"Yes, they did, and they found that Bryant's car was full of empty boxes, something that must have been done to make it appear that the car was still full of clothes and luggage."

"Jesus Christ! And our people fell for that? That's about one level of sophistication above telling someone to look down because their goddamn shoe is untied." Foster was literally shaking he was so mad. "So where the hell did they go, and what the hell are they doing for transportation?"

"One of our guys called Bryant's company and asked for him while pretending to be returning his call from the local BMW dealer. When he told the receptionist that he was following-up on Bryant's inquiry about possibly trading in his car, the lady told him that he was apparently having trouble with it that day because he left it at their office and took off for the weekend in one of the company cars, a Taurus."

"So he swaps cars right under our noses and waltzes right out the front door. That is just rich. Maybe I need to hire him as a goddamn agent and fire all of these supposed professionals I have working for me now down there in Charlottesville." Foster's voice was growing louder by the minute. "Tell me what we're doing to track them at this point. Have you tracked them via their cell phone GPS?"

Manning really didn't want to broach this subject, but since it was asked so directly he didn't see any way around it. "Right now we got nothing. The Bryant International company cars are not equipped with LoJack or any other type of tracking device, and both of them left their cell phones at his office. That's another reason that our teams didn't grow alarmed for several hours after they'd snuck out. I'm sure they left them there expecting us to be using their GPS signals against them. About all we have at this point is the license number and registration number for the car that Bryant took."

Foster thought his head was going to explode. "Then basically you have nothing," he seethed. "If they're smart enough to know to abandon their phones they're for goddamn sure smart enough to switch license plates on a regular basis." Foster tried shifting gears a bit, trying to will himself to calm down. "Do we know what they took with them? Are they going to try to live off of the land or are they going to try to hide out in a city? How much money do they have with them? Talk to me, people."

"All indications are that they have, at most, a few thousand dollars with them. That's based on the withdrawals they made yesterday. Obviously, they're not dumb enough to use their credit cards or ATM cards anymore, but maybe they'll get desperate for cash or food or gas at some point and make a mistake. As far as what they took with them, we don't know for sure. We need to send a team over to their house and see if we can get a better feel for it, but keep in mind that it's hard to know what's missing when we didn't know everything that was there to start with." Manning was growing weary of this discussion, to say nothing of this entire operation.

No shit, Foster thought to himself. "Alright, send a team to their farm and see what we can determine. In the interim, I want you to get two teams moving on tracking them down. Send one team west and the other team east. We know that they didn't go to The Greenbrier, but that doesn't mean that they didn't head west going somewhere. Have Mr. Hilton lead the team heading east; my money is on that direction. When we find them, I want them eliminated immediately. Preferably I'd like it to look like just another street crime, but at this point I am less concerned about covering our tracks than I am about stopping Bryant before he goes underground. If he hooks up with Let the Truth Be Told we could have a real problem on our hands and shit could spiral out of control very quickly. The last thing we need is a situation where we have to eliminate a half-dozen or more people. That just raises the possibility of something going wrong or someone asking too many questions."

Manning replied, "No problem, I can get that moving right away. Do you want to enlist the help of state or local law enforcement to find them? Maybe put out the word that we have some high-profile criminals on the run from the Feds and we think they're here in Virginia?"

"No, definitely not, at least not at this point," said Foster. "It may come to that, but right now I want to try to track them down and silence them with our own resources. Being picked up by state or local police might be the best thing that could happen for Dr. Bryant and Ms. Davis. Having them in police custody would make it difficult, if not impossible, for us to get to them to silence them. Plus, they may start talking to the authorities about what they know or what they think they know. That could prove very embarrassing for us, to say the least."

"That's valid. OK, I'll get our teams moving. If you have no objection I'm also going to call up a few reserve operatives to help expand the search grid a bit. There's really no reason to exclude the possibility that they ran north towards DC or south along Route 29 towards Lynchburg or Danville, right? It's not just an east versus west problem at this point. I think we should cover all of the bases until we have some definitive word or sighting, then we can swarm all of our people on one area."

"I'm OK with that," said Foster. "Just make sure that these people understand the mission and can keep their mouths shut. Let's have the searches start ASAP with the people we do have available. They should start tonight with a roadway search. Tomorrow morning the weather should be clearer so we should be able to put four choppers in the air to speed up the search."

"I'll get the helicopters prepped and ready to rendezvous with the teams at first light. This is going to be like finding a needle in a haystack. Hopefully we can count on them doing something stupid very soon, or at least their luck running out." Manning was pissed that this was all blowing up in their faces, particularly on a weekend.

"Maybe they will do something stupid. After all, they're not professionals. On the other hand, they're not stupid, either. I wouldn't want to bet my life on them making a mistake. They'll be cautious, scared. They'll stay out of the spotlight until it's time for the spotlight, meaning the press, to be their saving grace. We have to stop them before it gets to that point. That means monitoring every person we think they might possibly contact, including members of Let the Truth Be Told. They're going to be feeling very alone, very confused, and very much in over their heads in a very short time. It's our job, our mission, to be sure that we're cutting them off before they can forge any alliances with LTBT or any other group." Foster stood up to leave, and finally said, "I want hourly updates on this situation, and I want to know the second you track them down. And let our people know that we will be paying a $25,000 bonus to the person who eliminates both Dr. Bryant and Ms. Davis. That should get their juices flowing a bit."

Chapter 12

Bob Manning and his DCG teams worked throughout the night trying to track down Keith and Loren. One of the local Charlottesville teams had gone to the farm and searched their house. They had checked the registration for every hotel within a 500 mile radius of Charlottesville with no luck. Not surprising, he thought. Bryant would definitely be using a fake name and paying cash, and, in all likelihood, probably gravitating to small mom & pop motels well off the beaten path. They had accessed the traffic monitoring cameras that covered the interstate highways in Virginia, but that also proved fruitless; there were thousands of Ford Taurus's on the highways. Plus, there were tens of thousands of miles of roads in the state, at least, that weren't covered by cameras. They even went through the formality of checking all of the airline, train, and bus manifests nationwide, though they never expected any of those to pan out. Without any credit cards, a limited and finite amount of cash, and the impossibility of using their ID's to deal with any kind of security checks, it was highly unlikely that they would even attempt it. Although, Manning thought to himself, give them enough time on the run and they may figure out how to acquire the fake documents that they would need to travel anywhere and everywhere they wanted, including out of the country. That thought was enough to make him break into a cold sweat. On at least a dozen occasions throughout the night Manning caught himself muttering, *'I'm too old for this shit'* under his breath.

Around 5am Saturday morning Manning got together with his team in the conference room to do a quick reality check to see what progress, if any, they'd made. The consensus was that they were really no further along now than they were when they started more than twelve hours ago. They had not found Bryant and Davis, nor had they eliminated any particular location or geographic area. If anything, the search area had expanded since there was no way no exclude the possibility that they had continued driving away from the Charlottesville area for the last 14-15 hours, enough time to have put 1,000 miles or more behind them. Manning, feeling very tired and very frustrated, finally said, "Guys, we've been at this for 14 goddamn hours and we're no better off than we were when we started. If anything, we're further behind! We need to find a way to get a handle on this situation, and quickly, or we may lose these two forever."

"Any chance that Colonel Foster will reconsider bringing in the local police or state police to help? More feet and eyes on the street would definitely help at this point." Brad Hanover was the one that finally spoke what was on everyone's mind.

"Have you ever known him to change his mind once it's made up?" asked Manning. "But I gotta tell you, on this point I have to agree with him. If we bring in the locals, even with a decent cover story, the shit could blow up right in our faces. Those two would be singing like freakin' songbirds, especially once we tried coming in there to take them into custody. Even if they can't prove anything we still can't afford the visibility and the inevitable questions. We're on our own."

"I think I may have an idea," said Warren Adams. "Hear me out on this: we've been trying to track them using all of the conventional means, like looking for credit card usage, travel manifests on common carriers, road surveillance, etc., right?" Seeing nods all around, he continued. "So I was thinking, rather than try to track the subjects in an increasingly large universe, why don't we use Electra to look for buying patterns for the things that Bryant and Davis are most likely to need while they're on the run? Maybe that will help us narrow the search grid considerably, if not pinpoint the bastards."

"Goddamn," said Manning. "I think you're onto something." Turning to Les Mattox, he then said, "Les, you were in control of the team that searched Bryant's place last night. What did they come back with after the search?"

"The only unusual thing the search team found was that both of them had left their computers at the house, probably because they were suspicious about them being monitored. However, they did not find any backup disks or CD's, no flash drives, nothing. We know from our monitoring program that they both backed their shit up on a regular basis, including the night before they left, so the only thing I think we can safely conclude is that they took all of that with them. We also did not find any hard copy files or papers related to any of Dr. Bryant's current work, so we're suspecting that he also took that with them on the road. Let me see if there's anything else here worth noting," said Mattox as he looked through his notes one last time. "That looks like that's the gist of it."

"Thanks, Les. That helps ground us a little bit. Alright, guys. Where do you think we go from here? Other than home to bed, that is?"

"Let's try and knock this shit out quickly, and while we're back on the trail maybe somebody can make a quick run over to Einstein Brothers for some bagels and coffee? I'm starving, and the first few pots of coffee are wearing off." said Brad Hanover.

"Actually, that's not a half-bad idea. They open at 6am on weekends. How about we spend the next 15 minutes brainstorming on the program we need to have Electra run and then Brad can make a food and coffee run for us. Sound good to everyone?" asked Manning.

With that the DCG team got started trying to create the search parameters for Electra. What would the subjects need if they tried to go underground, maybe camping out and avoiding hotels and motels? What would they need if they went north versus south, or east versus west? What items were critical must-haves rather than nice-to-haves? After almost 25 minutes the team was obviously getting very tired, hungry, and punchy. They had a list of almost 100 items on their whiteboard, but it was too many items, too much 'noise'. They needed clear minds to think the situation through. It wouldn't do any good to load a bunch of useless search parameters into Electra. The data would be useless, just like the old adage of 'garbage in, garbage out'. Finally, Bob Manning decided that they'd hit the wall. "Alright guys, we're obviously dying here. Les, why don't you ride with Brad to get the bagels and coffee. And get lots of both, since God only knows how long we're going to be here. It's on the company, of course. I think we've earned it." He could see that everyone looked like zombies. "Let's meet back here in 30 minutes and we'll work through the rest of this shit and get Electra moving on it."

It was actually almost 45 minutes before Les Mattox and Brad Hanover made it back to the office from the bagel store. They came back with a dozen bagels, two gallons of coffee, at least a dozen bottles of various fruit juices, and assorted pastries and cookies. As the team got some caffeine and some food in them their mood improved considerably, as did their ability to think and focus. By 7:00 am they had narrowed the list of key items for Electra to search, as well as the search parameters they were going to use relative to distance from Charlottesville, time constraints, and so on.

Bob Manning stood before the whiteboard to summarize what they'd come up with and their plan for action. "OK, guys, here's what we've narrowed it down to: we believe that Dr. Bryant and Ms. Davis are going to want to purchase at least two throwaway cell phones, one for each of them. In addition, there's a good possibility that they'll want to get a PC in order to be able to communicate via e-mail, most likely with conspiracy groups or others that they think can help them stay on the run. It might be a low-priced PC since they have a relatively small and finite amount of cash, or, at least that's our assumption. They may also be trying to find someone to supply them with new credit cards or ID's, but we agreed that that's probably low on the list at this point, our assumption being that they don't have the contacts for such an undertaking, at least not yet. Last, they may be trying to buy one or more weapons, so we're going to search for purchases of guns and ammo. And finally, we agreed that the search parameters would be between the hours of 1pm and midnight yesterday, and within 300 miles of Charlottesville. Are we all aligned?"

There were nods and agreement from everyone at the table. "Alright, then, let's get going on it. I expect that we should have the programs and search parameters built and input into Electra within the hour, then she'll probably start spitting results back out pretty quickly after that. Keep me posted."

With that the meeting broke up, and the team, now energized with the prospect of having the end in sight – to say nothing of lots of caffeine now coursing through their systems – started to work with a vengeance. Manning slipped into his office and sent off a quick e-mail to Foster.

Colonel,

Starting with new search criteria. Should have input for Electra within the hour. Expect results within 60-90 minutes that will narrow, if not pinpoint, the search area.

Bob

Manning knew that the course he was taking was highly out of the ordinary. In fact, Electra had never been used for such a task. The DCG team was re-tasking her to act like a detective by sorting through all of the financial transactions of thousands of different retail facilities across a multi-state area. That change in direction for Electra was somewhat analogous to having the government intelligence community re-task a spy satellite to cover a different part of the world, or to change the time that it covered the same space on different days. He had no doubt that his team could do it, he just wasn't sure if they could pull it off as quickly as he wanted or as quickly as he committed in his e-mail to Colonel Foster.

It was just after 9:00 am when Electra started spitting out the data. Torres came into Manning's office with the information, noticeably excited and very wide awake at this point. "Bob, Electra's nailed their asses. Let me show you." He spread some printouts across Manning's desk as the rest of the team assembled to see for themselves. "Look at this. Yesterday afternoon an individual bought a new HP laptop and three new throwaway cell phones at the Best Buy just outside of Richmond. And, at virtually the same time another customer bought three more throwaway phones and a pair of Motorola walkie-talkies. Here's the clincher: they both paid cash."

"Hell, yes!" said Manning. "That has got to be them. Now the question is, where the hell did they go after they left that store yesterday? They've had more than twelve hours to run, and being right there in Richmond they could take either I-95 north or south or I-64 east or west. Although, I doubt they would risk heading back west since that would bring them right back past Charlottesville."

"I'm one step ahead of ya, boss," said Torres. "I had Electra correlate anything and everything in Bryant's life, or his girlfriend's for that matter, with the fact that they were in Richmond. I'm pretty sure we have our answer, or at least a damn good place to start."

"What is it? Don't keep us all in suspense," Brad Hanover said through nervous laughter.

"I think Bryant is running to his boat. He has a boat – actually a freakin' yacht, if you ask me – that he keeps in Gloucester, VA at a marina called York River Yacht Haven. It's only about an hour or hour and a half from Richmond, and the thing is nice enough that he could live on it for as long as he needs to. Plus, of course, it's mobile."

"What are the chances that he's already gotten on the boat and left?" asked Manning.

"Per Electra, pretty slim. And I'd have to agree. The weather has been flat-out terrible down in that area for the past couple of days. Windy as shit, raining cats and dogs, lots of flooding. I think he probably found somewhere to hole up last night and they plan to try to get down there today when the weather is supposed to be a little bit better."

"Did Electra pop out any other possibilities besides the boat angle?" asked Mattox.

"Yeah, several friends in the area, mostly from around the waterfront and marinas. Electra got that based on searches of his home phone and cell phones. Still, when I asked Electra to provide the probability for each, she came back with the boat as the highest probability. It was over 70%, and none of the other possibilities made it even as high as 15%. I think the boat is our best shot." Torres let all of this sink in with the team. He sat back and waited, actually feeling quite satisfied with himself, and deservedly so.

Finally Manning spoke. "I think our friend here has hit the nail on the head. Unless anybody has any reason to second-guess Mr. Torres or has any further questions, I think we need to move on this, and quickly. We need to plan a tactical response for our teams on the ground and get them moving on this ASAP. Anybody have any reservations about this data or any more questions for Torres?" Seeing that everyone was in agreement, Manning closed with, "Alright, let's have a tactical plan for our operatives in 30 minutes. Torres, great job."

While the rest of the team went to start working on the tactical plans, Manning closed his office door and called Foster. It was still pretty early on a Saturday morning, but Manning didn't really care. Fuck him if he gets upset, he thought. The prick got to go home last night to a hot meal and a warm, comfortable bed while the rest of them were here in the Bunker the whole goddamn night. Manning dialed the number and Foster answered on the first ring.

"Tell me something good," said Foster.

"We think we've found them. Per Electra, there's a better than 70% probability that he's heading to Gloucester to get to his boat. I have the team working on a tactical plan now for the field ops folks. Thought you'd want to know."

"I'm actually only about 2-3 minutes away from the office now. I'll meet you there in a few minutes and work with the team on the plans."

"A little early to be up and awake on a Saturday morning, isn't it?" Manning asked with a smile.

"Who the hell can sleep with this shit going on?" answered Foster, then hung up.

⌘

KEITH AND LOREN WOKE UP at 7:30am when the alarm clock went off. They should have been well rested; they'd both gone to bed just before 11pm, but neither had slept very well. The stress of the past few days made restful sleep impossible. They had walked down Richmond Road last night to one of the dozens of restaurants that had popped up in Williamsburg over the past 8-10 years. Their plan was to have a quick dinner and another glass of wine – they'd killed the entire bottle of Pinot Noir back in their hotel room – and still get to bed at a reasonable hour. They didn't dare spend too much time out in public, even though they felt relatively safe for this one night. After that, all bets were off and they knew it.

After they got up and showered and dressed, Keith packed up the laptop, the extra batteries, and the cell phones. The laptop, batteries, and two of the cell phones went into his PC bag, while Loren took two of the phones for her purse. All of the miscellaneous accessories like the car charger and home chargers for the cell phones went into one of the laundry bags that had been hanging in the room closet. When all of their clothes were together Keith carried the duffle bags down to the car and locked them in the trunk, all the while keeping an eye out for any suspicious people or vehicles. By the time he got back up to the room Loren was ready to go. They decided to have breakfast at their hotel in order to stay off the streets and to conserve their cash. Breakfast was included in the cost of their hotel room anyway, so while not exactly gourmet, to put it mildly, it did fill them up. Loren had two cups of coffee, or what she said was being passed off as coffee.

It was just after 9:00 when they got into the car and started heading out. "How long will it take us to get to Gloucester from here?" asked Loren.

"Not too long, maybe 45 minutes. We're going to go down the Colonial Parkway towards Yorktown, and then when we get there we'll just jump on

Route 17 for about a mile and go north across the Coleman Bridge. The marina is less than five minutes from the bridge."

"I don't think I've ever been to the marina from this direction before," Loren said.

"No, we've always come in from West Point and headed south on Route 17, so you've never been over this bridge. You've been under it a bunch of times as we cruised up the river, but you've never been over it."

"Do we need to get anything before we get to the marina?" Loren figured that was a pretty logical question since they had no idea how long they might be staying on the boat.

"I've brought some food from the pantry that is in the trunk, as well as some food from the refrigerator and freezer. It's in a cooler on ice, and thankfully it's been cold enough outside that I haven't had to worry about getting more ice yet. There's a case of bottled water on the back seat, and I've got plenty of water, beer, and sodas on the boat. Not to mention about 20 or so bottles of wine in the wine cooler."

"So it sounds like we don't have to worry about finding something to drink, at least, but what about eating? Let me guess: you brought bags of cookies, and crackers, and chips, and lots of junk food, right? But nothing healthy?" She smiled at him, knowing that left to his own devices he'd be glad to live off of cookies and junk food for days, his gourmet tendencies be damned.

"Actually, I'll have you know that I also brought bread, lots of deli meat and cheese, and even some frozen hamburger, steaks, and chicken. There are also some canned vegetables and some rice and risotto. It may not be four stars, but we definitely won't starve to death. Thankfully, the galley on the boat is almost as well stocked and equipped as any home kitchen, so we won't exactly be roughing it."

"I guess that's true," she said. "Being on the *Kismet* is not exactly like camping out in the wild and sleeping in a pup tent, that's for sure." Loren loved spending time on the boat, although this time was definitely not about going on a pleasure cruise. This was survival.

They drove on in silence, the usual beauty of the Colonial Parkway between Williamsburg and Yorktown not as noticeable today with the remnants of the nor'easter still evident. While better than the previous few days, it was still far from nice. The sky was still heavily overcast and the wind was still blowing steadily out of the northeast, though the winds had lessened considerably. The river looked dirty and muddy, the result of too much rain and too much dirt and soil running off of the rich land that bordered the river. The waters were usually calm this far upriver, but today the York was covered by whitecaps as far as the eye could see in all directions. With several large trees down along the road, to say nothing of hundreds of large tree limbs and tons of debris, Keith had to focus more on navigating the Parkway safely than on enjoying the view of the river. If there was this much debris on the road, he mused, then he can hardly wait to see how much is in the water....

When Keith took the exit for Route 17 off of the Parkway it snapped him back to reality. "Sweetie, could you get me a couple of dollars out of your wallet, please. We'll have to stop to pay the toll here in just a couple of minutes." Loren handed him the money, which he folded and held in his right hand. He was trying hard to hide his nervousness and anxiety, but he wasn't sure he was doing a very good job of it. He wanted to be strong for the both of them, but he was scared of what they were up against. *Whatever they were up against*, he reminded himself.

Keith stopped to pay the toll as they reached the Gloucester side of the bridge, and then he turned right within a half-mile of the toll booth. Within minutes they were pulling up to the marina, and Keith and Loren walked to get two of the wheelbarrow-like carts that the marina kept around for hauling lots of stuff to and from the boats. Keith hoped to get it all in one trip and get the hell out of here; he'd feel much more comfortable when they were out on the open water. He looked up at the flags snapping in the breeze. It was definitely still blowing today, but at least it was down to a Small Craft Warning versus the two straight days of Gale Warnings they'd had in this area. As he surveyed the area around him he saw that there were tons of tree limbs down everywhere, and the tide was still exceptionally high, probably at least 3-4 feet above normal. My God, he thought, as he looked around the marina and the harbor, the water is just full of debris and flotsam. He was going to have to be really vigilant when running the boat today. Heaven only knows what they might find floating around out there in the river, and the last thing they needed to do was hit something and damage the boat or its running gear.

With everything loaded from the car, Keith and Loren started down the docks. He had thought about trying to hide the car somewhere, but he didn't know anywhere close by to leave it while still being able to get back to the boat quickly. Plus, they both reasoned, if someone were tracking them and made it as far as the marina, the fact that the car was there wouldn't really tell them anything they didn't already know, namely, that their 78' boat was gone from its slip. Not wasting any time or motion, they walked quickly down the dock and threw all of their stuff quickly into the cockpit. They could spend some time straightening up as soon as they pulled out of the docks. Finally everything was onboard, and Keith went straight to the lower helm to fire up the engines. They both started effortlessly, as always. Thank God, he thought. He went ahead and fired up the generator as well, knowing that they'd be needing electricity for heat, refrigeration, and cooking while underway. Before leaving the helm to disconnect the shore power, Keith turned on his primary navigational electronics, including the VHF and Single Sideband (SSB) radios, color depth finder, GPS/chart plotter, and the radar. Although the radar could get readings as close as 1/8 of a mile and as far away as 72 miles, he opted to set it for a 10-mile view. That way he'd be able to see anything that was approaching from any direction and still have enough detail to make out their speed and approximate size, even in these messy conditions. As he let the engines warm up Loren started quickly moving their clothes into the salon area, along with Keith's PC bag, briefcase, and electronics accessories. The food and other things could wait until they pulled out, but now it was time to start helping with the dock lines. Keith came down and dropped the two bow lines onto the hooks on the pilings, telling Loren that the way the wind was blowing the last lines to drop were going to be the spring lines. Keith was proud of how well she had adapted to the boat and how quickly she had learned how to run the boat and handle the lines around the dock. She never needed to be asked twice to do anything, and most of the time she was intuitive enough to know what needed to be done without even being asked.

Loren yelled out to Keith from the stern. "I've got both stern lines dropped. I'm going to drop the port spring line first, but the winds may try to lay you against the starboard dock before I can get around there to drop the last line. Can you be ready to hold it off with the bow and stern thrusters?"

"No problem. I've already got the bow thruster engaged and using it to fight the wind. Once we're out of the lee of the Grand Banks beside us the wind is really going to try to take us, but nothing we can't handle." The

Grand Banks was a large motor yacht just a couple of feet shorter than *Kismet*, and, like *Kismet*, it was drop-dead gorgeous. As Keith liked to say, they both looked the way a proper yacht should look.

Loren scurried around to the starboard side and dropped the last spring line onto the dock. Keith used the thrusters to keep him lined up straight in the slip, and then slipped both engines into reverse. The two big Caterpillar diesel engines did not have any wasted motion; the second Keith put them in reverse the boat started moving backwards *right now*.

As they eased out of the marina, Loren popped up to the helm. "Great job of getting the boat away from the dock in this wind. It makes me nervous to have $10 million dollars worth of boats within a few yards of ours as we come in and out, just sitting there waiting to get damaged."

"Piece of cake, especially with my trusty first mate aboard." He smiled and gave her a little kiss on the nose. "As soon as we clear the first buoy you want to take her the rest of the way out to the main channel while I put the stuff away?"

"Sure, I can do that. Looks like it's going to be pretty rough, at least for the York River, but I don't think it's anything we can't handle."

"You're right. And we'll be going pretty much bow into it, so it won't be bad. It shouldn't take me more than 5-10 minutes to stow our things. I just want to make sure we get everything inside where it's dry, especially once we're out of the harbor and the spray starts flying in this wind. Oh, and keep a close eye out for debris and flotsam in the water. After the rains and flooding down here there's no telling what we may see floating along. I'm sure there's everything from tree limbs, to pier pilings, to entire pier structures out here today."

"I'll be careful," said Loren. "By the way, how much fuel do we have onboard? Enough that we don't need to stop and fill up I hope. That could put a serious dent in our cash."

"We're fine. I made sure that the tanks were full the last time I brought it in, so we have 3,000 gallons onboard. That should last us a while, especially since we're not planning to leave the Chesapeake Bay." As they reached the second red buoy Keith handed the helm over to Loren, and he was fully confident in her ability to get them out to the main channel. Even from here he could see the larger waves and white caps rolling up the river. Not a good day to be out in a small boat, he thought, but not bad at all in this, his luxurious 'mini-battleship'.

Keith proceeded to get all of their things stowed. All of their clothes went into the master stateroom, and his PC bag and all of the electronics were safely stowed in his office. He quickly took the new laptop out of the bag and set it up on his desk and connected the RJ45 Ethernet cable from the boat's LAN; the internet connection, as on most yachts, was provided by an external satellite communication connection. He fired up the PC and went to grab some more of their provisions while the laptop started its boot sequence. He stowed the water and the food, including the food for the refrigerator and the freezer. Then he went back down below to his office and, as he expected, the PC was waiting for him to enter his password before completing the boot-up. Password entered, the PC was quickly ready for action. That would be later, Keith thought to himself. For now, he just wanted it ready.

Heading back up to the helm area, he saw that Loren had already reached the main channel and had started downriver. The seas were short, steep, and sloppy, but *Kismet* slogged right on through. Knowing that it would be a lot nastier once they reached the bay, Keith went ahead and turned on the Naiad stabilizers. They would make the ride a lot more comfortable when the seas were larger or more on the beam. "I brought you up a beer. It must be noon somewhere," Keith said, taking a look at his watch. "Let's keep it to around 9-10 knots. No need to be in a real hurry, and it might do us well to conserve on fuel, just in case. Plus, there's enough crap floating in the water that we really have to keep an eye out."

"Are you still thinking that we'll set a course for St. Michaels?" St. Michaels was on the western side of Maryland's Eastern Shore and was a beautiful, idyllic place for boats that were cruising the bay. Plus, it was just hard enough to reach from the DC area and the Norfolk and Virginia Beach areas that any of the surveillance teams would have a tough time getting there in rapid fashion.

"I think so, but let's wait and see how it is when we hit the bay, especially out around New Point Comfort. If it's too snotty we can always plan to put in at Gwynn's Island, or, worst case, we can bag St. Michael's altogether and run down the Bay and put in somewhere off of Hampton Roads, like maybe the Nansemond River." Keith switched the VHF radio to the weather channel and listened for a few minutes as the automated, robot-like voice gave the weather forecast for their area. "Well, there's some good news. With the winds forecasted to drop to 10-15 mph later this afternoon and swing around to the southwest, conditions on the Bay should improve quite a bit. Maybe we should slide up into Mobjack Bay for a few hours and drop anchor, maybe have some lunch. Then we'll see if the wind actually starts laying down some and then make our move. We won't be able to make St. Michaels before nightfall, so maybe we can duck in somewhere around Deltaville for the night and just stay out on the hook until morning."

"Whatever you think is best. You want to go below and try to call LTBT and let them know what we're doing?"

"Yeah, I think I will. Just keep her heading down river and watch out for stuff in the water. We can't afford to get slowed down, or worse, by hitting anything. You see anything or need anything, you yell. Especially if you see another boat approaching on the radar, don't wait, just yell. Got it?"

"Got it. You go ahead; I've got things under control up here." And she did, too.

Keith went down below to his office and grabbed one of the cell phones. The signal meter showed almost full strength, but he decided to go back up into the salon area and sit on one of the couches. Mainly, he just felt better if he were up here and better able to help keep an eye out for any trouble. He called the number that Jeff Anders and Patrick Treadwell had provided him, and his call was answered on the second ring.

"This is Anders."

"Jeff, it's Keith Bryant. Can we talk?"

"Definitely. Hold one second while I conference in Patrick." The line went quiet for a few seconds while he set up the 3-way conference. When he came back on the line Patrick Treadwell had joined. "OK, Keith, we're both here. What's your situation?"

"Loren and I have left Charlottesville and we're currently on my boat heading down the York River. We've picked up a new PC and several prepaid cell phones, as you instructed, and we've made sure that we weren't followed as we headed out yesterday afternoon. Obviously, they probably caught on by late afternoon, but I think we probably got at least a 3-4 hour head start on them."

"Excellent," said Patrick. "Where do you plan to go now?"

"Our current thinking is up to Maryland's Eastern Shore. It's a bit off the beaten path, but more readily accessible by boat."

"Smart," said Jeff. "If you need to have us bring you in, you call us any time day or night. We'll make arrangements to get you somewhere, like maybe Atlanta or some other large city where we have resources. In the meantime, I'm guessing that you haven't had a lot of free time to continue your research since we last spoke, am I right?"

"Yes, you're definitely right. With all of the preparations for leaving town and all of the cloak and dagger stuff it hasn't left me any time for research at all this week."

"Completely understandable," said Patrick. "Do you know where your research is going to take you next? Anything that we might be able to help with from our end?"

Keith thought the offer through for a minute. He didn't know these guys from Adam, didn't know if he could really trust them. The fact that Lowell knew one of them didn't really help as a strong endorsement. The only thing in their favor was their reputation, or at least the collective reputation of LTBT. Keith considered that maybe it was time to bring someone else into the loop. He could no longer count on his Conspiracy class for research assistance, and it's quite possible that where he was headed with his research could benefit by having other skilled theorists involved. "Just before this shit storm started coming down this week I was getting ready to start researching an entirely different angle relative to 9/11. I had not shared this with my class, or anybody for that matter, other than Loren. Maybe if I work on this in parallel with you and other members of LTBT we'll get some answers much quicker."

"Tell us what you're thinking and how we can help," added Jeff.

"Have you guys ever heard of Daniels Robotics Corporation, or DRC? They're a defense contractor up in DC," Keith added.

"Sure. Big company, big hired-gun lobbyists, one of the lucky ones that always seem to profit from war and the resulting defense buildup. They just announced a couple of big contracts for new robotic and X-ray technology, as I recall." Patrick was definitely up on current events.

"Yeah, that's them. I was thinking, after reading their recent announcements, that they really seemed to have made an obscene amount of money in the years since 9/11, and maybe, just maybe, it's more than luck. Here's a theory: DRC, or some other members of the military-industrial complex, helps plan and finance the 9/11 operation, and in return they are rewarded by our government with multi-million, even multi-billion, dollar contracts to secure our nation and provide for our military – all for a war that they helped to instigate."

"Very interesting hypotheses, and definitely worth following if you ask me. You know, I can't remember all of the details, so I'll have to follow up on this, but I could swear that there were a few deaths around that time that set off alarms in the conspiracy world. One of them, I believe, was the CFO of DRC. Ostensibly, it was due to a heart attack, but what's a good conspiracy theory without some suspected foul play?" Jeff said with a chuckle, and they all got a laugh off of that.

"But be that as it may, Jeff, I think Keith raises a point that is definitely worth following up on. We should work with our teams to research every aspect of DRC and other key defense players, most notably their financial statements and bank accounts. If they did, in fact, help finance and plan the events of 9/11, there has to be some anomaly, something just a little out of whack, with their financial reporting. The amount of money we're talking about certainly has to be in the millions, and contrary to popular belief, that amount of money is just not that easy to hide, even in a privately held company like DRC." Patrick thought for a minute, and then added, "Keith, we would be honored to assist you with your research. All of us at LTBT, without exception, believe in uncovering the truth about 9/11, not seeking fame or glory for ourselves. Any assistance we can provide, whether research support, financial support, protection from the government agencies that are after you, anything – just reach out to us. It's in all of our best interest to keep you and Loren safe and for all of us to unlock the secrets of 9/11. Only by exposing the sick bastards behind that tragedy will we ever be safe."

"I appreciate your help, and like you, I want to see these bastards taken down. I'll keep working from my end as I'm able, and I'll try to stay in touch at least daily, if not more frequently."

Keith finished the call and checked on Loren at the helm. Everything was still looking good, so he ducked back down to the master stateroom. He went into his briefcase and removed the pistol, checking again to make sure that it was loaded and the safety was on. He tucked that gun into the back of his pants. Not the safest or most secure way to carry a pistol, he knew, but he didn't have a holster for it. He'd just have to carry it like your average street thug. He also took out the two rifles he had brought and loaded both of them. After ensuring that the safety was on, he left one beside the king size bed in the stateroom, and the other he took up to the helm area with him and sat it on the couch. Better to have one of them close at hand, he reasoned. Loren watched him handling the rifle, saw the gun tucked into his belt. She wasn't a big fan of guns, but right now, under these circumstances, she would have loved to have had a crate full of M-16's.

Keith stepped up to the helm and gave a quick glance at all of the main engine gauges; everything was perfect. He scanned the horizon for anything out of the ordinary but saw nothing. The river was empty, not unexpected on a day like this. He checked the GPS and chart plotter, confirming that it showed their position approximately parallel with the Coast Guard docks about a mile off their starboard side. He checked the radar and didn't see any other vessels anywhere, other than the large tanker currently tied at the oil refinery dock.

He went to the refrigerator and got them each another beer, then carried them back to the helm. "A toast to the lovely first mate for a job well done, and to the two of us for making the perfect getaway, if I do say so myself." With that, Keith reached his beer over to clink it against Loren's. "Great job at the helm, sweetie."

"Thanks, but I hope you're not jinxing us with that toast," she said in reply. She took a long sip from her beer, then reached up and gave Keith a kiss. "Let's just hope that our luck holds."

They didn't know it yet, but their luck was about to change, and not for the better.

⌘

As soon as Colonel Foster entered the Bunker he gave his first tactical order. "Get Hilton and the team that's been covering the eastern sector moving towards Gloucester ASAP. Send them the address and directions to their PDA's, and tell them not to waste any time dicking around over breakfast or coffee. Second, get those goddamn choppers moving that direction now."

Manning responded. "Already on both of those, boss. The choppers are at least an hour and a half out since we couldn't get them moving yesterday due to the weather. They're all airborne now, and two of them are heading in that general direction and waiting for our orders on a more detailed search grid. The other two birds are heading for rendezvous points with our other tactical teams to pick them up and get them moving towards the Hampton Roads area."

"Good job," said Foster. With that, he took his customary chair at the head of the conference table and jumped right into the fray with the rest of the team. It didn't take this group of experienced operatives very long to come up with a game plan. After studying maps and nautical charts of the area, the team had come up with a dozen or so possible places that they thought Bryant might try to reach for safe haven. While there were literally thousands of miles of coastline and thousands of places where he might be able to simply drop anchor and hide out, they all agreed that he'd want to be someplace that gave him access to major highways as well as necessities like food, water, and fuel. Just as important, they theorized, was the need to not be anywhere too isolated. That precluded just anchoring out in some private little cove off of the beaten path; Bryant had to assume that they'd eventually figure out that he was on his boat and begin an aerial or satellite search. A 78' boat would not be easy to hide under any circumstance, but at least it would be more likely to blend-in in at a marina that catered to larger boats and yachts. They came up with a list of the ten most likely destinations that ranged from marinas on the Elizabeth River in Norfolk and Portsmouth in the south all the way up to Annapolis and Baltimore, MD in the north.

"What do we know about his boat?" asked Foster. "Any idea how it's equipped or how much fuel he's carrying, the likely range, etc.?"

"We know that it's a 2-year old 78' Marlow Explorer, blue hull with cream superstructure. We have a copy of the original contract with the dealer and the Coast Guard documentation from the closing. Carries 3,000 gallons of fuel and a couple hundred of water, but we know it's equipped with a water maker, so he's pretty self-sufficient. The electronics list makes it look like he's equipped as well as your average fighter jet, if not better. They even have INMARSAT. Let me see what else…" Hanover trailed off as he read through the information. "Twin CAT diesels, two generators, speed about 20 knots at fast cruise. Probably consumes about 75 gallons per hour, at least, at cruise speed with those diesels. Oh, we also got his last fuel receipt from the marina.

Looks like he topped off the tanks about three weeks ago, put just over 1,100 gallons in."

"So basically, they're traveling in a well equipped condo that can move about 20 knots, if need be, and they have enough fuel to last a week or more if they're careful about where they go and how fast they try to get there." Then addressing the group and making sure he had their complete attention, Foster added, "And the fact that they're equipped with satcom tells us that he has internet access as well. What we've got here, essentially, are two people on the run that have every modern convenience at their disposal. I want our teams to track them down and take them both out ASAP, and I want it done quietly, before they reach any type of safe haven. There is no way that they have reached that safe haven yet; let's track them down and cut them off before that happens. Let's move it!"

In another 20 minutes the entire tactical plan was ready and the team ran through it quickly for Foster. Manning stood in front of the white board to lead the discussion. "Alright, Colonel, here's the plan. Hilton and his team are only about 10-15 minutes out from Bryant's marina in Gloucester. He will report in as soon as he reaches the place, but at this point we're working on the assumption that Bryant has at least a 1-3 hour head start on us. That tells us that our search needs to cover an area about this big." Manning drew a circle that extended about 35 miles upriver and all the way to the Chesapeake Bay and about 25 miles out in all directions. He continued, "Our best guess is that they probably wouldn't go upriver towards West Point. Too limiting. They'll almost certainly head downriver and either try to find cover in and around the Mobjack Bay area or head straight up or down the Chesapeake. I've ordered Hilton to commandeer the fastest boat he can find and start down the York River. The first two choppers should be able to provide him support and extra eyes within 30-45 minutes after he hits the river. I'm sending one of the birds towards Mobjack and the other towards Seaford and Poquoson on the south side of the river."

"Sounds like a good plan so far. What about the other teams?" asked Foster.

"After they pick up the two teams in our western sectors they're going to head to the Hampton Roads area as well. Team 3 will land at the Newport News/Williamsburg airport and secure a few rental cars in case we don't nail Bryant out on the water and he somehow makes it back to land. They'll keep the rental cars staged right near the airport and wait for our orders. Team 4 will do a quick search upriver, just in case, and then swing back downriver and coordinate their search with the other two groups."

'That works for now, and as always, we'll make adjustments as the situation warrants. Good work everyone. Bob, make it happen."

Within minutes the DCG team had sent the operations plan out to all of the teams and they were moving. Everyone had their orders and understood their roles. They also understood that there was serious money being offered to the person or team that made the hit on Bryant and Loren Davis. And no one, anywhere, was more about the money than a soldier of fortune.

⌘

HILTON AND HIS TEAM OF two operatives, Alan Hamilton and Derek Norman, got to York River Yacht Haven and quickly assessed that Bryant's boat was gone. They took a quick look around the marina to see what their choices were for something small and fast to use to go after their prey. Not too many choices, they were surprised to find. Lots of sailboats, totally worthless. Dozens of large motor yachts and sport convertibles, but nothing fast. Hell, most wouldn't be any faster, if even as fast, as Bryant's. Finally they spotted what they needed, and fortunately, it sat on one of the docks farthest from the marina office. "Let's go," said Hilton. "That center console over there."

They climbed on board the boat, a 27' Fountain with twin 250 horsepower Mercury outboard motors, and grabbed their gear. Hamilton found the battery switch and set it for 'Both' batteries while Norman and Hilton looked around for the keys. If necessary they had no qualms about hotwiring the boat, but they knew that most boat owners were just dumb or naïve enough to leave their keys hidden somewhere on board. "Found 'em," said Norman. "Tucked up here by the starboard rod racks."

Hilton grabbed the keys, tilted both motors down into the water, and then fired them up. Both motors put up a struggle before starting, and they both idled rough and smoked like hell. "Fucking two-stroke pieces of shit," Hilton muttered to the others. "Get these lines off and let's get out of here before somebody calls the fire department with all of this damn smoke."

They dropped the lines and Hilton idled out of the slip. He was tempted to just firewall the thing, but the last thing he needed was to call any attention to them. As it was, nobody would probably give them a second thought. "Bundle up boys, it's going to be a cold, wet ride." Like they didn't know that. They were all already freezing and they hadn't even starting running yet, and there was no doubt that this center console was going to be a wet ride with all of this wind and the choppy waves.

As soon as they cleared the first buoy Hilton hit the throttles. Once Hilton fire-walled them the boat took off like a bat out of hell, jumping quickly on plane and leaping over the waves at better than 55 mph. The Fountain was built for running fast over offshore swells on the way to the fishing grounds, but the waves on the river today were a whole different challenge. The waves were short, steep, and coming seemingly from all directions as the easterly winds pushed hard against a strong outgoing tide, and the fact that Hilton had, on several occasions, had to jerk the wheel to dodge debris floating in the water only made an already uncomfortable ride that much worse. Several times Hilton lost control of the boat, and Norman had already fallen hard against the starboard gunwale. There was nowhere to hide from the cold and the spray, either. They were all soaked within minutes, a problem only made worse when Hilton stuffed the bow in a large wave as he turned downriver after passing the last harbor entrance buoy. A virtual wall of water hit the 3 men, all of them able to maintain their footing only because of the death grip they had on the grab rails situated around the helm. Had the boat not had a self-bailing cockpit with large scuppers at the stern they would have been in trouble. Even as it was, they had cold, muddy water swirling around their ankles for the next few minutes. Hilton wisely slowed it down just a bit to maintain control and, hopefully, not beat the bottom right out of the boat.

About six miles ahead, *Kismet* was moving comfortably eastward at a steady 10 knots. Other than the occasional spray on the windshield you would have never known that conditions were so snotty. The interior of the boat was a very comfortable 68 degrees, and Keith had just made them each a little snack. As he was coming back to the helm, Loren said to him, "Uh oh. I see a boat on the radar, and they're coming from the direction of our marina."

"Let me see," said Keith, trying not to sound too alarmed. Nobody with any senses would be out on a day like today, he thought to himself. Hell, he hadn't even seen any of the commercial watermen out here today. As he studied the radar, he noted that the boat had in fact just left Sarah's Creek, the body of water where York River Yacht Haven is located. And the guy was flying! Watching the radar, it was evident that the guy had to be running nearly 50 knots. Shit, Keith thought. This can't be good. When the radar screen showed that the boat was turning downriver, that sealed it for Keith. "I think we're going to be having company," he said as calmly as he could. "Whoever the guy is, he's flying, and nobody in their right mind would be running at those speeds today, if they're even dumb enough to be out on the water in the first place."

Loren was fighting the growing panic she was feeling. "I didn't think there was any way they'd be able to track us this fast. God damn! What do we do? We can't outrun them, that's for sure."

"No, we definitely can't outrun them, but hopefully we can outsmart them. Let's start by increasing our speed to give us more time before they catch up to us. You keep the helm, but bump up the speed to about 18 knots. That should at least give us an extra 5-10 minutes before they catch up to us."

"What then?" Loren wanted to hear some sort of concrete plan, and quickly.

"I'm going to call Patrick Treadwell and Jeff Anders real quick and let them know what's happening. If nothing else, I want someone to be aware of what happened out here in case something does happen to us. Then, I'm going to take the .30 caliber rifle and my handgun up to the bridge, maybe see if I can hold them off from up high. They probably don't know that we're armed"

"God only knows what kind of guns these guys have. We're going to be sitting ducks."

"No, we won't. Sitting ducks don't shoot back." Keith hugged her from behind and kissed her neck. "I'm going to leave the other gun right here with you by the helm. If you have to, pick it up, click off the safety, and shoot at anything that moves. Except me, of course." He smiled at her, trying to put on a brave face. She didn't buy it for a second; she knew that he was scared shitless, just like she was.

"Should we call the Coast Guard for help?" she asked, almost imploring.

"No, we're on our own. The Coast Guard base is several miles back, and by the time they get one of their boats moving out of Wormley Creek it will be too late. These guys are moving way too fast for that. Let's just hope that the element of surprise is enough to give us an advantage. If things get too bad, you set the autopilot and head below for cover, but you keep that rifle with you. Got it?"

"Yes, I got it." Tears started welling in her eyes, but she didn't want to lose control now. Their lives depended on them keeping calm and springing a trap on the men that were out to kill them. She knew that Keith was just putting on a brave face for her, but she was so glad to be with him. He may have been a kind man, a gentle man, an academic, but she knew one thing: when it came down to it, he knew how to fight and he would fight. His time at the Naval Academy and in the Navy, as well as his many years as a top athlete, did a lot to toughen him up. They might well be outnumbered and outgunned, but she knew that he would take some of them down before he'd let anything happen to them, particularly to her. Before he went to make his call, she reached for him. "Keith?" He turned to her. "I love you. I just wanted you to know. I'm scared as hell, but I love you and I'm glad we're in this together."

"I love you, too," he said, giving her a long hug and a kiss. He wiped the tears from her eyes, then said, "Don't worry. We'll get out of this. Those assholes won't know what him them, and besides, we're the good guys. The good guys have to win, right?" he said with a smile.

"Let's hope so this time, at least. Go ahead and make your call, make sure that LTBT knows what's happening. And make sure, if anything should happen to us that they promise to follow-up on your research until they find The Truth and bring these bastards down!" The tears were starting to flow again, and she turned away from Keith and tried to focus her attention on the waves and all of the debris she saw floating in the water.

Keith grabbed the cell phone and called the next number in the sequence provided by the leaders of LTBT. This time Patrick Treadwell answered. "Keith, I didn't expect to hear back from you so soon. Is everything OK?"

'Probably not. I'm tracking a small boat approaching us at a very high rate of speed, coming from the same harbor where we left from earlier."

"Couldn't that just be a coincidence? After all, it is the weekend."

"No way," said Keith. "We've had several days of absolute shit weather, and today isn't a helluva lot better. Very overcast, very windy, and absolutely rough as hell. There's not another boat to be seen anywhere on the river, or anywhere on radar, for that matter. No, whoever this is they have to be after us. Nobody in their right mind would be out here today, and definitely not moving at 50+ mph."

"Shit. Not good. Whoever these people are, they're not stopping by for lunch. I take it you're in no position to outrun these guys, right?" asked Patrick.

"Not even close. On a good day I top out in the 20 knot range, and these guys are easily twice as fast as that. I figure I've got just a few minutes until they're on us." Keith tried looking out the salon door, and he was just able to make out the boat coming towards them in the distance. He could see the spray flying and knew that they must be taking a helluva beating, but it didn't appear that they were slowing down any to make the ride more comfortable.

"Do you have any way of defending yourselves?" Patrick wanted to know.

Keith didn't want to say too much, not just in the interest of time, but also because he was a little nervous about the call being monitored. "Yeah, I think we can hold them off for a bit, but it depends on how many of them there are and what they have for firepower."

"Look, there's nothing that we can do to help you in this situation, obviously. But let me tell you this: in our experience, every time we research reports of government action or hear from survivors of this kind of government action, they never send in just one guy or one team. If you're seeing one boat coming after you, that means that either (a) they're the closest ones to the scene, and others are on their way, or (b) you're not seeing everyone involved in the chase. Are there still no other boats on your radar?"

Keith went to the helm and checked the radar. "No, just our friends coming up from behind, a little less than 3 miles at this point."

"Then I'd start looking to the skies, my friend. If they have re-tasked satellites to look for you, we're screwed. But I doubt they've done that, at least not yet. That always raises too many questions around the other intelligence agencies. Instead, I'd keep my eye out for any helicopters that might be searching for you. I'd bet my ass that there is at least one or two up there looking for you right now, and even if the helicopters aren't armed military types, you can bet that the people on board are armed and ready to take you out."

"The news just keeps getting better and better, doesn't it?" said Keith. "If anything happens to us, I want you and LTBT to tell the world what happened here, and I want you to keep digging until you find the answers that these bastards are trying so hard to keep secret. Don't let The Truth stay hidden."

"We won't, my friend. You do what you can to defend yourself, and get back to us as soon as you can and let us know your status and if there's anything you need. If we need to get to you to bring you in, we'll do it. Just stay alive. I'm going to get to Jeff Anders right away and see if we can figure out a way to try to run some interference for you with the backup teams that I'm sure are out there. If you can get past the primary team maybe we can clear the way with the others, at least."

"I appreciate anything that you can do. Hopefully I'll be back in touch with you within the hour. If not, assume the worst and start doing whatever it takes to bring these fuckers down." With that, Keith clicked off and stowed the cell phone in his jacket pocket. He went below and got all of the ammunition that he could grab for both rifles and the pistol, along with the binoculars that he kept onboard. As he was about to head back up he remembered the Motorola walkie-talkies that they'd bought and decided to bring them up as well. They might prove useful while he stays hidden from sight up on the bridge.

"Alright, sweetie, here's what I'm going to do. I'm going up on the bridge and try to set up a little ambush for our friends. I'll leave you this rifle and extra ammunition, and I'm going to take the .30 caliber with the scope up on the bridge with me, along with the pistol and extra ammo. You keep the boat as steady as you can, and stay down low and away from the windows. The last thing we need is you getting cut by a lot of flying glass. And before the shooting starts, you set the autopilot and be ready to duck below. These guys will probably start shooting before they get close enough to be accurate, so God only knows what they're going to hit. The one thing in our favor is that it's so rough they probably can't get off a clean shot, but hopefully I'll be able to from up high. And here, take this walkie-talkie so we can communicate. I'll be trying to stay hidden, so I won't be able to use the bridge radio. Hopefully these will do the trick. Are you OK?"

"Yeah, I'm OK. I know what we have to do. You just be careful, and try to stay down. I don't want anything to happen to you." The tears were falling again, and she was trembling. Keith held her tight, lightly stroking her hair and whispering reassurances to her. He knew that anything he could say would ring hollow at this point. All he could think to say was, "I love you." Keith kissed her one long, last kiss, then took a quick look at the radar to see how much distance separated him from possible death. Just over 2 miles, maybe 4 or 5 minutes. He grabbed his things and headed for the bridge.

He was counting on the fact that the men that were following them were taking such a beating and hanging on so tightly for dear life that they wouldn't be able to see him scurry up to the bridge. He lay down prone on the bridge deck between the helm and the dinghy, a 13' Zodiac RIB. The Zodiac sat in chocks that held it about 12" off of the deck, and Keith brought the scoped rifle under the tender and pointed the long barrel straight down *Kismet*'s wake. He used the small duffel bag that held the extra ammunition to prop up the barrel and help keep it steady. He then reached behind him and brought the binoculars to his eyes, and he was just able to discern that there were three men onboard. Three against one, he thought. Hopefully the element of surprise would even those odds just a bit. "Keep on coming, you bastards. Just a little bit closer," Keith mumbled to himself. He had never asked for this fight, but this is one that he had every intention of winning.

Chapter 13

Hilton finally had the *Kismet* in his sights. Thank God, he thought. The waves had continued to grow as they moved further east and got closer to the Bay. With the wind still blowing hard out of the east-northeast, any land protection that they'd had as they'd started downriver was quickly fading. He and his team had tried to call Foster to let him know that they'd located Bryant, but between the wind, the spray, and the bouncing around, neither Hilton nor either member of his team could make the call. The boat was equipped with a VHF radio, but even if the antenna hadn't snapped off from the beating that the boat was taking there was no other team within range to hear them. It was all that they could do to hang on as the boat launched off one wave and then another, all the while lurching along right on the ragged edge. On more than one occasion both Hamilton and Norman almost went overboard, and Norman, especially, was having a hard time holding on since he'd taken a nasty fall on the deck and sprained his right wrist.

"Listen up guys," Hilton yelled, hoping to be heard over the whining of the two big outboards and the wind rushing past at more than 50 mph. "I'm going to try to come up just off the starboard stern of Bryant's boat, and you guys hit them with a few bursts from your AK-47's. I'm hoping that they'll just stop and we'll go onboard and take care of them once and for all, but it probably won't be that simple." Hilton stopped talking when he noticed an especially large wave getting ready to hit them just off the port bow, but before he could react and turn into it the wave hit them at an awkward angle, and the boat, moving as fast as it was, went totally airborne at an unnatural, twisting angle. The engines revved all the way to their limits, and all three men lost their footing. The boat hit with an almost sickening crash, more on its side than on its bottom, and only by the grace of God did it not turn over.

As the boat hit the water it snapped back hard to the left, allowing the boat's running surface to get tucked back under where it should be. Hilton was on the deck, barely hanging on to the steering wheel. He managed to reach up and yank back on the throttles to slow the boat down before even struggling to his feet, knowing that if he didn't get the boat under control they were surely going to be killed. As the boat lost forward momentum and started to rock in the swells, he immediately took stock of the situation and saw that Norman was barely able to get to his knees, and Hamilton had a major gash on his forehead that was pouring blood, as was his mouth. It appeared that a couple of teeth had been knocked out in the fall. Both men were moaning and in obvious pain. Christ, not exactly the type of warriors that Hilton wanted and needed to go into battle.

"Norman! Hamilton! Are you guys OK? Can you hear me?" screamed Hilton. Even with the boat idling in neutral it was still hard to hear over the wind and the motors.

"You goddamn idiot!" screamed Norman. "You almost got us killed! I told you that you needed to slow down and try to keep this goddamn boat under control!"

"Shut the fuck up, you whiny little bitch! We're almost caught up to Bryant's boat, so get up and get ready."

Hamilton could barely speak through the blood and the pain, but he managed to scream, "I swear, after we kill Bryant and the bitch I'm going to kill you next, you stupid bastard." If he hadn't dropped his sidearm pistol when he fell, he would have brought it out and killed Hilton right here on the spot. He looked around the boat as best he could, but his pistol was apparently gone, lost over the side of the boat. Just fucking great, he thought.

"You're going to have to keep this damn boat steady for us to be able to control our fire. We're not going to be able to get any shots into the engines or anywhere else that is going to shut it down, so we're probably going to have to board them after we've sent them running below with our first barrage. Can you run this goddamn boat well enough for us to board them?" Norman asked the question, but he had his doubts based on what he'd seen so far of Hilton's capabilities at the helm.

"Yeah, I can do that. You just make sure that you guys blast the shit out of that boat first, especially along the windows near the salon and the lower helm. That will send them scurrying for cover." Hilton was the only one that believed his own cockiness. Then he added, "Get your weapons ready. We're only a few hundred yards behind them, and as soon as you're locked and loaded I'm going to try to make a charge off of their starboard side and you guys open up on them."

Norman crawled forward and grabbed the two AK-47's from the waterproof canvas bag stowed in front of the helm. He handed one to Hamilton, along with three extra clips. He kept the other for himself, along with three spare clips. Since Hilton was concentrating on driving – and obviously, he wasn't worth a shit at that either – Norman didn't hand him another weapon. Hilton did have a 9mm in a holster on his belt, but if everything went as planned he shouldn't even need to draw his weapon. Norman and Hamilton each got slowly to their feet and readied their weapons. Norman wasn't sure how he was going to handle this, having one wrist sprained so badly that he could barely close it around the grab rail to steady himself, while the other hand held an automatic weapon that was going to be jerking wildly from the recoil. And on top of that, they're bouncing along off of 4-5 foot waves. Thankfully it wasn't precision shooting, he told himself. Just point and shoot at a 78' boat and hope that you hit something, anything.

"OK, guys, here we go!" shouted Hilton as he accelerated the boat once again. "Wait until I tell you to start shooting."

⌘

KEITH HAD SEEN THE BOAT almost flip over, and he was very disappointed, and shocked, to see it recover. He wondered if the three men on board had gotten cold feet after that or if they'd been injured. The boat had definitely stopped and was bobbing wildly in the swells. Probably just wishful thinking on his part, he realized. *Kismet* kept moving steadily east, still making the same 18 knots, and Keith kept a watchful eye on his pursuers with the binoculars. He could see that the helmsman was yelling at the others, but he couldn't see either one of them. Finally he saw one of them crawling on his hands and knees, and then slowly pulling himself up. Keith smiled to himself. That guy was obviously in a lot of pain, probably bumped and bruised from the rough ride and their near disaster of a few minutes ago. Maybe the third man is even worse off, Keith figured, since he still hadn't gotten up.

Keith called down to Loren using the walkie-talkie, but he kept it short just in case. "They've stopped, at least for the moment. They almost lost it a minute ago on a bad wave, so they're probably regrouping a bit. They might have even sustained injuries."

"OK. I'm maintaining course until you tell me different," was Loren's reply.

Keith looked back at the center console, and he saw them pick up speed once again. This is it, he thought to himself. They're going to come at us fast and hard, try to spray us with bullets and either kill us or stop and board us. Keith decided to let them get within about 150-200 yards and then try to take one of them out with the rifle before they'd even started shooting. He assumed that they'd be using automatic weapons, but what they'd gain in firepower they'd probably be losing in accuracy. Keith keyed the microphone of the walkie-talkie. "Here they come" is all he said. Down below, Loren was doing her best to keep a watchful eye on what was in front of them but still stay as far away from the windows as she could. She set the autopilot so she'd be ready to move immediately when the bullets started flying, but she was determined to keep a lookout for as long as possible in case she had to veer off to avoid the debris in the water.

Keith set down the binoculars and calmly brought the rifle scope to his eye. He clicked the safety off and had his finger resting on the trigger. He had to wait for just the right shot, he told himself. The pursuit boat was bouncing around like crazy in the waves, and even *Kismet* had a little bit of up and down motion as it punched through the head seas. Couple that with a 20-25 knot breeze, and even the best marksman would not consider any shot at this distance a slam-dunk. When they were about 125 yards off of his stern Keith saw one of the shooters start to get to a kneeling position at the bow. This was the shot he'd been waiting for. He breathed in, and then as he exhaled he squeezed the trigger. Shit! Just as he was pulling the trigger the center console lurched to the right and his shot missed altogether. Keith cursed under his breath. Fortunately, with the loud whine of the outboards and the wind the pursuers didn't even know they'd been shot at. Keith readied another shot. He needed to hurry because they were closing in on them quickly, but he didn't want to rush the shot and miss again. Wait for it…wait for it…now! Keith squeezed the trigger and he put a shot right into the chest of Derek Norman, killing him instantly. Hilton and Hamilton didn't see where the shot had come from, but they knew damn well they were taking fire.

Hamilton stood up and opened fire down the starboard side of *Kismet*. Bullets tore into the beautiful blue hull and windows along the salon area shattered as a dozen or more bullets hit the boat in a single blast. Loren headed down the companionway and kept low, knowing that there was virtually no way a bullet could penetrate to where she was. She wanted to rush out and see that Keith was alright, but she couldn't dare head through the salon now with bullets flying.

The center console was now only about 30 yards off the starboard stern of *Kismet*, and Hamilton was popping another clip into his weapon. Keith realized that this may be his only chance. Dropping the rifle on the bridge deck, he grabbed for his pistol and got up to his knees behind the dinghy. He clicked off the safety and then raised the pistol, taking the best aim that he could under the circumstances, and quickly squeezed off six quick shots. Only two of them hit Hamilton, one in the side of the head and one in the shoulder, but it was enough. He was dead before he hit the deck.

Hilton was shocked to be under attack and see two of his men down, but he quickly recovered. Drawing his own weapon he started firing at Bryant up on the flying bridge. The shots were scattered all over the place by the motion of the boat, none of them even coming close to the target. Realizing that he needed to back away from the yacht and regroup, if not wait for reinforcements, Hilton turned the wheel hard to starboard. Seconds later he felt a searing pain in his left shoulder as a large caliber bullet tore into him from behind. Hilton screamed and fell across the wheel, barely managing to pull back on the throttles as he fell to the deck. Then he heard two shots in pretty rapid succession, each shot putting a large hole into the back of the Mercury outboards. Both engines died, and as the boat lost all forward motion it slowly turned sideways into the waves and started rocking and rolling in the troughs.

Keith grabbed both of his weapons and descended from the bridge as fast as he could. "Loren! Loren! Are you OK?" Where are you?"

"I'm down here! I'm OK." That wasn't exactly true, she knew. She wasn't hurt, but she was more terrified than she'd ever been in her life.

Keith ran to the helm and pulled the boat back to neutral, then turned to look out the starboard side windows to see where the pursuit boat was. It was bobbing in the waves a couple of hundred yards behind them and off to the right. Loren came up from the stairs below and threw her arms around him, crying. "Are you OK? Are you hurt?" she wanted to know, between sobs.

"No, I'm fine. Really." He held her tight as she cried on his shoulder, though he never took his eye off the other boat. "I took out two of them, and I've wounded the guy at the helm pretty badly, if he's even still alive." He held her for several minutes, hoping this would give her some comfort or reassurance that things were really OK. Keith knew that, at best, things were OK for just a short period, but he didn't feel the need to bring that up to Loren at this point. Finally Keith whispered to Loren, "We need to go over there and see who these guys are and see if they're still alive. Think you can run us over there slowly while I keep them covered from up on the bridge?" Keith brushed the hair out of her eyes and looked directly at her, making sure that she was really OK.

"Yes, I can do that." Loren looked out the window to get her bearings on the target. "I'll spin us around and approach them from the far side so I can make sure that we don't drift down on them."

"Perfect," said Keith. "And go ahead and turn on the bow and stern thrusters as well. That may help you keep the boat positioned exactly where we need it. I'm heading back on up to the bridge." As soon as Keith was back up on the bridge he took a minute to reload each of the guns. There were some bullets left in each, but just in case things went to shit he wanted to be ready.

Loren spun the boat around and set a course for the center console, careful to allow for the waves and the wind and the tides by not getting too close. She was also giving the boat a fairly wide berth because she was aware that there could be a wounded killer onboard playing possum and just waiting for them to get close enough to open fire. She passed the boat about 20 yards off of the bow and then turned to put it on a parallel drift. Keith obviously had a much better vantage point from up on the bridge. She was able to see the bodies lying on the deck near the bow, but she hadn't yet seen the helmsman. She'd seen dead bodies before, and even come upon the scene of car accidents where people were injured, but this was the first time she'd ever seen a gunshot victim in real life, and it wasn't pretty. It was also, it went without saying, the first time that she'd ever been involved in causing another person's death, regardless of how justified that death might be. She wasn't sure what she was supposed to feel, but at this point she was too numb, too terrified, to feel much of anything. Then she heard Keith yell over to the other boat.

"You, get up slowly. Don't make me put another bullet in you." Keith waited a few seconds and saw the helmsman stir. "Get up. Now."

"I'm wounded, you bastard."

"Yes, and your friends are dead. And if you don't stand up right now, you're going to be dead, too. Stand up slowly, and drop your weapon overboard. If you make a move to use that gun I'll kill you where you sit."

Hilton threw his pistol overboard, as ordered, and then slowly pulled himself to his feet using his one good arm. His left shoulder was shattered, and he had no doubt that he'd probably bleed to death before he could get medical attention. As he stood up, he slowly lifted his head and looked up at Keith with a pained, but very sadistic, smile on his face.

Keith froze in disbelief, totally dumbstruck for a moment. The sick son of a bitch smiling back at him was Mathew Hilton, one of the students from his Conspiracy class. It took a minute for Keith to come back to reality after the shock of seeing Hilton, but when he did he yelled out so that Loren could hear him. "Loren, come out here and get a good look at this piece of shit. His name is Mathew Hilton, or at least that's what he tells everybody. He's a student in my Conspiracy class. I guess we now know how all of this information reached our friends in Washington and caused this whole clusterfuck. Our friend here must have been feeding them information ever since the class started."

Loren was stunned into silence. They had known all along that there could be someone at the school keeping an eye on them, but my God! This man, this…..assassin, sitting in Keith's class for the whole semester, listening to Keith teach, interacting with other students. He could have killed Keith on a hundred different occasions, yet the two of them had been totally oblivious. The thought almost made her ill.

"What's the matter, Dr. Bryant? Didn't expect to see one of your students leading the charge to take you down, did you? You should have just kept your nose out of business and politics that don't concern you. If your friend Lowell would have done that, I wouldn't have had to go in and snap his geeky little neck."

Keith knew that Hilton was trying to bait him, but he wasn't taking it. "I think right now you better be more concerned about your present situation, not your past little misdeeds. If you expect to live through this day, I suggest you start talking very quickly about who you're working for and why they're after us."

Hilton just laughed at Keith. "Fuck you, professor. Even if I knew who was paying me to kill you, do you think I'd ever tell you? What are you going to do? Torture me? Puhhh-lease… You can't do anything to me that real soldiers, real men, haven't done to me in the past. You don't have the skills, and even if you did, you don't have the stones. Go fuck yourself."

Keith had expected as much. No doubt Hilton was a tough son of a bitch, and even if Keith were inclined to inflict some serious pain, he knew that this was neither the time nor the place. He remembered what Patrick Treadwell had said: if one team is after you, it's a virtual certainty that there are others. After considering all of this for a moment, Keith finally spoke. "You know what? I think you're probably right. I can't break you. But that's OK with me. It just means that I don't have to waste my time with you." Keith raised his pistol and shot Hilton right between the eyes. He fell to the deck, right between the helm and the motors. "That's for Lowell Westbrook, you bastard."

Loren screamed when Keith fired the gun. She was shocked that he killed a man standing barely 25 feet from him, a man that was looking him right in the eye. Keith came down from the bridge and walked to the helm. He saw the look of shock on Loren's face. "I'm sorry that you had to be here to see that, but that man killed Lowell and led a team that tried to kill you and me. I couldn't let him walk away from that, especially when it's a virtual certainty that there are other hit teams out here looking for us right now."

"My God. I don't know what to say….It's just not something that I've ever seen happen, not in real life." She tried hard to be stoic, to keep herself from crying, but it just wasn't working. The tensions of the last few days had been bad enough, but now, with what they'd just lived through over the last half-hour or so…..Loren went and sat on the couch and buried her face in her hands.

"Hopefully you'll never have to see it again, but for now I did what had to be done." With that, Keith took the helm and swung *Kismet* around to the other side of the center console. He had to time this maneuver just right or he could be putting the two of them in danger. He brought the bow of the big Marlow slowly, ever so slowly, up to the port side of the center console, then using the engines in combination with the wave motion, he let his bow push the much smaller Fountain over on its side until it tipped completely and turned bottom up. He was able to see the three bodies go over the side and into the water, and he knew that their guns and everything else on deck had surely fallen to the bottom. He quickly put *Kismet* into reverse and backed well away from the now overturned boat. Once clear, he put the big boat up on plane and set a course for the south side of the river. All thoughts of trying to make it as far as St. Michaels were now out the window. "You take it easy for a few minutes, try to relax. I need to get us the hell out of here."

Keith set a course for a narrow cut between Goodwin Island and the tip of Seaford called the Thorofare, although he'd heard many of the locals call it by another, much more appropriate name over the years: The Sandbox. Normally, he would have never attempted to use this shortcut. *Kismet* had a draft of nearly 5 feet, and there was a section of the Sandbox where there was often barely 3 feet right in the middle of the marked channel. However, with the heavy rains and strong northeast winds of the past few days, Keith knew that the tides were running several feet above normal. If he could make it past the first two buoys he knew he could make it easily through the rest of the cut. It only took them about five minutes to reach the first set of channel markers, and Keith didn't even pull the boat back off of plane. It had been a few years since he'd been though here, and always in much smaller boats. He hoped that he still had enough local knowledge to keep from running this big beast aground. As he went past the first markers he kept a close eye on the depth finder. The transducer for the depth finder was made of heavy bronze and was set only about a foot shallower than the boat's keel, about 2/3 the way back towards the stern. Keith just hoped that he wouldn't stick the bow in mud while the depth finder was still showing several feet of water beneath them – a distinct possibility when the bow was 60' forward of the transducer. *Kismet* kept on rolling along at just a shade over 20 knots, and soon Keith realized that they were definitely past the shallowest parts. The depth finder had never shown less than 3.5 feet beneath them. He finally allowed himself to breathe a sigh of relief.

The channel brought them back out into the Bay, and he continued to follow the markers until he reached the distant end of the entry channel. He scanned the sky every few minutes for approaching helicopters, but the only thing he saw was an AirTran passenger jet on approach for Newport

News/Williamsburg airport a few miles away. Keith set his course for the entry channel to the Poquoson River, just a couple of miles away and easily within site even on this snotty day. He was tempted to set the autopilot for a few minutes so he could go sit with Loren, but he knew better than to leave the helm unattended on the nicest of days, much less today. The water still had lots of junk floating around, plus there were still a few crab pots out here. They really didn't need to hit anything or get one of the props tangled up in a pot.

Keith spoke to Loren. "Sweetie? Come up here and stand with me." He held out his hand for her.

Loren slowly got up from the couch and wiped her eyes with the back of her hands. "God, I need a tissue. I must look a mess. Is my mascara running?"

"Yes, but you're still beautiful to me." He pulled her gently to him and kissed her on the cheek. "Why don't you go below and get a tissue then come on back up here with me. I'm taking us towards Poquoson." She did as he suggested. As she came back up the steps Keith said, "Would you mind handing me that cell phone out of my jacket, please. I want to call Patrick and Jeff to let them know that we're OK, at least for now."

"What do you mean?" Loren asked.

"Hilton and those other goons on that boat aren't going to be the only team after us. There are, or soon will be, others. We're not going to be able to stay with the boat, that's for sure. Whoever is after us knew about the boat, knew where to look for us. They're smart, very well informed. We have to be even more careful than we've been so far. We're going to have to get back to land and get far away from this area, and quickly.

Keith dialed the number for LTBT and Patrick picked up on the first ring. "This is Patrick. Are you guys OK?" He was practically hyperventilating, Keith could hear.

'Yeah, we're OK. I managed to take care of our three friends in the boat that was pursuing us. I recognized one of them. He'd been posing as a student in my Conspiracy class and went by the name of Mathew Hilton."

"Holy shit! No wonder they seemed to know so much about what went on in your class. Did this Mathew Hilton individual have anything to do with killing Lowell Westbrook?"

"Yes, he admitted as much to me, actually bragging about it before I killed him." Keith was not proud of what he'd done but he knew it was what *had* to be done. "About those other hit teams, though, I haven't seen any of their *compadres* yet. I'm assuming that there are still others out there, right?"

"Right, but I do have some good news. We found out that there were a total of four choppers heading your way. Two of them had to make stops near Charlottesville and Lynchburg to pick up other teams of operatives before heading east, and they've been detained on the ground by the local police and the FBI is on their way to interrogate them."

"How the hell did you know about them in the first place, and then how did you manage to get the police and FBI to detain them?" Keith asked, just totally flabbergasted at the resourcefulness of LTBT.

"Let's just say that Jeff managed to access some information about flight plans and tap into some communications between the pilots and the local air traffic controllers. The authorities decided to pay both groups a little visit when they landed to pick up the hit teams because they received an anonymous tip that a group of terrorists were planning to disperse a chemical or biological agent using helicopters as the delivery vehicle. Pretty ingenious, don't you think?" Patrick was practically giggling.

Keith was awestruck but couldn't help a little chuckle, too. It definitely helped to break the tension a bit. "Genius. Absolute genius. So I guess our friends out there in Lynchburg and Charlottesville are getting a little interrogation and body cavity probe right about now, eh? That's great. What about the other two choppers, or should I ask?"

"One of them was sent to search along the Mobjack Bay area, including out around the Severn, East, and Ware rivers. With all of the distance they've traveled and the strong headwinds they've been contending with, they just reported that they were low on fuel and looking for a place to set down and fuel-up. I'm not sure where that will be, but the FBI has already sent an alert to the Gloucester and Mathews County sheriffs. I don't think they're going to be a threat, at least not today."

"So that leaves one that could be a threat, right?"

"Unfortunately, yes. At last report they were heading back downriver and were in the vicinity of the Naval Weapons Station. That's what, maybe 4-5 minutes flying time from your current position?" asked Patrick.

"Yeah, I'd say that's about right." Keith thought for a minute. "I might have an idea that can buy us an extra 5-10 minutes, maybe give us a chance to set a trap for these guys."

"OK, let's hear it." Patrick was eager to hear any idea that might put the other team of assassins out of commission.

Keith continued. "Can you send out a broadcast on their radio frequency asking them to be on the lookout for a small boat that was reported capsized near the mouth of the York River? Tell them that there were reports that three men were onboard, possible gunfire reported, and so on, and they'll probably want to haul-ass down there, assuming that it's their team."

"That just might work. I can't be sure, but I don't think they know the status of the team that was after you, or at least nothing that we've monitored makes it sound like they have any idea." Patrick considered this, and then said, "Maybe the team that was after you were never able to let anyone know that they'd located you or were getting ready to attack."

"I think that's probably the case. It's so rough, and they were taking such a beating chasing us, that I would doubt seriously that they were able to use any kind of cell phone or satellite communications. Their boat was an open center console, so there was no way for them to get out of the wind or the spray. Most communication devices would have been worthless under those conditions. And, I did notice that the VHF antenna on their boat was snapped in half and dangling from the coaxial cable. No way they'd have been able to use that to call anyone."

"Good," said Patrick. "I'll be back to you in just a couple of minutes and let you know if we were able to reach the chopper and get them redirected. In the meantime, you come up with something to take advantage of the situation."

Keith continued towards Poquoson, finally reaching the entrance channel between Red #6 and Red #8 markers. He got ready to turn the boat to starboard to follow the channel towards Poquoson Marina, but then it dawned on him that doing that could put them in even more peril. If he went into the Poquoson River and was forced to make a stand there, every person living along the waterfront would hear the gunfire and see the boat and the helicopter shooting at each other. The police and God only knows who else would be all over them in no time -- if they were still alive, that is. The police, and certainly the FBI and other Federal agencies, were simply not to be trusted at this point. If the government was capable of planting an assassin in his classroom and sending multiple hit teams to kill them, there's no telling what kind of stories they might be willing to tell the police if they were captured or killed. No, he and Loren couldn't just try to outrun this hit team. They had to take them out of the game before trying to ditch the boat and leave the area.

"Loren, can you get our emergency ditch bag from down below and bring it up here, please? Bring the cash as well, and see if you can find some waterproof bags, maybe a couple of garbage bags, to put it in. Oh, and grab something warm to wear, too. For both of us."

"What's wrong? Are we taking on water?"

"No," replied Keith. "I have an idea about how we're going to even the odds with our next group of visitors." While Loren went below to gather their things, Keith turned the boat back out towards the Bay. He was about to try something that was probably a little bit insane, but what the hell was not insane at this point? Keith turned the boat out of the channel and started towards the Poquoson Flats, a notoriously tricky and shallow area right off of the marshes that protect Poquoson from the Chesapeake Bay. The flats extended out for several miles, and though you sometimes saw skiffs or boats designed for shallow water running along in here, you definitely didn't see large motor yachts. Once again, though, the storm tides were working in his favor, at least until low tide. Thankfully that wasn't for a few more hours. He managed to get the boat about a mile outside of the channel, and when he looked at the depth finder he still had a little over 3 feet of water under the keel. That's probably close enough, Keith thought to himself. He released the bow anchor, afraid to risk having the boat drift aground.

Loren came up from below with all of their stuff. Looking around at where they were sitting, she was stunned. "I can't believe you were able to get all the way over here, even with these tides. So what are we going to do now, sit here and wait for them with a big bulls-eye on our backs?"

"No, actually. We're going to abandon ship. I'm going to drop the Zodiac in the water and we're going to take it away from the boat."

"And do what? Cut through the marsh channels and make a run for the marina? If these guys are in a helicopter they're still going to be able to see us if they get here before we get to the marina."

"That's true. That's why we're not running to the marina, or anywhere for that matter. That's probably what they'll assume, but hopefully by then it will be too late for them."

"So where do we go then?" she asked.

"Right over there," Keith said as he pointed out the window. Keith pointed in the direction of a duck blind that was about 150' away from the boat. "We're going to take cover in there, and when they come to check out *Kismet* we're going to open fire on the bastards and try to take them down. Simple as that."

"I'm sorry, did you say 'simple as that'?" She laughed a little bit at that statement. "Did one of the bullets graze that brain of yours back there earlier? You think the two of us are going to be able to shoot down a helicopter that is probably carrying three or four armed men? Do the words 'David versus Goliath' mean anything to you?" she said with a smile. The smile didn't really hide the fear and trepidation she was feeling.

"Hey, remember that David actually won that little fight. Look, I know that it won't be easy, but I can't come up with a better idea, and this at least gives us the element of surprise. If we can make it past these guys we can get the hell out of here and go…wherever. We'll have to figure that part out."

The cell phone rang and Keith picked it up. "Patrick? Tell me something good."

Patrick responded. "They took the bait. They're heading towards the mouth of the York now, so you better be ready."

"We're almost ready," replied Keith. He told Patrick what they were planning, and his response was essentially the same as Loren's. After a moment, though, Patrick had to agree with Keith's assessment that it probably was at least worth the chance. Keith clicked off and told Loren, "We need to move."

They went up on the bridge and Keith started getting the Zodiac uncovered. Thankfully the dinghy and the lifting davit were unhurt in the earlier attack, and Keith had the boat floating behind the swim platform in about 2 minutes. The dinghy was generally used as a floating taxi to carry passengers from the big boat to other boats in the anchorage, or up to a marina or restaurant. It could also be used as an emergency lifeboat, but it was not a great boat to be in on a day like this. While the waves weren't too bad here on the flats, it was still damn cold. They loaded the Zodiac with their emergency ditch kit, a couple of life jackets, both rifles and spare ammo, and the garbage bag full of cash – just in case. They put on heavy coats and gloves, but at Keith's urging they did not put on their foul weather gear, even though, God knows, this was the perfect day for it. He was afraid that the bright colors – hers was a bright yellow and his was a bright red – might give away their position. They climbed into the boat and Keith started the small Yamaha outboard. Once it was running he untied the line from the swim platform and they made their way over to the duck blind. Neither of them had ever been inside a duck blind, and they were amazed at how well constructed this one was. Not only was it sturdily built, it was extremely well camouflaged. Keith felt pretty confident that they wouldn't be able to be seen in here, even from the air.

Keith removed the binoculars from the bag and did a quick scan of the horizon back in the direction of the York River. Nothing yet. He turned to face Loren. "Not exactly a luxury cruise ship we're sitting on, is it?"

"No, definitely not." Loren shifted subjects. "So, Mr. Bond, how do you intend to play this?" Her wicked sense of humor was coming back. That was a good thing.

"I expect that they're going to fly in and circle *Kismet*, look for any signs of life. When they don't, I think they're going to hover and just open fire on her, hoping that they'll either kill us or scare us up on deck to surrender. While they're hovering, that's our chance. We want to try to take out the pilot. As low as they'll be, I don't think they'll have a chance to get the chopper back under control, even if one of the others knows how to fly the thing. What we can't afford to do is get into a shootout with these guys. They have the high ground, to put it mildly, and they have automatic weapons. We need to get that pilot before they get a line on us."

"I think I hear something," Loren said. She stopped and listened, as did Keith. "Yes, I do hear something. It sounds like a helicopter off in the distance."

Keith listened, and then he heard it too. He focused the binoculars and saw the chopper heading their way over top of Goodwin Island. No doubt they already had *Kismet* in their sights from their high vantage point. He sat down the binoculars and handed Loren her rifle, then he picked up his. "When they're in range click your safety off, back there near the trigger guard," Keith pointed. "Let me try to take the money shot since I've got the scope. After that, unload on them as best as you can, but be careful. That gun has some kick and I don't want you getting knocked overboard from the recoil. And if they start shooting back, get down as low as you can." He could feel the tension building with each passing second. *'Breathe, damn it'*, he kept telling himself, desperately trying to stay calm.

It didn't take long at all for the chopper to close the gap, and as Keith had predicted, the pilot did a quick circle around the boat. Seeing nothing, the chopper quickly came back around and positioned itself about 20 feet off of the port side. Unfortunately, that put the pilot on the far side and there was no way that Keith could get a shot at him. Two of the passengers leaned out from the side of the chopper and raked *Kismet* with automatic weapon fire, and Keith could hear the fiberglass splintering and the windows being shattered. It took everything he had in him not to stand up and shoot them right now, but he knew that even if he took out both of these shooters they'd be easy targets for the others in the chopper. Very few things in his life he loved as much as that boat, and to see someone destroying it was heartbreaking. "Come on around, you cocksuckers, and you're all going down," he muttered just barely loud enough for Loren to hear.

As if on queue, the pilot swung the chopper around to the starboard side and turned parallel to it so that the person in the jump seat to his right could get a clean shot. As the shooter started spraying *Kismet* with bullets Keith realized that this was his chance. He stuck the barrel of the gun through an opening in the duck blind and took a sighting on the pilot's head. *Steady… Steady…squeeze.* His shot was right on target and the pilot's head literally exploded. Keith could see blood all over the inside windshield of the chopper, and the craft was immediately out of control. It rocked violently as one of the passengers scrambled to try to grab the controls. The chopper banked sharply to the left, its momentum carrying it about 50 yards astern of the damaged yacht, and then it simply dropped straight down into the water. No dramatic spin, no Hollywood explosion or disintegration, it just flopped down into the water from an altitude of maybe 60 feet. The water was less than six feet deep where it hit, so most of the helicopter stuck right up out of the water

Keith moved quickly. "Quick, untie us." He started the motor and threw it into reverse to back out of the blind. "Hold on, and be ready. Anything that moves, shoot it." They bounced across the waves and were beside the helicopter in mere seconds. Keith had his pistol in his hand, but so far they had not seen any movement. The chopper's cockpit was filled about halfway with water, but had someone been conscious they could have made their way out. They looked in through the canopy; if anyone was alive, they definitely weren't moving. "I smell gas," Keith said. As they looked around, a sheen was on the water, obviously coming from the helicopter. "Come on, let's get back to the boat and see if we can get the hell out of here." They rushed back up to *Kismet* and tied the dinghy to the small cleat on the swim platform. Keith climbed into the cockpit and went through what was left of the heavy glass sliding door separating the cockpit from the salon. What he saw was enough to make him cry.

"God damn! Look what they've done to my boat!" he screamed.

"I know, sweetie, but at least it's still floating and we're still alive. Let's see if everything is working enough to get us the hell out of here before someone comes looking for us or that chopper."

She was right, of course. Count your blessings, you lucky bastard. You just survived two assassination attempts in one day. Keith ran up to the helm. All of the electronics looked ruined, but he didn't need them right now, he just needed the boat to run. He put the keys in and tried to start the engines Yes! They both fired right up. He tried the throttles and clutches and found that all were working, as was the steering. That's all that really mattered at this point. "Loren, while I raise the anchor, see if you can get a decent line attached to the dink and we'll tow it with us. We don't have time to hoist it back up and stow it, assuming that the controls for the davit still work. There should be a 50' piece of ½ inch line down in the starboard locker under the gunwale. Keith hit the button to raise the anchor, but nothing happened. Shit. He ran up to the bow and tried using the switch mounted on the deck near the windlass. Thankfully that one worked. He didn't have that much anchor chain out, but with the huge anchor and heavy chain that a boat the size of *Kismet* required it was not something that one man wanted to try to handle manually. Especially when that man was being chased by people that wanted to kill him. The anchor was up and stowed quickly, and Keith hustled back to the helm to get them moving.

"Is the dink secured?" he yelled back to Loren.

"Yes," she answered. "And I've gotten everything out of the dink and into the cockpit. We're good to go."

"Do me one more thing real quick, please. Can you bring me the flare gun kit out of the ditch bag?"

Loren dug through the bag and found the flare gun and flares, then brought it to Keith at the helm. "What are you planning to do? Signal for help?"

"No, not at all. Can you watch the helm for a second, just make sure we don't drift any closer in? With the depth finder shot to shit we're going to have to crawl our way out of this area and back to the channel, so we definitely don't want to get into any shallower water." Keith took the flare gun from Loren and walked back to the cockpit. He snapped open the gun breach and popped in one of the flares. Closing the breach he calmly walked to the stern, then lifted the gun and took aim. He launched the flare at the helicopter sitting like a washed up whale about 75' feet away. The hot flare hit the side of the chopper and the sparks and flame quickly ignited the fuel that was leaking from the tanks and surrounding the bird. Within seconds it was engulfed, and soon after there was finally the Hollywood-like explosion that Keith had been expecting when it first crashed into the water. That gave him some small matter of satisfaction. *"Burn in hell, you bastards,"* Keith muttered to himself.

Walking back up to the helm, Keith took the wheel and slowly started making his way back to the channel. Loren stood beside him and held him tight, and he put his arm around her shoulder. "Where to now?" she asked.

"I don't know. I need some time to think about that." He looked around the water to get his visual bearings – no glass to cause any distortion or glare, he told himself – and then checked behind him to make sure they weren't kicking up any mud from the shallows. Everything was looking good, or at least as well as could be expected under the circumstances. "I think we're past the worst of the shallow water," he announced. "We should be good from here on back to the channel. When we get a little nearer to the channel I'm going to put her on plane and try to put some distance between us and the little barbeque we left behind. Hopefully the Zodiac will tow OK."

"I think it will. I made a bridle out of the 50' line and tied a 100' foot line between the dinghy and the bridle. That should help it ride a little better and tow a lot straighter than just using the shorter line tied to one of the stern cleats."

Keith smiled. "My little Gilligan comes through again."

Without any windshield or side windows in the boat it was a lot colder and noisier at the helm, but Keith knew that he should call Patrick and Jeff to let them know that they were safe, at least for the moment. He ended up talking to both of them via a quickly established conference call, and they were very relieved, to say nothing of impressed, that he and Loren were still alive. They were equally impressed that *Kismet* was still running after taking probably a hundred or more rounds of automatic weapon fire. Keith told them that he hadn't yet come up with a plan for getting out of the area, but he was sure that he'd come up with something quickly. They committed to talk later this evening to make sure that he and Loren had gotten safely away, and Patrick and Jeff both said that they expected to have an update on their research into Daniels Robotics when they next spoke. Keith thanked them profusely for all of their help and support, especially for Patrick creating that little diversion for two of the hit teams.

After he hung up from his call, he asked Loren where she had stowed the stuff from the dinghy. She said that she'd put the money bag on the couch, along with the rifles. The ditch bag was just inside the salon door. "Could you please look in the ditch bag and get the handheld VHF radio out for me, please." A plan was taking shape in his mind.

Loren dug around in the emergency bag and she found the radio. She turned it on to make sure it was working; of course it was. Keith was meticulous about maintaining his emergency equipment, making sure that he always had fresh batteries in the handheld radio and GPS, and making sure that everything was at least as good, if not better, as recommended or required by the Coast Guard. She handed him the radio and he pressed the button to change to the standard calling channel. "*C-Note, C-Note, C-Note*, this is *Explorer* calling on Channel 1-6". He waited a few seconds for a reply, hoping that using a fake hailing vessel name wouldn't confuse his friend David if he was monitoring the VHF, as he usually was on weekends while hanging out on his boat tinkering, drinking beer, and listening to Jimmy Buffet. After 15 seconds without a reply, he tried hailing *C-Note* one last time.

"This is the *C-Note*. Who's this again?"

"This is *Explorer*, from Yacht Haven." He was hoping that David would pick up on his voice. "Can you switch to channel 68, I repeat, channel 68."

"Yeah, this is *C-Note* switching to 68."

Keith turned his handheld to channel 68 and hailed David. "*C-Note*, you there?"

"*C-Note* is here. Keith, that you?"

"Yes. Please, just listen, OK. Is there still that old payphone there in your marina?"

"Sure, but you can just call me on my cell phone if you need to talk to me."

"No. We can't do that. I'll explain later. Go to that phone and call the number I'm going to give you, and when the person answers ask him to conference you in with me. Got it?"

"Yeah, I got it, but I don't understand..."

Keith cut him off in mid-sentence. "Trust me, I'll explain everything to you. But right now I really, really need you to go to the phone and call this number. Please. This is not a joke, I swear it. Got something to write with?" After David acknowledged that he could write the number down, Keith gave him the number for LTBT and told him to call there as quickly as possible. He could tell that David was confused and probably assuming that this was just another practical joke like guys played on each other all of the time. As soon as he signed off with David he placed a quick call to LTBT. This time Jeff picked up, and Keith explained the plan. No problem at all, Jeff assured him.

About two minutes later Keith's cell phone rang, and Jeff patched David through. "David, I need a favor, a big one. I'll explain everything when I see you, but right now Loren and I desperately need your help. I need you to pick us up in maybe 10 minutes. Can you do that?"

"Yeah, buddy, I can do that. Where and when?"

"I've got to get my boat out of sight. There's an old boathouse and abandoned pier back on Easton Cove, about a half mile further up White House Cove. The building is also abandoned and looks like it used to be a crab or fish processing place. You know where I'm talking about?"

"Yeah, I know that place. I've anchored out near there a few times. Harder to find by car than it is by boat, but I'm pretty sure I know which road to turn down to get there. What's the matter, dude? IRS trying to seize your boat? You ain't got an ex-wife to be coming after your stuff."

"I wish it were that simple. I'll explain it when I see you. I'm about 10-15 minutes from there now. Can you please come pick us up?"

"No problem. I'll go button my boat up real quick and I'll be right on over there."

"Thanks, man. I'm going to owe you a big one. See you in a few minutes." Keith turned to Loren. "How the hell do you explain this to someone? Even your best friend will get suspicious, especially when reports of dead bodies, overturned boats, and flambéed helicopters hit the news."

"A wise man once said, 'the truth will set you free'. Maybe you just tell him everything that is going on. At least then he has some reasonable basis to make a decision on whether or not to believe you and help you. If you try and keep him in the dark he can't help but be suspicious."

Keith just looked at her, and a smile crossed his face. "You know, every day you amaze me more and more. Come here." She slowly came to him and he wrapped his arms around her, realizing again what a lucky man he was to have found her. "I don't know what I'd do without you in my life."

"I don't know what I'd do either. Probably live a lot safer, saner life, that's for sure. No more gun fights, no crazed assassins out to kill me." She gave him that killer smile and reached up to kiss him. Keith reached up and pulled back the throttles as he entered the No Wake area. Only about another ½ mile to go; he'd be a lot more relaxed once they got the boat out of sight.

As they approached the abandoned shed Loren went to get dock lines from the lazarette. Once they got her tied up as well as they could they'd try to put some fenders out to keep the boat from rubbing against the pier. Considering that the hull was shot and splintered all to hell it didn't really matter so much for the boat, but from what Keith remembered, a few good rubs might just bring the pier and boathouse crashing into the water. The only good news was that the boat shed was actually big enough to completely cover *Kismet*. With a little luck the boat would be safe here for a few days. If anything, Keith thought to himself, the boat was more likely to be discovered by a bunch of high school kids coming down here to the abandoned building to drink beer and smoke pot. He rounded the last bend and the shed was in sight. Pulling back on the throttles, the boat settled down to its lowest idle speed. He eased into the shed bow first and, when he was far enough in, kicked the engines into reverse for a couple of seconds to stop all forward motion and then put both engines in neutral. Loren managed to drop a loop over the piling on the port bow side, and Keith went forward to try to get a couple of lines over the piling near the starboard bow, one for the bow cleat and one for the forward spring. It took them almost 15 minutes to get all of the lines on and a couple of fenders out, but when they were done the boat was about as secure as they could hope for under the circumstances.

Just as Keith was mentioning that David was late, as usual, he heard the distinctive rumbling of a diesel engine rolling down the long driveway. He instinctively reached for his pistol, but as he looked out he was able to see that it was David's truck. They had been trying to decide what they needed to take with them and what they should leave. Keith could always ask David to come back to salvage some of the stuff that they couldn't carry now. At the very least they needed everything that they'd brought on board just this morning, like their clothes, cell phones, PC, weapons, and money. Everything else might just have to stay; there was just no way to carry it all.

They heard David approaching. "Goddamn, somebody could get killed walking down this dock! What a pile of shit." As he reached the door to the shed and walked in he stopped in his tracks, his jaw dropping open in stunned disbelief. "Holy shit! What in the hell happened to you? Were you guys being used for target practice down near the Navy base or something?" Then seriously, "My God, are you guys OK?"

"Yeah, we're both fine, which is more than I can say for the good ship *Kismet*. I told you it wasn't the IRS or an ex-wife out to repossess the thing." David got aboard the boat and looked around, helped himself, as well as Loren and Keith, to a beer (*'can't let them go to waste, or risk them getting bruised if the weather turns warm, right?'*). Both of them took turns filling David in on the events of the last week, particularly the Wild West show that took place today, as they carried stuff off the boat and up to David's truck. For one of the few times since Keith had known him, David was practically speechless. Other than a frequent refrain of 'holy shit', he was almost struck dumb. Finally, with the truck loaded with the gear, they were ready to get the hell out of Poquoson.

As they pulled out, David asked the obvious question. "So where are you guys gonna go now, and how the hell you going to get there?"

"I'm not certain at this point, to be honest," Keith said. I think the best thing, and the safest thing, for us to do, is find a car and head out of town ASAP."

"Why don't you guys just stay at the house with me and the family? At least for a few days. We got plenty of room. Then you guys can borrow the mini-van for as long as you need it. It's not real sexy, but it'll get you from Point A to Point B."

"Thanks, friend, but we can't do that. It would be putting your life and your family's lives at risk. These people have already killed someone who works with me, and we're damn lucky to be sitting here now having this conversation after the shit we've been through today. You've done enough. We can't ask you to risk any more."

Loren added, "It's really sweet of you to offer, but this is our problem. I couldn't stand it if anybody else was killed on account of us."

"Tell you what then," said David. "I'll call Susan and tell her to meet us up at the airport and we'll rent you a car in my name, make it like a two-week reservation. That way it can't be traced back to you. Then you guys get on the road and get the hell away from here. How about that? That should work, right?"

Keith considered the offer for a moment. He didn't really like involving David even that much, but he quite honestly couldn't think of a better plan. "Yeah, that should work. And David, for your own good, please don't go telling anybody – and I mean anybody – that you've seen us. These people will kill you without even thinking twice. You hear me?"

"Yeah, man. I hear ya."

Keith felt better. They had a plan, or at least the beginning of a plan. He didn't know where he and Loren would go next, but as long as it was far away from here it would be an improvement over the current situation. He planned to touch base this evening with Patrick and Jeff, so maybe together they'd make a decision about where he and Loren should go to escape this craziness. *If* they can escape the craziness, he thought to himself.

Chapter 14

Saturday afternoon was not a pleasant time to be working in the clandestine division of DCG. In fact, it was probably the single worst, most stressful time in its history. Colonel Ed Foster was beyond out of control. He and Manning had not heard from Hilton since he and his team had arrived at York River Yacht Haven, but based on reports from the police in Gloucester, three men were seen stealing a small, high-speed fishing boat and heading out into the rough waters of the York River. Why hadn't the team called in? That question was on everyone's mind. Was it just Hilton, as team leader, being too stupid or too cocky to let someone know that they were going after Bryant, or was it something even more basic, like greed? With the bonus that Foster had offered to the person or team that took out the targets maybe Hilton wanted the opportunity all for himself.

Foster knew that they'd been played and he was determined to find out who was behind it, and when he did, they would pay the price for interfering in his mission. No doubt Dr. Bryant had enlisted help from someone, probably those troublemaking bastards from LTBT. How else to explain the so-called 'anonymous tip' to law enforcement about an imminent terrorist attack using helicopters that had caused three of his teams to be detained and questioned? Those teams were effectively taken out of commission for the day, and the choppers probably would not be released until at least tomorrow or Monday. This is a textbook example, Foster thought to himself, of why he always preached the necessity of knowing your quarry and never underestimating their resourcefulness. One little phone call, made to the right people and saying the right words, like 'terrorists' and 'chemical or biological agents', had taken his teams out of the game as surely as if they'd been shot out of the sky by a shoulder-fired rocket.

The mood in the room had darkened even more when the crew of the last operational chopper had called in to say that they'd been asked to check out reports of an overturned small boat near the mouth of the York River. Once on site they reported back that they had found the boat, approximately 25'-30' feet long with twin outboard motors, capsized near the right side of the main shipping channel, exactly where the report had indicated. No sign of any survivors. Manning asked over the radio, "Can you tell what happened to the boat to cause it to capsize? Like any signs of gunfire or explosion?"

"No, we can't tell anything from this vantage point," responded the pilot. "Maybe they just capsized the boat in the rough seas. Certainly possible as rough as it is today, especially if he was pushing too hard while chasing Bryant."

"Alright, nothing we can do about this now. Let's get you back on the trail of Dr. Bryant. He can't have gone far."

"Roger, that," said the pilot. "We're moving."

Things brightened for everyone in the room about 5 minutes later when the pilot called back to report that he had spotted Bryant about 1.5 miles south of their present position. The onboard camera brought *Kismet* into view as they closed in on it at better than 100 knots. "Damn, that is one fine looking boat," exclaimed Warren Adams. "It's almost going to be a shame to have to blow it to hell and back."

Foster spoke to the pilot. "Circle around one quick time and let's see if anyone's on board."

The pilot did as requested, and everyone's eyes were glued to the video feed. "I don't see anyone," said Manning. "They could be hiding below."

"Yeah, or they may have taken the dinghy and tried to hide somewhere up in those marshes or around those small islands. It looks like their davit was left in position to launch and retrieve," said Hanover.

"Give them a couple of blasts of machine gun fire from all sides, see if that scares them up from below," ordered Foster. The DCG crew watched as automatic weapon fire rained down on the boat below and sent chunks of glass and fiberglass flying.

"Still no movement," said the pilot, "moving around to the other side. OK, we're in position, let 'er rip…"

No sooner were those words out of the pilot's mouth than Foster and the others heard what sounded like a shot from a high-caliber rifle come across the radio, and the camera immediately lost its focus on *Kismet*. One of the operatives on board yelled into the radio, *"the pilot's hit, he's down!"* From the wild swinging of the video feed they could tell that the chopper was tilting and spinning, then within seconds the video feed was lost altogether as the chopper crashed into the water.

"What the fuck happened?" yelled Foster. "Try to get the chopper back on the radio!"

"We're trying, sir. Nobody's responding," yelled Adams.

"Goddamn it! How the hell could we lose the only fucking asset we have left in the whole area?" yelled Foster. His face was beet red and any semblance of his usual professional demeanor was definitely out the window. "Rewind that video feed and run it frame by frame."

"I'm on it," said Manning. "OK, here's the video capture. Everything looks good right here as they're swinging around from the port side to the starboard side. I still don't see any movement on the boat…And right…here….is what sounds like a gunshot, but I don't see any sign of anybody on the boat, nor do I see any rifle sticking out of any window, or any muzzle flash, nothing."

"Well somebody goddamn well took a shot and killed our pilot, and may have very well killed our whole damn team. Run that video feed back slowly," said Foster. Manning ran through that 15 second section in slow motion, and as the helicopter and camera were swinging around the boat, Foster suddenly yelled, "freeze it, right there."

Manning stopped the video and was wondering what it was that Foster was focused on. Then Foster said, "There's our answer, right there. Goddamn it! Look, a fucking duck blind just a couple of hundred feet, maybe less, off the starboard side of the boat. Bryant was sitting in a freakin' duck blind setting up an ambush! Keep that tape rolling, slowly." As the feed went a few more seconds, Foster added, "Keep it moving after the shot is fired until the end of the feed."

As the video moved in slow motion after the shot, the footage was as out of control as the helicopter had been, but after about 3 seconds following the shot, Foster said, "Stop. There it is. Zoom in on the duck blind." Manning did as he said. "Right there! There's the rifle muzzle sticking out through the camouflage." He pointed at the screen, and finally everybody saw exactly what he was focusing on.

"You're right. And look down there where the bottom of the duck blind almost touches the water; you can just make out what looks like a dinghy hiding there," said Manning.

"Son of a bitch!" Foster screamed, as he threw the phone and virtually all of the contents of the desk onto the floor. "This *cannot* be happening! One man, a goddamn school teacher, for Christ's sake, shoots down a helicopter and kills a whole fucking team of Special Forces trained operatives by playing Elmer Fudd in a duck blind?" Foster was incredulous.

"We don't know that the rest of the team is dead yet, sir. They could still be alive and just not able to use their radios," offered Hanover, trying to put a positive spin on things. From the look on Foster's face, that was probably not the right thing to say.

"Oh really, Mr. Hanover? So you think that our dear Dr. Bryant, who apparently *does* have the balls to blow a man's brains out at fairly close range, is going to let the rest of a hit squad live and risk them catching up with him later? Bullshit! If those men didn't die when the chopper hit the water, you can be assured that Bryant did not leave them alive when he left." Foster's heart was racing and he was sweating like he'd just run a 10k race. If he didn't get himself under control, he was afraid, he was going to have a heart attack or stroke right on the spot.

"I'm with the Colonel on this one," added Manning. "And after what we've seen, I'm willing to go a step further. I got a hundred bucks that says that Hilton and his team didn't just roll their boat over in rough water. I'm betting that we find that Bryant had a hand in their deaths, as well."

"Gentlemen, we need to regroup." Foster was back under control, more or less, and was trying to get the group back on task. "We obviously have a very bright, very capable, and very adaptable quarry in Dr. Bryant. Perhaps we've underestimated him; we will not make that mistake again. We've lost seven men today – seven good men, patriots all – and I know I speak for us all when I say that we don't want to lose any more." He looked around the room at each of them. "Obviously, this operation is going to be a marathon, not a sprint. Bob, I want you to set a schedule to have your team here in staggered 12-hour shifts until this mission is finished. I will be here, too. All of my DCG business commitments are going to be put on hold. Let's meet in the conference room in 15 minutes with a plan for moving forward and closing this shit out for good."

It took the team less than a half hour to set up a new work schedule and to come up with an action plan. As Foster pointed out so succinctly, they had lost the trail of their prey. They didn't know where they were running or, for that matter, how they were running. Of one thing he was pretty sure, and that was that they were getting assistance from LTBT. No calls had been made or monitored between Bryant and any of the known LTBT members, nor had there been any e-mails. Still, Foster knew that the people at LTBT were some smart, crafty bastards, and he did not for one minute assume that just because DCG didn't know of any contact that no contact had taken place. It had always been an unwritten rule that killing someone involved in the conspiracy movement was always a last resort since that only tended to make the conspiracy voices even stronger. The team realized that the time may very well be upon them to put that rule aside and take out the leadership of LTBT, at a minimum. Bottom line, at this point in time, unless and until Bryant made a mistake, they were flying blind.

It was Colonel Foster that finally came up with the most important aspects of the plan. Simply put, Bryant had not yet contacted any of their friends and relatives. Most subjects don't, at least initially, for fear of putting others in danger. That usually changed, though, as soon as the bullets started flying and the bodies started piling up. DCG knew that he had at least three, and probably six, cell phones, and most likely pre-paid calling cards to be used from public phones. That made tracking them much more difficult. What they did have a reasonable knowledge of, courtesy of Electra, were the most likely people that Bryant and his girlfriend would try to contact, whether via phone or e-mail. Foster's orders were simple: monitor all of the people on the list of most likely contacts, and if and when Bryant contacts them record the call and capture the phone number and location information. If it's via e-mail, try to capture the user name and the IP address. Then, Foster planned to call Bryant back personally, and, in his words, 'put the fear of God in him'. Threatening Bryant and Ms. Davis would ring hollow; they had to be found first. Threatening their friends and family, though, that would be much more effective. Better yet, they had to be *shown* that these were not idle threats.

"We are going to have to make a very bold, very profound statement that Dr. Bryant can't help but notice, gentleman. And we need to make sure that, even if he's on the run, that he can't help but take notice. When he wakes up tomorrow morning, wherever he is, I want his world to be rocked. If we've spoken to him between now and then, so much the better. He can have a night of fear and dread wondering what we're going to do. But either way, he needs to understand that he is definitely tangled up in something that he should have never gotten involved in. And there's no way out. He's going to die, that much is assured. It's just a matter of how many more people that are close to him that he wants to take down with him." Foster could be a cold, calculating bastard when he needed to be. And in his world, right now, he needed to be.

⌘

KEITH AND LOREN WERE TRAVELING westbound on Interstate 64 between Williamsburg and Richmond in their rented Chevy Impala, still not sure where they were heading but at least moving away from the Hampton Roads area. Knowing that they'd be at the crossroads for Interstates 64 and 95 within the next 20 minutes, Keith decided that this was an opportune time to call Patrick and Jeff to apprise them of the situation and see if they had ideas about where they should go.

"Our suggestion is to head towards the Raleigh-Durham area and lie low for a day or two," said Patrick. "We have an associate there – you met him briefly, the pizza delivery man – who is ready to assist you in whatever you need. We've made reservations for you under the name of William Moore at the Marriott in Durham, and we've already sent over a fax authorization form for the room to be billed to a corporate AMEX belonging to one of Jeff's offshore companies."

"Won't the hotel clerk demand identification from me when I try to check-in?" asked Keith.

"Possibly, so you'll need to come up with some song and dance about losing your wallet, getting robbed, whatever. Have the front-desk clerk call me at the next phone number in the sequence, and we'll be sure to answer it using the corporate name on the credit card authorization. By the way, that corporate name is Cypress Associates, Inc., just in case you're asked. We'll provide the authorization to the hotel, verbally, should they call."

Luckily, Keith was familiar with the Marriott where they were heading since it was located just a couple of miles from the beautiful campus of Duke University. He had visited Duke on a number of occasions and had even stayed at the same hotel several years ago. With the precautions that they were all taking he felt that they'd probably be reasonably safe for a couple of days. After that, who knows? One thing was certain: they could not count on staying in any one place too long. Their pursuers were too smart, too experienced, and too well-connected.

"What have you and your associates found out about Daniels Robotics? Anything interesting yet?" Keith asked.

Patrick answered. "Actually, there does appear to be something to your theory, at least based on our preliminary research. No smoking gun yet, but I think you're on to something. We've seen a few too many coincidences for our liking. For example, the Daniels Robotics CFO died hours after completing the 2001 financial statements, purportedly of a massive heart attack. On its own that might not be that big of a deal, but we've found at least two other instances of very high ranking men and women in major defense and security firms that died within months of 9/11. In all cases, the firms we're talking about have made billions from government contracts since then. Statistically, we're way beyond 'improbable'. I'd say there's definitely something going on here."

Keith replied, "I'm going to spend some time over the next day or two, hopefully, following the thread around Daniels Robotics. I'd like to start with the CFO's death. Obviously, if someone had him killed because he stumbled on some financial involvement in 9/11, there must be some paper trail, or at least someone that he talked to about his suspicions. What was the CFO's name?"

"Fred Abraham," said Jeff. "Lived in Arlington, VA, survived by a wife of 25 years, per the obituary we pulled up."

"I'm going to start there. What I'd like to ask you guys to look into is to see if you can determine any link between the deaths of 9/11 conspiracy researchers and the various sites they had visited, blogs they had posted, etc. in the days or weeks before their death." Keith was feeling inspired again, mostly because his hypotheses about DRC seemed to have at least some basis in fact.

"Why do you want to follow that path?" asked Patrick. "We'll gladly pursue it, just curious what's driving you there."

"Simple. This whole mess got started for two reasons. First, because I was teaching a class on Conspiracy Theory and my students were pinging tons of conspiracy sites, conspiracy blogs, and basically trying to dig up dirt related to 9/11. We were causing enough of a spike in the traffic for these sites that someone in the government obviously took notice, including sending in a spy, Mathew Hilton, into our class. And second, Lowell Westbrook's relationship with LTBT and the government's fear that you and I would hook-up and combine forces sent them into a major snit."

"And you're assuming that the same thing has probably happened in the past? Up to and including the possible murders of other researchers or theorists," added Jeff.

"Exactly. These bastards came after us with everything but the kitchen sink. Listening devices. Classroom spies. Helicopters and automatic weapons. This can't be the first time this kind of thing has happened. They've probably tried to cover their tracks as best they can, but if we find enough instances of people disappearing or turning up dead, we're right back to our statistical improbability that rules out coincidence."

All three agreed that the research would move forward along the lines they'd discussed, and Keith committed to touch base with LTBT tomorrow morning. Before hanging up they all agreed to one other thing: the next morning LTBT was going to post an account of today's attempts on Keith's and Loren's lives on their website. They all knew that that was going to push their pursuers right over the edge and probably result in more danger for everyone involved and everyone connected to Keith and Loren. Still, they had to make sure that their story made its way into the public eye before it's too late. All they could hope to do was warn friends and family as best they could and as discretely as they could.

Keith took the exit to Interstate 95 south when they reached the edge of downtown Richmond, and from there they would head south for about 30 miles to Petersburg, VA before picking up I-85 south. They should be hitting the Raleigh-Durham area in a little less than three hours. "I think I want to call my sister and let her know what's going on, at least at a high level. Maybe she's safe being all the way out in California, but who knows with these people? She definitely needs to at least be aware of the potential danger."

"I agree", said Loren. "And I'd like to call my mom and dad. Maybe I can convince them to get out of town for at least a few days, maybe go stay with her sister out near Pittsburgh. Do you really think our families could be in danger?" The thought of putting her parents at risk, as well as her friends and other relatives, made her ill.

"I don't know what to believe. Part of me says that they'll do anything to keep their secrets and to stop us, but then another part of me says that they have to be so paranoid about being exposed that they don't like to risk anything too public or anything that would raise too many questions. Otherwise, why haven't they killed Patrick, Jeff, and everyone else even remotely associated with LTBT?"

"True. Do you think it's safe for us to make those calls?" Loren had no idea how sophisticated their pursuers might be when it came to monitoring phone calls and e-mails, but she assumed that they were keeping an eye on the people that she and Keith would most likely reach out to.

"Probably not, at least not if we stay on the phone long. The best we can do is put in the code to block the Caller ID information and then throw the phone away when we're done with the call so they can't pinpoint us via the built-in GPS." Keith sounded like he knew what he was talking about, but in reality he was only making an educated guess. This was way outside of his core area of expertise.

Loren took the chance and made the call, and she caught her mother just as she was heading out the door to the grocery store. Her mom wasn't going to make this easy or quick. At first she didn't believe her, and then when she was convinced that what Loren was saying was true, she broke down. "Please mom, you and dad go to Aunt Laura's and stay until I call you to let you know that it's safe. I don't want you caught up in this mess." Loren was fighting back her own tears, trying to be brave in front of her mom, show her that she was as under control and rational as possible. They talked about another five minutes before Loren told her mom that it wasn't safe for them to keep talking, lest they be tracked. Her mom promised to convince her dad that this was a serious threat and to leave town tonight. It wouldn't be easy, they both knew. Loren's dad was a proud man, someone who believes in taking care of and defending his family. It's not in his nature to run, not from anything. "Mom, you've got to make him understand," Loren had said. "These people are professionals, probably ex-military. They've got big guns and lots of them, to say nothing of helicopters and God knows what other resources. Trust me. I've seen what these guys can do up close. They will kill you without the slightest compunction. Go, please. Tonight."

When she got off the phone the tears couldn't be held back any longer. "My family should not have to be a part of this, goddamn it. They have nothing to do with this. It's us, not them."

"I know, sweetie," Keith said as he put his arm around her. "It's not right and it's not fair, but better they be warned and have a chance to get somewhere safe. We'll go see them as soon as this mess is all over, I promise."

"That's what I'm scared of, that something will happen to us, or something will happen to them, and I'll never get to see them again," she said through the tears.

"We're not going to let that happen. We're going to stay safe, and we're going to bring these bastards down so that nobody ever has to fear them again. *Ever.*"

Keith consoled Loren as best as he could, but it still took more than five minutes for her to calm down. He knew that she had been through a lot over the past few days. Hell, they both had. And then surviving two attempts on their life in one afternoon, well, that was just enough to drive anyone over the edge. He had never known terror like he'd felt today, and he hoped to God he would never experience it again. The fear and the tension were making his neck and shoulders ache, and his head was pounding. He'd probably had a year's worth of adrenalin pumping through his body today, he reasoned. Maybe that's why every muscle in his body felt so tight. On the other hand, maybe it's what had kept him alive.

With Loren somewhat calmer, Keith picked up the same cell phone and called his sister's mobile number. There was no reason to think that the government wouldn't have that phone number monitored as well, he just assumed that there was a better chance of catching her on her cell since it was early afternoon California time. Julia answered on the third ring, assuming it was a wrong number since no caller information popped up on the display of her cell phone.

"Julia, it's Keith." He realized there was probably no good reason to try to hide his identity since anybody monitoring would know it was him right away. After all, they'd probably been expecting this moment.

"Hi, Keith. What's up? Wait, let me tell you where I am first, so you can be green with envy. I'm having lunch at Pebble Beach, looking out over the golf course and the Pacific Ocean. Jealous?"

"Very. That's definitely much better and much more glamorous than where we are." Keith spent the next few minutes explaining the situation that he and Loren found themselves in, being careful not to divulge too many particulars since he assumed their call was being monitored. Julia didn't take the news much better than Loren's mother had. She was starting to cry and finally excused herself from her lunch companions and moved outside, partly out of embarrassment and partly out of a need for privacy. "Look, I don't think you're in any danger, but I need you to know what's happening to me and Loren. We're safe, at least for the moment. You need to make sure that you're safe, too. Get away from your house and your regular routine, at least for a while until I call you and let you know it's safe. Take as much cash as you can and go. Don't use your credit cards or ATM card, and you should probably throw away your cell phone since they might track you via GPS."

"Well for once I'm lucky, then. My cell phone is kinda old, pre-GPS. I guess it can still be monitored, but at least it can't be easily tracked." Julia hoped that she was right about that tracking statement.

"Good. Lie low, get somewhere off the beaten path. I'll contact you as soon as I can. Take care of yourself, and please, stay alive. You're all the family I have." Keith talked to her a few more minutes before hanging up, wondering if he'd ever have the chance to see her, or even talk to her, again. He checked the road signs to see exactly where they were and soon came upon a sign that said 'South Hill 8 miles'. That was the last major town before crossing the Virginia-North Carolina border. "Let's make a quick pit stop in South Hill and grab something to eat and drink, then I'll dump the cell phone in the trash and we'll get back on the road."

"That sounds good," said Loren. "I am getting hungry. Are you going to leave the battery in the cell phone? Won't they be able to track us via the GPS?"

"Yeah, we may as well leave it on, just to fuck with them for a few minutes if nothing else. Let them think we're that dumb or naïve. I'd say it's a virtual certainty that they've just monitored both of those calls and they know exactly where we are via the GPS. Fortunately, they don't know what kind of car we're in and they definitely don't have any agents close enough to South Hill to be a threat. Since they know we're on I-85 they're aware that we could be taking this road somewhere like Raleigh-Durham or Atlanta."

"You're not afraid that they'll get the local cops after us if they know where we are?"

"No, not really. If they'd wanted the local or state police to bring us in they'd have had us in custody within a few hours of leaving Charlottesville. No, I think they're too worried about keeping this compartmentalized to ever bring in the locals." He knew that his logic was sound, he just hoped that it was right. Logic had always worked for him his whole life, but would it work for him now when the stakes were this high – literally life and death?

⌘

"COLONEL, I'VE GOT SOMETHING HERE," yelled Warren Adams with obvious excitement in his voice. "I've got a call going from Bryant's girlfriend to her parents in Alexandria." He brought up the audio so that everyone in the Bunker could hear it. They all listened as Loren tried to explain the unexplainable to her mother, listened as they cried together and tried to make plans to run from people that, in reality, they couldn't run from.

"Keep on recording, and let's look at the GPS information to see where they are," said Colonel Foster, for the first time today actually having some positive emotion on his face and in his voice. He was back into the thrill of the hunt, feeling like he was one step closer to having his prey trapped and, eventually, dispatched. "Have you got the phone number yet from the cell phone they're using?"

"Yes, sir. It's coming up on the monitor now. I knew he'd have to make a mistake sooner or later. He's no professional."

Foster laughed at the bravado. "Don't sell him short. Let me assure you, this is no mistake on Bryant's part. He's very aware of exactly what he's doing. He's simply looked at the risk versus reward of making the calls to his friends and family in a ridiculous attempt to warn them about the danger. He knows we're monitoring these people. He's just willing to take the risk."

"OK, here's the phone number he's calling from. 804-555-2355. And it looks like we have his location pinpointed. He's on 1-85 heading south, maybe about 25 miles south of Petersburg. Should we try to scramble the teams?" asked Adams.

"No need at this point," said Foster. "Let's just listen for a few minutes, and then I think I'll reach out and touch Dr. Bryant personally, by phone. I imagine that will make his asshole pucker enough to be able to turn a piece of coal into a flawless diamond." Foster smiled. God, how he enjoyed the game, at least during the good times.

Foster, Manning, and the two operatives currently on duty, Adams and Hanover, listened to the entire call between Loren and her mother. When the call was over they went back over it and analyzed the words looking for hidden meanings or code words, but their conclusion was that the call was as it appeared: a daughter trying to save her mother's life. Nothing clandestine, no subterfuge, just an emotional appeal to her mother to please get away and to stay safe. Ironic that Ms. Davis would tell her mother to leave and go to her sister's house, the team discussed. They had to know that the location of Loren's aunt's house was no mystery, nor were the names and addresses of every relative and virtually every friend she'd had since high school. If Foster ordered her parents killed it didn't really matter if they were at their house in Alexandria, the aunt's house in Pittsburgh, or at the North Pole. They would be dead. End of story.

"Sir, I've got a call coming in to Julia Bryant's cell phone out in California. It's coming from the same cell phone that Ms. Davis used a few minutes ago," said Hanover. "Putting it up on the speakers for everyone to hear."

It was all that Foster could do not to laugh with glee at hearing the panic and the terror in Julia's voice, as well as the stress and fear in Keith's. The fact that Julia was in Monterey was not going to save her life should Foster decide to up the pressure. That bitch would be dead by morning if that's what he wanted. "Same drill as the last call, Mr. Hanover. Record it, analyze it, and check to see if Dr. Bryant is still heading in the same direction." Foster was sure that he was; why bother to make any changes in direction now? Much better to wait until after the cell phone is dumped.

"The second that Dr. Bryant drops that call with his sister, I want to call him back and have a little talk with him. Make sure he's feeling the love that we're feeling for him." Foster was thinking through the dialogue in his mind, thinking about how to instill the greatest fear and panic, how to cause the most pain.

"Colonel, I think I've got a lead on Bryant's car," Manning said. "I had Electra check out all of the usual things in the Hampton Roads area, like reports of stolen cars, rental cars, and so on. Obviously, Bryant would never be dumb enough to rent a car, right? But we did find that one of his best friends, a David Ward, rented a car this afternoon from Avis at the Newport News/Williamsburg airport. Booked it for two weeks. Unless our Mr. Ward is taking off on vacation I gotta believe that this car was rented for Dr. Bryant and Ms. Davis."

"Excellent," Foster smiled. "God, I love it when things start going our way! Get all of the particulars on the car to Adams and Hanover, and then see if we can start monitoring I-85 cameras from the Virginia and North Carolina departments of transportation. I have no doubt that Dr. Bryant will be disposing of his cell phone very shortly, probably the second he hangs up after talking to me. It would be nice to see if we can keep an eye on him as he continues moving away from the area."

"Will do, sir. Anything else?" asked Manning.

Foster thought for a second. "Yes, actually. Have one of our teams pay a visit to this David Ward and his family tonight, and let's make sure that a little accident befalls them. No survivors. I want to give Dr. Bryant a little something extra to think about the next time he reaches out to friends or family for help. We want him to feel very isolated and very, very alone."

Foster got the word that Keith had hung up with his sister. As he started punching in the numbers to call Keith's cell phone everyone else at DCG stood by to listen over the speakers. Every word was being recorded, every sound, every nuance. Voice stress analyzers would be used to determine if and when Bryant was lying, as well as keying in on any statements, phrases, or threats that Foster made that looked particularly useful or effective. "Here we go," announced Foster.

⌘

KEITH AND LOREN WERE ONLY a couple of minutes from exiting I-85 and grabbing something quick to eat when the phone rang. Weird, thought Keith, that Patrick or Jeff would be calling him back so quickly. They'd just spoken about 45 minutes ago, but maybe they'd had a breakthrough in their research. "Hello?"

"Good evening Dr. Bryant." Foster planned to keep his voice calm and controlled, having learned long ago that subjects found it much more disconcerting when the interrogator was cold and detached, never letting their tempers flare or raising their voice. It established dominance and control, and the subject would usually shiver with fear when they realized that the interrogator had no emotions or would feel no remorse for beating, torturing, or killing them. Many a hardened criminal and terrorist had been broken using this method; the threat or fear of what might happen was often worse than actually experiencing the beatings, the chemicals, and the pain. Foster had every intention of putting a chill down Dr. Bryant's spine.

"Who the hell is this?" asked Keith. The voice on the other end had the warning sirens in his head screaming. Loren looked over at Keith in alarm.

"My name isn't really important, but if it makes things easier, you can just call me Ed."

"OK, then, Ed, why don't you tell me who you are and what you want before I end this call and toss away this cell phone."

"Well, Dr. Bryant, you can certainly do that if you wish. In the end, it won't make a whole lot of difference, but I think it might be better for you, and the lovely Ms. Davis, if you stay on the phone and we have a chance to get to know each other a little bit better."

"Why? So you can keep me on the phone to track us?" Loren was clearly getting frightened as it became obvious that 'they' were on the other end of the call, and she couldn't begin to understand how they could have found them and made contact.

"Oh, please. We already know where you are, as I'm sure you're aware. And I know you'll be throwing this phone away as soon as we're done with this call, and that's OK, too. So the GPS signal that tells us that right now you're almost to South Hill, VA on I-85 isn't really critical. Right now I just want to make sure that I have your undivided attention."

"I'm listening. What is it that you think I need to hear?" asked Keith, feeling somewhat defiant.

"You need to understand, Dr. Bryant, that you have really stuck your nose in where it doesn't belong. You're going down paths that are going to cause you nothing but pain and misery unless you decide to back off, and you need to do it immediately. The blood of Lowell Westbrook is already on your hands, so you should be concerned that more innocent blood isn't spilled on account of your pigheadedness."

Keith decided to try a little verbal jab, see how Ed reacted to it. "Actually, I'd say that Lowell Westbrook's blood is on your hands. The blood of Mathew Hilton and six other so-called professionals is on *my* hands. I would think that with all of the resources that you obviously have – multiple helicopters and hit teams, automatic weapons, top-notch communications and monitoring capabilities – that you wouldn't have to deal with such a bunch of pussies and amateurs."

Foster had to mute the phone momentarily as he felt his blood start to boil. Insolent little prick! He fought to get himself back under control. "My dear Dr. Bryant, while I must commend you for your resourcefulness today, and your good luck, I can assure you that it won't happen again. If anything, you have saved me the trouble of having to deal with Mr. Hilton. The other operatives, quite honestly, are expendable. Nothing but collateral damage, if you will. I'll actually save a significant amount of money by not having to pay them for work performed, truth be told. Perhaps I should thank you."

"Glad to help you out. And I'll be glad to help you out some more if you try to send others after us," Keith added. His show of cockiness and bravado was as much for his own good as it was for the people listening in on the other end.

"Very good, Dr. Bryant. You put on a brave front, probably trying to convince yourself as much as Ms. Davis. Let me get to the point. As I said, you are dealing in matters that don't concern you. You are endangering your lives and the lives of your friends, your families, and your new acquaintances at Let the Truth Be Told. The only way out of this for you, and by extension, the people I just mentioned, is for you to stop your silly conspiracy theory research and return to your quiet life in academia and business."

Well, that's certainly now out in the open, Keith thought to himself, meaning the statement by his enemies that they knew he was collaborating with LTBT. That shouldn't come as a surprise, he figured. Keith decided to take another poke at his quarry, see if he could stimulate a real reaction. "You know, Ed, I really hate to do that. I mean, we're feeling like we're really onto something right now, especially with the research we're doing into Daniels Robotics and the death of their CFO right after the fiscal 2001 filings. It's just amazing how many companies we're finding that had suspicious deaths of high-ranking officials shortly after 9/11, and those same companies seem to be making enormous profits off of the so-called 'War on Terror' and the increased security here in the US. We just don't seem to think it's a coincidence, you know what I mean?"

"Listen to me, you son of a bitch!" Foster almost screamed. So much for maintaining his composure and the psychological upper hand. "You are playing a very dangerous game, and it's a game you cannot win. Let me tell you what's going to happen, Dr. Bryant." Foster tried taking a couple of deep breaths before continuing, trying to regain the calm, detached tone he had been using just moments earlier. "Tomorrow morning I want you to turn on the news or pick up a newspaper, and I want you to see the death and destruction that occurred overnight as a direct result of your insolence and your stubbornness. You needn't worry; you'll know it when you see it. And you remember, as you sit there looking at the images of the people that are dead because of your stubbornness and stupidity, that their blood is on your hands. Yours. Not mine. You could have prevented it but you chose not to. You chose your own selfish needs for knowledge, or recognition, or money – whatever the hell it is that drives you – over the lives of the people you're going to be reading about tomorrow. Live with that, Dr. Bryant, if you can."

"And you live with this," said Keith, "if you touch anyone, any of our friends or family, anybody associated with LTBT, I'll be coming for you. You won't have to keep hunting me because I'll be hunting you, right to your front door. Believe it."

Foster just laughed derisively. "That was rich, Dr. Bryant. Thank you for lightening the mood considerably. I'll be sure to sleep with one eye open, lest the great white hunter, Dr. Keith Bryant, track me down and kill me." Then in a much more serious tone he added, "Don't let the good luck you had today be confused with real skills, son. The next encounter you have with me or any member of my team – and as you said, I do have considerable resources – will be your last. Have a good evening, Dr. Bryant, and sleep well. Tomorrow when you awake you're going to see that your world has changed forever. It's up to you when your world gets back to normal, or for that matter, when your world ends. Oh, and one last thing. Should you feel the need in the coming hours or days to talk with me again, day or night, call the number that you are seeing now on your cell phone display. And don't bother trying to have the number traced or investigated by your little friends at LTBT. They mean well, but they're out of their league, too. Until then...." Foster clicked off. His team would have plenty of time for analysis, but for now they were feeling pretty good about the message and the tone. Foster turned to the team and said, "I expect that Dr. Bryant will be disposing of that phone shortly, so let's see if we get lucky with the video cameras along the interstate highways and the other main routes into the major cities. I would think that they'd probably want to stop for the night within the next few hours. Let's keep our eyes open."

About 200 miles south of DCG's Reston headquarters, Dr. Keith Bryant rolled down his car window and tossed the cell phone out into the middle of I-85, smashing it into a hundred little pieces. He gave Loren a word by word replay of the call with the mysterious Ed and they spent the next hour or so dissecting every bit of the conversation. Stopping in South Hill for food and drinks was forgotten; it would be another 60-plus miles before they finally stopped and grabbed some fast food at one of the exits off of I-85.

Loren looked at Keith as they both picked at their burgers and fries. "So what do you think he meant when he said that our world was going to be forever changed when we woke up tomorrow morning? Do you think he was serious or just trying to threaten you?"

"Oh, I think he was deadly serious. Sorry, bad choice of words," Keith said sheepishly after seeing the expression on Loren's face. "Whoever this person is, I'd say that he has every intention of making something bad happen tonight, something that will be very evident to us in the morning when we read about it or see it on the news."

"Not like another terrorist attack or some huge catastrophe, right? Probably something more personal?" asked Loren.

"Oh, yeah. I don't have any doubt that it will be very personal. We just better pray that everybody we know stays safe tonight."

Loren tried a slight smile, and said, "You've never been much on praying. You thinking about starting now?"

"Hell, at this point it might be worth a try. Probably better to cover all of our bases." He smiled at Loren. "There's one thing, though, that I didn't share with Ed either. The whole time that he was trying to frighten me and manipulate me and telling me how much my world is going to change tomorrow, I held back one important piece of information for him."

"What was that?" Loren asked.

"I didn't tell him that we're about to change his world, too. Tomorrow LTBT is going to put a posting on their website and put postings on other blogs about the attacks on us today. Nothing will send a clandestine group into a tizzy faster than shining the spotlight on them. The only downside is that we don't have any idea who they are as the postings are created. It would be great to be able to name names."

"It would also be great if we had some sort of evidence to back up our story. Aren't you afraid that whatever they post will just be discounted as the ravings of another group of conspiracy whackos?"

"Normally I would. But this time, they're going to have a little bit of proof to back them up," Keith answered.

"What kind of proof?"

Keith just smiled. "This kind of proof." With that, he pulled his digital camera out of the bag and showed her the pictures he'd taken. The pictures weren't the best quality, but you could easily make out Hilton and his team attacking *Kismet*, along with pictures of the dead people in the center console, the overturned boat, the helicopter circling and shooting up *Kismet*, and the wreckage of the helicopter and the bodies inside after it erupted in flames.

"Oh my God! You're a genius!" Loren reached over and kissed him, burger breath and all. "Is it any wonder that I love you?" she asked.

"No wonder to me at all," he said with a smile. "Let's just see if you think I'm so great in the morning if our new friends have actually carried out their threats."

"Boy, you do know how to kill a mood," Loren sighed.

Chapter 15

After checking into the Marriott, Keith called Patrick and Jeff to fill them in on the conversation he'd had with Ed on the drive down. The LTBT leaders were very concerned about what they were told, so concerned, in fact, that they insisted on holding off on posting anything about the attempts to kill Keith and Loren. At first Keith objected, loudly, but then he was slowly swayed to their way of thinking. Patrick, especially, had argued that nothing was to be gained by posting an account of the assassination attempts, even with the pictures that Keith was promising to send to them via e-mail, that couldn't hold for a day or two. Even more so, he insisted, since the people pursuing them would probably just up the ante by attacking other people close to Keith and Loren.

"It's great that you have these pictures, Keith," said Patrick. "But we can always run them, along with an account of today's events, anytime we want to. Maybe it's better that we keep this information as our own ace up the sleeve in case we ever have to use it for extra leverage?"

Jeff added, "I agree. If we run this now all it does is give our enemies a chance to downplay what we've got by creating false 'proof' that this never happened, or that it happened in the course of an accident caused by bad weather, whatever. I think we should hold this until we absolutely need it, or, better yet, use it in conjunction with the proof we're seeking for the whole 9/11 conspiracy. We can show that Keith was onto them about their involvement and they tried to kill him to stop the information from leaking out."

Keith pondered what they said for a few minutes, even putting Patrick and Keith on Mute for a short period so he could discuss the options with Loren. After considering all of the angles, they both concluded that the LTBT leaders were probably right; nothing to be gained by going public with this now, but possibly plenty to gain by holding the information close until it was most beneficial. Keith un-muted the phone. "Loren and I have discussed it, and we agree with your logic. Let's hold the information and the supporting pictures until we can use it for maximum effect. But I'll still go ahead and e-mail you the pictures for safekeeping so there's no risk of losing them if something happens to the camera, or me, for that matter."

"Great, then. We're all aligned," said Jeff. Then he added, "Man, I would have loved to have been listening in on that call, especially when you mentioned our research into Daniels Robotics. It sounds like that sent him right over the edge."

"Oh, man, did it ever," laughed Keith. "I'd like to play poker with this Ed asshole. Apparently keeping his emotions in check isn't one of his strong suits. It was immediately obvious that I'd struck a major nerve. That was the highlight of the call for me; at least it gave me a few seconds of pleasure to offset the minutes of sheer terror I was feeling as he threatened to kill our friends, our family, even you guys, for 'sticking our nose in where it doesn't belong', in his words."

They all talked for a few minutes longer and then made arrangements to speak the next morning at 10am Eastern Time. Patrick and Jeff said that they'd like to have the rest of their core leadership team on the call so that they'd have a chance to hear firsthand from Keith and Loren about what they'd been up against. They also wanted all of them to put their heads together to decide on the best direction to move the research. Everyone agreed that they were definitely on the right track with the investigation of Daniels Robotics, and that research would continue. Still, the fact that Daniels appeared to be a promising path meant that they had to start to think about what other paths they might try. Certainly there were going to be links and overlaps in the paths, they just needed to figure out where they may be. Keith asked if there might be a way that he and Loren could participate with the LTBT leadership team via their video bridge. Everybody agreed that it would certainly be helpful to put names with faces at this point, so Patrick committed to having the local LTBT associate – the pizza delivery man – pick Keith and Loren up at 9:00am to take them to a secure location with video link capabilities.

"Last request, if I may," said Keith. "Would it be possible for your associate to rent us a new car that we can use for a while? Call me crazy, but I feel safer changing vehicles and hotels as frequently as possible. He could hold our current rental car for a few days or a week and then turn it in at the Raleigh-Durham Airport."

"I don't think that will be any problem, and as you say, it's probably a good practice," said Patrick.

"You guys have a good evening and we'll talk to you at 10am tomorrow, regardless of what happens. And we look forward to meeting your 'pizza delivery man' tomorrow morning."

It had been a long, stressful day for Keith and Loren. They were too tired to go out for dinner, even if there had been any decent restaurants open on a Sunday night anywhere near their hotel. Besides, they reasoned, better to keep their rental car hidden in the parking garage instead of rolling around the streets of Durham. They decided to just order dinner from room service and stay in for the evening.

When the room service food was delivered Loren had the waiter set hers on the desk and asked if they could hold onto the service cart to give Keith somewhere to rest his tray. With the computer set up on the desk and their duffel bags and other stuff strewn across the room, they didn't exactly have the ideal setup for dining. Neither of them was especially hungry, but they figured it was best to eat now since there was no way to know what tomorrow might bring. Keith joked that if it brought nothing else he hoped it would bring some better food. Like hotels all across America, the room service food offered at the Marriott was mediocre at best. Still, better to have an expensive but disappointing meal in their room than to be spotted out of the streets by the government agents that wanted them dead.

They were both being quieter than usual while they ate, both lost in their own thoughts. Loren finally broke the silence. "I think I may have an idea for tracking down who's behind all of this."

Keith looked up from his food. "OK, let's hear it. We could use a new direction right about now."

"OK, here goes. This government agency, whoever they are, seems to be concerned with people getting too close to the real story behind 9/11, agreed?" Loren saw Keith nod in agreement, so she continued. "If that's the case, then it stands to reason that this government agency may not have existed prior to 9/11. So far, so good?"

"Not necessarily," said Keith, as he thought through her reasoning. "Why can't it just be another division of an existing agency, like the CIA or NSA?"

"That's a good point," Loren responded, "but I don't think so, for several reasons. First, even though the CIA, NSA, and God knows how many other groups are covert spy agencies, they definitely have very public budgets and a lot of Congressional oversight. I'm not saying that they can't or don't keep some things hidden from Congress and the public, but I think we can at least agree that it's something they'd have to work at to keep hidden versus a new agency that might be totally off the grid."

Keith considered this point. "OK, I can buy that. Not exactly a 100% certainty, but I can definitely see where there is a higher probability that you're on the right track with looking at a new agency or group versus the usual suspects. What else you got?"

"Second point: Putting spy novels and Hollywood movies aside, the CIA and NSA and the rest of the 'usual suspects', as you so eloquently described them, don't have a charter for domestic spying, and they certainly don't have a charter for murdering people, especially American citizens. With all of the constant oversight from Congress, as well as constantly being under the microscope of the American and foreign press, I don't think it's too likely that any of those agencies would be involved with this kind of operation."

"I would have to agree. I hadn't really considered that, but what you're saying definitely makes sense," said Keith. "The FBI certainly has a charter for keeping tabs on Americans, but to your earlier point, they're not really in the business of murdering American citizens, or anyone, for that matter."

"Good. Now let's try point #3. There are tens of thousands of employees at the CIA, the NSA, and the rest of the better-known players in the intelligence world. What's the one sure thing you can count on if you have something you want to keep secret and you entrust it to thousands of people?"

"Shit. You're right," said Keith. "You can't have something like domestic spying on conspiracy groups and the murder of American citizens going on in these agencies, because with their thousands of employees someone is certain to be leaking it to a friend, the press, or to Congress. All it takes is one disloyal or disgruntled employee to bring the whole thing down like a house of cards."

"Exactly. If you want to keep a secret, you have to keep it as compartmentalized as possible. I mean, think about it," she continued. "The events of 9/11 were one of the most tragic, defining moments in this country's history. While I completely agree that there was most likely a conspiracy behind it, I can't for one second believe that many people knew about it. If there was a large number of people it would have *had* to come out by now. My guess is that there are probably only a handful of people in the whole country, maybe the whole world, that really know the true story."

He reached over and gave her a big kiss. "You are brilliant, you know that? I think you're definitely onto something with your reasoning."

"Thanks," she said with a smile. "The only problem is, I don't know how we're going to identify who this group is. My opinion is that they're probably chartered by an Executive Order and they don't have a single bit of Congressional oversight. For that matter, I'm willing to bet that there is not a single line item in any budget anywhere in DC that is tied to these people."

"I'd have to agree with you on that. Domestic spying would definitely raise a flag if it were any agency that has oversight." Keith grew silent for a moment while his brain went into that internal chess game mode where he looked at all of the variations and outcomes of different scenarios. Some people claimed to do the same thing, often referring to it as 'vector analysis' or some other high and mighty term. For Keith, it was much simpler than that; he just thought of it as 'what-if' scenarios. Basically, he was looking at cause and effect, but he tried to play it out several steps or moves ahead. After a few minutes, Keith had an idea that was starting to formulate and gel in his mind.

"How about this: we definitely have one of the associates at LTBT check on the federal budgets and various Congressional oversight committees for any possible mention of our friends and/or their mission, just to be certain. As you said, I don't think there's much chance that we'll find anything. I think where we might find something, though, is to look for correlations out there between people *leaving* the employ of agencies like the CIA, NSA, DIA, etc., around the time of 9/11 and then going to other agencies, or going into private consulting, or setting up their own shop, whatever."

"I'm not sure I'm following your logic," responded Loren.

"Sorry, I was thinking out loud and probably not making myself very clear. Let me try it this way: I'm guessing that whoever is running this agency or group probably didn't just walk in off the street and set up shop, right? Possible, but not probable. Then, whoever is setting up the shop has to find employees, and obviously, these are not the kind of positions that your average headhunter agency gets involved with. More likely, you'd have better luck finding these kinds of people by running ads in *Soldier of Fortune*," Keith said, only half-jokingly. "I'm guessing that it's much more likely that some high-ranking person at some other spy agency left their gig shortly before or after 9/11 and created this new agency from scratch. Maybe if we try to dig up information on these shitbags in the clandestine world that either left their position to go to another spy agency or left to go out on their own, we might find our friend Ed."

"Most likely in the DC area?" Loren inquired.

"Most likely, but not necessarily. With today's communications there is really no reason to think that it has to be in or near DC. Still, with the critical mass of trained spooks in that area, at least relative to the rest of the country, you'd almost have to expect them to be there. I'm not sure if that fact will be really relevant, though, when we start our research. We'll see."

They continued to refine their ideas as they finished their meals and desserts. It was getting late, and as awful and stressful as today had been, both Keith and Loren recognized that tomorrow could be just as bad, if not worse. They were too keyed up to sleep, plus they both felt too dirty, too gritty from their time spent on the water, particularly in the Zodiac. Loren decided that a nice hot shower might be just the ticket to help her unwind enough to be able to sleep. Keith agreed and said that he could really use a shower, too. And, he added with a smile, they should probably be good stewards of the Earth and help conserve water by showering together. She just gave him that wicked little smile back, knowing exactly where his mind was going. "After all we've been through today, old man, you can still manage to be a pervert. I don't know why I put up with you," she said as she wrapped her arms around his neck and kissed him softly on the lips. That was all the convincing that either of them needed.

The long, hot shower was indeed a much needed luxury, but it was the chance to slow down, hold each other closely, and make that deep connection that only two people in love can make that really made them feel better. They kissed passionately, breathlessly. They made love with the water running over their bodies, fighting to keep their balance in the too-narrow, too-slippery space. Is sex in the shower ever the way that the movies portray, they wondered? Can two people really have hot, lustful, sex when they're fighting to maintain their balance and, hopefully, not be heard by every guest in every hotel room within ear shot? The thought made them both laugh, even as they continued to make the best of an awkward situation. Regardless of how awkward it was physically, it was exactly what they both needed emotionally.

"Oh my God, that felt so wonderful," Loren said breathlessly. She kissed him deeply and told him, again, how much she loved him. "Only problem is now I feel dirtier than I did when we got into the shower, not cleaner," she said with a giggle.

"I wish we could just stay here in this shower and make love for days, let the world go on without us," Keith said with a smile and glazed eyes.

Still catching her breath, Loren replied, "That would be nice, except for the pruney skin. We're already starting to look a little shriveled," she laughed. "Besides that, I think someone needs to have the dexterity and balance of a Cirque de Soleil performer to have sex in this shower unless they want to risk life and limb."

Keith laughed at her comment. "True. It reminds me of all of those people that claim to be members of the 'Mile High Club' when there's barely enough room in one of those damn airplane bathrooms to unzip your pants and pee standing up. I just don't understand the physics of how two people supposedly get in that little space and have sex. And don't even get me started on being able to do it without people hearing, especially since every damn flight nowadays is full."

Loren was laughing now, too. She put her arms around him and kissed him deeply one last time. "I guess we really better get out of this shower before we empty every drop of hot water the hotel has."

They finally got out of the shower and dried off. Checking the door locks one last time, they finally turned off the lights and crawled into bed. They cuddled underneath the covers and Loren laid her head on Keith's shoulder, his arm around her. Despite all that had happened today, and the threat of what might happen tonight, they both managed to doze off quickly and to get some much needed rest. Apparently that long, hot shower *was* exactly what they needed.

⌘

By Sunday night the winds had diminished almost completely, and for the first time in several days stars could be seen in between the last of the light, wispy clouds that were slowly marching off to the east. The temperature had dropped into the high 30's, a little bit cooler than normal for this time of year, and the half-moon gave just enough light through the cloud layer to keep it from being another pitch-black night. At 2:30am there were not a lot of cars on the road in Hampton, VA, and even fewer once the black Ford Fusion pulled off of Mercury Boulevard and started making its way up Fox Hill Road. The car's three occupants were dressed for business, though not the kind of business dress that most people associate with their daily jobs. No nice suits, no button down shirts, no ties, and no wingtips. No Burberry trench coat or nice camel hair overcoat. Their clothes were suited for a different type of work, simply, the work of staying hidden late at night in the middle of a residential area. Dark pants, dark shirts and pullover jackets, black balaclavas to hide their faces, soft-soled black shoes, and even black gloves to keep their hands hidden. This was the uniform of the assassin, at least for tonight's mission. The plan was simple: create an accident that resulted in the deaths of three civilians, including one child, at their home in the Willow Oaks subdivision in Hampton. The fact that the targets were non-combatants, including a child, had absolutely no effect on any of the operatives. They could not have been any less caring if the target had been Osama bin Laden himself.

They pulled the car into a cul-de-sac about one block from the target's house. Grabbing their tools from the backseat, they noiselessly made their way across the backyards that separated them from their goal. They had to go over a few chain link fences to reach the house, but even that presented no problem for these seasoned professionals. When they reached the target's house they entered through the back garage door. The door was equipped with only the basic lock built into the doorknob, so getting inside took mere seconds. Once inside, two members of the team immediately went to work on the knob and deadbolt on the door from the garage into the house. They both wore night vision goggles, and with the ambient light filtering from outside tonight they had no problem seeing all that they needed to see. In less than a minute they were past both and silently slipping inside. They stealthily moved towards the stairs, making sure to avoid bumping into any furniture or stepping on any of the toys left lying around the living room floor. Moving silently up the stairs, the killers made their way to the master bedroom. It was obvious that everyone was asleep; they could hear the snoring coming from both occupants of the bedroom. Working with quick precision, each moved into place, one on each side of the bed. With no hesitation and no words spoken, they each put two silenced shots into the heads of the man and his wife. Heading back down the hall, they slowly opened the door to the bedroom where the couple's twelve year old son was sleeping. They each put a shot into his head as well, the fact that he was a mere child not weighing on their minds in the least. The entire operation had taken less than two minutes from the time they'd entered the house.

As the killers slipped out of the house and into the garage, the third member of their team was just finishing his part of the mission. He had rigged a very simple, actually very amateurish, explosive device. Foster had been clear that there were to be no military grade explosives or no signature fuses or timing devices that would scream 'military' to the fire investigators. Keep it simple, make it look like the mark of someone without any real skills. The killer had even gone so far as to use the simplest fuse possible: a burning cigarette and a book of matches. The plan was simple. He had cut a hole in the gas line at the furnace and the garage was quickly filling with natural gas. Even after just a few minutes it was noticeable. The other team members went quickly back inside and turned on all four burners of the gas stove, further filling the house with the gas. The cigarette was lit just outside of the garage and placed inside the folded cover of a book of matches, then brought back into the garage and set just inches away from the furnace. From there, it was just a matter of time. It usually took about five minutes for the cigarette to burn down far enough to ignite the matches, and when the matches sparked in the presence of the gas, the resulting explosion was usually forceful enough to obliterate the entire house. With everything in place, the hit team slipped back out the way they came. They were back in their car, hit accomplished, less than 10 minutes after they had parked it.

The team slowly made their way around a few blocks, careful not to drive too fast or otherwise be too loud at this time of night lest they catch the attention of a roving police patrol or the eye of a nosy neighbor with insomnia. When approximately four minutes had passed since setting the fuse they started making their way towards the street where the target house was located. As they made their approach, now just a few hundred yards away, the house exploded in a huge fireball, with flames reaching more than 25 feet engulfing the house in seconds. The team gave each other high-fives and were whooping and hooting like college kids after their team scored the winning touchdown. "Goddamn, now, that's a pretty fucking site," laughed the team leader. The others just laughed and nodded in agreement. They slowly drove away from the neighborhood and made their way back towards their hotel in Newport News. The mission had been, by all measures, a success, and they were ready to get back to their rooms and have a celebratory drink.

⌘

ON MONDAY MORNING KEITH WOKE up earlier than he had hoped. He really didn't want to be facing this day. There was no reason to doubt that Ed had done exactly as he had threatened, namely, hurt or killed someone close to him. Exactly who that might be was anyone's guess, but Keith had no doubt that he'd recognize it when he saw it on the news, in the newspaper, or on the internet. Quietly rolling out of bed, he made his way to the bathroom without waking Loren. That was good; this was sure to be a helluva day for both of them, and the longer she was able to sleep the less time she'd have to deal with the terror and the grief. Unfortunately, the flushing of the toilet finally woke her. Keith apologized for waking her, then walked over and sat beside her on the bed. Bending over, he gave her a light kiss on the lips. "How'd you sleep?" he asked.

"As well as can be expected, I guess. I had some weird dreams and tossed and turned part of the night. How about you?"

"OK, not great. I sure would like to be back in our own bed, though."

Keith went to the door of their hotel room and looked through the peephole. The hallway was clear, at least as far as he could see. He opened the door just a crack and grabbed the *USA Today* that was lying there and quickly brought it back into the room, making certain, as always, to lock the deadbolt and put the security chain on. He quickly read through the day's headlines and all of the national news but nothing jumped out at him. Loren turned on the '*Today*' show, but as with the paper, she saw nothing that seemed to affect them. Even when they checked the local news nothing really resonated, though that didn't surprise either of them since they were seeing local news out of Raleigh and they really had no connection with anyone in the area. Keith then went to his PC to try looking at the Charlottesville newspaper online. He paid close attention to the news from the area, assuming that their hometown was a likely candidate for something bad to happen. It took nearly a half hour to get through all of the local news stories, but he could find nothing that was tied to them.

"What about trying the local news down around Hampton and Newport News where we were yesterday? That might make sense, especially since so much else went on there." Loren had a point.

Keith pulled up the website for *The Daily Press*, the local paper for the Hampton and Newport News areas, and went straight to the local news section. The first headline jumped out at him: 'Family of Three Killed in Apparent Gas Explosion.' "Please, God. Don't let this be them..." He scrolled down and saw the story. *David Ward, his wife Susan Ward, and their son Jason Ward all dead from a massive explosion in their home overnight.* The realization hit him full in the gut, waves of nausea rolling over him. He barely made it to the bathroom in time, hanging his head and throwing up, barely able to steady himself on his knees as his hands clutched the sides of the toilet. Loren ran to him, dropping to her knees and wrapping her arms around him to try to offer comfort as best she could, realizing that she was trying to console the man she loved under inconsolable circumstances.

"I am so sorry," she whispered to Keith as she held him. "You can't blame yourself for what these sick bastards did to them. You had no way of knowing that this would happen." She realized how hollow and cliché that sounded, but she didn't know what words could possibly comfort him at this time. Keith and David had been friends for 20 years, and he'd even been best man at his wedding and godfather to his son.

Keith reached up to flush the toilet. He couldn't stop himself from sobbing and buried his head in Loren's shoulder. She held him and let him cry. It was several minutes before he was able to speak, but finally he was able to talk between the tears and the sobs. "Those mother fuckers! I can't believe they would go after an innocent family, and for what? Because they're our friends? Because they rented a car for us?"

"It may be just that simple. Ed threatened to rock our world by harming the people close to us, and I guess this is their way of getting to us, trying to make us give up the search for the truth about 9/11." Loren's voice was low and calming, trying to get Keith to settle down a bit before he made himself sick again. She was shocked that their pursuers had linked them with David so quickly, mere hours since they had been with him. As Keith had said, it must have been through the rental car that David had been so anxious to provide. Ed must have found some correlation between their phone records and David's car rental, she surmised, and it had taken their pursuers only a few hours to pick up on that connection. My God! What were these people capable of? More accurately, what weren't they capable of? The thought gave her a chill.

"Fuck Ed and his whole crew! I will kill him and every last one of his people for this!" He was almost screaming, his anger was so hot. His face was a mask of hate, something that Loren had never seen in him. "And I will not stop searching for the truth about 9/11, because it's a goddamn certainty that our friend Ed is ass-deep in the whole thing, from the actual operation all the way to the massive cover-up. We've got to take him, and the whole goddamn bunch of them, down for this."

"And we will. We'll do whatever it takes to find the truth and bring these people to justice. You, me, and LTBT. We will hunt them down and get to the bottom of this. They need to pay for what they've done. Not just to David and his family, but to the 3,000 people that they sacrificed on 9/11." Loren was just as mad, just as determined, as Keith.

It was almost twenty minutes before Keith finally made it to his feet, barely, as Loren held him and helped him up. As he moved to the bathroom sink to try to clean himself up, Loren went back to the PC and read the full text of the story. Basically, the story said that the house had exploded in the middle of the night from an apparent gas leak, and no family members were able to make it out of the house alive. Burned virtually beyond recognition, still in their beds. An explosion so powerful that it rattled the windows of homes a block away, and at least a dozen people called 911 to report the fire. It was a 3-alarm fire, and when the fire department arrived the house was totally consumed by the fire, what was left of it. Bullshit, she thought to herself. That explosion was certainly no accident, and eventually the fire department inspectors would realize that once they opened their eyes and investigated. She also didn't believe, not for one second, that David and his family were killed by the explosion and fire. No way would the people they'd come up against ever risk something as fraught with potential problems as a gas explosion as a means of assassination. No, they might use the explosion and fire as a cover-up, but she'd bet her last dollar that the family was already dead before the explosion ever occurred. Not exactly a comforting thought, she realized, but better than thinking of people being trapped in their home and burned alive.

When Keith finally made his way back to her side, his face still red, his eyes swollen from crying, Loren went to him and held him. She had never seen the man she loved in so much pain. They sat together on the bed and Loren explained to him about the rest of the article, doing her best to talk about it in a way that would upset Keith the least. He listened closely, though his eyes stared off into the distance, almost lifeless. Finally, after hearing her review of the article, he simply said, "There's no way the hit team left anything to chance, not with an explosion and fire. They killed them all before blowing the place up."

"I know, I totally agree," said Loren. "I assume that will come out in a day or so, after the fire marshal and the coroner look more closely."

"This won't be the end of it, you know," Keith said quietly, dispassionately. "They're going to go after others, whether it's our families, our friends, our colleagues, whoever. They're not going to stop. Not unless we stop them." He looked up at Loren, and life was starting to come back in his eyes. The distant look he'd had, the hurt and the helplessness, were fading. Now she saw only the growing hatred, rage, and determination. Under other circumstances she would be worried that these were bad, unhealthy emotions. But for now, she welcomed seeing any emotion, and she had to admit to herself that, given the present situation, hate and rage and determination may be just what they need to stay alive.

Chapter 16

Keith and Loren arrived at the non-descript low-rise office building on the outskirts of Chapel Hill around 9:30am, having followed the local LTBT associate – he offered, upon meeting them, that his name was Richard – from their hotel. Richard had brought a new rental car for them, a 2007 Dodge Charger, and Keith drove that to the meeting while Richard drove their old rental Chevrolet. The new rental car was totally, according to Richard, "untraceable". Keith smiled politely when he'd said it, but he couldn't stop himself from thinking that nothing seemed to be untraceable for Ed and his team of killers. Richard had also brought them an unexpected, and potentially even more valuable, surprise: new drivers' licenses and credit cards for both of them. He explained that Patrick had insisted on providing them with new identities and drivers' licenses in case they were stopped for a traffic violation or needed to purchase anything that required an ID. Or, in the worst case scenario, they needed to get on a plane and get the hell out of town. Apparently creating fake documents was another one of Richard's special skills in addition to being a crackerjack paralegal. Keith's ID and credit cards were in the name of Adam Moss, and Loren's were in the name of Katherine Moss. The licenses showed their place of residence to be Williamsburg, VA.

At precisely 10:00am the video link came up and Keith and Loren found themselves face to face, or at least a close facsimile of face to face, with the core leadership team of LTBT. Patrick took the lead in introducing everyone and gave a brief synopsis of their background, and both Keith and Loren found themselves incredibly impressed with the caliber of people running this organization. These were not your average nutcases by any stretch of the imagination; they'd never assumed they would be, really, having read and reviewed some of their work as well as having spoken with Patrick and Jeff. Still, this was a very impressive group with a strong, diverse background in business and academia. Keith would have considered it an honor and a privilege to work with any of them, whether at UVA or at Bryant International.

After going through the introductions and background, Patrick turned to Keith and Loren and asked if they had, in fact, woken up to find that Ed had made good on his threat. Keith had to fight to hold himself together, but he finally managed to tell them about the deaths of David and his family. Loren, seeing that he was in pain, took over for him and filled in the details about the apparent 'accidental' explosion, how David had rented a car for them to flee the Hampton Roads area, and the long, close relationship that Keith and David had had over the past 20 years. The LTBT leaders looked shocked and pained as well, though, truth be told, they weren't especially shocked that the killings had occurred. Not just because Ed had threatened it, but because they had researched enough supposedly random killings and accidents over the past few years that having it happen again was, well, expected. Still, Patrick and his team weren't insensitive. They knew that this was new to Keith and Loren, and they knew that he, especially, was in a lot of pain at the loss of his best friend.

"Moving on," said Keith, still fighting back tears, "First, before we forget, we want to thank you guys for the new ID's and credit cards. We're still doing pretty well as far as cash goes, but you never know; these could come in handy, and it's a virtual certainty that the drivers licenses will. Obviously, we'll make sure that you guys get paid back for any charges that we put on those cards."

Before he could continue, Patrick jumped in. "Don't worry about the credit cards or paying us back. If you can down the line, you will. If not, it doesn't matter. Not in the least. Oh, and the cards are totally legitimate so you should not have any problems using them anywhere. They're being paid out of one of Jeff's offshore company accounts."

"Thanks, we both really appreciate so much all that you guys have done for us. I'm not sure where we'd be without you." Keith then added, "Shifting gears back to business, I think Loren and I may have come up with a new angle that we should explore. Loren, since this all started from your idea, why don't you explain it?"

"Sure," she replied. "Simply stated, we deduced that there is a distinct possibility that whoever is behind these assassination attempts is probably employed by a new intelligence agency rather than someone like the CIA or NSA. We came to this conclusion based on the fact that domestic spying, to say nothing of the murder of US citizens, is well outside their charter and their typical modus operandi. Hollywood notwithstanding, of course." She paused momentarily and saw that everyone was still with her, then continued. "Our assumption is that this agency is totally dark and off the books. No Congressional oversight, no published charter or budgets, nothing."

"So you're assuming that they were probably created by an Executive Order from the President then." This from Terrell Jackson.

"Most likely," replied Loren. "And we're assuming that this group was chartered and formed around the time of 9/11 with the specific task of making sure that nobody gets too close to the truth about those events. That's why they were on Keith and his Conspiracy class so quickly; they saw a huge increase in traffic to various conspiracy websites coming out of the little town of Charlottesville, and that spike caught their attention."

"That sounds reasonable to me," said Karen Richardson. "We know that the government is definitely monitoring some sites and some traffic on the internet, and we also know for a fact that they are sometimes planting false flags and misinformation to keep people wandering down the wrong paths and away from what we affectionately call 'The Truth'."

"Good, I'm glad that our ideas resonate with you guys. With all of your experience working in this area we realize that we may be coming up with theories that you've already considered and discounted a long time ago." Loren collected her thoughts for a moment, then asked, "Assuming that we're right about this new shadow group, how do we find them if they don't officially exist?"

Tony Winchester answered. "We can always go searching and digging to see if we can crack into the servers and sites of places like the White House, CIA, NSA, and so on, but obviously that runs a lot of risk. That being the case, we often find it useful to come up with one piece of relevant search criteria and expand outward from there."

"Like what kind of information?" Loren asked. She knew that Tony Winchester was a mathematician, and she was worried that he might go off on some theoretical tangent that she wouldn't be able to follow. She knew her limits; while brilliant in her field, she knew that math was definitely not one of her strong suits.

"It might be anything, sometimes even something innocuous," Tony answered. "For example, it could be when they were created, or where they're based, or the name or names of some of their people."

Tony's statement snapped Keith back to full attention. "Tony, one of the other criteria that we considered might be just what you're describing. See if this makes sense to you all: We posit that the leader of this new group or agency probably worked for another intelligence agency, probably in a very senior position. He, or she, would have probably resigned or retired from that position prior to taking this new role. If that is the case, perhaps we can correlate the retirement or reassignment of a key intelligence or DoD individual with a new role." Keith was not getting any signals that he was barking up the wrong tree from the others, so he continued. "One other thought. I can see the possibility that this new agency or group might be operating and hiding in plain sight. What I mean is, why not have this new group set up under the auspices of a private corporation? Maybe they, in whole or in part, operate as a legitimate business. That could provide them cover as well as an easy source of cash, remembering, as we said earlier, that they're probably totally off the books of the federal government."

Jeff Anders spoke. "I think you may be on to something here, and the concept is almost brilliant in its simplicity. We'll look for both civilians and military, keeping in mind that the head folks at our clandestine agencies are often high-ranking career officers with intelligence backgrounds."

Patrick spoke. "Can anybody think of any other parameters that we might use to narrow our search, or if not, at least to use as additional confirmation or support for any hits we get in our search?"

"I think I've got one," offered Tony, leaning back in his chair and starting to stare up at his ceiling, almost as if he were looking to the heavens for some divine answer. Finally, after a few seconds of thinking, he brought his chair back down and around to face the camera. It was evident from his eyes that he'd just had his own small epiphany. "We all agree that there is some group of government ne'er-do-wells that are monitoring everything that Dr. Bryant and his students are doing relative to 9/11, and in addition, they must certainly be monitoring all of the hits these websites get from all over the world. Right? Otherwise, how would they have stumbled on Dr.

Bryant? Obviously, they weren't just focusing on Charlottesville, VA in their monitoring. They're looking worldwide. They're looking for patterns, they're looking for anomalies. Agreed?"

Everyone on the video link agreed, so Tony continued. "Alright then. What are the two things that our government friends would have to have in order to accomplish this monumental task?" Tony couldn't help himself from slipping into his professorial mode, asking questions of his peers as if he were putting his own students on the spot during one of his lectures.

Jeff Anders spoke up. "Shit, it's so obvious. Massive computer power and massive amounts of bandwidth."

"Exactly. We've got these guys keeping tabs on God knows how many different websites and how many individuals, and that is going to require a shitload of processing power and the bandwidth to connect it to the Internet. If we start with the variables that Dr. Bryant and Loren have already brought us, and then correlate those results against any purchases of supercomputers and huge amounts of bandwidth around the time of 9/11 we may be able to build a stronger case, and a faster case, against our friend Ed." Tony was smiling from ear to ear, quite pleased with himself for thinking of it.

"That's a fantastic idea," said Patrick. "We'll all put our heads together on this and figure out how to divvy up the work. And Karen, with your background in telecommunications, you'll be a big help in identifying the likely bandwidth requirements that this new agency needed to order and who they may have ordered it from. That way we can narrow our search more quickly."

Karen Richardson responded, "Yes, I can certainly do that. Once we figure out what they have in the way of computing power and capacity I think we can make a pretty good estimate of their bandwidth needs, and as you can probably imagine, there are only a handful of service providers that could probably meet their needs."

"I think Tony, Terrell, and I can help develop a likely scenario for their computing needs," said Jeff. "It may take a few hours for us to develop some reasonable ideas about what they would require, but the good news is, at least in my mind, that we don't have to be perfect. If we just come up with some reasonable concept of what they need it may be close enough, because I'm guessing that purchases of computer processing power anywhere close to their requirements is pretty rare. It probably puts them in pretty specialized company, like a handful of large research universities, an even smaller group of government agencies, etc."

"I'd have to agree with your assessment," added Terrell. "Computing power on this scale you might see used for working on extremely complex problems like the Human Genome project, huge engineering projects like the proposed suspension bridge between Sicily and the Italian mainland, or for mapping the known universe. No matter how well the government would have tried to hide this kind of purchase, like splitting it among several contracts, it had to have created a spike in revenues, and maybe even employment, among the handful of companies that are capable of building this kind of supercomputer."

"Agreed. That's good for us then, since that spike in revenues and/or employment is one other data point we can use for our search, or at least for corroboration," said Keith.

The whole group was obviously getting pumped, their mood definitely brightening as well. With the fresh perspectives added by Keith and Loren, the core leaders of LTBT felt that they had, for the first time in a long time, a new and viable direction for uncovering The Truth. They were no longer being reactive, simply researching other conspiracy theories and, more often than not, shooting them down. They were no longer waiting to disprove all of the other theories that were out there and then, magically, back into their own answers. Now they were moving forward, proactively going after the bastards responsible for 9/11, to say nothing of the latest killings of Lowell Westbrook and David Ward and his family. Without really intending to, Keith and Loren had given the LTBT leadership team the shot in the arm that they needed to go on the offensive, to attack. If there was any fear, any apprehension, or any second thoughts at all among anyone on the call, it was certainly not evident. They were primed for the fight.

The call went on for about another forty five minutes, during which time Keith told the leadership team about Ed giving him a number that he could call should he want to talk. They all discussed the pros and cons of Keith calling him and how such a call should be handled. Keith wanted to go on the offensive, tell Ed that he was going to track him down and kill him, or maybe threaten to go to the press. Fortunately, cooler heads prevailed. In this case, the voices of reason came from the two females in the group, Loren and Karen Richardson. They suggested a more passive role, maybe showing fear, or even some contrition, to Ed. Make him feel superior, make him think that he has scared Keith to the point of hopelessness. They reasoned that maybe, just maybe, it might throw him off or make him overconfident and thus more likely to make his own mistake.

Keith listened to all of the back and forth, then finally said, "Look, with all due respect to everyone here, I think we're being naïve if we play it the way that Loren and Karen are suggesting. It's not just a matter of whether or not someone like Ed can be fooled or whether I'm a good enough actor to convince him. Frankly, I don't think either one matters one iota. He's a man on an ego and power trip. He likes that he's in control, most likely has been in control of others throughout most of his career. He is up to his ass in the conspiracy behind 9/11, and he will kill anyone that creates a risk of exposure for him and the other conspirators. The truth is, I don't think what you're proposing as a way to deal with him will work, but to be honest, I'm not convinced that my way will, either. I think that no matter what I do or say, he's going to keep on hurting and killing the people that we love until he can catch me and Loren and kill us both." The thought gave him chills, and he could see the frightened look in Loren's eyes. He had never put it quite so bluntly, so matter-of-factly, up until now. Keith may not have accepted the fact that he was going to die, but he had definitely accepted the fact that somebody was trying to kill him and would not stop trying to kill him unless he got to them first.

"You two are the ones most in the line of fire here," said Patrick, breaking the awkward silence. "We'll support you either way you want to go, or, for that matter, if you choose not to contact him at all."

"Thanks. I'm definitely going to contact him, though. I want to hear his voice again, really listen closely to what he says and how he says it. I need to get to know him, understand what makes him tick, what sets him off. Maybe learn which of his buttons to push, if you catch my drift."

"I think we do," smiled Patrick. "By the way, have you decided where you're going next? As you said before, it's probably not a good idea to stay in any one place too long."

"Actually, Loren and I haven't really discussed it at this point. I had been thinking about making it to Atlanta since it was a big enough city to hide, plus there are tons of major roads leading in and out of the city if we have to run. But now, I'm thinking about heading back closer to DC." Keith saw Loren look at him quizzically out of the corner of his eye.

"What's your logic there?" asked Jeff.

"There probably isn't any really good logic," Keith replied with a smile. "But somehow I keep coming back to the fact that, somewhere along the line, we're going to have to take this fight right to Ed, right to his doorstep. I know there's no concrete proof that he and his group are necessarily in the DC area, but I think we can all agree that's the odds-on favorite if we had to guess a location. I want to be somewhere in the area in case the opportunity arises for us to nail his ass." He looked at Loren to see if she would be with him on this; she simply smiled at him and reached out and put her hand on top of his. That was all he needed to feel reassured.

"Again, we defer to you. You're on the front lines. Obviously we'll continue to support you in any way we can. Just continue to check in with us regularly so we know you're safe and so we can let you know how the research is progressing." Patrick tried not to sound too worried about his new friends, but he wasn't doing a very good job.

"Before we sign off, I'd like to ask you guys one thing, if you don't mind." Keith had been holding back on asking this question, not wanting to say anything to offend his new friends or to make them feel defensive.

"Ask us anything," said Patrick.

"OK, here goes. How do you guys manage to stay safe from the bad guys, like Ed and all of his friends? You guys have a high-profile within the conspiracy theory community, so I'd think that you'd be pretty easy targets if they wanted to eliminate you."

"That's a valid question, although I think we're probably not feeling as safe and insulated as we did prior to learning about this new agency that's focusing in on conspiracy groups, to say nothing of killing people that get in their way. But to answer your question," Patrick continued, "we've never tried to publish or promote our names or our credentials. In fact, we go to great lengths to stay anonymous. We're not naïve enough to think that our identities might not be compromised, but until now we've never had any real concerns. Truthfully, that may be simply because we've never stumbled onto anything of any great value. We've often been the clearinghouse, if you will, for debunking theories that other people and groups have put forth. Beyond that, though, we've always gone to great lengths to keep things around here compartmentalized. That is, each of the core team leaders has their own extended team of associates that assist them with research and other tasks. In most cases, we tend to have maybe 4-5 associates aligned with each core team leader at any given time. Those associates, in turn, don't know who any of the other core team leaders are, nor do they know any of the other associates in our network. So, to answer your question, we strive to make sure that everybody that works with our group knows only one other member, that being the core team leader that recruited them."

"Ingenious, I have to admit," said Keith admiringly. "It sounds a lot like the methods our clandestine services use with their operatives, making sure that they don't know anyone involved with their mission other than their assigned handler."

"Exactly. That's actually where we got the idea," said Jeff. "Since our founding we've adopted many best practices from different private companies and government agencies, and when it comes to compartmentalization of information there's probably no one better than our spy agencies."

The call concluded shortly thereafter, and Keith and Loren both agreed that they were fortunate to have been taken in by a group of such bright, dedicated, professionals. They were all certainly kindred spirits, not just in their intellectual and academic backgrounds, but in their belief in uncovering the lies and deceptions that had taken the place of truth and honesty and integrity in our country. Nobody would ever ask for the risk or the terror that they were now faced with, but they knew that, if it was something that they had to endure, they could never ask for a better group of compatriots to align themselves with. And for that, they were both very, very grateful.

⌘

KEITH AND LOREN LEFT THE Raleigh/Durham area and headed north, their destination Annapolis, MD. A beautiful town hard beside the Chesapeake Bay, it was both quaint and picturesque, but more importantly, it was within an hour or two of virtually the entire DC metropolitan area. Plus, it was a town where Keith knew his way around intimately, having spent four years at the Naval Academy.

Loren drove while Keith jotted down some notes and questions that he wanted to cover during his forthcoming conversation with Ed. They discussed the benefits and liabilities surrounding each question, what they'd hope to gain by asking it, and what the probable responses might be. Action, reaction. It was as simple, and as complex, as that. You ask a question; hopefully you get an answer or provoke a response. Depending on the answer you get, you respond appropriately or ask another question. You're always working to gain the upper hand, always working to keep your valuable information hidden. Move. Countermove. Check. Checkmate. Always thinking, always planning, several steps ahead. Life as the ultimate game of chess.

Finally satisfied with their game plan, Keith asked Loren to pull off at the next exit. They were in Henderson, NC, the last city of any size before they reached the Virginia border. The plan was to use one of the pre-paid AT&T calling cards from a pay phone, hoping that that might impede Ed from locating their position as quickly as from a cell phone. They had no illusion of it being completely secure, at least not for long. Ironically, the hardest thing about their plan turned out to be finding a pay phone; it hadn't dawned on them that pay phones were virtually relics of the past. Other than the payphone in the Cracker Barrel restaurant they weren't able to find one indoors at the first exit they tried, and there was definitely too much background noise to make it a good choice. They finally found what they were looking for at the next exit, a phone in a reasonably quiet, reasonably empty barbeque shack. While Loren ordered some food for the two of them, Keith went to the payphone in the small hallway next to the bathrooms. Not ideal, he realized, but under the circumstances it would have to do.

Once he had entered the interminable string of numbers, it took only two rings before Ed picked up. Even though Keith was expecting him to answer, hearing his voice again scared him to the core.

"Well, well, Dr. Bryant. I've been expecting your call. Actually, I'm a little surprised that it's taken you quite so long to reach me. I trust you've seen the news."

Keith fought to keep his emotions in check. They weren't yet 10 seconds into the conversation and already Ed was pushing his buttons. "Yes, I saw the news. Why did you have to kill an innocent family? They had done nothing to you. And my God, you killed a woman and young child, for what? To punish me?" Keith tried his best to let his emotions, his fear come out through his voice, while at the same time trying to control his anger and his instinct to lash out.

"Of course it was to punish you, Dr. Bryant. Don't act so surprised. After all, I only did exactly as I promised. And don't give me that shit about how your friend was just an innocent bystander in all of this. He chose to become involved in this little affair by renting a car for you the other day and helping you evade capture. And, I'm sure, you undoubtedly told him about your little high-seas adventure. Face it, Dr. Bryant. His death, and the death of his family, is your fault. No one else's." His voice was as cold and detached as if he were describing the local high school sports scores.

"Even if you think you can justify killing David, you can't use the same justification for killing his wife and son! They had nothing to do with this."

"You're right, of course. But again, their blood is on your hands, Dr. Bryant. In all wars there is collateral damage. In this case, they had to be sacrificed for the greater good. It's a shame that such drastic measures have to be taken sometimes, but you've brought us to this point. Despite what you may think of me, Dr. Bryant, I don't relish the thought of having a mother and child turned into 'crispy critters' simply to prove my point."

Bastard! Making a joke out of murdering innocent people and incinerating them! Keith fought hard to control himself, knowing that Ed was trying to provoke his own response. He also had no doubt that there were others listening in on the call and recording it for analysis. He had to control himself, continue with his tone of helplessness. Continue to sound like a man that has lost hope, a man that has accepted the inevitability of defeat. "I don't want any more people to die, not on my account. I'm begging you, please don't hurt anyone else. Just tell me what I need to do to stop this. I'll do whatever it takes."

Ed hesitated a few seconds before answering, no doubt getting input from others that were listening in, or, perhaps, just playing his own internal chess game. "It's quite simple, really. You and Ms. Davis need to be brought in, and all information you have related to your 9/11 research has to be turned over to me. All disks, all external drives, all hard copies, everything. And that includes any copies that you may have decided to try to hide in safe deposit boxes, or under a rock, or with your little friends at LTBT. Until such time as you and Ms. Davis are standing in front of me and I'm convinced that I have everything, and I do mean everything, in my hands, you are going to continue to be responsible for a lot of needless pain and suffering. Is that what you want for your friends, for your family?"

"No, of course that's not what I want, and I'll do anything to stop it, I swear. But what's it going to take for you to be convinced that you have everything? No matter what I turn over to you, you're always going to assume that there's more," Keith said with a feigned rising panic in his voice.

"Very true, sir, and, might I add, a very astute observation. I will certainly assume that you're lying to me. People always try, you see, and I'm sure that you're no different. Everyone always thinks they're so much smarter than me, so much cleverer." Then his tone turned more menacing. "But they're wrong, I assure you, and let me tell you why lying is utterly futile: I will test you, both mentally and physically, to ensure that you're telling the truth. Depending on how obstinate you want to be, that may include physical pain or it may require some chemical persuasion. Oh, and don't forget, of course, that the lovely Ms. Davis will be here as well. After seeing her and hearing her during your little romantic trysts, my team is absolutely salivating at the prospect of getting their hands on her. If you decide to be less than straight with us, Dr. Bryant, I promise you this: you won't even recognize her when we finish carving her up. And once again, the blood of someone you love will be on your hands."

"No, please, God no! I'll do whatever you ask; I'll give you everything you want. I can be in DC tomorrow, but please, just don't hurt anyone until we can get there." Keith was hoping that the reference to DC would elicit a response from Ed.

"Well, I'll certainly look forward to seeing you tomorrow then. You can call me and I'll let you know where we can rendezvous. But, you know, Dr. Bryant, I can't help but feel that you're being disingenuous with me. Call me suspicious, but in my experience people in your position often change their minds at the last minute, essentially chicken out, if you will. I can't afford to have that happen here, nor can you. So, what I'm about to tell you is really quite simple, but I want to be crystal clear and make sure that there is absolutely no room -- zero -- for any misunderstanding." Ed's voice was practically dripping with venom. "Now you hear me, and you hear me well: Apparently you haven't learned your lesson yet and somebody else is going to have to die to convince you that I mean exactly what I say, and once again, their blood is going to be on your hands! Somebody else has to be sacrificed because you continue to stall for time!" His voice was growing louder, getting angrier. "If you wanted to be here today you could be and you would be, and we both know it. You're not nearly that far away. You're trying my patience, to be honest. And because you're intent on trying to prove that you're smarter than me, and tougher than me, I'm afraid that you're going to need just a little bit more convincing. Now it's just a matter of deciding who's next on the list to die. Any preferences? Maybe it's someone from Bryant International? Or maybe one or more of your students, or a faculty member? Or maybe it's Ms. Davis' parents, all snuggled up at her aunt's house in Pittsburgh? So many choices, so little time, unfortunately."

"Please, no, you don't have to do this," Keith pleaded. This time the pleading was for real. All pretenses of being in control or feigning fear were over. The fear and dread he was feeling were far too real.

"Oh, but I do. It's like I told you, someone around you is going to die every single day until I have what I want. And what I want is quite simple, but you refuse to listen to reason. So again, don't be surprised when, for the second day in a row, you wake up to a nightmare. This conversation is over, Dr. Bryant. I suggest you quit wasting my time and do as I've instructed. The people around you can't afford for you to continue to be this stupid and selfish." With that, Ed disconnected the call.

Keith was wobbly and lightheaded as he hung up the phone, actually having to lean against the wall for support. The call had not started off badly, but by the end all he had really come away with is confirmation, more or less, that Ed and his group were based somewhere in the DC area. Not much of a stretch there, he reasoned. It was always considered the most likely location. In this little chess game, Ed had Keith at checkmate in just a few moves. He was very disappointed that he'd let Ed drive the conversation and ratchet-up the threat level. And, from what he'd seen, there was no reason to think that Ed's threats wouldn't be carried out, and soon.

Keith walked into the main part of the restaurant and sat down with Loren, his face ashen. "I can tell by the look on your face that the call didn't go as we'd hoped," Loren said to Keith, trying to control the rising panic and fear that she felt.

"No, it didn't." Keith looked around to make sure that no one was within earshot. "Let's take the food and go eat out in the car where we can talk a little bit easier." He stood up and started grabbing food, drinks, and napkins and heading for the door, though his appetite had pretty much vanished.

Once they were in the car, Keith started telling her about the call. "Basically, he's threatened to keep on killing until we've turned ourselves into him and turned over every shred of information we have about 9/11. Even then, it's obvious that he's going to have to be 100% convinced that we've given him everything, and I don't know how we're ever going to convince him of that."

Loren thought for a second, fighting the rising fear inside. "He'll never be satisfied, not completely. Even if he beats us and tortures us and gives us some kind of truth serum chemicals, once he's through with us he's going to kill us, right? No way that he's going to let us live to tell our story."

"You're right, of course," Keith replied flatly. "They can't let us live, or, for that matter, anyone that's been involved with this along the way, like LTBT. All we can do is minimize the fallout by turning ourselves, and everything we've got, over to him and pray that the killing stops with us. The longer we wait, the more people around us die."

"Bullshit!" Loren screamed. "You're not considering for one second giving yourself up to that maniac, are you? Forget what he'll do to us. What about the fact that he'll be able to continue to bury the truth about 9/11 from the American public? That's something that has to be uncovered and shared with the world, our lives be damned! This is bigger than the two of us, or even bigger than all of us. We need to take this son of a bitch, and all of the other conspirators, down for good!"

Keith was still in shock from the conversation with Ed and his mind was working in slow motion. He felt like he was running in molasses while the rest of the world was passing him by at hyper-speed. "I don't know how we're going to do that. We don't even know where or how to find them, and they seem to know where to find every person in the world that means anything to us. They'll kill them all before they're done."

"We are not going to let that happen. They're only going after other people because they don't know where to find us, right? I say, let's let them know where we are and have them put the focus back on us, where it belongs."

Keith looked at her like she had lost her mind. "How the hell do you propose that we do that? And what makes you think that they won't continue to go after our friends and our families even as they come after us?"

"I'll tell you why," Loren shot back with fire and determination in her eyes. "Because we are going to do exactly what you said earlier, we're going to take the fight to them, right to their front goddamn door. We are going to find out where they work or where they live and we will hunt *them* down! Let's turn the tables on these bastards and put them on the defensive. That's the last thing they'd be expecting, right? They expect everyone to run for their lives until their hit squads track them down and kill them. I say we do it differently. Let's track them down."

Keith looked at Loren and saw the fear in her eyes being replaced by anger and hope and determination. That snapped him out of his momentary mental hell. Thank God they had each other, he thought. Whenever one was down, the other was there to help pick them up and bring them back to reality. She was ready to face the fact that they might well be killed, but she would be damned if she was going down without a fight. The government had brought this fight to them, and then they'd escalated it by killing people around them and threatening everyone that was important to them. Loren was right; the only way that they were going to have a chance of surviving this – and even then the chances were pretty slim, he admitted to himself – was to turn this whole situation on its head.

"So what kind of plan is floating around in that pretty little head of yours?" Keith asked.

"I say we get Patrick and the LTBT to step up their efforts to identify Ed and pinpoint his agency's location. As you said, we've got pretty definite confirmation that they're in the Washington, DC area. Once we find them, maybe we'll be able to identify the individual players, maybe take them out of commission one at a time. One way or the other though, we're going to track down Ed and uncover the real 9/11 story and tell the whole world, and when this is over he's going to be as dead as those hired killers you left in the middle of the Bay."

Keith had never heard Loren talk this way or be this cold, this calculating. Rather than be repulsed by it, though, Keith actually embraced it. She'd been pushed as far as she was going to be pushed. 'Fight or flight' had been decided, and in her case it was definitely 'fight'. He had to agree. If they continued to flee, they'd eventually be tracked down, and in the interim, probably every person they knew or cared about would be killed. Outside of LTBT, they had nowhere to turn for help. The police would scoff at them, at the very least, and probably arrest them. The press, or at least the legitimate press, would probably ignore them unless there was an incredible amount of unassailable evidence to back their story up. References to 9/11 conspiracies, shootouts on the high seas, and tales of friends killed by shadowy hit teams might make for great fiction or the cover of the *National Enquirer*, but the *Washington Post* wouldn't touch it with a ten foot pole.

Looking over at Loren, Keith reached out and took her hand. "You know, you're probably right. No matter what we do, no matter what we say, we're as good as dead if Ed finds us or if we turn ourselves in. Our only hope is to get him before he gets us, and we need to get to him before he has a chance to kill everyone that we care about." Then, squeezing her hand, he added, "Thanks for giving me the little kick in the ass I needed to see things clearly."

Loren just smiled over at him, and then said, "Hey, you've been keeping watch over me and saving my bacon for the past few days. It's time for me to step it up a bit instead of letting you have all the fun."

"Tell you what we need to do then," he said, re-energized. The fog and the funk were lifting and he was once again thinking strategically and acting tactically, his mind going a million miles an hour. "We'll be crossing over into Virginia in about another 30 miles, and Virginia is the home of easy gun purchases. I know of a store a little bit south of Richmond that sells just about every firearm known to mankind, and they're not really too concerned about what you buy or how much you buy, especially if you're paying cash."

"Are you talking about handguns or rifles?"

"I've already got the one pistol, so I think we need to concentrate on more firepower, like assault-type rifles. This store will have it all, including ammunition and anything else we need, like camouflage gear or night-vision goggles. You know, in case a hunter needs to be out stalking Bambi in the dead of night with their big guns." He hoped that would bring a little smile and help ease the tension a bit.

Loren did, in fact, smile. "Yeah, those hunters nowadays, they're quite the sportsmen, aren't they?"

It took just over an hour to reach the exit for the gun store on the south side of Richmond. Even on this weekday the parking lot was almost full, and virtually every vehicle sported a dozen or more bumper stickers -- Keith figured that in at least a few instances the bumper stickers were the only things holding them together -- praising God, country, and the NRA. Keith went in alone while Loren waited outside and kept watch for any signs of trouble or surveillance. As he walked into the store he was awestruck at the incredible volume and variety of instruments of death. There were guns of every size, shape, and description, and enough ammunition to support a small army in war. He saw every type of hunting and outdoor clothing, plus every possible accessory for hunting and survival in the woods. Keith took a look at the assortment of rifles, which, to his mind, was overwhelming. There were rifles of all types, from simple bolt-action hunting rifles to guns that were, in virtually every detail, no different from the weapons currently being used by SWAT teams and armies all over the world. Stepping up to the counter Keith started taking a closer look at his options.

"Can I help you find something there, partner?" asked a clerk named Kyle.

"Yeah, I'm looking for a high-end rifle, semi-automatic. Something that holds a decent number of rounds and has the option for a nice scope. It doesn't have to be especially long-range, but something accurate out to a couple of hundred yards, at least."

"Got something you might like right here," offered Kyle. "Got two of 'em left in stock. Been on sale for a couple of weeks and we've sold a boatload of 'em." Kyle pulled down a rifle off the rack. The assault style gun practically screamed 'killing machine'. "This here's a Heckler and Koch HK 416, their version of the AR-15 Carbine that's used by police SWAT teams and the military the world over. Got a magazine that holds 30 rounds and can shoot either the 5.56mm NATO rounds or the .223 caliber Remingtons. You can add a scope to 'er as well."

Keith looked the gun over, and what he saw was really impressive. Solid, with flawless craftsmanship. The empty magazine popped in and out easily, and the standard sight looked adequate for all but the longest shots he might be tempted to attempt. "How much for both of them?" Keith asked.

Kyle's eyes lit up. Not too often he had customers willing to pop for two guns in this price range. "I can let you have 'em for $950 each. I'll even throw in a box of ammo for each one."

"That sounds good. I'm also going to want to get some extra 30-round magazines for these, as well as some extra ammo. Can you handle that?"

"Oh, hell yes, partner. Let me take a look on the computer here to see what I've got in inventory." Kyle took a couple of minutes to check, then came back to Keith. "I've got 10 of the 30-round magazines in stock for the

H&K, and I've got several dozen boxes of the ammo here in the store. How much you want?"

"Tell you what, give me all 10 of those magazines and 20 boxes of the .223 caliber Remington rounds. And one last thing: what do you have in stock in the way of silencers or suppressors?"

"Well, sir, normally we don't keep them in stock since the law requires us to fill out a shitload of forms, get your fingerprints, then have the sheriff or police sign-off on the paperwork after the requisite background check. Whole process usually takes 60-120 days, and we can't hand over the silencers until we have that paperwork back here in our hands. With that much lead time, we usually wait to order the silencers once we know the paperwork is completed."

"Damn, that's too bad. I would really like to get some suppression for both of these. It gets awfully loud sitting out on the range firing these things, even with earplugs."

Kyle grew quiet for a moment, thinking, and then signaled for Keith to follow him. He led the way back to the stockroom just off of the sales floor, and seeing that they were alone, spoke to Keith in a voice barely above a whisper. "Tell ya what. I got two silencers right here in the backroom that will fit those H&K guns. We ordered them a while back for a man but screwed up and did it way too early in the process. It turns out that his paperwork was rejected because of a felony arrest on his record. Now we're stuck with them. We just don't have a big market for silencers since they're pretty expensive and the process is so damn cumbersome."

"So what's the chance of you being convinced to part with both of them – today? Unfortunately, I'm not inclined to wait the 60-120 days for the paperwork." Keith was hoping that Kyle could be persuaded to sell him the silencers. Somehow, it didn't appear that he was the type to be a stickler for regulations, especially if it would put cash in his pocket.

"Well, if you're sure you're not a Fed – you're not the police or ATF, right?" Seeing that Keith was answering in the negative, Kyle continued. "We paid about $450 each for these babies and retail is about $595. They've been sitting here in inventory for damn near a year and I'd like to see them the hell out of here. What do you say to $750 for the pair?"

"I'd say that you have yourself a deal. I assume that you'd like to keep that part of the deal separate and just between us guys, right?"

Keith stayed a little bit longer and had Kyle help him pick out a good scope for one of the rifles, as well as two sets of night vision goggles. The whole little shopping spree set him back several thousand dollars, but it was well worth it. Now he had the firepower he needed to go up against Ed and his army of killers. Once they found them, he reminded himself. Keith paid cash, of course, and even turned over his new driver's license without hesitation when making his purchases. Kyle was so excited about the large sale that he invited Keith to come back down one weekend so they could go out hunting and shooting together. 'Boy, I can't wait', Keith thought to himself. Back out in the car, Keith put the guns and other purchases in the trunk. The pistol and other guns he'd brought from Charlottesville were up front with them, just in case.

"So, how'd it go? Make any new friends in there?" Loren asked with a giggle.

"Yeah, several. I think I saw them all in *Deliverance*. At least we've got some fire power now for when we need it."

"Good," Loren responded. "I have a feeling we're going to need it sooner rather than later."

They headed back out to I-95 North and headed for Annapolis, MD. Close, but not too close, to their quarry. They both knew that, one way or the other, they were going to be very close to them, very, very soon. And without question, they intended to make Ed and his group pay for what they'd done – or die trying.

Chapter 17

KEITH MADE A STRATEGIC DECISION to stay a couple of miles outside of downtown Annapolis at a small Comfort Inn on Route 50, the main road in and out of the area. While he would have much preferred to be downtown near the crowds, the bars, and the restaurants for both convenience and nostalgic reasons, he had to keep reminding himself that he wasn't here on vacation, he was fighting to stay alive. Better to be out here on the main road where he could make a hasty exit toward DC, Baltimore, or, worst case, across the Bay Bridge to Maryland's Eastern Shore. He and Loren decided to pop downtown for dinner and a little stroll around the harbor, she having convinced him that a little walk and exercise would probably do them both a world of good. The town area wasn't that crowded, a scenario that they considered a mixed blessing: easier to get into your favorite bars and restaurants, but a lot less people to blend in with. The situation would have been radically different just a couple of weeks ago here in town. In October Annapolis is home to the United States Sailboat Show for four days early in the month and then the United States Powerboat show for four days the following week. The powerboat show, especially, brought thousands of visitors to the area, and, as luck would have it, each year it was scheduled for the same weekend as the Naval Academy's Homecoming. Hotel rooms were always booked solid, and every bar and restaurant was bursting at the seams.

They stopped in at Riordan's and had a couple of drinks at the bar, the alcohol slowly but surely easing some of the day's tensions. The stress was really starting to take a toll on them both, as were the constant nights in strange beds and the hours spent in rental cars. Both longed for a night at home in their own bed, eating their own food and drinking their own wine. Soon, they promised themselves. Soon, this would all be over. One way or the other. They talked about where they should go for dinner, nothing really being that tempting after days and days of eating on the road.

They were so engrossed in their drinks and their conversation that neither Keith nor Loren noticed the man who came into the restaurant and sat on the barstool about twenty feet away. He had noticed them walking along the sidewalks and looking in shop windows, perusing restaurant menu choices, and ogling some of the gorgeous go-fast type boats tied along the quay in the section of the harbor known as 'Ego Alley'. The man's name, at least according to his identification, was Thomas A Julian, a former Army Ranger now working under contract to Ed Foster and Bob Manning. It hadn't exactly been hardship duty for him the past few days, essentially hanging out in Annapolis, keeping an eye out for Dr. Keith Bryant and Ms. Loren Davis, and reporting in on a regular basis. He'd actually grown quite bored. The small town of Annapolis, while charming, was not exactly a major metropolis with a seemingly unlimited number of restaurants, museums, or stores to keep you occupied. As Julian walked along the harbor admiring the boats, he managed to get several reasonably good photos of both Keith and Loren using his camera phone. After they popped into Riordan's, he kept an eye on the entrance to make sure that they didn't leave, while at the same time sending their pictures to Foster and Manning for confirmation. Julian had no doubt that these were the subjects he'd been on the lookout for, and he was anxious to hear back from his employers. More than anything, he hoped that Colonel Foster might give him the plum assignment of taking these two out. It would be his first for-hire killing since going freelance, and there was no better way to make your bones than to kill both subjects – a twofer, Julian smiled to himself – without assistance from the DC boys. Plus, he didn't need to remind himself, he could certainly use the money that would come with killing these two. Doing this job for Foster and his team might even lead to additional work in the future, perhaps be the start of a very long, very lucrative relationship.

Within minutes Julian's phone rang and both Foster and Manning were on the line. "Mr. Julian, it looks like you have found the elusive Dr. Bryant and Ms. Davis. Good work. What can you tell us at this point?"

Julian took on his best military affectation, assuming – correctly – that Foster had been a superior officer. "Well, sir, not a lot, at least not yet. I just spotted them a few minutes ago and haven't done anything but observe them and call you. Right now they're in Riordan's, a local restaurant and pub, having drinks at the bar. I was reconnoitering the downtown area, as I've been doing several times a day, and I just happened to see them walking along the street, just like any other couple out for a little shopping or early dinner. I followed them for a few blocks before they ended up down here by the harbor, then, as I said, they ducked into Riordan's for a drink."

"Any indication where they came from, or if maybe they're staying right there in town versus coming there by car?" asked Bob Manning.

"No sir, any answer I could give you would be a pure guess and speculation on my part. As I said, I picked them up a couple of blocks up from the harbor, but I couldn't tell you at this point if they're staying in one of the nearby hotels or inns or if they're parked somewhere here in town just to grab some dinner. I'm going to assume that you guys already have every possible type of electronic surveillance on their credit cards, bank accounts, and ID's, correct, sirs?"

Foster answered. "Yes, that's correct, Mr. Julian. We've checked, of course, just to be thorough. We don't expect Dr. Bryant to make that kind of mistake, and we've found no activity on his cards or any hotel reservations of any kind using his name. Dr. Bryant is very careful, and all indications are that he's getting substantial outside assistance, which might even include new identities and new credit cards. That's why we've had to resort to a more old-fashioned game of cat and mouse and why we've had you, and others like you, staking out places where we believe he might go for comfort or familiarity."

"Well, then, lucky for me to be at the right place at the right time," said Julian. He decided to go for the assumptive close, just like a good salesman. "Sirs, I recognize that you probably have considerable resources, but since I'm on the scene, right here and now, I'd like to offer you my services to take whatever steps you require with regards to Dr. Bryant and Ms. Davis. I can probably have the job done before you can even get additional resources up here to Annapolis."

Foster and Manning had expected as much. These contractors were always eager to make the kill, get their money and get out. They had laughed about it earlier, about how you had to admire the blatant entrepreneurship of some of these guys – and girls. Neither of them doubted Julian's abilities or his resolve. At the same time though, they no longer underestimated Keith's abilities or, in their view, his damnable luck. Foster spoke. "Mr. Julian, as you say, it would take a while for us to get additional resources to Annapolis, probably at least an hour or two. Then, of course, we have to concern ourselves with where we stage our people, where we set up the hit, and so on. You're by now intimately familiar with the town and the traffic patterns, probably even know the best places to make a kill and guarantee a safe exit. I'm asking you to eliminate both Dr. Bryant and Ms. Davis, tonight. I will offer you $25,000 for the job. Will that suit you?"

That would suit him just fine, Julian thought to himself. These are obviously some very high value targets. He had thought maybe $10,000 for the pair, not $25,000. Sweet. "That will work just fine for me, sir. Do you have any preferences for how this should be done? I can accommodate whatever you want; I just want to make sure I'm delivering something that's consistent with your overall strategy and plan." Here he was talking about killing two human beings, and he could have just as easily been talking about a strategic business plan for a new retail store or restaurant.

"Our first preference is to make it look like a mugging or robbery gone wrong," said Foster. "But the most important thing is that it be done tonight, without fail. If circumstances should keep you from completing the mission such that it looks like a mugging or robbery, consider yourself to have the green light to take them out by any means necessary. Of course, we'd like to eliminate, or certainly minimize, any collateral damage, as I'm sure you can appreciate. We don't need any more people hurt, or any more people asking questions, than is absolutely necessary. Is that clear?" Foster felt compelled to ask, these hired killers seemingly having no compunction about killing the entire human race so long as it meant taking out the one person that they were targeting and being paid to kill. There is certainly nothing subtle about them, he mused to himself. No art to their killing, no close-in combat or quiet assassinations. They'd rather use a machine gun than a garrote or five pounds of plastic explosives instead of one smaller, shaped charge. Nothing elegant, just simple brute force. Philistines, he thought to himself.

"I hear you loud and clear, sir."

"And Mr. Julian, one last thing," said Foster. "If you find yourself, for whatever reason, unable to complete your mission within the next few hours, I want you to call me or Mr. Manning immediately. We'll send whatever additional resources you may need, no questions asked. And we'll still pay you $10,000 as a finder's fee for leading us to Dr. Bryant and Ms. Davis even if you don't make the kill. So, bottom line, there is no reason whatsoever that this mission should not be completed tonight. And, there is no reason that you should not walk away from tonight with a significant amount of money even if you don't end up with blood on your hands. Do we understand each other?"

"Yes, sir. Crystal clear," said Julian. "I will not let you down, sir. I will be in touch as soon as the mission is complete."

⌘

BACK INSIDE RIORDAN'S, JULIAN SAT at the bar nursing a beer and talking nonchalantly with the bartender, a gorgeous young thing that, on any other night, he would have been hitting on in a major way. Based on the looks she was giving him and the very flirtatious and barely disguised sexual references, he had very little doubt that she would have welcomed his advances. "Just my luck," he muttered under his breath. The first chance he'd had to get laid in the three days he'd been here in Annapolis and he had to walk away. He had to stay focused, get the thought of her beautiful smile, perfect breasts, and incredible ass and legs out of his mind and back to the task at hand. Fortunately, there was a mirror over the bar that let him observe his prey without having to look directly at them down the bar.

Keith and Loren were just finishing their second drink and had finally settled on a choice for dinner. Rather than hit the restaurants right there around the harbor that serve mostly pub-type food, they decided to go for something a little more chic, a little more upscale. A lady sitting next to Loren had heard them discussing places to eat, and she offered that she'd had a fantastic meal at a restaurant that was just about a half-mile from downtown. She raved about the Asian fusion cuisine that she and her friends had enjoyed there, including the sushi, the crab cakes, the tiger prawns, and the yellow fin tuna. That certainly sounds more interesting than going for another burger or sandwich with fries, they both agreed. Keith called to the bartender for their tab, and while she was ringing them up he took a look around the restaurant to see if anyone, or anything, looked out of place. Was there anyone there that seemed to be paying too much attention to them, or someone that he'd seen somewhere else over the past few days? He no longer considered this a sign of paranoia; events had proven him correct. Now it was just survival instinct.

He'd even encouraged Loren to develop the same habit, which was, at its most basic, to simply be observant and vigilant. Seeing nobody or nothing out of the ordinary, they headed for the door.

As they walked out of Riordan's, Keith took her by the hand. "Let's walk this way," he said, nodding towards the far side of the street. "I want to get a good view of the street before we head back towards the car."

"Is something wrong?" Loren asked with a bit of unease in her voice.

"Probably not, but better to be careful, right? I'm just feeling a little bit uneasy, like my internal radar is starting to go off, but I don't know why. I'd rather play it safe, if you know what I mean."

"I know exactly what you mean, and believe me, I'm not going to second-guess your sixth sense at this point."

They walked hand in hand to the far side of the street, and then they stopped and embraced, like two people in love do when they're sharing a special moment. Keith held Loren tight, but he let his eyes scan up and down the street. It was now dark, but the streetlights and the light pouring out from the restaurants made it plenty bright. He saw the door of Riordan's open, and he felt the hairs on his neck bristle. The man had been at the end of bar and didn't appear to be paying any undue attention to them, but suddenly here he was, barely a minute since they had walked out. The man looked quickly up and down the street before he caught sight of Keith and Loren, allowing his eyes to settle on them for just a second too long for it to have been a coincidence. Keith knew that the man couldn't see his eyes from this distance, especially with he and Loren standing in the shadows cast by a streetlight. Keith studied the man: about 6'1", maybe 200-225 pounds. He was wearing jeans and a pullover sweater over a tee-shirt, and there was no mistaking the guy's massive chest, shoulders, and arms even from that distance. His look, his posture, his hair, everything about him screamed military, probably even Special Forces. Keith watched as the man slowly made his way down the block, ostensibly looking in the shop windows but surely, he knew, watching them through the reflection of the glass.

Keith gave Loren a kiss on the lips, then hugging her closely whispered, "We've got someone following us, other side of the street. Big guy, jeans and a maroon sweater. Looks like he just walked out of a recruiting poster for the Army Rangers."

"Are you sure?" she asked.

"Yeah, definitely. He was at the bar in Riordan's, left just after us, obviously looking for us as he came out the door. He must have been staking out the whole Annapolis area in case we came through here. Pretty stupid of me to lead us right here to their lair."

"You couldn't have known. Christ, how many people do they have that they can just stake out places in case we decide to pop into town?"

"I don't know. I'm guessing that our friend Ed is just hiring a bunch of mercenaries to do his dirty work. They're probably not a part of his game. For that matter, they probably don't even have a clue what his game is. They're just in this for the money, killers for hire."

"So how are we going to get back to the car and make it the hell out of here?"

"I'm kinda making that up as I go along," he said with a smirk, hoping to ease the tension. Obviously humor wasn't working real well, judging from the look of fear on Loren's face. "I think he's alone, at least for now. He might have the cavalry on the way though, so we need to get our asses out of here as quickly as we can. We've got to get back to the car, and I'm guessing that he doesn't know where we're parked. More likely he just stumbled onto us on the street. I'm going to give you the keys, then when we get to the garage we're going to separate. I'll lead him away from you so you can get to the car, and I'll try to spring a trap on him somewhere there in the garage. There aren't many cars in there tonight, but there are enough to provide some cover, at least. After I take care of our little friend, you pick me up on the street outside the exit."

"That's it? That's your big plan? Kinda sparse on the details, don't you think?" she said with her own smirk. She was so scared that she had to fight to maintain control. She had stepped back from Keith just enough to get a look at their pursuer across the street, and even from here she could tell that he looked like he was chiseled from stone.

"Trust me," he said. "We can make this work. Just keep cool, don't look his way or let on that you know he's following us. He'll be behind us; I don't think we need to worry about that. We've got the element of surprise on our side, and we need to keep it that way."

"Yeah, but he's probably got the element of big guns and the experience of being a trained killer on his side." Loren was silent for a minute, then said,

"How do we know that he hasn't done something like planting a bomb in our car, or have other people waiting there to kill us?"

"We can't be certain, but we have to play the odds at this point. There's a very, very slim chance that they would know what kind of rental car we're driving. We didn't rent it, remember? Richard rented it for us, and it's in the name of one of Jeff's offshore companies. Plus, it's not like they'd have a public parking lot in downtown Annapolis staked out just in case we'd ever come along and park there. Instead they'd maybe have one or two people canvassing the whole downtown area. Right now, I don't think our friend over there has any idea where we've been, where we're going, or where we're staying. And I think he may even be alone, at least for right now. Bottom line, I think he has to follow us to see where we're going, and, I'm guessing, if the timing and the place are right, try to kill us before we can get out of here."

Keith led Loren up the block, stopping every now and again to look in the shop windows, just typical tourists. They could see their friend, slowly meandering up the street on the opposite side, clearly in the shop windows' reflection. That actually gave them comfort; better to know your enemy's location than to have him gain the element of surprise. As they approached one of the street corners Keith directed Loren into a small wine and liquor/convenience store, a place that had been in business there in downtown Annapolis for at least as long as he could remember. They browsed for a few minutes, and Keith started gathering some items and carrying them towards the register. Loren gave him a quizzical look and Keith just smiled and said, "Just go with it."

She gave him a nervous smile and said, "It scares me what goes on in that little mind of yours."

"Me, too," he snickered.

Keith carried their purchases as they left the store and headed up the street towards the parking garage. Their apprehension grew with every step, but they both knew that their only hope was to outsmart their quarry and get away from this town immediately. The streets were almost empty now, and Keith didn't even have to look back to know that the man was still following them. He felt for the 9mm pistol in his back waistband, and felt around again, for probably the hundredth time in the last few minutes, for the extra magazines he had in his jacket pocket. They were parked on the second floor of the parking garage, and Keith had given Loren the keys and told her to head straight for the car, get inside and lock the doors. The rifles that Keith had brought from Charlottesville were both loaded and ready to go on the back floorboard, so should the killer come after her she would at least have a chance to fight him off. The plan was to draw the killer away from Loren and lead him up to the third floor and away from the stairwell. The good news is that would give Loren a chance to make it out of the garage before the killer could get to her if things got ugly. The bad news, this being a weeknight, is that there were virtually no cars parked on the third floor of the garage. Keith ran the risk of being caught out in the open, and he knew that he was as good as dead if that happened.

When they reached the parking garage they tried to pick up the pace just a bit, hoping that they were at least partially shielded from view. Keith had no doubt that this would be the place that the killer would try to take them. It was quiet, dark, and deserted, and he imagined that it would just be written off by the police as another street crime gone badly. As they reached the stairwell inside the garage, Keith gave Loren a quick kiss and told her to run as fast and as quietly as possible and to stay out of sight. He, meanwhile, kept moving up towards the third floor, and made sure to make plenty of noise as he did it. Stopping between the second and third floor landings, Keith reached into the shopping bag and pulled out two quart sized bottles of Wesson Oil. Opening both, he poured the oil on the stairs and handrail as he made his way up. He continued up to the third floor and squatted down behind one of the few cars on the upper deck. Working quickly, Keith removed some more items from the shopping bag and constructed a poor-man's silencer for his pistol using a two-liter Coke bottle, cotton, and duct tape. His military training had not all been forgotten. His creation was not as good as the real thing, but it was at least good enough to suppress most of the sound from his gun. The last thing he needed was someone calling the police if they heard gunfire right here in the middle of town.

Julian reached the garage just as Loren was reaching their car. He surveyed the first floor for any movement, and seeing none, sprinted for the stairwell and quickly made his way to the second floor. He walked out of the stairwell and repeated the same process, but again, he saw nothing untoward. His hand rested on his gun, but he still hadn't brought it out. All he needed was to come upon some easily startled civilian that would scream bloody murder and ruin the whole operation. He watched, listened, his senses on high alert.

Then he heard it: car doors slamming up on the parking deck above. He flew back to the stairwell and started rushing up the stairs two at a time. Suddenly, only a few feet from the top of the stairs, his feet slipped from under him as he hit the vegetable oil-covered steps that Keith had set as a booby-trap. He went down hard on his right knee, screaming in pain, and his head hit the steps and cut a wide, deep gash above the eye. A welt rose over his eye almost immediately and blood started running down the right side of his face. His knee was not broken, but it was badly bruised and bleeding, and he was not going to be doing too much running on it for quite a while. It took him several minutes to recover from the fall enough to start to get to his feet; the pain in his leg and head were both excruciating. He used his sweater to wipe the blood from his face. Julian looked around, gathering his bearings. Seeing all of the oil on the steps and the handrails, he felt the rage boil within him. *'Motherfucker'* he swore to himself. *'This was no goddamn accident'*. He was pissed at himself for letting this amateur, this fucking college professor, for Christ's sake, get the drop on him.

Keith heard the scream when Julian went down and allowed himself a little bit of a self-satisfied smile. Keith was counting on the fact that the killer would be so pissed that he would let his rage take over and make a mistake, as well as that he'd be too proud and too greedy to call for reinforcements. He didn't have long to wait before his assumptions were proven true. Julian was making his way, slowly and painfully, up the steps to the third floor deck. When he emerged out of the doorway, Keith could see the rage etched on his face as well as the blood running from the wounds to his head and knee.

Julian looked around, his gun now out and in his hand as he hobbled around the deck, slowly making his way towards the cars that were providing Keith cover. He spoke in a loud, menacing whisper, making sure that Bryant could hear him but still ensuring that his voice didn't carry up and down the street. "Very clever, Dr. Bryant, the oil on the stairway. Touché. Now it's my turn. When I'm finished you'll be begging me to kill you. Maybe I'll put a bullet in your knee so you can appreciate the pain I'm feeling right now. It will be the worst pain you've ever felt, I promise you. You'll survive, at least as long as I choose to let you survive. I want you to be around for a while, though. I want you to watch while I beat and rape that little bitch of yours right in front of your eyes, watch you lay there helpless as she begs you to come to her rescue." Julian was slowly limping around the area, trying to draw Keith out from his hiding spot. He slowly made his way further and further away from the doorway to the stairwell, knowing that he was more exposed but not fearing Keith, or any man, at that moment.

Keith heard the words, and he was finding it hard to control his own rage. He fought hard to control the anger, knowing that his quarry was trying to goad him into making a mistake. Keith wasn't about to let that happen. He had the upper hand in this encounter, Army Rangers be damned. This killer, this assassin, was as good as dead. *'Keep on coming motherfucker, just a little bit further, and you're a dead man.'* Finally Julian came from around the back of the Buick Century that Keith had used to lure him up here, having actually broken the passenger side window and unlocked the door before slamming it a couple of times to simulate the sound of two people getting in a car. There were four parking spaces between the old Buick and the Pontiac Grand Prix that Keith was now lying behind. He was flat on his stomach, watching Julian walk closer and closer towards him, his weapon trained on the injured assassin as he approached.

Julian continued to move forward, continued his taunting rant. "Come on, Dr. Bryant. This is absurd. You know that you can't hide up here forever, and there's no way out of here but past me. And even on my worst day, you don't stand a chance against me. I may be slowed down, but I can drop you like a bad habit with just one shot."

"And I can do the same to you," Keith whispered, as he squeezed off a shot that hit Julian in his right ankle. The homemade silencer had done as intended, and barely a spit or whisper was heard from Keith's 9mm.

As Julian went down he shot off three wild rounds that went harmlessly into the night, his own, government-issued silencer also doing its job. He screamed in pain, and the pistol fell from his grip as he hit the pavement.

Keith was on him quickly, and before Julian could let out any more screams he had secured a piece of duct tape over his mouth. "Well, well, Mr. Hired Assassin. Looks like you're having a pretty bad day of it. Busted knee, a nice little gash on the head, and now a bum ankle. I don't think you're employer is going to be too happy with you. You missed the hit, and now you're going to cost him a lot on his medical insurance. You do have medical insurance, don't you?"

Julian's eyes flashed with anger and pain. He was screaming through the tape on his mouth, and though Keith couldn't make out the words, he definitely caught the sentiment.

"So let me break this down for you in very simple terms that even a douche bag like you can understand. If you tell me what I want to know I won't have to kill you; I don't think I can say it any simpler than that. You may not be running any marathons, but you will be alive. It's your choice. If you don't tell me what I want to know, I'm going to kill you right here. Your choice. What's it going to be?"

Keith slowly pulled the tape back from a corner of Julian's mouth, giving him the chance to speak. Julian's response was spoken with more hatred and venom than Keith had ever seen or heard in his entire life. "You go fuck yourself, Professor. I have no idea who hired me to kill you, and if I did know you're not man enough to ever get it out of me." His teeth were clenched in pain, but he didn't show any fear at all of dying here on this parking deck. "But I promise you this, the people who hired me are going to come after you and fucking destroy you and that bitch you're with. You can't win. You got lucky here, but your luck is going to run out. The best thing you can do is kill yourself right here, right now, beside me. You have no idea the shit storm that is going to be raining down on you."

"I'll take my chances. But if you're the best they can find, maybe I don't have that much to worry about anyway." Keith had to get that last little dig in on him just to see the rage, the hatred, one more time. He put the tape back over Julian's mouth as he tried to scream and squirm. Keith just looked down at him and smiled, actually laughing at him to make the pain and rage that much stronger. As Julian tried everything he could to lash out, even trying to kick out with his shattered ankle, Keith slowly walked over and picked up Julian's silenced pistol. As he looked down at the fallen assassin he didn't see fear, or sorrow, or any kind of human emotion in his face. All he saw was contempt and loathing. That just made what he had to do that much easier. Keith lifted the pistol and shot Julian twice between the eyes. Only then did the contempt and the loathing leave Julian's face.

Keith figured that he should work quickly now and get out of the area as fast as possible. He removed the silencer from Julian's pistol and then stuck both in the shopping bag, and then he searched quickly through the pockets and took the dead man's wallet and cell phone. Keith assumed that any identification would be fake, but he was counting on the fact that his cell phone probably had a direct number to Ed and/or whoever was pulling his strings. No way that the killer would have attempted the hit without letting someone know, and more than likely that someone with the authority, as well as the purse strings, was Ed. After searching through the pockets, he grabbed him beneath the arms and dragged him back over to the old Buick. He opened the back door and struggled to lift him up into the car; he was, literally, 200-plus pounds of dead weight. It took a couple of minutes, but Keith finally got him into the back seat and closed the doors. Going to the shopping bag, he pulled out a bottle of cheap vodka and proceeded to empty the contents all over the interior of the car, paying special attention to Julian's body. Then, retrieving a second bottle from the bag, he doused some more on the interior and spread a little bit on the exterior. He carefully placed both vodka bottles, the vegetable oil bottles, and the now-destroyed two-liter Coke bottle in the shopping bag, taking no chances on the police department's forensic unit tracking him down through the purchase at the liquor store. Satisfied that he'd done the best he could at cleaning up, Keith took a pack of matches from his pocket and, without a second thought, lit them and tossed them into the alcohol-soaked car. It immediately erupted in flames, and Keith started making his way carefully towards the stairwell. He had to be careful going down, making sure not to have the same fate that had befallen Julian just a few minutes earlier.

When Keith reached the first floor he quickly made his way outside and, as expected, found Loren waiting just up the street with the car running. He slipped into the passenger seat and they headed towards Route 50, slow so as not to attract any undue attention. Keith looked back over his shoulder and could see the flames from the fire that was raging on the top deck of the parking structure. It wouldn't take long for the Annapolis Fire Department to reach the garage, but Keith was counting on the fact that the alcohol-fueled fire would have effectively destroyed the car by the time they could get there and get set up. Plus, the fire would make identification of the body difficult, but not impossible. Assuming, of course, that the corpse even had an identity, he reminded himself.

"We need to head back to the hotel, grab our things, and head out of town. It's not safe for us to stay here any longer. And I need to get rid of this bag and its contents, too. We can't afford to be caught with stuff that links us to what just happened." Even as Keith said this he was reaching into the bag to remove the pistol and silencer he had taken off of Julian. No way that he could or would risk disposing of the weapon, not to mention that it may come in handy somewhere down the line.

"And what did happen?" Loren asked.

"He tried to kill me, I killed him first. I put his body in a car on the third deck and torched the car. That's the net of it." He realized, as he said it, that the statement came out very cold and detached.

Loren understood. She didn't like it, or the fact that it had to happen, but she understood. They were definitely in a kill or be killed mode, and she knew that Keith was doing all that he could to keep them alive. She reached over and put her hand on his. That said it all, without really saying a word.

⌘

FOSTER WAS PACING THE BUNKER, anxious to hear from his man. Even to a seasoned professional, time spent waiting was the slowest time imaginable. He had no way of knowing how far Julian would have to go or how long he would have to wait for the right opportunity to kill the targets. It could be just a few minutes or it could take an hour or more. Foster knew better than to call Julian, though he was still tempted to call to get an update. Having a cell phone ring could put his man, and the whole mission, in danger. Julian, he reminded himself, was expendable. All of the hired specialists and hit teams were. The mission is all that mattered.

"Colonel Foster, I'm picking up something from the Annapolis E-911 center," shouted Eric Torres. Torres and Brad Hanover were working this evening's shift, along with Bob Manning and Colonel Foster. Manning and Foster had barely left the Bunker over the past few days, and the men that served with them were amazed at their ability to continue pulling the hours and the workload that they'd been doing.

Foster moved quickly over to Torres' workstation. "What have you got?"

"Sir, there was a call that just came in to the E-911 center reporting a vehicle on fire on the third floor parking deck of a public garage in downtown Annapolis. I would suspect that that's the handiwork of your contractor, sir." Torres couldn't contain his smile. Like everyone else under Foster's command, they desperately wanted this to be over, though for different reasons. Foster was concerned about concealing his role in the deadliest terrorist attack in US history. Torres and the other men were more concerned about getting back to some semblance of normalcy, to spending some quality time with their wives and their families. To them this was just a job, and though it may be a job they loved and took seriously, it was still a *job*. Sometimes you just want to leave the job behind and *live*. Not much of a life when you're working 70 hours a week in an underground Bunker, Torres figured.

"Good. Keep me posted on the radio chatter from Annapolis PD and Fire Department and let me know the minute anything substantial is reported," said Foster. "Bob, I suspect we should be hearing from Mr. Julian within the next few minutes, wouldn't you?" he asked Bob Manning.

"Probably so, sir, but it may take a few minutes if he needs to worry about safely clearing the area first," was Manning's reply.

It was about 10 more minutes before Foster's phone rang and he saw Julian's number pop up on the screen. "Put this up on the speaker, please" he instructed Torres. "Everybody should be able to enjoy this." Foster was smiling from ear to ear, the first time that anyone in the room had seen him happy in the past week.

Clicking on the 'answer' button on the console, Foster said, "Mr. Julian, I trust that you have some wonderful news to report. We've been monitoring the emergency channels in Annapolis and it seems that they're on the scene of what I can only assume is your handiwork?"

"Why yes, it is my handiwork, Ed", said Keith. "Too bad you're admiring it from afar, though. Why don't you come down here and we can roast some marshmallows?"

Foster and everyone in the room sat in stunned silence for several seconds. It was the first time that anyone had ever seen Foster dumbfounded. His face reddened and his lips were quivering with rage. "You are a fucking dead man, Dr. Bryant, do you hear me. Dead." His voice was probably a half-octave higher than usual and he was teetering on the brink of losing control altogether.

"What's the matter, Ed? It sounds like someone has you by the balls or something. Everything OK?" Keith was intentionally goading him, trying to enrage him.

"I will have *your* balls in a vice, you son of a bitch! I swear to God that I am going to string you up and gut you like a fucking fish!" Foster practically screamed.

Keith lowered his voice, forcing them to listen closely, and spoke in his most threatening, menacing tone. "Now you listen, Ed. You keep sending these Special Forces pussies to do a man's job, and they're failing miserably. I'm not sure who does your hiring, but you may want to rethink your interview and hiring process. In the meantime, if you keep sending them after me, I'll keep sending them back to you in body bags."

Foster was trying to bring himself back under control, to regain the composure and the upper hand that he had always considered practically a birthright. Unfortunately, he realized, he didn't have the upper hand tonight. Not even close. "Don't confuse a little bit of luck with skill, Dr. Bryant. Remember, it's just like they say in the War on Terror: '*We have to be perfect every day, but they only have to be lucky once*'. Your luck won't last nearly as long as our skill."

Keith laughed at Foster's attempt at bravado. "Don't make me laugh, you pretentious little cocksucker. Talking about the War on Terror, as if you, of all people, have ever done anything noble in your whole life. You're nothing but a little desk jockey, probably never were anything more than a pathetic little analyst. I'll bet you've never even fought in a war, just sat there behind your desk and your computer while real men did the fighting." Keith was laying it on heavy, intentionally goading him. "Listen up, Ed. The rules of the game are changing, and they're changing as of tonight. You don't need to keep coming after me. You've already shown that you're totally incompetent and incapable of doing that successfully." *Stick that knife in and twist*, Keith thought to himself. "Starting tonight, *I'm coming after you*. I'm coming to kill you and your whole team. Everyone that's there with you now, listening in – they're all going to die. You, though, Ed, I'm saving you for last. You're going to see everyone around you die, and you're going to know that your time is coming. And very soon."

Everyone, including Colonel Foster, grew silent. They all felt that same twinge of fear, that same sensation of having chills after hearing the words, the threats, spoken by Keith. They were all too proud, too macho, to ever admit it, but it was there. Finally Foster spoke. "You forget Dr. Bryant, that we know who you are, as well as everyone and everything that is important in your life. You, on the other hand, don't know the first thing about me or any member of my team. I'd say that still gives us the upper hand in this little pissing contest, wouldn't you?"

"You just keep on thinking that way, Ed. You think about that, right up until the second you feel the bullet enter your brain." Keith let that last little remark hang out there for a second. "Goodnight, Ed. And please, pay my respects to the family of your latest incompetent contractor. I thought you'd appreciate the irony, as I chose to leave him in the same condition that you left my friend David Ward and his family. I think you referred to them as 'crispy critters'. I'm sure that the family will enjoy identifying the body." With that, Keith disconnected the call.

Foster was again silent, and none of the others in the room dared to say a word. They were all shaken by what they'd heard. This supposed soft-spoken, mild-mannered college professor had taken on a totally different persona. Having been pushed too far, he had become as hard and as cold as the very people that had been hired to kill him.

Finally Foster spoke, trying to bring some semblance of normalcy back to the operation. "Mr. Hanover, where did that call from Dr. Bryant come from? I assume we were able to track it?"

"Yes, sir. I showed the signal heading northbound on Route 197 away from the Annapolis area. The signal terminated shortly after the call ended, but at that point he was about 10 miles north of the intersection of Route 197 and Route 50 and heading towards Baltimore." Hanover watched Foster digesting the information and waited for a response or assignment.

"I assume that Dr. Bryant simply threw the phone out the window once it had served its purpose, which seems to be his usual M.O. I expect that his current direction is nothing more than an attempt to put some distance between him and the events in Annapolis. I would guess that he will most likely make his way back down toward the DC area, if not tonight then certainly tomorrow. Let's make sure that all of our people are on the lookout for him and Ms. Davis."

"What do you think about the threats he made?" asked Torres.

That brought the fire back into Foster's eyes. "What I believe, Mr. Torres, is that Dr. Bryant has become a very cold, very skilled killer, and we continue to underestimate him. It was my error to allow Mr. Julian to try to take them out tonight without backup, and I accept the responsibility. I put expediency over thoughtful preparation, and I shall not make that mistake again. Beyond that, I don't believe that Dr. Bryant has any knowledge of who we are or where we are, nor do I think he has any chance – at all – of finding out who and where we are. And even if he were to be so lucky, again, I know that he does not have the proverbial snowball's chance in hell of killing me or any of the fine members of this team."

"I think we may need to continue to raise the stakes with Dr. Bryant, sir. Let's put some additional pressure on him tonight, as we said we would. Make him see that his threats did nothing to deter us." This suggestion came from Bob Manning.

"I completely agree," said Colonel Foster. "I want Dr. Bryant to understand, clearly, that he has absolutely picked the wrong people to fuck with." His tone was as menacing as the team had ever seen. "Get me the team from Charlottesville on the phone."

⌘

"So how do you think it went?" asked Loren after Keith disconnected from the call.

Before Keith answered he rolled down the car window and threw the cell phone out into the middle of Route 197, the road they were currently on heading north towards Baltimore. "I think, for the first time, I heard fear and apprehension on the other end. I don't think they know what we do and don't know at this point, and it worries them. They've always been able to remain secretive, and now I've threatened to break that veil of secrecy and insulation. They're probably concerned that we can actually cause them harm after we've survived this long, and with so many casualties on their side."

"Of course, we really don't know anything at this point, at least nothing substantive." Loren was simply stating the obvious.

"True, but we're slowly picking up more clues. Maybe with this new phone number that we just used we can trace our way to Ed, or maybe we can find some information on the recently departed Mr. Julian that will lead us to the people that hired him. Like we talked about this morning with LTBT, every piece of information can help fill in the puzzle."

They talked a bit more about the call and Keith's perceptions of what was said, what meanings or nuances were conveyed, and Ed's state of mind. Keith smiled when he recounted how many times he'd been able to push his buttons. They decided to continue north to Baltimore and then pick up Interstate 70 west. They'd stop for a quick dinner somewhere along the way, and then try to grab a room somewhere around Frederick, MD for the evening. Another night, another bad meal and lousy hotel room. But at least, they agreed, they had survived another day.

"I just realized something," said Keith. "We've been through so much the past few days that I'd totally forgotten that we're supposed to be back home tonight from our little romantic getaway to The Greenbrier. That's means we're supposed to be back at school and back at work tomorrow morning."

"God, I'd totally forgotten about that, too," said Loren. "I guess we better stop somewhere along the way tonight and call in to have someone cover your classes and both of our schedules. What do you think we should say?"

"I don't know. I'll have to give that some thought. Obviously we can't tell the truth," Keith said with a smile. "Who'd believe this wild-assed tale anyway?"

"True. I'm living through this nightmare, and I don't even believe it."

Chapter 18

It was late Monday night, or more accurately, very early Tuesday morning, as the black Chevy Tahoe made its way down Route 20 towards Scottsville, a small town just south of Charlottesville, VA. Had it been daytime the car's occupants could have looked out on beautiful estates with expansive green pastures, white rail fences, and the Blue Ridge Mountains. They would have been able to see beautiful horses roaming the pastures and herd after herd of Angus and Hereford cattle grazing. They would have seen acre after acre of grapevines, this area of Virginia having seen an explosive growth in both the number of wineries and the total acreage planted with vines over the past decade. It was a small town in an area full of small towns; Scottsville, like many of the small towns in and around Charlottesville, had a lot of residents that were, to put it mildly, filthy rich. Industrialists. Media moguls. Bankers. Hollywood actors. They all came here to live, at least on a part-time basis, and enjoy the beauty and the grandeur of Virginia's horse country.

The occupants of the Tahoe were not, by any stretch of the imagination, gentrified folk or gentleman farmers. They were killers, pure and simple. Ex-military and Special Forces all, they had long ago traded in their allegiance to the United States or anything it stood for. Now all they stood for was the almighty dollar, though Euros, gold, or diamonds would work just as nicely. The team was led by Justin Knight, a former SEAL team leader from Coronado, CA. He and his team had been on this mission for a couple of weeks and they were growing weary of it. They preferred a bit more action than just following a subject around town, planting listening devices, and monitoring phone calls and wiretaps. Boring. The money was great, though, so that minimized the complaints. The team was excited to finally get into the game on Sunday when they went after Dr. Bryant and Ms. Davis in one of the choppers. Unfortunately for Knight's team, their chopper was one of the ones that got grounded by the Feds when someone – Bryant and his people, obviously – called in an anonymous tip that they were terrorists. That had really pissed him off, though he had to give a tip of the hat to whoever came up with the idea. He swore that if given the chance, he'd be sure to pay Bryant that compliment. Right before he blew his head off.

When the Tahoe reached a small dirt road on the right hand side of Route 20 they turned off and proceeded about 200 yards off of the road. The night was cold, dark, and overcast with a brisk breeze blowing out of the northeast. Not that this part of Scottsville was ever very lit up at night; even on nights with a full moon and a sky full of stars, it could still be scary-dark on the back roads and in the woods. The three members of the team exited the Tahoe, making sure that the interior light did not come on as they opened the doors. They grabbed their gear and assembled at the back of the car. Knight spoke to his team. "Alright, we're going to approach from the southwest, and the target is just a couple of clicks back over the hill. Once we're on top of the ridge we want to maintain silence; fortunately all of the trees rustling in this breeze should help mask our approach even more, but we can't afford to take any chances. Everybody knows the plan, right? So any last questions?" Seeing that there were none, he gave his final orders. "Alright, then, from here on out it's night vision goggles on and an absolute minimum of noise. Let's move out."

The team spent better than 30 minutes slowly and silently approaching the target. In other circumstances they could have covered this distance in a fraction of the time, but the mission put a premium on stealth over speed. As they approached the target building they stopped about 50 yards out to regroup. Knight used hand signals with his two team members and signaled them to move to their positions. Both moved forward silently while Knight covered them, his eyes constantly sweeping for movement anywhere around them and his ears attuned to any sound that was out of place. He watched as his team attached a simple pipe bomb to the propane tank located next to the building, propane often being the only choice for homes in areas not served by natural gas. The pipe bomb had a simple timer made from a Timex wristwatch, essentially an explosive device that any reasonably intelligent kid could make from directions readily available on the internet. The timer was set to give them a half-hour to reach the Tahoe and head out of the area. That was more than enough time for these battle-hardened men.

The team was back in the Tahoe and slowly making their way through Scottsville on the main road, at most a quarter mile from the target, when they heard the explosion and saw the fireball above the trees. The concussion from the explosion actually made the Tahoe shudder even at that distance. They all drove on in silence, being careful to make their way out of the area and back to Charlottesville without doing anything to arouse any suspicion. The team drove in silence the entire way back to Charlottesville. Usually it was whoops and screaming and high-fives all around, often followed by a night of celebration and drinking. Tonight they found it impossible to revel in their mission. They'd all killed many men, and even women and children for that matter, both in the US and abroad. None had ever batted an eye. It's the mission. It's what they're paid to do. Fuck 'em all. Tonight was different though, and to a man, the team was sad, even a little heartbroken. It was the first time they'd ever been contracted to do a hit on a couple of dogs, and to a man they all hoped they'd never be asked to do it again.

⌘

KEITH TOSSED AND TURNED ALL night. He had gone to bed Monday night at a reasonable hour, but by 4:00am Tuesday morning he realized that trying to sleep was useless. He felt physically and mentally exhausted, but sleep just would not come. The events of the last few days kept playing over again and again in his mind. He felt no real remorse in the fact that he had killed eight men; he'd done what he'd had to do to keep them alive. But still, eight men? Is that more people than psycho serial killers like Jeffrey Dahmer and Son of Sam had killed? He couldn't remember. Christ. Of one thing he was sure: he needed rest. *'Rest is a weapon'*. Figuring out how to bring this hell to an end was certainly not conducive to getting a good night's sleep.

Around 5:00am he finally gave up and got out of bed, trying his best to keep quiet and let Loren get some rest. She had to be exhausted, too, he told himself. The stress and strain of everyday life takes a toll, so what kind of toll must it take when government agents are killing your friends and threatening you and your family? Keith opened the PC and booted it up. In minutes he was on the internet and surfing through some of his favorite news sites, like CNN.com and MSN.com. Nothing caught his eye, thankfully. At least nothing outside of the usual disasters, political infighting, and the Iraq war. He decided to send a message to the School and to his leadership team at Bryant International explaining that he would be out for at least the rest of the week due to a family emergency. Using one of the many alias e-mail addresses that he'd set up on Hotmail.com he sent the communiqués with an explanation that he was having trouble getting into the University's VPN so he was using the account of a family member. In reality, he was sending the e-mail to Jeff Anders at an anonymous Yahoo e-mail address and Jeff was then scrubbing it and forwarding it to the University in order to eliminate, or at least minimize, the chance that Ed and his team would be able to track the e-mails back to him and determine his location. He requested that one of the graduate assistants lead his classes for the balance of the week. Keith also sent the same type of message to Loren's boss/graduate advisor explaining her absence for the remainder of the week. No sooner had Keith sent those messages than he started worrying about how he'd explain their continued absence if they were still on the run a week from now. That is, assuming that they were still alive a week from now.

E-mails done, Keith decided to take a shower, hopefully without waking Loren. While their room at the Hampton Inn was certainly adequate and comfortable there was still a limited amount of space, so trying to stay quiet enough to not wake the other person was a special challenge. Keith took a long, hot shower, as if standing in the stream of hot water would cleanse him of the sins of the past few days. It did at least relax him a bit and gave him a chance to think more clearly about what might lie ahead. He didn't know what today would bring. God, how he longed for his old routine, *that life of just a week ago*, he reminded himself, when he knew when he got up that he would be teaching a couple of classes, going to client meetings, and cooking dinner and spending time with Loren. Now, every day was filled with fear and dread. Each day he wakes up knowing that he and Loren are most likely facing more death and destruction, maybe even waking up for the last time.

Keith was starting to feel overwhelmed by the constant fear and tension. Recent events had changed him, jaded him. Instead of imagining a beautiful life spent in a beautiful place with the people he loved all he could imagine was darkness and killing. If he only had one day left on this Earth, he wanted to spend it hunting down and killing Ed and every member of his team, watching them suffer for the things they had done. Watching them pay, along with every other member of the conspiracy, for the pain and suffering they inflicted on America when they conspired to make the events of 9/11 unfold. Prison is too good for them, he constantly reminded himself. They need to be exposed to the world, the full story told. Then they need to die.

When he got out of the shower it was still only about 6:30, but he decided it was probably best to go ahead and wake Loren and let her start getting ready. They left the hotel around 7:45 and decided to grab some breakfast before getting on the road. They loaded all of their things into the car but intentionally didn't check out of the hotel. Check-out time wasn't until noon, so they reasoned that it was better to have the option of going back to the hotel if they needed to. Both of them realized that at this point they really didn't know where they were going to go. All they could do is get in the car and keep moving, do everything they can to avoid being trapped by the teams of assassins that were, without a doubt, still out there looking for them. Since dinner the night before had been a quick stop at a KFC restaurant just outside of Baltimore, they were both a little bit hungry this morning and in the mood for a hot breakfast. Checking with the front desk clerk, they found out that there was a Cracker Barrel less than a mile away. That actually sounded great to both of them. Eggs, bacon, pancakes, and hash brown casserole instead of a rock-hard biscuit sandwich from McDonald's. Not exactly *haute cuisine*, but compared to what they'd had the past few days it felt like dining at The French Laundry in Napa Valley. *'They don't call it comfort food for nothing'*, Loren had said on one of their prior visits to Cracker Barrel long ago. At this point he couldn't agree more.

They lingered over their breakfast for over an hour, enjoying the food and taking the time to talk, quietly, about their plans for the day. Keith suggested that they head back to the hotel, assuming that they didn't see any surveillance or anything out of the ordinary, and take a few minutes to check the news and the internet. Everything looked normal as they road past the Hampton Inn, but still they sat across the road and observed things for a few minutes before deciding to head back to their room. Once there, Keith headed to the bathroom while Loren turned on the TV. As she surfed the channels she realized just how pathetic daytime television is and how thankful she was not to have to sit around and watch it all day. She finally settled on CNN, figuring that no matter how bad the day's news was it couldn't be worse than watching the mindless drivel on the other channels. Keith finally joined her and sat with her on the bed.

"Are you OK? You don't look like you feel too well," said Loren.

"I've had better days, that's for sure. But I'm OK. I feel better now, but I wouldn't mind hanging around here for just a little while to make sure that I don't have to go to the bathroom again."

"Maybe when we leave we can stop at a drugstore and get you some Pepto-Bismol or something. That might help. It's a wonder that we're not both sick, considering all of the crap we've been eating the last few days, to say nothing of the stress."

"Yeah, you're right. We really can't afford for either of us to be sick at this point." Even as Keith said this he realized what an understatement it was.

They sat in silence and listened to the news headlines. An airplane crash in South America. Another political scandal in Congress. Speculation about who would seek the Republican presidential nomination in the next election. Flooding in the Midwest. Then Keith said, "You know, it might not be a bad idea for us to find a local news station and see if there's anything about the events last night in Annapolis. Mind if I change the channel?"

"No, go ahead. That's a good idea. I think I saw one of the local affiliates down on Channel 9."

Keith turned to Channel 9 and saw that it was the local CBS affiliate station out of Washington, DC. They were just starting the coverage of local news after talking about some of the national and, typical for DC, political stories. The anchor, a generic Barbie-doll type that could have been reading the news in any major US market, looked at the camera with a look of studied concern on her face. *"In our top story for the local Metropolitan area, Annapolis police and fire crews responded to a fire last night on the third floor of the public parking garage on Main Street in the capital city. When crews arrived they found a 1999 Buick Century fully engulfed in flames. Firefighters were able to contain the blaze and extinguish it, and fortunately, no other cars were in close enough proximity to sustain any major damage. However, when the fire was out police discovered the body of a male victim in the back seat, the apparent victim of a homicide. Police and city officials are not commenting on a cause of death, and no word has yet been released regarding the victim's identity. Our news team will provide continued coverage on this story today at noon and again at 5:00".*

"Pretty much as I suspected," said Keith. "My guess is that they'll get nowhere in identifying him. He's probably a ghost that our government buddies found somewhere along the way."

The Channel 9 Barbie-doll turned to her colleague, a handsome African-American version of a Ken-doll, for the next headline. *"Our next story is a sad one, Connie. It really tears at my heartstrings. There was a violent explosion overnight in the small community of Scottsville, VA, a town in the middle of the Albemarle County horse country just a few miles south of Charlottesville. Fire crews from around the area were called to the scene after an apparent propane tank explosion at Stonehenge Kennels destroyed the building housing the kennels and killed all eight dogs currently being boarded there..."*

Keith and Loren didn't hear another word. They both collapsed onto the bed and burst into tears and screams of anguish. They held each other and sobbed uncontrollably, unable to say or do anything. For Keith, only the pain and hurt of losing his parents even came close to what he was feeling now. He had raised those dogs from puppies, and in all respects they were his 'kids'. While he hoped someday to have children with Loren, he never wanted to be without his dogs, his best friends. Unconditional love, that's what they felt for Keith and what he felt for them. In the short time that Loren had lived with them, she had come to feel the same way. She felt this loss as much as Keith did, plus she felt so much hurt and helplessness as she saw him in so much pain for the second time in just a few days.

They lay together on the bed and held each other and cried with each other for over an hour. Finally Keith was spent; he had no more tears to shed. God, he felt so guilty for letting this happen. Why didn't he just back off and save them, and everyone, from this terror, from this death and destruction? Guilt was only one of the many emotions flooding through his mind at this point. Sadness was certainly still there, probably always would be there. Anger and rage were there as well, but he was fighting hard to keep them bottled-up at this point. Better to let that anger and rage fuel the fire when he had the chance to confront the cowardly bastards who did this. And he planned on ensuring that such a confrontation would happen very, very soon.

He was startled by a knock on the door. "Housekeeping", he heard from a Latino female on the other side of the door. "Housekeeping."

"Can you come back later please? We'll be checking out in just a few minutes" said Keith, cautiously standing back and away from the door.

That seemed to satisfy the housekeeper and Keith heard her move off down the hall. He walked back over to the bed and sat down beside Loren. She was still crying quietly, face down on her pillow. He reached out and rubbed her back and shoulder lightly. "Come on, honey. We better go. It's probably not safe for us to stay here any longer. We need to find a new place to lie low."

"I can't believe that this has happened to our sweet fellas. Goddamn it! They never hurt anyone or anything. What kind of sick bastards goes after innocent animals? And it wasn't just Bo and Winston. The news said that there were six other dogs staying at the kennel when this happened. Fuck!" This sent her into spasms of crying again. It took several minutes for her to be able to compose herself enough to be able to speak. "Promise me one thing. Please."

"What's that, sweetie?" Keith asked, still having trouble talking through his own crying and sniffling.

"Promise me you'll kill the sons of bitches that did this. Please."

"Oh, trust me. That's not a problem. As far as I'm concerned, Ed just signed his own death warrant. I promise you, he'll fucking pay for this, as will the people he paid to blow the place up. They will pay, and they will suffer."

Both of them took a few minutes to try to get cleaned up a bit before hitting the road. Their faces were red and their eyes were swollen from crying. Loren could at least put on some makeup to cover up the puffiness and to make herself look better. For Keith, he just had to go out and face the day looking like he'd just lost his best friends. Which, in point of fact, he had.

⌘

KEITH AND LOREN CHECKED INTO a Hampton Inn & Suites in Leesburg, VA, a city in Northern Virginia just west of Dulles Airport and about a 45 minute drive south from Frederick, MD on Route 15. The once sleepy town of Leesburg, smack dab in the middle of Virginia's horse country about an hour or so west of Washington, DC, had boomed in the last 15-20 years into one of the fastest growing cities in the fastest growing county in the state. Where Leesburg was once considered the boondocks, albeit boondocks with tons of money, it was now suburbia.

Once they were checked in and settled, Loren set up the PC and checked to see if there were any more developments in Annapolis, but so far nothing new was being reported. That's a good thing, she reminded herself. She and Keith had decided that they would call on Patrick and Jeff straight away to see if they had developed any leads. Keith called the next number in the sequence using the prepaid AT&T calling card from the hotel phone. This allowed both he and Loren to listen in and talk on the call, though the built-in speakerphone on the room phone was less than ideal.

Patrick answered on the second ring, and after speaking to Keith and Loren for a minute he asked them to stand by for several minutes while he reached out to the other core team leaders and brought them all together for an audio conference call. It took about five minutes to get everyone together, but even that was amazing to Keith. These were people with real careers and real responsibilities, yet they were able to come together on this short a notice to work on something that they found this important to their country. Once they were all assembled, Keith gave the team a synopsis of all that had transpired since they last spoke, including the attempted hit on them in Annapolis, his killing of the assassin and the torching of the car, and the explosion at the kennel that had killed Bo and Winston. As Keith and Loren relayed this story, they couldn't stop the tears from falling again. There were more than a few sniffles and tears from others on the conference bridge as well, and they knew that this had to be devastating for Keith and Loren. Trying to change the subject, lest he and Loren both start blubbering right there on the call, Keith asked if LTBT had uncovered anything of value on Ed and his team.

"We've come up with a few possibilities that we wanted to run by you. I don't want to skew your thinking, but this first scenario seems like a highly probable target to us," offered Jeff. "Tony, since you put together most of the parameters for the search that uncovered our first likely suspect, why don't you explain our findings."

"Gladly," said Tony. "We ran the parameters that we discussed yesterday, things like high-ranking officials that retired or quit around the time of 9/11, leaders that showed up in new positions of leadership in either government or private industry, and companies that made purchases of large supercomputers and huge amounts of bandwidth around that same time. As I'm sure you can imagine, the search for retiring leaders started us off with several hundred possibilities, and each subsequent search narrowed the field down a little bit at a time. When all was said and done, we came up with one name that looks to have a substantial probability of being our guy."

"How high a probability?" asked Keith, feeling his excitement growing but not wanting to be overly optimistic, not just yet.

"Better than 90%," Tony answered. "And to answer your next question, our next highest suspects are all less than a 20% probability. The bottom line is, assuming that we've used reasonable and accurate search parameters, and I feel confident that we have, this is almost certainly our guy."

"Don't keep us in suspense any longer, please. It's already been a helluva day," said Keith, trying to sound somewhat upbeat.

"His name is Colonel Ed Foster, retired after 25 years in the Army just a few weeks after 9/11. Apparently your boy was ballsy enough to throw his real first name out there when talking to you. Cocky bastard. At any rate, his background was intelligence, cryptography, all the usual spook shit. His last assignment, by the way, was at the NSA. After he retired he founded a very successful telecom dealership called Destiny Communications Group in Reston, VA and – get this – he ordered enough freakin' bandwidth to practically build his own internet provider company. Oh, and here's the best part. Not all of the bandwidth that was ordered was delivered to his headquarters in Reston. It's all billed to him there, but according to the cable and assignment records we found at the major carriers, the bulk of the connections are at a supposedly empty space a couple of doors down."

"What kind of bandwidth are we talking about?" asked Jeff.

Karen Richardson answered. "Destiny has their own SONET ring, which is not unheard of for large companies or universities but extremely rare, to say the least, for small private companies. Considering that Colonel Foster's company has less than 200 employees we would typically expect them to have just a very small fraction of this bandwidth, even with all of the demo equipment they have there to show off their switches, routers, and phone systems." Karen had put in a considerable amount of effort in a very short time to analyze the communications capability of Foster's company, and she was in desperate need of some sleep.

"What were you able to find in the way of computer and processing power?" asked Loren.

Terrell Jackson jumped in. "We had to be careful where we poked and prodded on that information since we were concerned that it might set off some alarms with our friends. What we found was a little strange, at least at first. We didn't find any orders for a single supercomputer. What we found were components that were purchased from a number of different suppliers that would allow someone to build a massively parallel supercomputer that would likely rival anything currently in use anywhere in the world. We found orders, for example, for 20,000 AMD Opteron 64-bit processors, and that could make you a helluva computer. We figure somewhere in the 40-60 teraflop range. That's fuckin' huge."

"Don't forget the other thing that we found that was just as important at pointing the finger towards the presence of a massive supercomputer: the orders we found for humongous Uninterruptible Power Supplies and DC power isolation equipment, not to mention absolutely gargantuan air conditioning units to keep this beast cooled and operating efficiently." Tony threw this out there as the final nail in the coffin.

"I'd say that's pretty open and shut," said Keith. "Is there any reasonable doubt in anybody's mind that we've found our man?"

No one spoke up. "I think we're all in agreement. This has to be our guy." This from Patrick.

Loren spoke. "Before we move on, I'd just like to understand a bit about your search methodology. I'm not challenging it, of course. Obviously, it worked and you guys have done a fantastic job, especially in such a short time frame. What I'm asking is if there's any chance that your search may have set off any alarms or flags for Ed and his team at Destiny? We just all need to be prepared for their reaction if they know that you've stumbled on them. I would guess that they'd come after all of us with guns blazing if they know that we've gotten this far."

"That's a valid point," responded Jeff. "We've minimized our exposure by sticking to publicly available documents such as newspapers, newsletters, archived media reports, and that sort of thing. That doesn't include, of course, the purchase orders that we mentioned for the SONET circuits or the computer components. In those searches we never touched anything to do with Destiny Communications Group. Instead, we tried coming through the backdoor to see what orders were placed with targeted companies around the time of 9/11, so basically, we looked at the systems of AT&T, MCI, Sprint, AMD, Intel, and others. I can't promise that we got through this 100% clean; you can just never be completely certain. But I can say with absolute confidence that we did everything to limit our possible exposure, including spoofed logins, multipoint routing from around the world, and so on. I feel pretty safe."

"I think that's all we could ask for. You guys are just phenomenal! I can't believe that you gathered all of this information in just a day. That's incredible." Loren's praise was enthusiastic and heartfelt.

Patrick quickly added, "Don't forget though, that without you and Keith pointing us in the right direction we never would have gotten there. You guys definitely provided us with the breakthrough that we've been hoping for."

"I'd like to propose some next steps and see if you guys are aligned," offered Keith. "First, I'd like to dig up every piece of personal information you can find on Colonel Foster. I want to know where he lives, where he shops, what he eats. I want his home address and phone number, and I want every bit of personal information we can dig up on his family. I want pictures; I want to know these people on sight. In addition, I want to check out the background on every person on the Destiny payroll. I'm guessing that Foster's real team of operatives aren't going to be listed as regular Destiny employees, but maybe we'll uncover something. There has to be some record of these people somewhere. I suspect that they still have paychecks and pay taxes and have homes and mortgages. I want to know who these people are and where they live, too."

Jeff sounded a bit nervous as he asked Keith, "Where are you going with this? Sounds almost like you're thinking about going after them. Tell me that's not what you're planning."

"That is exactly what I'm planning. Every one of them is going down. No exceptions. Our days of running are over. We'll still be cautious and keep moving from place to place until this is over, but we're not running. It's like I told Ed yesterday, from this point forward, we're going after them."

"But Keith, not only do we fear for your safety, we're worried that Colonel Foster and his team may destroy any evidence of their involvement in 9/11 if you get too close. Or for that matter, they may be more than willing to take their secrets to the grave with them rather than implicate other conspirators. Bottom line, if they die, the secrets behind the 9/11 conspiracy die with them." Patrick's concern was evident in his voice.

"With all due respect, I think you're all being a little bit naïve if you believe that. I'll grant you that Foster may know everything, or most everything, about 9/11. But I'll bet you that the rest of these yahoos don't have a clue.

They probably think that they do, but what they know is probably 10% truth and 90% bullshit courtesy of Colonel Foster. Why would he have them in on the secret? For every person that Foster brings into the loop the greater the chance of someone leaking the information, right? And wouldn't Foster be putting his own life, his own freedom, at risk by sharing the truth with others and opening himself up to blackmail? Or assassination? I don't think so folks. I think Foster is the key, at least within this cell at Destiny Communications Group. Everybody else? They're just soldiers."

"So assuming that we need him alive to get this information, what are you proposing to do?" Karen Richardson was feeling uncomfortable with the direction that this was heading.

Keith wasn't ready to go down that rat hole, at least not yet. He needed LTBT to back his play, not scare them off by talking about the death that he planned to rain down on Foster and his team. "I'm not sure at this point. My assumption is that he's a pretty tough guy and won't want to give up the information too willingly. If we want to learn the truth from him, including the names of all of his co-conspirators, I think we're going to have to figure out what makes him tick. What he holds dear, what he values even above himself." Keith looked at Loren to get her read on how the conversation was going. She jotted a quick note on the hotel stationary. *'You're freaking them out. Stop or we may lose them'*. Keith nodded his agreement. "Anyway, guys, let's not put the cart before the horse. Let's just collect the information as best we can and then plan our next move together. In the end, we all want the same thing: the people responsible for the events of 9/11 to be exposed and brought to justice."

Patrick was glad that Keith brought things back on track. He could feel the vibe on the call even without seeing the faces of his team. "Agreed. For now, we'll forward you everything we've uncovered relative to Colonel Foster and his company. You should have that in your email within the hour. So what are your plans for the rest of the day?"

Keith pondered that for a second. "After we get the e-mail and review it, I think we'll head over to Reston to scope out the DCG building and the surrounding area. I'd like to take a look at the complex where they're headquartered and see how that relates to the location where Karen found the SONET ring circuit. Maybe we'll even get lucky and ID some of Foster's men as they come and go. That could be a help down the line."

"That sounds like a good plan. Do be careful, though. God only knows what kind of security and surveillance they have around there. Might I suggest that you rent yourself a second car, just in case you're spotted in the one you're presently driving? Better to be prepared." Jeff was very concerned for Keith's and Loren's safety, as were the others.

"I like that idea. We'll do that this afternoon." Both Keith and Loren were glad to have other keen minds tossing out the ideas; no way that they could ever think of everything on their own.

Patrick decided to wrap things up. "Alright, then. We'll get you guys the information that we discussed and we'll keep working on our end to find even more on Foster and his team. Check in with us this evening and we'll be able to let you know what else we've discovered, and of course, we'll be anxious to hear the results of your stakeout at Destiny."

After hanging up from the conference call, Keith and Loren recognized that their desire for revenge, though totally justified, was inconsistent with the end goals of LTBT. LTBT was laser-focused on uncovering The Truth and achieving justice for the families of those killed in 9/11. They also wanted to make sure that America, and the world, learned from this horrendous conspiracy and series of events so that nothing like this could ever occur again. Keith and Loren agreed that these were noble goals, but none of the LTBT members had just had their lives turned upside down, or had their friends and family killed or threatened. Revenge was a totally appropriate emotion under such circumstances, and neither of them felt that they had anything to apologize for. Still, it was obvious that LTBT was their best -- their *only* -- ally in this fight, and they both knew that they needed to work closely with them if there was to be any chance of accomplishing any of their goals. Whatever steps were necessary to learn The Truth from Colonel Ed Foster they were prepared to take. Other members of his team were expendable, but he had to be taken alive. If he died after revealing his secrets, well, then so much the better. Perhaps they could help hasten his death a bit and save the American taxpayer the trouble of jailing him for mass murder.

Chapter 19

By mid-afternoon Keith and Loren had read through all of the information that LTBT had developed. They both lamented the absence of a printer, finding the task of reading page after page of text on the laptop PC screen to be quite tedious. Still, they couldn't complain about the amount or the quality of the information that LTBT had uncovered, especially in such a short period of time. Even more impressive, they were receiving additional information in real-time regarding Colonel Foster. They now knew virtually everything about his military background, where he had served, even the awards and decorations he'd received. They even had his home address, home and cell phone numbers, wife's name, and the names and current addresses of his two college age children. Most importantly, though, they had his picture. Now they knew the face of the man that was trying to kill them, the face of the man that had taken their lives and turned them upside down. The face of the man that they planned to make pay for all of the pain, suffering, and death that he had caused.

"This is interesting," said Keith as he read through the information on Foster. "It says here that he lives in the Claremont Country Club section of Ashburn. That's just a few minutes from here. Maybe we can take a swing through there this afternoon and get a feel for the area."

"Sounds like it might be sort of upper-crusty and private. What if they have security at their entrance? That could possibly alert Foster, don't you think?"

"Hmmm, good point."

"Why don't we check the web and see if they have a sales office on site for the neighborhood? That way we can make an appointment to see the place tomorrow, and once we're in the neighborhood we can poke around a little, maybe see where Foster lives."

Keith just smiled. "That's why I love you. You think things through and keep me out of trouble, especially when I'm pissed off and prone to be impulsive." Keith did as she suggested and checked out the neighborhood on the web and then called to make an appointment for the next morning.

After making the appointment at Claremont, they decided to head over to Dulles Airport to pick up another rental car that Keith had booked online. Thank God for the fake licenses and credit cards provided by LTBT. Trying to rent a car without them, even if you're willing to pay cash, is all but impossible. After picking up the new car from Hertz -- another Taurus, Keith lamented -- they decided to park the Dodge Charger that they'd driven from Raleigh in the long-term parking section at the airport. That way it was there when they needed it but not so close as to be associated with them, a scenario they could envision if they left it parked at their hotel. Keith moved the two H&K rifles over to the Taurus but left the other two rifles that he'd brought from Charlottesville under the seat of the Charger. That was another one of Loren's ideas; with all the firepower they had with the H&K's, better to leave the other two guns in the Charger in case they had to grab that car and run without time to prepare. Keith kept his pistol and all of the spare magazines with him at all times, though. That gun was never out of his reach, not even when sleeping.

They exited Dulles Airport and headed east on the Dulles Toll Road. The exit for Destiny Communications Group was only a few mile away at Reston Parkway. Keith took the exit and turned left towards Reston Town Center, an office/restaurant/shopping area less than a mile off of the Toll Road. He was very familiar with this area, having come up here to meet with clients on numerous occasions. On most trips he stayed at the Hyatt in the middle of Town Center, and he had entertained employees and clients at many of the area restaurants and watering holes. Too bad, they both realized, that they weren't here for a more leisurely visit. Hiding from teams of assassins and trying to stay alive against incredible odds was not conducive to a relaxing day of shopping, eating, and spa treatments.

Destiny Communications Group was located in a three-building complex on Sunset Hills Drive about a quarter mile from Reston Town Center. They took up three of the five floors of one of the buildings, and it was immediately evident which one. Their name, or at least their initials, DCG, were in large letters across the top of the building. "They're obviously not trying to hide their business, that's for sure," said Keith. "Or more accurately, at least they're not trying to hide the legitimate business front that they show to the world."

"I didn't really expect that they would, not after reading the information that LTBT sent over. It said that Foster had built DCG into a business with more than $250 million dollars of annual revenue and about 200 employees. That's pretty impressive for such a short time in business, especially when you consider that that's more than a million dollars of revenue per employee. Most businesses would kill for that kind of production." Loren remembered her facts well.

"That's true." Keith couldn't help but wonder how much advantage Foster was having over his competitors with his ongoing links to the government.

They rode through the complex slowly, as if looking for a particular address. They were paying particular attention to the building next door to DCG. LTBT had indicated that a lot of the telecommunications circuits were supposedly connected to that building rather than to DCG's building. "I want to check something out," said Keith. "Something about this just doesn't feel right."

"What is it?" asked Loren.

"I want to go into the lobbies of both of these other buildings, see what companies are there. Maybe even check them out a bit on the web. It's possible that one of them is a front for DCG, but I'm guessing that there may be something else at play here." Keith was quiet for a few seconds, formulating his thoughts. "Think about this: if one of the companies in that building is a false front for DCG, there will probably be little or no information about them if we run a background search, right? They may have a website and some glossy pictures, but it's probably not something that would hold up to scrutiny if we, or LTBT, did some real investigation. Agree so far?"

Loren didn't yet understand where he was going, but she was at least with him to this point. She nodded her agreement.

"OK then, next logical step. Let's suppose that every company that is in those other buildings checks out 100% legitimate, maybe even names we're familiar with." Keith looked up and saw that one of the buildings had the name of one of the country's largest accounting firms on it, and the third building had the initials of one of America's largest oil companies. "Check out the names on those buildings. Even though this is not their world or American headquarters, it's a virtual certainty that they have a significant amount of the space in their respective buildings. So what I'm thinking is that if the preponderance of the space is leased by companies that we know are legitimate or we can prove are legitimate, then we know that they don't have the SONET ring that Karen Richardson talked about or the supercomputer that Tony and the rest of the team talked about."

The light bulb went off in Loren's head. "I see where you're going. If we find a false front company we can be sure that they're part of Foster's operation, but if everyone turns out to be legitimate, then the whole idea that Foster has an operation in one of these other buildings is a ruse."

"Exactly. He has another base somewhere, because there's no way he's got all 200 of his employees in on this kind of operation. Like we talked about before, it would be impossible to keep the lid on this type of thing if he had that many people in the loop."

"So if things check out as you're suggesting, where does that leave us? Foster's base could be anywhere."

"I don't think so. I think it's right here in front of us. It's just not *in* one of these buildings. It's *beneath* one of them."

"Oh, my God! That makes perfect sense. They build some sort of underground facility that houses all of their computers, all of their power equipment, their air conditioning equipment, telecommunications equipment, everything, and it's hidden from view. If they put it in regular office space in one of these buildings, or any public type of office building, for that matter, it would be nearly impossible to keep that hidden from the world."

"That's my point exactly. Here's what I want to do. I'm going to take the digital camera and get a picture of the building directory from the lobby of each of those two buildings. Then we'll get back to the hotel and do a little research on the companies that we find listed. How's that sound?"

Loren looked at him like he'd lost his mind. "It sounds scary as hell to me! How can we be sure that Foster doesn't have security cameras, or some of his killers, working in the other buildings? He knows us on sight and probably wouldn't hesitate to kill us, even right here in the middle of Reston."

She actually raised a valid point. Keith thought things through for a minute. "Maybe I have a better idea. We still have an hour or two before they lock the lobbies to these buildings, so what if we go somewhere close by and try to get something to use as a disguise? Nothing too outrageous that will have the lobby guards giving us a second glance, but subtle enough to change our appearance in case anybody's watching the security monitors. Maybe a wig, glasses, that kind of thing."

Loren considered this. "That might work. But we don't have a lot of time, and we don't know where to go to find that kind of stuff around here. It's not like there's a theatrical store on every corner." Loren thought for a minute. "You know, there are probably a lot more wigs around for women than men, so why don't we concentrate on getting enough to disguise me? Maybe a local beauty shop, or we can check the phone book real quick to see if there is a wig store somewhere close by. Then we can grab a pair of cheap reader glasses from a local pharmacy, hussy up the makeup a bit, or whatever. That should hopefully be enough to get me in and out of two building lobbies over the course of a few minutes. Then we'll get out of here as fast as we can before we raise any alarms."

Keith didn't like putting her in harm's way, but still, he knew she was right. It was much easier to change her looks on short notice than his. "I don't like it, but you're right. Let's get going so maybe we can blend-in with all of the people that will be leaving there at the end of the business day."

They drove quickly back over to the Hyatt in Reston Town Center and Keith ran inside to find a payphone and Yellow Pages. Not finding what he needed in the lobby, Keith asked the front desk clerk if he might borrow their phone book for a moment. He immediately flipped to 'Wigs' and found that there were three choices within a few miles of their present location. He would have preferred to just rip the page from the directory, but being as he was standing right at the front desk he took a minute to write down the three names, addresses, and phone numbers. Thanking the clerk and handing back the directory, Keith asked, "By the way, is there a pharmacy anywhere close by?"

"Yes, sir," came the reply from the young lady. "If you continue on Reston Parkway, away from the Toll Road, there will be a Walgreen's about a mile down on your left."

Keith thanked her again and hurried back to the car. He headed straight to the pharmacy, and it only took Loren about five minutes to find a suitable pair of reading glasses that made a subtle change to her look without hurting her eyes. She was lucky to have 20/20 vision and found that many of the glasses were so strong that they made everything totally out of focus. The last thing she needed was to call attention to herself by tripping or bumping into a wall. With that part done, Keith headed over to a wig store on Centerville Turnpike in Herndon. Fortunately it was still open when they got there, the afternoon rush hour traffic slowing them down considerably. They went inside and took a look around. Thank God they weren't trying to be fashionable, Keith thought. Most of these wigs would have been more appropriate for streetwalkers or old ladies. There were only a few that Loren thought she should consider, afraid that most of the others were so ugly or outlandish that they would cause people to pay even more attention to her. She finally settled on an auburn wig fashioned into a stylish bob cut. It was far from flattering, but compared to the other available options Loren looked like she'd just stepped out of a Beverly Hills salon. They paid the shop owner and headed out quickly to try to get back to Reston before all of the office workers had left and the lobbies were empty. Plus, Keith hoped to take a little closer look around to see if he might notice people entering or leaving from unusual areas of the building or surrounding property, or possibly parking in places that didn't seem to fit with their eventual destination. Loren wasn't too thrilled with that part of the plan, but she agreed to go along with Keith since it might help them identify some of the DCG operatives.

They reached the DCG complex of buildings around 5:30, and Keith dropped Loren off in front of the second building. She went inside and observed the building directory, then managed to snap a few quick pictures with the digital camera stashed under her coat. Thankfully, there was enough light in the lobby that the flash didn't go off and arouse suspicion. She kept her head down and headed back outside. Climbing into the car she quickly reviewed the pictures while Keith rolled towards the third and final building. "They look pretty good. No problem reading the names on the directory," she announced.

"Any names jump out at you?" Keith asked.

"No, it looks like Arthur Andersen has most of the building, and the other offices appear to be occupied by law firms and one public relations firm. I don't recognize any of the names, though, so we'll need to check them out later."

Keith reached the third building and Loren repeated the same process, actually making it back to the car in less than two minutes from the time she first stepped out at the curb. As she climbed into the car Loren said, "Something just dawned on me while I was in there. We've got pictures of the directories for the other two buildings in the complex, but we don't know who the other tenants are in DCG's building. Their name is on that building but they surely don't have all of the space, not with only 200 employees. We need to check out the directory in their building, too."

Shit, Keith thought. She was right. There was no reason why DCG couldn't be using extra space in their own building to run their clandestine operations as easily as one of the other buildings. Still, he really hated to run the risk of having Loren walking into the lion's den. "You're right, but do you think it's worth the risk? We'd be taking a helluva chance."

"I know, but if we don't eliminate the tenants in their HQ building as possible fronts then we've really risked everything we've just done for nothing."

"I really hate you taking the risk walking in there, but I can't argue with your reasoning. Are you sure that you want to take that chance?"

"I'd rather not have to, but like I said, if we don't do it now everything is for naught. Let's follow the same routine, except you drop me off further from the door and let me walk in there alone. At least that way we minimize the risk of someone in the building looking out and seeing you sitting there by the curb."

Keith pulled into a Visitor's parking space closer to the Arthur Anderson building and Loren walked the 100 yards to the lobby. For all practical purposes, she couldn't see any differences between this lobby and the others. If DCG had extra security it was certainly hidden from her view, though she expected that they probably had extensive security in their own space. Walking up to the building directory, she was grateful for the large number of people coming through the lobby on their way home. She was able to get her pictures of the building directory and get back out without raising any alarms or notice, at least as far as she could tell. Once she reached the car she finally took a deep breath and tried to will herself to be calm.

"Let's get the hell out of here while the getting is good," Keith said as soon as she closed the door. Keith had changed his mind about staying around to look for anything or anyone suspicious, deciding that they had probably pressed their luck as far as they should for one day. Loren was all in favor of that, admitting that she'd had more than enough excitement to last her a lifetime. They quickly made their way back out to the Dulles Toll Road and headed west towards Leesburg.

⌘

WHILE LOREN WAS ON HER mission of photographing the building directories, Les Mattox was working at his station down in the Bunker and the security cameras that were linked to all three buildings in their complex fed the video images into their proprietary facial recognition software. Most facial recognition programs used a database of pictures to match against a live video feed, such as picking a face out of a crowd. DCG's program went a step further by learning every face of every person that entered these buildings each day and added it to the database. If a person came in whose face wasn't in the database it sent a signal to the person in charge of monitoring. At the same time it started a search of the expanded database that included criminals, terrorists, or other high-value targets. Like Keith and Loren.

When the facial recognition software didn't recognize Loren, it set off the alarm at Mattox's console. This wasn't an unusual occurrence; the same thing happened at least several dozen times per day. It just gave the team a heads-up to give the subject a little more scrutiny. The system checked its expanded database and compared it against the female image on the security monitor. It ran through the entire database several times but was unable to lock in on the image, probably because the images captured by the cameras were less than ideal since she had on a large coat, glasses, and a scarf up high around her neck. Nothing suspicious about that; dozens of people come into these buildings every day for the first time and are unknown to the program. They might be clients of the firms that have offices in these buildings, or they might be family members, or vendors and suppliers. It was not really a concern to DCG, but they did continue to improve their system by adding every single person to the ever-expanding database. Over the course of the next 10 minutes Mattox saw the same lady walking into both remaining buildings, again walking straight to the directory. Apparently, she was just another person unable to find the company that she was looking for. Just like before, the facial recognition software was unable to identify her, nor was he able to get a good look at her face. Not an unusual occurrence, Mattox told himself. Time to get back to concentrating on the task at hand: tracking down Dr. Keith Bryant and Ms. Loren Davis.

Keith and Loren had no idea how closely they had dodged a bullet. Lucky for them, or they may have decided against continuing this suicide mission.

⌘

BACK AT THE HOTEL IN Leesburg, Keith and Loren spent about an hour researching the companies that had offices in the DCG complex and, as expected, none of them raised any red flags. Keith checked-in with Patrick and Jeff and made arrangements to have a call at 8:30pm Eastern Time to discuss the latest developments, then he and Loren popped out for a quick dinner. They still weren't feeling much like eating after the day's events, particularly the deaths of Bo and Winston. Both of them realized that they had to keep moving forward, had to keep busy. That was the only way they could keep their minds off of their pain and sorrow and on the mission to destroy Colonel Foster and his co-conspirators.

At 8:30 everyone was assembled on the conference bridge. Keith really wished that he had video capability, but at this point he realized that he was lucky to have a decent audio bridge and a reasonably effective speakerphone in the hotel. They started off with Keith telling them about their little adventure at the DCG office complex and how they had checked out all of the companies located there. Everyone on the call was taken aback that he and Loren had done anything quite so risky.

"Weren't you worried that someone might see you and recognize you?" asked Karen Richardson.

"Yes and no, really," said Keith. "We took the best precautions that we could under the circumstances, but we thought it was critical that we try to identify the location for Foster's headquarters, and to do that we needed to know if any of the companies in those other buildings were acting as a front for him. I think that with Loren's efforts at disguising herself, particularly with the wig and the glasses, it would have been tough for her own mother to recognize her."

"While that may be true, Keith, it doesn't mean that facial recognition software couldn't have identified her," said Jeff. "I actually wrote a number of algorithms used in the government's facial recognition programs, and I can tell you they're pretty sophisticated. I've seen it work to identify someone on the terrorist watch list as they got off of a plane in New York, and this guy had on a disguise while walking in a crowd of several hundred people. It's some scary shit."

Actually that thought was scary to both Keith and Loren. "Maybe it's good that we didn't know that before or we probably would have chickened out. Fortunately, from all indications, we got in and out of there without setting off any alarms or anyone following us. Maybe it was just beginner's luck. We won't try to press our luck again, I promise you."

"We're not second guessing you guys or your decisions. As we've said before, you guys are the ones with your butts on the front lines here, so we defer to you. Obviously, though, we are very concerned for your safety and want to make sure you survive this ordeal." This from Patrick. "So what do you see as the next steps?"

"Loren and I actually came up with a theory that we think we should investigate. We believe that Foster is running his clandestine operation from some sort of underground bunker beneath DCG headquarters, not in one of the other buildings. He may have to access the bunker from another building, but I'm betting it's been right under everyone's noses the entire time."

Terrell, having the strongest engineering background, spoke up. "We could probably pull the county building records or architectural plans and verify if there's some sort of sub-basement."

'I don't think so," replied Keith. "My gut says that this bunker, if it exists, won't show up on any architectural drawings or county records. In addition, I think that if we go poking around in the county systems or the building owner's systems looking for it we're going to trip some alarms."

"I would tend to agree with that," said Jeff. "Since that's the logical path that most people will follow if they're trying to get information on the complex, it would only make sense to add some safeguards there."

"Exactly. That's why I came up with another way to approach the problem. Basically, we find out who built their complex and who was used for excavation and hauling. If I'm right about this there had to be some sort of plan when the building was first being constructed to have something underground, right? My guess is that they had plans for a parking garage. Regardless, you can't hide a hole. And there's one other thing you can't hide, and that's all of the truckloads of dirt that had to be hauled away from there."

"You're right about that," said Tony. "It would have taken hundreds, if not thousands, of dump truck loads to excavate the type of bunker that you're talking about. My money is on them originally planning for underground parking and then magically deciding against it once the shell was built. Pretty damn ingenious, actually."

"I agree," said Keith. "It's brilliant in its simplicity. And somewhere along the line they probably tried to conceal how much dirt was hauled out of there, because that would really set off the alarms with the county and state. So what do you guys think? Think this is something that you can dig into quickly and see if we're on the right track?"

"Absolutely. In fact, I think I already have it," said Jeff. "My apologies for multitasking, but I took a quick look and found that the building was constructed by Cherry & Wilson Construction out of Bethesda, MD. It was completed and had first occupancy in early October, 2001, about two months behind schedule. And I also found that Keith was correct about that hole. They had planned a 3-level parking garage under the building now occupied by DCG, but for some reason it was never completed and they moved to surface parking garages instead. No explanation of why. The excavation company was Seitz Hauling, and it looks like they definitely hauled out enough truckloads to fill a football stadium. And here's the clincher, at least in my mind: they hauled away hundreds more truckloads of dirt from the DCG building than they did from the other buildings in the complex even though they're all the same size. And, they never hauled any dirt back when the parking garage was mysteriously cancelled. I'll let Terrell and Tony review the findings and let them do their engineering and math voodoo to validate the assumptions, just to be sure." Jeff was getting excited again and he was ready to jump on this quickly.

Loren said, "So, to net it out, there is a structure under DCG's building that no one knows exists, and they've converted it from a shell of a parking garage into a clandestine monitoring facility to ensure that the world never learns the secrets of 9/11."

"Yeah, I'd say that pretty well sums it up," said Patrick. "Now, the tricky part is how do we prove it and how do we expose them to the world?"

"Actually, I think I have a few ideas there as well," said Keith. "Let me think them through a little bit more and flesh them out a bit and then we can talk about it in the morning. Will that work for everyone?" Keith already had a plan of action in mind, he just didn't want to share it with the others on the call and have them try to talk him out of it. He knew that his idea would sound crazy to everyone else, but so far crazy had been working pretty well.

⌘

Colonel Ed Foster was in an ugly mood, and nothing that anyone did or nothing that anyone said seemed to make things any better. To make things even more stressful, nobody had a clue as to why he was acting like such a horse's ass. The mission the night before in Scottsville had gone off without a hitch. The police in Annapolis were no closer to identifying their dead contractor than they were the minute they found the body. Some of the guys commented – very quietly, lest they provoke the wrath of God – that maybe Foster just wasn't getting laid enough at home. That at least lightened the mood a little bit in the room.

Foster was in a bad mood for one very simple reason: the situation with Dr. Keith Bryant and Ms. Loren Davis was not resolving itself the way he expected. It was dragging on much too long, and he knew from experience that the longer a bad situation drags out the better the chances that it will blow up in your face. What more could he do? He'd sent two operatives posing as FBI agents to Bryant's house and gave him a less-than-subtle warning, and then he took things a step further and had Lowell Westbrook terminated. Rather than doing the smart thing and heeding Foster's warnings, Bryant had instead taken off and joined forces with LTBT -- the very people that Foster had been trying to keep him away from in the first place. Even the killing of his best friend and his friend's family didn't seem to have dissuaded him one bit. Hell, just yesterday Bryant had threatened to come after *him*. He'd never had a subject stay alive this long, much less threaten his life. And from what he'd seen so far of his resourcefulness, Foster didn't think for one minute that Bryant wouldn't try it.

Probably most disconcerting for Foster was the fact that the events of last night had not provoked the expected response, or any response for that matter. To think that he had taken the extraordinary step, God forgive him, of killing their dogs, and now to have Bryant and Davis go quiet, he didn't know what to make of that. Surely they were grieving, but that didn't mean that they would give up the fight, at least not for long. Probably anything but. He wanted, even needed, to have Bryant respond. That's how this game worked. I poke you, you poke me. Action. Reaction. Bryant should have reached out to him today and either agreed to turn himself in or threatened to kill him and everyone around him. It was pretty apparent that Bryant was not going to give up, and any fear that he had for his own life, or his girlfriend's, was outweighed by his thirst for vengeance. He wanted to find The Truth. And he wanted Foster dead. It was that simple.

It was almost 9:30pm when Foster called Bob Manning into his office and closed the door. "I don't understand why we haven't heard from Bryant today. I expected a reaction of some kind, so not hearing from him shocks me. What do you think?"

Manning had been thinking about the same thing all day. "I'm not sure what to think either. I mean, I can see him running off somewhere to lick his wounds a bit after the operation last night at the kennel, but I would have expected him to contact you by the end of the day. If nothing else, just to tell you what an asshole you are. You don't expect that he's given up the fight and decided to run, maybe try to leave the country or anything, do you?"

"I'm not sure what to think. He doesn't strike me as a quitter, and all of the profiling we've done on him, and Ms. Davis for that matter, doesn't point towards people that are going to run from a fight. If anything, he's grown a lot bolder over the past few days as he's managed to get the better of our contractors. I was hoping that might make him overconfident enough to do something stupid, but he seems to have taken a step back."

"Maybe he's working on his grand plan for killing us all," Manning said, only half-jokingly.

"Oh, I'm sure that's crossed his mind a million times in the past week, but you know what they say: *'You can't kill what you can't catch'* and he doesn't have any way to identify us or find us." He certainly hadn't lost any of his self-confidence and arrogance. "So what do you think our next steps should be?"

"I'm not sure that I see any point in continuing to kill the people around him. So far that doesn't seem to have done much good, plus there's always the possibility that some overzealous reporter might connect the dots between all the deaths and connect it back to Dr. Bryant." Manning thought that through for a second. "On the other hand, if someone does connect it back to Bryant and then realizes that he's been AWOL for the past few days – about the time the killings started – they might start to point the finger at him as a possible murder suspect."

"Interesting. Still, I'm reluctant to have him in police custody. Once they start interrogating him about all of these murders he'll most likely start talking about his conspiracy theories and how the government is out to get him. At this point he knows little and can prove even less, but it might be enough to start someone snooping around where they don't belong. Not the least of which could be some nosy-assed congressman or senator looking for a little free publicity and spotlight."

"True enough," agreed Manning. "I think we just need to redouble our efforts around finding Dr. Bryant and Ms. Davis and bringing them in for interrogation and eventual elimination. If we're not able to do that soon we're going to be in the position of having to eliminate too many others, including their families, their work associates, etc. That could definitely shine too bright a light on us."

"Don't forget that while we're identifying people for elimination we need to include those pesky sons of bitches from Let the Truth Be Told. They're obviously in close touch and collaboration with Bryant, and if things don't get resolved pretty quickly we're going to have to start thinking seriously about eliminating all of them, or at least the leadership team. I really don't want to have to do that. Not just the logistics of eliminating that many people, but you know what happens when conspiracy theorists start dying: the other conspiracy theorists just get that much more vocal." Just thinking about having to contract hits on that many people spread all across the country was enough to give Foster a headache.

"So what's the plan then? What do we do to kick it up a notch in our search for Bryant?" Manning was ready to get his orders and head back out to the trenches. He was way past ready for this whole operation to be over.

"I was giving that some thought. Here's what I've come up with, and you let me know if it makes sense. First, we know that Bryant and Davis checked into a hotel somewhere in the general vicinity of Annapolis yesterday, and we know that it was their first day there because they traveled north from somewhere in North Carolina, presumably somewhere in the Raleigh/Durham area. Then, after the events unfolded in Annapolis we assume that they took off, right? At most they probably went back to their hotel to grab their things and then got on the road, and we've got that pretty much confirmed because we took a call from them using Mr. Julian's phone when they were heading north towards Baltimore. You with me so far?"

Manning nodded his head in the affirmative, so Foster continued.

"So that begs the question of where they stayed last night. I'm guessing that they got another room somewhere within a 50-100 mile circle of DC, and, if we're lucky, they may have used the same name for the registration."

Manning saw where this was going. "I follow you. And then they probably checked out of that hotel today and into another hotel for this evening, perhaps again using the same name on the registration."

"Exactly," said Foster. "Maybe we can get Electra to check the registrations at all hotels within 100 miles of DC for duplicate names used over the past few days. We'll surely get a lot of false hits, what with all the tourists and business travelers that stay all over this area, but I'm guessing that we'll be able to drill down to a few probable targets pretty quickly."

"I think we can make that work. The biggest issue is creating the program and getting Electra re-tasked. We can probably have that completed by mid-morning tomorrow."

That was not the answer that Foster was looking for, and Manning was able to see the blood rising in his face. "Why not tonight?" Foster practically yelled, barely able to contain his growing anger and frustration. "It can't be that goddamn difficult, can it?"

"Yes, it is, actually. But besides that, I'm down one man on the night shift. Torres and Hanover were scheduled tonight, but Torres is out with the flu or some kind of bug and Hanover is not a strong programmer. Adams and Mattox could do the work, but they just left here after their fourth straight eighteen-hour day. They're fried. It's better to let them get some rest tonight and then have one of them jump on it first thing in the morning. That way it will be done right the first time and save us hours on rework or sorting through false positives."

Foster had to bite his lip. Here he sat with tens of millions of dollars in computing power and more bandwidth than God, and what happens? No matter how much money you spend on technology you can always be brought to your knees by that one weakest link, i.e., people. One man stays out sick with the flu – a*nd he damn well better be sick*, thought Foster – and the whole fucking operation gets delayed by 8-12 hours. Foster worried that, by the time the team had Electra spitting out information, Bryant and Davis would be on the move again. They weren't stupid, and they definitely didn't appear to be staying in one place too long. If he were in their place neither would he. For that matter, he probably would have just gone off the grid from Day One.

"Get on the phone with Adams and Mattox ASAP and tell them to report here tomorrow morning no later than 6:00am, and make sure that Torres is here bright and early, too. This is too critical to waste time. If we lose them tomorrow morning we don't know where they'll surface or when. We don't even know if they'll risk using the same names again if they realize that we're on to them. I don't want to have to start this search all over again, so make sure that they get it done and get it done right the first time."

Foster knew that it was time to head home before his head absolutely exploded. A nice, stiff drink is what this kind of day called for. He called his wife to tell her that he was on the way home and instead of the usual pleasantries he was hit with an earful of bitching and moaning about problems with the house, problems with the gardeners, problems with their oldest son away at school, problems, problems, problems. He really didn't need this shit today, of all days. So he did what men always do. He lied and told her that he had to leave to go up to New York so he could be there for a meeting and 8:00 the next morning. Sorry, last minute thing. Sure, I'll miss you, too. Like a case of the fuckin' clap.

It was time to get some sanity back into his life, if only for one night. Foster picked up the phone and dialed the private phone number known only to him. It went to someone very special.

"Hello, this is Jennifer."

God, just the sound of her voice was enough to get him aroused. He could picture her long, gorgeous legs and her beautiful green eyes and it almost made him shudder. "It's Foster. Can I see you tonight? Strictly pleasure, no business." Of course, he realized that even though it was pleasure for him – and he hoped for her as well – he would be paying dearly for it.

"Colonel, nice to hear from you. Always a pleasure. Just tell me where and when."

"How about the Willard Hotel in about an hour? I'll be registered as Clinton J. Williams." Foster thought he was clever registering using the reverse of Bill Clinton's name when he was going for a romantic evening with someone other than his wife. In this case, someone that was the *polar opposite* of his wife.

"I'll be there. And I hope you will be bringing me some other business sometime soon. I wouldn't want my skills to get too rusty, if you know what I mean. There has to be someone in your world that's been a bad boy and needs to be dealt with."

Once again Foster had to admire the entrepreneurial spirit of these killers-for-hire. Here was Jennifer, about to spend the evening with him having dinner and making love, and she was already thinking forward to another opportunity to kill someone. Foster loved spending time with her, but he was certain that he would never, ever, want her on his trail if there were a contract on his head. Over the years they had spent time together enjoying fabulous meals and wine, sailing the Chesapeake Bay, traveling to the world's most exclusive and exotic locations, and untold nights in world-class hotels having the best sex of his life, yet he could never really trust her. He always slept with one eye open, as they say. He'd seen her considerable skills in action, and heaven help him, or any man, who was in her sights. She was as deadly as she was beautiful, and God knows she was one of the most beautiful women that Foster had ever seen. And without question, the most beautiful woman he'd ever been with or ever will be with. The fact that he'd be paying her $5,000 to have dinner with him and spend the night with him at a grand hotel didn't faze him in the least. It was a small price to pay for a night of pure pleasure, to say nothing of a small price to pay for maintaining your sanity.

Chapter 20

Wednesday morning found Keith and Loren waking up in a hotel in Leesburg, VA.

"Have you lost your mind?" Loren practically shouted, her voice at least a half-octave higher than usual. Thankfully they were alone in their hotel room and not out in public when the outburst occurred. Hopefully no other hotel guests could hear her through the thin walls.

Not exactly the response Keith was hoping for, but it is the one that he pretty much expected. "Hear me out on this, OK. I know it sounds crazy…"

"*Sounds* crazy? I'd say that's a bit of a goddamn understatement!"

Keith couldn't help but love her fire and passion. "Look, right now we have an advantage." Seeing Loren's eyes get wide with incredulity he held up his hand to stop her from interrupting. She didn't like being silenced and he could see the rising anger in her eyes. *'God, she is so hot when she's got that look in her eyes….'* "I know that he's got all of his computers and all of his killers and weapons, but we *do* have an advantage, at least in the short term. He doesn't know that we've found him. We need to hit him head on while we have that advantage. You know that it's just a matter of time before he finds us, and I'll be goddamn if I'm going to live my life like this forever."

Loren's tone softened somewhat. "Look, I know we can't go on living like this, and I'm sure that Foster wouldn't stop hunting us even if we moved to some island in the South Pacific. As far as he's concerned, as long as we're alive and as long as there are global communications, we're a threat. But Jesus, Keith, you're talking about walking right into his own house and then letting him know that you've been there. I'd say that you're definitely going to provoke a response. You could probably accomplish the same thing by taking a stick and poking a sleeping pit bull."

Keith smiled. "I like your analogy. And that's exactly what I think we need to do. Maybe if he gets pissed he'll make a mistake, let his guard down. He's already changed the rules of the game, right? He threatened to kill someone every day until we turned ourselves in or until he caught and killed us. I'd say that's pretty clear and unambiguous, wouldn't you? So what happened last night? We've checked the local and national news, we've checked the newspapers and internet, and there's nothing. I think maybe Foster's come to the realization that he's risking his own exposure by continuing down that path, so now he's taking time to regroup. This is our chance. Hit the motherfucker while he's already dazed and confused."

Loren saw his point. She wasn't comfortable with it, but she acknowledged that he could be correct. "Alright, let's say for the sake of argument that I agree with your lunatic plan. Before we run off half-cocked I think we need to take a few minutes to reach out to my family and your sister to make sure that they really are OK and safe. You're predicating your plan on the fact that Foster has changed the game and I'm OK with that. But let's make sure the game really has changed. For all we know, Foster may have killed someone, anyone, and the police haven't found the body, or it was too late to make the papers or the news."

"That makes sense, actually. If nothing else it's probably a good idea to check in with our families and let them know that we're safe, at least for now. We've been focusing so hard on staying alive that we haven't taken any time to let them know that we're OK. They're probably worried sick. I say we get packed up and get on the road, and we'll call everyone while we're driving around and mobile. We know that Foster will be monitoring the calls and trying to home in on us, so it doesn't make any sense to be sitting still when we call. They'd probably be on us like white on rice."

"I can be ready to go in 15 minutes. Why don't you get everything packed up while I throw my clothes on and we'll get checked out. Then maybe you can find me a Starbucks or a decent coffee shop somewhere around here. If I have one more cup of lousy hotel coffee I think I'll just turn myself over to Foster and have him put me out of my misery."

They left the hotel about 8:30am and found a nice little coffee shop on a street corner in the old downtown section of Leesburg. It was the first decent cup of Kona coffee she'd had since they'd left Charlottesville, and she raved about the coffee, the pastries, and the atmosphere. "God, this is heaven," she said. "If we had this place near us in Charlottesville I swear I'd never have to set foot in another Starbucks for the rest of my life. This is *so* much better."

Keith was glad it made her happy. She deserved a little bit of happiness and relaxation after the week of hell she'd lived through. If a decent cup of coffee made her feel better, he'd buy her a hundred. For that matter, he'd take her to Kona and let her buy it straight from the plantation. Hell, maybe just buy her the plantation. Since he wasn't a coffee drinker he just made due with a bottle of orange juice and a bagel, which, he had to admit, was pretty good. Not as good as Bodo's Bagels back home, but pretty darn good for a small store in the middle of downtown Leesburg.

As they left the coffee shop they decided to drive south from Leesburg on Route 15 while they made their first call to Keith's sister. They'd keep the call short, just long enough to let her know that they were OK. Foster, of course, would hear every word and know exactly where they were. As soon as the call was completed, Keith would shut down the phone and pull the battery to disable the GPS signal. Then, they'd drive for about another half-hour in a different direction, probably on I-66 towards Washington, and make the second call to Loren's parents. Once that call was completed they'd disable the phone for good. Keith expected Foster to try to play mind games and call them back after intercepting the calls to the families, so he decided to play his own mind games by disabling the phones and not being online to take Foster's calls. That would probably send him right over the edge.

As they were heading from the coffee shop to Route 15 Loren was fumbling in her purse. "Have you seen that piece of hotel notepaper that had my aunt's cell phone number on it? Maybe it fell out of my purse and on the floor." She tried looking around and feeling around on the floor of the rental car. Not finding it, she said, "Damn. It must have fallen out of my purse back at the hotel when we were rushing to get out of there. Do you think it's safe for us to swing back by there to see if I can find it? I'd rather try to reach my mom and dad through that cell phone than by calling them on their cells. Maybe my aunt's won't be monitored."

"I don't know. I hate to retrace our steps, 'cause you never know when someone might be following your trail." Keith thought about it for a few moments. "Tell you what, we'll ride past there and scope things out. If everything looks clear we'll let you run in to the front desk while I keep the car running near the front door. How about that?"

"That sounds good. I'm sorry. I know this is taking a risk."

They drove on in silence, but both of them were on constant high alert for anyone or anything that looked suspicious. When they reached the hotel Keith drove past the driveway and pulled into the McDonald's next door. They surveyed the hotel's parking lot and everything seemed normal. "Let's keep an eye on the place for a few minutes before we approach, just in case," said Keith. "Can you reach into the duffle bag on the back floor and grab me the binoculars? I'll try to get a closer look."

Loren handed him the binoculars and Keith raised them to his eyes; fortunately, there was no one parked close enough in the McDonald's parking lot to notice him. They watched the front entrance of the hotel for about five minutes and were just beginning to feel secure in their plan when Loren noticed an SUV approaching. "Keith, take a look. See it? That black Suburban that just turned into the Hampton Inn." Something about that big, black SUV set her nerves to jangling.

Keith took a closer look using the binoculars, and he saw immediately why it had set off Loren's radar. Black Suburban, dark tinted windows, government license plates. This could not be a coincidence. "Shit," Keith muttered. "This can't be good." They watched as two men climbed out of the vehicle, took a quick look around, and headed into the hotel lobby. Both men were wearing suits, but there was no mistaking their size and their build, even their look and the way they moved. These guys weren't FBI and they weren't Secret Service. These guys were ex-military, just like the other teams that had come after them.

"Maybe we should try to get out of here while they're inside," offered Loren. "Obviously they're here looking for us."

"I think we're safer if we stay put for a few minutes. Let's see how long they stay in there and what they do when they come back out. I'm betting that they're on the phone or radio to Foster before their car even moves."

"You're not thinking about trying to follow them are you?" asked Loren, almost praying that Keith would answer in the negative.

"I was thinking about it for a minute, but I'm not sure what good it would do us. Probably just expose us to more risk, actually. No, I think we'll wait for them to leave and then try to stick with our original plans. We'll just make sure to go in the opposite direction once they hit the main road," he said with a smirk.

"Thank God," Loren said. "I'm not sure I can take another 'Shootout at the OK Corral' just yet." Then, in a more serious tone, she added, "I'm sorry that I insisted on coming back here. We could have been caught or killed."

"Are you kidding? This probably saved our lives. We would have never known that Foster was on to us and we probably would have checked into a hotel tonight using the same name, then we'd be sitting ducks. Hell, this was a great thing to happen! Now we know better and we can register with a different name and be safe, or..." The wheels were turning at warp speed in Keith's brain again. "Or, we can set a trap for Foster by checking into a hotel using the alias that he's looking for and take his hit team out. That could send a pretty strong message to the son of a bitch."

"Oy vey!" she said, breaking into a laugh. "You're starting to take this spy stuff too seriously. Can't we just find a nice little place to stay and do without the terror and the killing for one night?"

"Hey, they brought the fight to us, not the other way around. And for all we know, Foster may end up sending the same team that he sent to kill Bo and Winston. If that's the case, I really want the chance to pay them back." There was no smile on Keith's face, no warmth in his voice. He was reverting back to that same cold, hard persona that he'd had when facing down the hit teams on the Bay and in Annapolis.

She wanted to protest but then thought better of it. Maybe the only way they were going to survive is for both of them to keep that edge. "Look, I wanted to get back at them as much as you, but let's keep our eyes on the real prize here, and that's Foster. Let's worry about taking him down first and then we can worry about everyone else. There's no need for us to take on the extra risk that you're talking about because all it does is put us in danger and does nothing to help us get closer to Foster. I say we stick to the current plan and concentrate on nailing his ass. What do you think?"

Keith was growing angry and sullen, but not because Loren was wrong. He knew that she was right. This was just one time he wished that he could go with his gut and follow through on the path that his anger was taking him. At any other time he would be happy that she was watching out for his best interest, but right now he was hell-bent on revenge and acting rationally wasn't his highest priority. It took him several minutes to cool down enough to be able to admit that she was right and agree to stick to their original plan. "I'm sorry for getting angry and so caught-up in this shit. You're right; we need to focus our sights on Foster. If he falls, they all fall." He reached over and held Loren's hand, and she just smiled back at him.

"It's OK, don't worry about it. Let's just keep pressing forward. You never know, this could be our lucky day, as in the day that we end this nightmare." She reached over and gave him a peck on the cheek.

"God, let's hope," he answered. They drove on in silence.

⌘

FOSTER WOKE UP WHEN HIS internal alarm clock hit 6:00am. He'd slept great. There was nothing like spending the evening wining and dining a beautiful girl to make a middle-aged man feel vital and special again. And then, to be able to have a night of incredible sex with that beautiful girl, well, it just didn't get any better than that. How lucky, how alive he felt waking up next to Jennifer. My God, she was even beautiful waking up this early in the morning. Certainly not the scary sight he was used to when waking up next to his wife, although, if he were honest with himself, he'd have to admit that he isn't a real prize first thing in the mornings either. Still, he convinced himself, it's different for men. Apparently 25 years in the military had instilled a great deal of chauvinism in Colonel Ed Foster, and he didn't know any other way to think or behave. That's OK, though, he thought to himself. This is starting off to be a great day.

Foster's day went quickly downhill after he arrived at the Bunker around 9:00am. It had taken longer than he'd been promised for his team to get the complex program written for Electra, so by the time they started getting any information back it was already 8:45am. Then, by the time he was able to dispatch a team it was almost 9:30, and when they finally got to the Hampton Inn in Leesburg they had missed Bryant and Davis by at least an hour. Manning had apologized for the fact that it had taken longer than estimated. If he'd left it at that Foster probably would have eventually calmed down, but then he had to add, *'Well, at least we know what name they're using now, so we should be able to track them down tonight once they register at a hotel.'* Foster almost exploded.

"Why the hell do you find that to be an acceptable scenario, goddamn it? We should have fucking had them last night or this morning, and we would have if not for your incompetence and the incompetence of your so-called team of professionals. Who the fuck knows what today will bring? This whole thing could blow up on us today for all we know and all because of your delays." His voice was so loud that everyone in the Bunker could hear even through his closed door. If it had been much louder even the Bunker probably couldn't have sealed it in.

Torres was at his workstation when he got a hit on the cell phone of Julia Bryant, Keith's sister. The recording started automatically, and he was able to pinpoint Keith's location from the GPS tracking. He wasn't able to pinpoint Julia's location since her older phone didn't have built-in GPS. He could go to the trouble of trying to triangulate the signal using several cell towers in the area from where she was transmitting – in this case, somewhere near La Jolla, CA – but they weren't really concerned with her at this point. No need to waste the time and cycles when Bryant was the real target. He really didn't want to go in and interrupt Foster while he was in the middle of his tirade since he was almost as likely to shoot someone as fire them when he's in this kind of mood. Finally mustering his courage, Torres headed for Foster's door and knocked loudly.

"I don't want to be disturbed, goddamn it," he yelled even without knowing who was at the door.

Fuck you', Torres muttered to himself, then reached out and opened the door anyway. If Foster came at him, and he halfway wished that he would, he'd snap the little analyst geek like a fucking twig. "Sorry, sir, but I knew you'd want to know that we have Bryant currently on a call with his sister, apparently just checking in to let her know that he's OK. We tracked him to a point on southbound Route 15, just a few miles north of the merge with Route 29 in Gainesville."

Foster stopped his yelling and led Torres and Manning back out to the workstations. He heard Bryant on the call and could tell that he wasn't overly concerned with keeping the call short. Foster looked up at the call timer and saw that they'd already been talking almost three minutes. "That arrogant bastard knows that we're monitoring and tracking him but he doesn't seem to care. His cockiness is going to be his undoing. Fucking amateur."

"*If that's not the pot calling the kettle black, I don't know what is,*" Torres whispered to Manning. "We'll continue to monitor the call and then go back over it for a more thorough analysis."

Just then they heard Keith and Julia saying their goodbyes. After Julia disconnected, Keith kept the line up just long enough to say, "And goodbye, Ed. Hope you're having a good day". With that Keith disconnected the call and pulled the battery.

Foster's face turned beet red. He wasn't used to people mocking him. Not the people he worked for, worked with, or that worked under him. And certainly, goddamn it, not some pansy-assed college professor that was lucky to still be alive. "Let me know immediately if he makes any more calls." With that Foster stormed back to his office and slammed the door.

It was barely a half-hour later when Torres was back at his door. "Colonel, we have Ms. Davis making a call to her mother. They've been on about 30 seconds at this point, and we're tracking the signal to eastbound I-66 around the Vienna Metro area."

Foster was seething, fighting to keep himself under control. He got up from his desk and walked with Torres back to the workstation. He heard Loren talking to her mom, reassuring her that she and Keith were doing fine but warning her mom and dad to stay away from home until they heard otherwise from Loren. The fact that she was talking about it so openly with her mom, knowing full well that the call was being monitored, pissed Foster off all over again. "Maybe I should have someone kill her parents just out of spite, just to take this little bitch down a couple of notches," Foster muttered.

Just as with Keith's call, Loren waited for her mother to hang up and then said, "Goodbye, Ed. Looking forward to seeing you real soon." At that point she disconnected the call and pulled the battery.

"They're gone, sir. GPS signal is history." Torres was stating the obvious, even though he knew that doing so would piss off Foster even worse.

"As I expected. They know that we can track their signals so they're not going to make any calls sitting still or heading to any real destination. They'd drive in circles all day before they'd let us use their GPS signals against them. You can bet that they've probably just tossed that phone out the window and turned off of I-66 by now." Foster's voice was starting to rise again as the anger built back up. "Gentleman, we've already lost our chance at ending this thing this morning due to your inability to meet your commitments. We may not get another chance, but if we do you damn well better be ready to move and ready to make it happen. Do not let me down again, or I promise you, you will pay a very heavy price for your fucking incompetence." With that Foster stormed off back to his office. *'Could this day, this situation, possibly get any worse?'* he wondered to himself.

As bad as his day was starting off, Colonel Foster had no idea just how bad it was going to get.

⌘

JUST BEFORE 11:00AM KEITH AND Loren pulled up to the security gate at Claremont Country Club Estates and told the security officer that they had an appointment at the developer's model homes. They waited while he called to confirm the appointment with the on-duty sales agent; being such an exclusive community they couldn't let just *anybody* come wandering through the neighborhood. Keith had commented earlier to Loren that he was surprised that they hadn't demanded a credit report before setting the appointment. Single family homes ranged from just under a million to several million dollars. Still, as far as Keith was concerned, they could have it. He had no use for 5,000 to 10,000 square foot houses that were set on postage stamp sized lots. He'd take his farm any day versus the 'McMansions' that were so common in the suburbs of Washington, DC. To each his own.

Once through the security gate they drove straight to the sales office. It was, to say the least, stunning. The model homes were beautifully decorated, and from all indications no expense was spared. They were greeted by the sales agent, a bubbly blonde in her early 40's that just reeked of money. Not her money, necessarily. Keith and Loren both took her to be a former trophy wife of some rich guy that probably replaced her after 5-10 years by an even younger, more attractive trophy wife. After being kicked to the curb – with a pretty large divorce settlement, they imagined – she had probably decided to enter the workforce as a realtor in the high-end DC market. Either that or she's sleeping with the builder or developer, they giggled. They sat through the agent's sales talk and looked at the brochures and other information about the neighborhood, and even walked through a few of the model homes with her. After about an hour together the agent realized that they weren't serious buyers, just lookers. At that point she was more than happy to help usher them through and out the door, politely and professionally, of course. Keith and Loren were glad to be done with her, despite her friendliness and charm, so they could get moving on to more important things.

"Well, all I have to say is, that's an hour of our lives we'll never get back," Keith said.

"True. We better get this show on the road. Are you planning to call Patrick and Jeff to let them know what we're up to, or are you still thinking about playing this a little close to the vest?" Loren was a little nervous about their plan, but she was game to try.

"Unless you feel strongly otherwise, I say we leave them out of this for now. They'll probably all freak out and come up with a hundred reasons why we shouldn't be doing this. Then again, I can probably come up with 99 reasons not to be doing this myself."

Loren shook her head. "No, I think you're probably right. Let's just touch base afterwards. It's probably better to beg forgiveness later than to ask permission now."

They drove the few blocks to Colonel Foster's home in silence. Once on his street they pulled to the curb a few doors away and took stock of the situation, both scanning up and down the street for any sign of Foster, members of his team, or any obvious surveillance equipment. They knew that once they were committed and moved in they could find themselves trapped. Nothing looked out of place; just a typical midday in an upper class, or at least upper-middle class, suburban community.

"I don't see anything out of the ordinary. Let's move," Keith said. With that, he pulled the car away from the curb and drove past a few more houses before pulling into Foster's driveway. The only car in the driveway was a Mercedes E350. "I'll grab the bag from the back."

They left the car and walked to the front door, both of them so nervous they were practically shaking. Keith's hand never left the pistol, ready to pull it out and fire at the slightest threat. Loren reached out and rung the bell. A few seconds later they heard someone approaching, a female, they deduced, as they heard her heels clicking on the floor. "Please, God, let it be Alexis Foster, and let her be alone," he whispered to Loren.

The door opened, and before them stood an attractive, well dressed woman in her mid-50's. Apparently they hadn't caught her at the best of times, though. It was pretty apparent that she was upset and had been crying earlier. Her makeup had been refreshed, but her eyes were red and puffy. "May I help you?" she asked politely. Obviously, this neighborhood didn't get a lot of strangers or solicitors coming through, especially with a 24-hour security gate.

"Hi, Mrs. Foster, I'm Keith Bryant from *Business Telecommunications* magazine, and this is my colleague Loren Davis. We're here to do the interview with you as part of our article on Mr. Foster and DCG."

"Excuse me? I haven't heard anything about this. Who did you say you're with?" She didn't seem the least bit suspicious, thankfully, just confused by the fact that she hadn't heard about it.

"*Business Telecommunications.* We're doing a feature article on your husband and his company for our February issue. He's had such great success in the industry, and we can't wait to bring his story to our readers. We've already met with Mr. Foster twice and spoken with him over the course of several hours, and we told him that we'd like to meet with you to get a woman's perspective on his success, how his former career positioned him to build such a successful organization like DCG, and so on. We like to think of it as the human interest side of the technology story."

Loren interjected, "When we last spoke with Mr. Foster, just a few days ago, he indicated that he'd made arrangements for us to meet you here today for the interview. Let me guess, though. He probably forgot to tell you anything about this, right?" Loren smiled, trying to give her that look that said *'Men, what can you expect'*.

Alexis Foster just smiled demurely. "No, he hasn't told me anything. He tends to work long hours and we are often coming and going at different times. It must have slipped his mind." She seemed momentarily unsure of what to do. Let these strangers into her house? Call her husband to verify their story, or maybe to berate him for having time to do everything else that needed to be done for the business but precious little time for her? *'Bastard'* she thought to herself. "You know what? Come on in. I assume that this won't take too long, right? I have some errands to run that have to get done today, but I think we should be able to spend about an hour together. Will that work for you?"

"That's great, Mrs. Foster, and thank you for being so flexible." Keith and Loren both breathed a sign of relief. If she hadn't invited them in they were fully prepared to force their way in at gunpoint, but much better to do it this way. Who knows when a nosy neighbor might be looking out the window and get suspicious.

"Please, call me Alexis," she said, trying her best to put on a smile and a brave front, even though the redness of her eyes betrayed her sadness. About what, Keith and Loren had no idea. She showed them to a beautifully decorated living room and offered them a seat. It was obvious that this was one of those 'force field' living rooms, as Keith liked to call them. Beautiful to look at, impeccably decorated, perfect furniture, but rarely used. "Please, make yourselves comfortable. May I offer you something to drink; a cup of coffee, a soda, or some ice water perhaps?"

"That's very kind of you," said Loren. "If it's not too much trouble I'd love a cup of coffee. But please, only if you don't mind."

"And I'd love a glass of ice water. Thank you very much for being so gracious, especially when it's obvious that we've caught you unaware here today."

"Not at all. Please give me just a few moments to get things together in the kitchen and I'll be right back. Or, if you like, please follow me and I'll show you around while the coffee is brewing." Alexis headed off to the kitchen with Keith and Loren close behind.

"You're house is simply beautiful," Loren said. She didn't have to play the role when she made that statement; the house truly was one of the most beautiful, most tastefully decorated, she'd ever seen. "Did you do the decorating yourself? It's just magnificent, so gorgeous, but at the same time so comfortable and homey."

"Thank you dear," said Alexis. "You're too kind. Yes, I did the decorating, at least for the most part. I had a little bit of help on some of the window treatments, but most everything else I bought or designed. Before my husband's new career with DCG I actually worked as a designer and decorator for a firm in Chevy Chase."

'Oh, how interesting. Did you guys move in here right after he founded DCG back in late 2001 or were you already living here?" Loren started moving things along.

"Oh, gosh no, we could have never afforded something like this on Ed's income when he was in the military. I mean, he always made a good living, and we were certainly comfortable, but things took a substantial turn for us financially when he started his own business. We actually didn't move into this house until late 2003. Before that we were in a nice but significantly smaller house over in Alexandria."

"You must be quite proud of him," said Keith. "He's built a very successful business by any standard, especially in such a short period of time."

"Yes, I am quite proud of him. He's worked hard his entire career, but never more so than the past six years since founding DCG." She tried to smile while making this statement, but it was obvious that she was feeling something more than pride. Was it hurt? Anger? Her eyes started to water slightly, and it was clear that she was fighting to hold back the tears. Keith and Loren could see it in her eyes, though they weren't completely sure what 'it' was. "Could you two please excuse me for just one second? I'm afraid that talking about my husband and how hard he's worked, how much he's sacrificed, sometimes makes me a bit emotional." Alexis turned and walked towards a back stairway that led upstairs, and even as she climbed the stairs Keith and Loren could hear the tell-tale sniffles of someone starting to cry.

"What do you think that's all about?" Keith whispered to Loren.

"I don't know, but she's certainly upset about something. I could tell that she'd been crying when she opened the door for us. It could probably be anything; her husband, her kids, her friends, maybe just her whole life. Who knows? One thing's for sure though: it's not just her getting emotional over some soap opera."

"And it's definitely more than getting emotional talking about his hard work and sacrifice, too. My money is on marriage trouble, especially since she's married to a killer and an asshole of the highest order."

"Yes, but she doesn't know that. At least the killer part. Maybe if she's still willing to continue the interview with us we can broach some questions that might have her sharing those feelings with us. There might be something useful there if we can pull it out of her, assuming, of course, that we're even on the right track with your marriage trouble theory."

"Maybe you should take the lead on some of those questions, don't you think? You know, talk to her woman to woman."

"Yeah, I can do that. We'll play it by ear and hopefully find a smooth way to segue into it."

It was another few minutes before Alexis came back downstairs, and she apologized profusely for her emotions and for leaving them alone. "I'm so sorry; I just don't know what's gotten into me today. Here, let me get that coffee and your ice water and we'll sit down and talk."

"Please, there's no need to apologize. These kinds of things just creep up on us sometimes. I know it does me. Heck, some days I'm just sitting around watching *Oprah,* and next thing you know the tears are just rolling." Loren was reaching out, woman to woman, to establish a common ground.

"I know what you mean," sniffed Alexis. "I guess sometimes we all just need a good cry." She managed a slight smile as she said this.

They spent the next half hour talking about Foster's background, though it was obvious that Alexis Foster's knowledge of his real background at the NSA was minimal, at best. While Keith considered the possibility that she was simply a very skilled liar and able to talk convincingly about his cover story in the world of intelligence, he didn't believe that was true. Foster had probably followed the appropriate protocol and never shared the most secret details of his assignments with her, especially about his time at NSA.

"So I understand that you two have been married for quite a while, " Keith stated.

"Actually, we celebrated our 32nd anniversary just a few months ago," Alexis replied. The look in her eyes betrayed the smile on her face as she answered.

"Wow, that's incredible, especially in this day and age," added Loren. "Congratulations. What's your recipe for such a long, happy marriage?" Loren saw this as the type of probing question that might get her to open up, or at the very least make the tears starts to flow again.

Alexis's eyes were starting to moisten again. "I guess I'd have to say it's open and honest communication, along with a healthy dose of trust. If you can't trust your partner, then there is probably no hope of having a healthy relationship."

"That's for sure. God knows I had enough days and nights crying when I went through my divorce a couple of years ago, and it was all because I knew that I could no longer trust him." Loren was making this up as she went along, but she was doing it beautifully. "It was really an emotional roller-coaster. Part of me was hurt, devastated really, because he cheated on me, and then the separation and divorce turned ugly. Part of me was feeling guilty, feeling that there must have been something I did that made him want or need to cheat. Then finally, I felt relief that it was over. I didn't have to see him anymore, didn't have to put up with his lies, his cheating, and his emotional abuse. And once the divorce was final, I haven't wasted a tear on him, not even at the holidays or when I'm feeling lonely. I just thank God that I'm free of him and able to stand on my own two feet and keep moving forward."

"How did you know that he was cheating? Were there signs?" Alexis asked, still fighting the tears but starting to lose the battle.

"Oh, yes, there were signs. The amount of business travel suddenly picked up, and there were more and more business trips, especially last minute ones. And of course, I was able to do the usual things, like checking his cell phone bills, sneak in and read his e-mail, that sort of thing. At first I felt guilty about spying on him and not trusting him, but it didn't take long before I found out that my suspicions were correct. Worst of all, the woman he was cheating with wasn't his first. He'd been with several other women over the years, almost from the time we were married." Loren was going for broke, feeling more and more confident in their assumption as she watched the pained reaction on Alexis' face grow with each passing second.

Alexis finally just broke down in sobs, her head in her hands. Loren moved over and sat beside her and put her arm around her shoulder. "I'm sorry, Alexis. I didn't mean to upset you. Was it something I said?"

Alexis could barely speak through the sobs. "My husband has been cheating on me, too. I'm sorry; I shouldn't be telling anybody about this, least of all a couple of journalists, but I don't have anybody I can talk to. I've been keeping it bottled up for so long I sometimes think I'm going to lose my mind! I'm too embarrassed to talk to my friends about it, and I certainly can't confide in my children. They certainly don't need this burden."

"Don't worry about us," said Loren. "This will all be off the record. It's not what our magazine is about. Right, Keith?"

"Definitely, Alexis. We're not a tabloid, and this doesn't concern us, or our readers, in the least. If you need someone to talk to, we're here. None of this will be shared outside of this room, believe me."

"You're certain about his cheating?" Loren asked.

"Yes. Let me show you something." With that, Alexis got up and motioned for them to follow her. As they followed her up the stairs to her study, she continued. "I found out, purely by accident, that Ed cheated on me a few years back. He was in New York and one of my friends saw him there having dinner with an attractive young redhead. They seemed to be quite cozy, so my friend followed them back to his hotel at the Westin on Times Square, and the two of them headed off together to his room." Alexis paused, trying to regain her composure. "Ed was supposed to be in Chicago, or at least that's what he had told me. So when he got home and I asked him how Chicago had been he said it was fine, just business, or whatever. No mention was made of New York. I finally confronted him and we had a major blowup, but finally he admitted the truth. He promised never to stray again, and like a fool I believed him. Or at least I did for a while."

"What changed your mind?" asked Keith.

"I'm not sure, really. Just little things. The way he acted towards me. Or as Loren said, the number of supposed last minute business trips." Reaching her study, Alexis picked up several pieces of paper from her desk. "At any rate, a few weeks ago I hired a private detective to follow Ed to see if he's really where he says he is and if he's really being faithful. Last night he told me that he had to fly up to New York City to be there for an early morning meeting today. My private detective sent me a message, along with pictures, to show me that Ed never made that trip. Instead, he was with some woman right here in DC."

She handed the e-mail and pictures to Keith and Loren. The woman in the picture was stunning. Keith looked over the e-mail and saw that the pictures were taken inside the restaurant at the Willard InterContinental Hotel in downtown Washington, DC. Keith had to ask the question: "Did your detective indicate that they stayed the night together?"

"Yes," Alexis sniffed. "Even worse, he managed to identify the young woman and provided some background information on her. Her name is reportedly Jennifer Chambers and she lives in a $1.4 million condominium in Crystal City. She also drives a top of the line Mercedes and appears to travel all over the world. But here's the best part: per my detective, she has 'no visible means of support'. He can't even find where a 'Jennifer Chambers' even exists, officially, at least not in this area. His best guess is that she's a high-end call girl of some sort."

"That actually seems like a reasonable deduction," Keith said, though in the back of his mind there was another equally plausible, but even more disturbing possibility. Would it be possible that the beautiful girl in the picture was part of Foster's organization?

"I'm so sorry, Alexis. And for us to have come barging in here today, of all days. Is there anything that we can do to help?" Loren asked sincerely. Even though she and Keith both wanted Ed Foster dead, it was obvious that Alexis Foster was a good, caring, and decent person. Loren felt bad for her. Maybe the fact that Colonel Ed Foster was cheating on her, repeatedly, would make it easier for Alexis to accept his death when the time comes, she reasoned.

"Thank you, dear, but no. I've already made up my mind to confront him tonight when he comes home, and I'm simply going to end this sham of a marriage and try to move on with my life. I may not have my marriage, but I have my family, my friends, and what's left of my dignity. I'll be OK," she smiled.

"How do you think that will play out?" asked Loren.

"Oh, he'll deny it to start with, just like he did last time. Then once I show him the proof, the e-mails and the pictures, he'll grudgingly admit what he's done but then try to make me feel guilty for doubting him in the first place and having him followed. In the end he'll do what men always do in these situations – sorry, Keith, no offense intended – and blame me. I didn't pay enough attention to his needs, or I didn't provide something that he needed to feel good about himself." Alexis just sighed and dabbed her eyes with a tissue. "It doesn't matter though. I promised myself last time that if he ever strayed again or played me for a fool that I would leave him, and I intend to do just that."

Keith couldn't help but admire this woman. She was as charming as any Southern lady he had ever met, but at the same time she was so strong, so resolute. What an asshole Ed Foster had to be to have treated this wonderful woman, this loving wife that had stood by him for 32 years, with such callous disregard.

Alexis stood up and said, "Would you two excuse me again for just one moment? I'd like to go to the bathroom to splash some cold water on my face. I know that I must look quite the sight."

As Alexis headed off to the powder room, Loren turned to Keith and whispered, "I have an idea. It sounds crazy, but it might just work."

"Alright, let's hear it. At this point I'm pretty likely to want to follow your intuition. It's really been right on the money with Alexis." Keith smiled at her.

"I think we should confide in her why we're really here, tell her everything we know about Ed Foster and how he's killed our friends, our dogs, tried to kill us, everything. We should even tell her about his involvement with 9/11. Who knows? She might even know something that will prove valuable, or at least have some suspicions. It's hard for a husband and wife to hide everything from each other."

"What if she freaks out on us, or threatens to call him or the cops?" Keith wasn't sure he wanted to follow her intuition this far, at least not without some more convincing.

"So what do we have to lose? We high-tail it out of here and then we call Foster to tell him that we were just in his house, with his wife, like we originally planned to do. Or maybe we don't even have to, since she might call him herself."

Keith had to admit that much was true. That's all they had ever planned for, just to piss off Colonel Foster by letting him know that they'd broken through his vaunted layer of security. "I guess that's true. We're going to have to be really, really careful as we choose our words here or she could really lose it. She's been through a lot already; the last thing we need is to scare the hell out of her."

Loren had another thought. "Let's say that she buys into what we're saying, and I think she will. She already doubts him on several levels, so why not this? What if we can convince her to help us set him up?"

"What are you thinking?"

"How about this: we stage some pictures showing her held hostage, maybe even murdered, and then we send those pictures to Foster. If anything will provoke a reaction I'd say that's it. Of course we'll leave her alive and supposedly traumatized by our home invasion, but we will have already gotten the reaction that we want. He will probably come running with his posse in tow, and that could give us the opening we've been looking for to identify Foster and his entire team."

"I can't believe you're coming up with something that sick and twisted," Keith said. Then he smiled. "I love it. Like you said, we really have nothing to lose. I'll follow your lead."

Alexis returned to the room just a few minutes later and sat down. She had washed her face and freshened up her makeup, doing her best to keep the stiff upper lip appearance. "Thank you for being here, and I feel that I should apologize for burdening you with my problems. That's not the job that you people came here to do, and I'm sure that you didn't come here to hear the ramblings and sob stories of an old lady."

"Please, there really is nothing to be sorry about, and we're both glad that we could be here for you. This is not something that you should have to go through alone." Loren hesitated for a moment, trying to choose her words carefully. "But Alexis, we need to be honest with you. Or rather, we need to *start* being honest with you. Keith and I have a confession to make: we did not come here today to interview you for a magazine. In fact, we really came here today under totally false pretenses."

Alexis was taken aback by the statement. *'God,'* she thought, *'what have I gotten myself into by opening my home to these two strangers?*

Chapter 21

"What do you mean?" asked Alexis. "Who are you people?"

"We're who we said we are, but we don't work for a magazine and we're not journalists. Keith is a professor of Government and International Relations at UVA, and I'm a graduate assistant and doctoral student there." Loren was trying to speak calmly and rationally in the hopes that Alexis would remain somewhat at ease.

"Then why are you here, why have you come to my house?"

Loren and Keith looked at each other, and Keith decided to answer her question. "Alexis, what I'm about to tell you is completely true. Some of it we can prove to you, if necessary, and some other things you may have to take on faith, at least for a while. I understand that we haven't done anything to earn your trust or your faith, and for that we're truly sorry. But nonetheless, what we're going to share with you is true."

For the next 45 minutes Keith and Loren laid out the entire saga of the past week, including the background on the Politics of Conspiracy class, the murders of Lowell Westbrook, David Ward and his family, and even their beloved Bo and Winston. They told her about the multiple attempts on their lives, both on the York River and Chesapeake Bay as well as in Annapolis. Most importantly, they told her how they, along with LTBT, had cobbled together the truth behind Destiny Communications Group and the conspiracy behind 9/11. When Alexis asked questions, they gave her straight and honest answers. If they didn't know the answers, they admitted that as well, or, in cases where they expressed an opinion or were merely speculating, they were honest and upfront about it. Both Keith and Loren knew that the only way that Alexis could possibly go along with their plan was to earn her trust, and the only way to do that was to be 100% honest with her at this point.

Finally, Alexis asked the million dollar question. "So why are you here now? Why haven't you just run away, tried to get far away from Ed and the people that you say are after you?"

"That's a fair question," Keith responded. "So let me give you a completely honest answer. We know that there is no running from Colonel Foster and his people. He'll keep hunting us until we're dead, and in all likelihood he'll kill everyone that's important to us along the way, as we've already been witness to. So long as we're alive, we're a threat. It doesn't matter where we run. With today's instantaneous communications, particularly the internet, we could post the proof of his involvement in 9/11 from anywhere in the world, anytime. He can't allow that, nor can the other conspirators. Bottom line, if he won't stop until he kills us, we have to stop him first. That's why we're still in Washington. We plan to take him down first. It's really that simple."

"Even if you have to kill him?" Alexis asked.

"Yes, even if we have to kill him. For what he's done, he deserves to die. But more importantly, we need him to be held to account for what he's done. Not just to us; that's minor in the scheme of things. He needs to be held accountable for the lives he took and the lives he ruined when he took it upon himself, along with a handful of conspirators, to unleash the terror of 9/11 on America." Keith waited and watched for a response, a sign, from Alexis. At least she was not screaming and hysterical, or running for the phone to call the police as he thought might happen.

Finally Alexis spoke, very quietly, very thoughtfully. "As much as it pains me to say it, even in light of the fact that the bastard has cheated on me and hurt me, I believe you. That may make me a bad person, the fact that I can think so terribly of the man I've loved my whole adult life, but I do believe that you're telling me the truth. God help me, and my family. This will devastate them. They're not particularly close to their father, but they do love him and believe him to be a good person, a man of honor."

Keith tried to say something to make her feel a little better about the tragic turn her life was taking. "If I had to guess, I'd say that for many years he probably was a man of honor, doing his best to serve God and country. Sometimes though, somewhere along the way, men make a wrong turn, make one wrong decision. Or maybe it's just that they follow one wrong leader. Even in a case as extreme as this, he probably thought he was doing what his leaders wanted, the strategy that they wanted to take."

"Thank you," she smiled. "Thank you for saying that and at least trying to make me feel better. And you're probably right. He hasn't always been a monster, not to me or to the world. But now he's crossed a line for which he can never be forgiven. If he had anything to do with either causing the events of 9/11 to happen, or even, for that matter, knew about them beforehand and did nothing to prevent them, then he deserves whatever punishment he receives." Tears started to flow lightly. "Dear God, to have had anything to do with that tragedy, to have had a hand in killing all of those people. I've never been able to shake the visions of people panicking and jumping to their deaths from the Twin Towers, or the vision of people held hostage in those planes knowing they're about to die as they go hurtling into those buildings..." Her voice trailed off and she cried quietly, her hands covering her eyes.

They sat in silence for a few minutes, Keith and Loren realizing that everything that could be said had been said. All they could do now was wait to see how Alexis wanted to proceed. Keith looked and Loren and squeezed her hand.

Alexis wiped her eyes dry, and then sitting up straight on the sofa asked with steely resolve, "What can I do to help?"

Both Keith and Loren breathed a silent sigh of relief. "For starters, do you know if your husband keeps anything here at the house that may prove his involvement in 9/11, or even in the murders of the past week? That would be a great start," said Keith.

"Not that I know of, but let me take you to his private study to take a look. I know that he has two computers in his office, one that he uses for personal work and the other for business, but I don't know what's on them. I do know that he's fanatical about his passwords, which I guess stands to reason when he's been in intelligence and cryptography all of these years. He told me one time that his files are encrypted and his passwords for logging into the system and opening the files are 64 characters long, and he changes them daily." They all walked to Foster's first floor study, a room with a decidedly male touch. Heavy leather furniture, large mahogany desk, executive-type chair, plus a flat screen TV and surround sound stereo. There were also pictures of Foster all around the office with various dignitaries, including four different presidents.

"There's no way that we'd ever guess the password on that system, that's for sure. Do you know if he can access his computer system at DCG from here?" Loren asked. She was hoping that the answer was 'yes', which would mean that there was remote access via a Virtual Private Network (VPN), albeit a VPN that was probably as secure as any in the world.

"Yes, he can work from here. I don't know what a VPN is, but I have heard him say that he had one that allowed him to access the office computers without being there on site. He used that for nights and weekends, or during bad weather. I don't have a clue about how it works, but I know that he does use it pretty frequently." Alexis knew how to use a computer, surf the internet, and send and receive e-mail, but she was far from a technical guru.

Keith and Loren looked at each other. They were both thinking the same thing. "If he's got VPN access from here that means that there is a way to get into DCG's mainframe and find out everything about their operation. We just need to know how to get in there and then, once in, how to navigate around and find what we're looking for. God only knows how much data there is to sort through, but considering the size of the supercomputer they have, I figure it must be massive," Keith stated.

"True," said Loren. "But we do have some pretty skilled friends that should be able to help us in that area…" she offered, referring to LTBT.

"Good point. Maybe I should step out into the other room and give them a call."

Keith went back out into the family room and took a seat on the couch. Reaching for one of the cell phones in his bag, he punched in the next number in the sequence. Jeff answered on the first ring. "Keith, I'm glad to hear from you. We were getting a bit concerned when we didn't hear from you all morning, and now it's already mid-afternoon on the east coast. I hope that everything is OK?"

"Yes, everything is going pretty well. In fact, Loren and I have come up with a plan that we wanted to talk to you guys about."

"Uh, oh. I've come to learn not to like the sound of that," Jeff said with only a slight touch of humor in his voice. "Hold on and let me conference Patrick in with us."

Keith couldn't help smiling to himself. These guys were going to go nuclear when they found out where he was and what he was planning. It only took about 30 seconds for Jeff and Patrick to be back on the call.

"Keith, how are you?" asked Patrick. "I was hoping we'd here from you. We didn't find anything on the news that jumped out at us as being tied to you or Loren after last night, but we couldn't be sure."

"No, nothing happened. It looks like our friend Colonel Foster took the night off, thankfully."

"So where are you today? Still in the DC area?" asked Patrick.

"Yes. As a matter of fact, we're still in the Leesburg area. Right now, I'm calling you from inside Colonel Foster's house." Now Keith couldn't keep the smile inside, just waiting to hear what these guys have to say.

"You're WHERE?" yelled Jeff. "Please, God, tell me you're fucking with us. You are fucking with us, right?"

"Actually, no. Loren and I have been here with Mrs. Foster for several hours. Great lady, by the way." Keith was toying with them intentionally.

"What do you mean *she's a great lady*, for Christ's sake? Have you lost your goddamn mind?" yelled Patrick. It's the first time Keith had ever heard either man raise their voice.

"No, I don't think so. Well, maybe a little, to be honest," he smirked. "Loren and I came here under the guise of a couple of journalists doing an article on Foster and DCG. We even used our real names, the plan being that Mrs. Foster would tell the good Colonel about our visit sometime later today or this evening and he'd go absolutely apeshit. Maybe do something stupid, something that we could take advantage of."

"Oh my God, you have lost your mind. You're goddamn certifiable," said Jeff.

Keith was on the verge of busting out laughing. "Wait, I haven't gotten to the best part yet!"

"Oh Christ. What?" asked Patrick, finally resigning himself to the fact that this guy was a loose cannon and not to be controlled. Or saved, he feared.

"Well, it turns out that Mrs. Foster – Alexis – just found out this morning, via a private detective, that Colonel Foster is cheating on her. She has the pictures to prove it. She confided this to us and, long story short, said that she was going to demand a divorce tonight when he got home."

"Interesting, at least in an *Access Hollywood* kind of way, but that helps us how?" asked Jeff.

Keith replied, "Loren and I ended up telling Alexis the whole story about the 9/11 conspiracy and his involvement, including how he's been trying to kill us."

"Holy shit!" exclaimed Jeff. "Tell me you didn't…"

"We did. And she wants to help us. Already is helping us, I should say. She is as appalled at the prospect of him being involved in 9/11 as any spouse would be. The fact that she was ready to demand a divorce anyway, well, that just makes it work out even better."

"So how can she help us in all this?" asked Patrick.

"She's shown us his private study, and we're currently looking around for any incriminating papers or files, not that we expect to find any. There's a wall safe, as expected, but if there's anything in there we don't have a prayer of getting to it, not unless we blow the place up. More importantly, there's a DCG-issued laptop on his desk that he uses here at home to access their office systems via a VPN. From what Alexis has told us he uses a 64-character password for access and encryption on all files, and he changes passwords daily. That's where I was hoping you guys might be able to help."

Jeff responded. "Well, if what she's telling you is correct, and knowing Foster's background, I suspect it is, there's no practical way for us to crack the code for his password. By the time we can break it, even with a computer, he'll have changed it. I only see two possibilities here. First, we have to find his password written down somewhere. There's no way that he can remember a 64-character sequence, so he either has it written down or has it referenced some other way."

"Like maybe taking a passage out of a book or something like that?" Keith asked.

"Yes, actually, that would be a perfect way. He could change passages or lines every day. We would just have to figure out which book and which line or passage. I don't suppose you see any books hanging around his study, do you?" Jeff inquired.

"Yeah. Too many," replied Keith. "There must be several hundred books lining the walls of his study. I guess that means that we're out of luck on that idea."

"I assumed as much," smirked Jeff. "That leads me to Option Number Two. We have to watch him enter his password and then access his computer after he leaves but before he changes his password again."

"If it's all the same to you, Jeff, I'd prefer not to be hanging around the house when Foster gets home and just peer over his shoulder while he's at the PC. Somehow I think he might notice me lurking in the background and get a little mad, maybe even try to kill me."

Jeff just smiled to himself. "Good. Thank God we finally found a death-wish kind of idea that you didn't want to attempt. So, since you can't just peer over Foster's shoulder, we're going to need to try something a little different. What we need to do is find a simple video camera and set it up in Colonel Foster's study, and then we'll have a live feed of him logging into the PC uploaded to a secure web site. Basically, it's like setting up a 'nanny cam' to watch the kids. All we need are a video camera, a laptop, and an internet connection. If you can gather that stuff I can walk you guys through setting it up."

"And, of course, a hiding place for the video camera that allows us to view Foster at his computer without him seeing our setup," Keith said, thinking aloud.

"Yes, agreed. Why don't you check with Mrs. Foster and see if you can rustle up those things, then I'll help walk you through the setup, including the upload to the website."

"I can do that. Oh, and one more thing I forgot to tell you guys…" Keith didn't get to complete his thought before Patrick and Jeff started moaning.

"I shudder to think what else might be going on in that crazed mind of yours," said Patrick.

"It's simple, really. I still want to provoke a response from Foster, push him over the edge. And when he goes over the edge I want to be sitting somewhere near his underground bunker to see if we can find out exactly where it is, or maybe even find a way in."

"And how are you proposing to provoke that response?" Patrick wanted to know.

"We're going to take some digital pictures of Alexis lying on the floor in a pool of simulated blood, basically make it look like she's been murdered. Then we're going to send an e-mail with the pictures attached to Foster and tell him that this is the price he paid for what he's done to us. I'm betting that he'll come running back here, probably with some of his team in tow. That should help us ID some of the other players."

"And what happens when he gets home and finds his wife still alive?" Jeff asked. It was a fair and reasonable question.

"She will have simply escaped her bindings, and she'll just tell them that we forced her to stage the scene. Once she tells him that we had access to the whole house, including his study, he'll probably go straight there to check on his computer or anything he may have secretly stashed around here.

"And you're provoking this response in a man that has killed your friends, your coworker, and even your pets, to say nothing of multiple attempts on your lives, on purpose? I really think you're nuts. Do you go around poking a sharp stick at a sleeping dog just so you can get a response from him, too?" Patrick was incredulous.

"That's funny," said Keith. "That's the exact same response that Loren had earlier when I suggested it to her. But to answer your question, no, I'm not crazy. But I intend to do everything I can to make Foster crazy and hopefully cause him to make a fatal mistake." Keith took a more serious tone. "Look, this idea of Jeff's, using the video camera, just might work. If we can capture his login and password we should be able to access anything and everything we need to bring them down, and that might even include anyone and everyone involved with 9/11, not just Foster. Think of what this could mean. It's worth the risk. It's crunch time."

"I'll give you one thing, my friend. You must have balls the size of church bells," said Jeff.

Patrick and Jeff weren't thrilled with the methods, but they certainly couldn't criticize the results that Keith and Loren were having. In one week LTBT was further along on their quest for The Truth than they had been after years of study and research. Finally, Patrick spoke up. "We're still in this with you guys, with you 'til the end. Let's get going on gathering this stuff and setting up so you can get the hell out of there. Last thing we need is Foster walking in on you guys while you're trying to set your own trap for him."

Keith went back to the study and filled Loren and Alexis in on the plan to videotape Foster and capture the login and password. Fortunately, Alexis had everything they needed, including a video camera, but it still took almost a half hour to get things set up to a point that Patrick and Jeff could read the keystrokes while keeping the video camera out of sight. Keith sat at the PC and simulated typing at the keyboard while Loren moved the video camera around on the bookshelves as Jeff instructed. Once everything was lined up,

Alexis and Loren went about the task of making sure that everything was concealed from view. After everything was set, Jeff did one more look at the feed via the web and saw that they still had a clear, close-up picture of the keyboard.

Next, Keith sat down with Loren and Alexis and explained that he wanted to take pictures of Alexis showing her held captive and then additional pictures in a simulated murder scene. He explained how he wanted to stage the scenes and how he intended to send the pictures to Colonel Foster. He was actually surprised at how willing Alexis was to participate in this part of the plan. It must be disconcerting, he thought to himself, to have pictures taken of yourself in such a state. Being bound and gagged was disconcerting enough, he was sure, but simulation of your own murder? That was actually kind of creepy.

Alexis went around the house and found her digital camera, as well as rope and duct tape to allow Keith to tie her to a chair. She also brought a bottle of ketchup from the pantry; not the perfect ingredient for fake blood, but a reasonable enough facsimile for their purposes. Then he and Loren went about preparing the staging. They tied Alexis to a chair, and then when everything was set just right they put a piece of duct tape over her mouth. Keith instructed her to try to show a look of terror on her face, and Alexis responded perfectly. It only took a few minutes to stage that scene, and within a few more minutes they had the death scene staged. Loren apologized for ruining the carpet with the ketchup, but Alexis didn't seem to mind at all. She knew that the problems and the danger they were facing were much greater than the issue of a carpet, even a handmade Oriental carpet worth almost $10,000.

Once all the pictures were completed, Keith reviewed them with Loren and Alexis. When all were in agreement, Keith brought out his laptop from the duffel bag and set it up in Foster's study. While it was booting, Keith called Patrick and Jeff again. "Hey Jeff, I'm getting ready to e-mail you a few pictures. What I'd like you to do is send them to Foster at his work email address; I'll call you and let you know when we're in position. Make sure you sign the e-mail to show it's from Loren and me. That should send him right over the edge."

"How can you be sure that he'll be checking his e-mail? What if he's in a meeting or on the road or something?" Reasonable question, Jeff thought.

"Already thought of that. I'm going to call him about 10-15 minutes after leaving here, just to yank his chain. Tell him he's a douche bag; tell him we have a special surprise coming for him. Remember, he doesn't even know that we know his real identity at this point. When I call him 'Colonel Foster' instead of the usual Ed, then tell him that I have an e-mail heading his way, he's probably going to shit himself."

"God, you love to just poke and poke and poke, don't you?" Jeff said with a laugh.

"Yeah, I guess I do," laughed Keith. "Keep an eye out for my email. You should have it in about another five minutes. As soon as you have it let me know, then we're clearing out of here. Thanks again for your help."

In less than 10 minutes Keith and Loren had completed the email uploads and said their goodbyes to Alexis. They thanked her profusely for all she was doing and all that she was putting at risk. What she was doing and risking was nothing, she told them, compared to what they were doing, to say nothing of what they'd already been through. Both Keith and Loren hugged her as they left, grateful for having had the chance to meet such a lovely and gracious woman in the midst of all this craziness. "If you need anything, and we mean anything, please reach out to us or our friends at LTBT. If they can't find us, or if something should happen to us, they'll provide you with whatever assistance you need. I've already arranged that with two leaders of their core team, and I've let them know that what we're about to do, what we're about to accomplish, couldn't have been down without you. They won't forget that."

⌘

ON THE RIDE FROM FOSTER'S house to the DCG headquarters in Reston Keith and Loren were discussing where they should be positioned to see Foster and his men as they left the facility after hearing about Alexis. "I'm afraid that we might be positioned in one place and they end up leaving from another and we'll miss them altogether," said Loren. "Since we don't know how they get in and out of this underground bunker that's a distinct possibility."

"You're right. Let's think about this logically. What's the easiest way for Foster to get from his office on the top floor down to this so-called bunker?"

"Obviously an elevator is the easiest way. Second choice would be a stairway, and I'm sure that their building has at least a couple for emergencies."

Loren thought for a moment. "You know what, though, they can't be using an elevator. Think about all of the people in that building that ride those elevators; there would be too many chances for someone to take notice if someone stayed on the elevator when it reached the lobby and somehow magically went down to floors that don't exist."

"Exactly. To say nothing of the fact that an elevator company would have had to install at least one car that went probably 3-5 stories below the building's ground floor. Even if they managed to keep it a secret when they built it, it would be really tough to keep it secret after that when their technicians had to come by for maintenance." Keith continued. "My guess is that an internal stairwell going down to this bunker would also raise the same kind of questions that the elevator would: where does it go since there are no floors below the lobby?"

"So if they don't get down there via an elevator or a stairwell, how the heck do they get there?" Loren didn't really see that they were any closer to the answer.

"I've got an idea, but it sounds kinda crazy. Maybe there's a secret entrance of some kind located away from the building."

"And this secret entrance would be located where?" she asked.

"My first guess would be the parking garage closest to the DCG building, probably an entrance near the edge of the woods. Maybe there's a stairwell that they take, maybe behind a hidden door or something, that let's them get down there without being seen. I'm thinking a stairwell that the other building tenants never see and wouldn't even know existed."

"Actually, that idea isn't that crazy. I was half-expecting you to come up with some kind of whacky Bat Cave scenario," she said jokingly.

"Once we get over there we'll try to scope the place out a bit. Maybe we'll get lucky."

They finally arrived at DCG headquarters, and after circling the complex one time looking for anything or anyone unusual, they parked the car on the first level of one of the parking decks. Heaving the duffel bag that held the binoculars, both H&K assault rifles, a cell phone, and extra ammunition over his shoulder, Keith led the way out the back of the parking garage and into the woods that ran behind the buildings. He hoped that his hunch was right. The wooded area wasn't that deep, maybe 100-200 yards at the most, but it was enough to offer them some protection and coverage while they looked around.

"How far into the woods do you think we should go?" asked Loren.

"Not too much further. God only knows what they have in the way of security. There may be cameras, motion sensors, or some other type of alarms out here. Let's set our stuff down here and try to take a look around, see if anything looks wrong or out of place." Keith set down the bag, actually glad to get the weight off of his shoulder. Pulling out the binoculars, he made a slow sweep of the area.

"See anything that looks unusual?" Loren sat down on the ground beside Keith.

"Not yet," he answered, his eyes still scanning slowly, carefully. Then he saw it. "I think I got it."

"Where?" Loren reached for the binoculars from Keith.

"Check out that small outbuilding that's sort of attached to the back of the garage. I guess you'd call it a utility room of some sort. Take a look through the binoculars, about 75 yards ahead and to the right. It's just a small, simple, brick building that has probably been there since the complex was built. There's probably even a legitimate purpose for it, like maybe some of the water pipes or electrical service for the complex gets routed through there. Foster hasn't been using some secret location or trap door out in the middle of the woods. The goddamn access to the underground bunker is somewhere inside that little building."

Loren took the binoculars and checked things out for herself. "Smart. Hiding right there in plain sight. Nobody would think twice if they saw someone going in and out of there since the building has a real purpose, something to do with the complex facilities. We can't see the entrance, though, not from this side. Maybe we should make a wide circle around to the right and get in a position where we can see people coming and going."

"I agree. Let's swing around there and get into position, then I'll give Foster a call." They grabbed the bag and quietly made a wide arc around to the other side, both being very cognizant of the fact that they could be setting alarms off at any time, especially if they tried to get much closer. Once they reached a point about 85 yards from the building they set their stuff down behind a large tree and scoped out the entrance one more time.

"Think it would do any good to try to get a picture of these guys as they leave the building? I think there's still enough available light to do that without the camera's flash coming on." Loren was already fishing around in the duffel for the camera.

"That might be a good idea, but for God's sake let's test the thing to make sure that the flash won't go off. If there's any chance of that it's probably not worth the risk." Keith pulled out both of the assault rifles and made sure that they were ready to go. He had no intention of using them at this point, but he did want to be prepared in case things didn't go according to plan.

"Do you think you should call Patrick and Jeff first, before calling Foster, and ask them if they can mask or reroute your call? Otherwise, won't he be able to pinpoint your location in like two seconds flat?"

"Damn, I hadn't even thought about that, but you're right. I got so caught up in all of the other details of our plan that I totally lost focus on the most basic thing, namely, keeping ourselves safe." Keith reached over and squeezed her hand. "Thanks for keeping me from doing something really stupid," he said with a smile.

"Hey, it's my ass on the line here, too. No problem for me if I occasionally have to pitch-in to keep us from getting them blown off."

Keith picked up the cell phone and called Jeff and Patrick. After explaining the dilemma, Jeff said that he could easily mask or spoof the call, at least so long as Keith kept the call relatively short, say 30 seconds. "Let's do it then." Keith waited while Jeff did his magic, essentially routing the call through five different systems before making the connection to Foster's number.

"OK, you should be ready to go, but keep in mind that the volume of the call could be a little bit lower than normal due to all of the decibel loss incurred with each hop on the route," explained Jeff.

Keith turned up the volume on the cell phone to the maximum level. Not great, but certainly acceptable, if he were able to judge by the volume of the ringing. On the third ring Foster picked up.

"Dr. Bryant, so good of you to finally call. I was afraid that maybe I'd hurt your feelings when you didn't call for so long."

"That's OK, Ed, I think we're going to be talking or seeing a lot of each other very soon. In fact, *Colonel Ed Foster*, I want you to take a look in your e-mail, your *Destiny Communications Group* e-mail, in just a few minutes, and see a little surprise I have waiting for you."

The line went silent for a few seconds; no doubt Foster and his team had to pick themselves up from the floor. Keith would have loved to have been able to see his face at that second.

"What's the matter, *Colonel Foster*? Cat got your tongue? Now you listen to me, you worthless piece of shit. I told you that I was coming to get you, and now you're going to know that I meant every word. You're a dead man." With that last statement Keith dropped the call. He turned to Loren and smiled. "Think I got my point across?"

"I would think so. You were giving *me* goose bumps."

Chapter 22

Inside the Bunker it was complete pandemonium. Foster's face was drained of all color, and had he not been leaning heavily on the workstation he would have surely hit the floor. Bob Manning was in the room, as were Brad Hanover and Eric Torres. They were all screaming at each other, at Foster, at God. *'How could this have happened'* they all yelled. *'Who allowed this breach of security?'* Suddenly a group of men that only moments ago had been confident, even cocky, in their own anonymity, their own secure little womb, were feeling scared and vulnerable. Would Bryant come after them and their families? Who did he know about beyond Foster? One of them? All of them? Would they die, or maybe rot in prison? They all started rationalizing in their minds their role in the cover-up of 9/11. *'I was only following orders'. 'I don't know anything about what actually happened, I just monitor internet chatter'. 'I never had a hand in any of the killings. That was all Foster and his goon squads'.*

The color was slowly returning to Foster's face, and his anger was rising. "Everyone shut up and listen. I don't know how Bryant knows what he knows, but I aim to find out. If one of you allowed this breach you can rest assured that I will find out, and when I do, I will personally see to it that your body ends up at a rendering plant and ground up into cow feed."

'Hey, fuck you, Colonel!' yelled Torres as he jumped up from his chair. He closed the distance between he and Foster in less than a second and was nose to nose with him. "How do we know that it wasn't one of your stupid moves that led him here to our doorsteps, you arrogant little prick. You had to keep pushing him and pushing him, had to keep on killing!"

Foster was stunned that Torres, or anybody, would have the balls to get up in his face. No one had done that in many, many years, and the fear was evident in his eyes. Before Foster could even respond Hanover and Manning were pulling Torres back and trying to separate the men. Though, truth be told, neither of them would have minded seeing Torres kick the shit out of Foster right here on the spot. Torres struggled against both of the men, his rage growing even as he was pulled away.

"Sit him down and everybody shut up, for Christ's sake. Mr. Torres, I'll deal with you later." Foster threw that last sentence out there knowing full well that it would send Torres off of the deep end again. Now Hanover and Manning had to struggle even more to hold Torres back and move him away from Foster and try to get him calmed down. The Colonel moved to one of the work stations and typed in his login and password, then opened his DCG business e-mail account. There were over 50 new e-mails in his Inbox, but he immediately saw the one that was from Bryant. Not only did it stick out by having a Yahoo address -- something that his business e-mails never had -- but also because the subject line said *'Pictures from your friends Keith and Loren'*. He felt his blood boil at their smugness.

Nothing could have prepared him for what he was saw when he opened the file with the first picture, the one with Alexis tied to the chair. Her mouth was covered with tape and she had a look of sheer terror in her eyes. "Oh my God," he practically screamed. Hanover and Manning rushed back to his side to see what was going on. Torres stayed where he was, not caring in the least what was causing Foster pain.

"Jesus," exclaimed Manning. "Bryant has found out where you live and gone after your wife?"

Foster clicked on the second attachment in the e-mail and another picture opened, this one far more horrific than the first. "Dear God," he said as he practically fell into a chair. The scene depicted in the picture was so horrific that the others had to turn away.

Foster was nearly in tears, fighting hard to remain stoic in front of his men. That was becoming increasingly difficult as he stared at the picture of his wife lying murdered on the floor of their home. He may have cheated on her occasionally, and he may have grown more cold and distant with age, but he had never stopped loving her. The fact that they were still together proved that, at least in his mind. To others, perhaps being more cynical, they assumed that he stayed with his wife partly out of convenience and partly out of a desire to not have to go through the hell of a divorce. Particularly the financial hell.

The room was silent for several minutes. Hanover and Manning didn't really know what to say, and Torres was too concerned with killing Foster and saving his own skin to really care about the Colonel's wife. He was over Colonel Ed Foster and his whole fucking world, and while he wouldn't wish death or harm to Alexis Foster, the fact that it caused pain to Colonel Foster made the whole thing palatable in his mind. Finally Manning spoke. "Come on, Colonel. We need to get to your house and check things out for ourselves. If nothing else, and I'm sorry to sound callous, we need to get over there to be able to control the situation. Things are already starting to spiral out of control, the fact that Bryant, not to mention possible others like LTBT, have uncovered you and our group."

Foster looked at him, the pain evident in his eyes. His voice was low and almost distant. "You're right. If nothing else we have to make sure that this looks like some random act of violence, a home invasion of some sort. If we don't this whole thing could come tumbling down like a house of cards and none of our lives will be worth a dime. To say nothing of what it might do to our country."

Foster got up from his chair looking very wobbly and weak, far from his usual arrogant swagger. Torres, at least, was enjoying Foster's pain and was tempted to make some snide remark about how he'd brought this all on himself with his stupidity and arrogance, but he thought better of it. Maybe it would be better to wait until later when he can follow up his comments by beating the living shit out of this man that he had grown to despise. Manning led them all through the Bunker and up the stairs to the utility building behind the garage. Reaching the ground level, they checked the security monitors and saw that everything was clear. Only then did they open the door and emerge from the building single file and head for their cars in the parking garage.

⌘

"Here they come," Loren whispered. She raised the digital camera and set it for maximum zoom. The pictures would be far from close-up quality, but she and Keith had no doubt that the pictures would be able to be enhanced if necessary. Loren managed to get multiple shots of each of the four people as they emerged.

"There's Foster," Keith whispered as he nodded towards the door. "The last one coming out of the door. I'm tempted to kill him right here and now."

"I know, but you know that we can't. Killing him now won't put us any closer to learning the secrets behind 9/11, and that's what we have to focus on first. After that, we can turn him over to the authorities or we can kill him, whatever the situation dictates."

"No way am I turning that bastard over to the authorities, and I don't care which authorities we're talking about. I'm not going to risk him being protected or spirited out of the country. For that matter, the President might even pardon the son of a bitch, especially since it was most likely the President that authorized the existence of this group to start with. No, that is *not* going to happen."

"Let me have the binoculars and I'll see if I can get a look at their cars as they leave the parking garage. Come on; let's try to move a little bit closer so we can see them as they come out of the exit." Loren started moving slowly through the woods, doing everything that she could to minimize the sound. When she realized that Foster and his men had reached the parking garage she looked back at Keith and said, "They're in the garage and out of sight now. Let's hurry while we still have a chance to get into position." Keith moved as quickly as he could, but Loren had already moved at least 35 yards away from him before he'd gotten their equipment back into the duffel bag.

Manning led Foster through the garage and told him to jump into the passenger seat of his car. "Come on Colonel, you're in no real shape to drive. Hop in and I'll get us there." Foster did as he was told.

"What about Torres and Hanover?" Foster asked.

"They're both taking their own cars and they'll meet us there. That way, if we have to split up later we'll have options." What he wasn't saying was that they'd have other cars to use if they had to dump Alexis Foster's body while Colonel Foster stayed at the house.

Hanover was parked a couple of rows over from Manning. He started his Jeep and started backing out of the space and moving towards Manning. Torres was parked the furthest away, his car being all the way up against the back wall on the third level overlooking the woods. As he reached his car and started to climb in his attention was drawn to movement down in the woods. At first he assumed it was a deer, a not unusual occurrence in this area particularly as it got close to their feeding time at dusk. Then he saw the movement again and realized, without question, that this was no deer. It was a person, a person that was out there in the woods right near their entrance to the Bunker. Torres turned, planning to yell for Hanover and the others, but he saw that they were already making their way through the garage and heading for the ramp to take them down the three levels to the ground. 'Shit,' he muttered to himself. 'I'll just have to check this out for myself.' More than anything, Torres was looking for a reason not to have to go with Foster.

Torres made his way quickly down the three flights of steps and was at the edge of the woods in no time. Pulling his gun from its holster, he slowly made his way into the woods, taking time to watch and listen for any movement. Then he saw it again. This time he realized that it was a woman trying to move quickly towards the far edge of the woods. What could she possibly be doing out here, he wondered. Torres moved quickly towards her at an angle, his movements much more fluid, much more practiced. Special Forces training had obviously served him well. He was on her in mere seconds. As he closed the distance, now less than 50 feet away, he saw her raising a camera to her eye as if to photograph....what?

"Hold it right there or you're dead," Torres said menacingly. He continued walking slowly in her direction, his gun never wavering.

Loren froze, and then slowly started to raise her hands. Thank God her back was to him and he couldn't yet see her face. "Please, I haven't done anything. I'm just here taking some nature pictures."

"Funny places to be taking pictures. Not a whole lot of nature here in Reston lady. Now, slowly put your hands down and turn towards me. Slowly." When Loren didn't start doing as he had said quickly enough, Torres made a point of pulling back on the slide on his semi-automatic pistol. That sound usually helped get the point across, he had learned long ago.

Loren didn't know what to do. She didn't know how far away Keith was or if he was in any position to help. The man holding the gun was surely one of Foster's men, and there was little doubt that he would recognize her as soon as she turned around. He'd probably shoot first and ask questions later, especially since he'd almost certainly seen the pictures of Alexis. She looked down at the camera, barely able to make out the buttons in the growing twilight, but fumbling around nonetheless. "How do I know that you won't kill me?" she asked, stalling for time.

"Lady, if I wanted you dead you'd already be dead. But if you don't turn around by the time I count to three, I can promise you that you will have a bullet right in the back of your head. Am I making myself clear?" His tone was threatening, but he never raised his voice. He generally didn't have to for people to get his point, especially when he was holding a .45. At this point he was probably less than 20 feet away from her. Putting a bullet in her head, or anywhere he chose, would be child's play for him at this distance.

Loren started turning slowly around, her head hung low in an effort to keep him from seeing her face. As she turned almost facing him, she turned the camera up towards him and pressed the shutter. A bright flash erupted from the camera, temporarily blinding and disorienting Torres. At the same time, Loren dove for the ground. Then she heard it, the 'pop' of a weapon and Torres' head being impacted, and she looked up as blood and tissue exploded all around. Torres collapsed in horrific slow motion, his head half blown off.

Loren fought hard to stifle a scream, made all the more difficult as she caught sight of Torres with much of the right side of his head missing, blood and body tissue sprayed all over him and the surrounding area. Still, she kept her head enough to stay down on the ground, not knowing if there were others out here in the woods. The sight was so grotesque and disturbing that she finally had to avert her eyes. Seconds passed and still Keith had not yelled for her or started moving in her direction. God, where was he?

"Loren, stay down! Are you OK?" she heard him say from about 100 feet away, speaking only as loud as was needed to make himself heard but, hopefully, not loud enough to be heard much further away. Keith had taken a quick look around the woods and didn't see anybody else, but he didn't take for granted that there wasn't someone else there. He realized that the man he'd shot was one of the four that had just come out of the building with Foster, and that fact gave him a little bit of confidence that he might be alone and not some sort of security patrol. Still, he used the scope on the rifle to scan the area and check for any movement. Seeing none, he quickly got up from the ground and made his way to Loren, always staying low and moving in a serpentine route. He hoped that his attempt at being evasive would be enough should there be anyone still out there in the woods with plans to kill them, but he didn't kid himself. These people were professionals, with training and skills that went far beyond his basic military training.

Finally reaching Loren he plopped down on the ground beside her, reaching out to comfort her as best he could while still keeping an eye out for any threat. Even as he held her his hand did not leave the H&K. "Are you OK?" he asked as he raised her head to look into her eyes. She was trying to hold back the tears, but the shock of what she had just witnessed was too much. "It's OK, babe, you can let it out." And she did, the days of continued stress combined with the sheer horror of what had just happened being more than she could take. Keith tried talking to her while holding her, her head buried in his shoulders. "You did a great job of keeping control of the situation, keeping your face hidden and slowing things down until I could get into position. And using the camera's flash to startle him was brilliant. I think you have a definite future in the spy business, should you choose to accept the assignment." He hoped that his little attempt at humor, referring to the old line from *Mission Impossible*, might help to lighten things a bit. Not so much this time, he realized as she continued to sob.

They just sat there on the ground, silent except for Loren's quiet crying, for almost a half hour. As she started to get herself a little more back together, Keith said, "We should probably head out of here and find a place to crash for the evening. I don't think there's much more we can do today. From here I think it's all in the hands of LTBT. We can call them once we're on the road and see if they're having any luck capturing Foster's login and passwords. Surely Foster will be home soon, even in rush hour."

Keith helped Loren from the ground and they collected their things. Everything went back into the bag except for the H&K assault rifle that Keith was holding; he wasn't putting that back into the bag until they were closer to their car. "Let me check our friend here and see what he has on him. He might have something useful." Keith removed Torres' wallet and did a quick check of the ID, then grabbed his cell phone and shoved them into the bag for examination once they got to a hotel. He also took the pistol that Torres had been holding, partly because he thought it might come in handy down the road and partly because he was scared that some kid might come upon it out here in the woods.

"Does he have any kind of keys on him that might get us into their bunker, or maybe some kind of card key?" Loren asked.

"It appears that Mr. Eric Torres has some car keys and what looks like a house key. I'll take them just in case. I don't see any card keys but I'm not really surprised. I expect that their place is probably secured like Fort Knox. You know, lots of secure areas with cameras, biometric readers, and probably even some kind of scanners or X-rays to see if people are carrying weapons. I'm guessing that our chances of getting in there without the Marines are probably about zilch."

"Maybe when all of this is over," she said hopefully. "Of course, with our luck, they probably have the whole place booby-trapped to self-destruct."

Keith was about to ask her again if maybe she'd seen one too many action movies, then realized that, kidding or not, she might actually be right. That wasn't a pleasant thought. "C'mon, let's get out of here. We'll grab our car and then see if we can find Torres' car in the garage. His keys are for a Ford Expedition, so hopefully there won't be too many of them." It took them less than five minutes to reach their car and stow their gear in the backseat. Keith elected to keep the one H&K close at hand and asked Loren to hold it after first ensuring that the safety was on.

"While I drive through the garage looking for an Expedition, why don't you look through his wallet and cell phone to see if there's anything useful there," Keith suggested. As they circled through the parking garage he didn't note any Expeditions on the first two floors. Finally, on the third floor, Keith saw a black Expedition parked by the wall overlooking the woods. "That's got to be it", he said to Loren. Trying the key fob, he was immediately rewarded with the interior lights coming on. Pulling into a parking space next to the Expedition Keith jumped out quickly and left the rental car running.

Rummaging through the interior, including the glove box and the center console storage, Keith found nothing of any use. Car registration, some CD's, coupons for fast food restaurants, that was about it. He locked the car back and returned to the rental. "Nothing worth much in there," he announced to Loren. "Looks like a typical car of your average working guy. I was hoping to find weapons, communications equipment, something. This guy's car looks like it could have belonged to 'Joe Suburbia'."

"You know, that's probably the point," Loren responded, thinking things through. "This guy, this Eric Torres, probably was just your basic 9-5 suburban dad or something, he got up every morning and went to work and sat at a desk, just like tens of millions of other guys." Loren had found pictures of

Torres with his wife and kids, something that she hadn't been quite prepared for. Much easier to think of all of these people as monsters, people that love no one and no one loves them.

"Let's get out of here. I think it's time we found a place for the night, and I vote that we put at least 10-20 miles between us and this place." Keith headed out of the garage and away from Reston, pointing the car in the general direction of DC. That decision was dictated as much by his impatience with the rush hour traffic heading west towards Leesburg as it was by the large number of hotels to be found in Tysons Corner and other areas closer to the Capital Beltway.

⌘

BOB MANNING PULLED HIS CAR up to the curb in front of Foster's house, and Brad Hanover pulled his car up right behind. The three men headed for the door, none of them looking forward to what they were about to find once they headed inside. Even with as much death as they all had seen - to say nothing of how much death they had all *caused* - this time was different. It was personal. It was one of their loved ones.

"Should we wait for Torres to get here?" Brad Hanover asked.

"No. Screw him. I'll deal with him and his insubordination later," answered Foster.

When they reached the door Foster put his key in the lock with some trepidation. His hand was shaking so badly that he could barely guide the key to the slot. Holding his breath for the inevitable shock, he turned the knob and slowly opened the door and moved into the foyer. Then he had the biggest shock of his life: he heard Alexis screaming for help, her screams muted by a tape at least partially covering her mouth. Foster ran into the living room and found Alexis there, struggling to free herself from the ropes that were binding her wrists. Tears filled his eyes as he ran to her and quickly untied the ropes binding her and then slowly, delicately removed the tape from her mouth. She was crying, too shaken to even speak.

"My God, I thought that you were dead. The pictures…"

"I know," she sniffed. "They made me pose for them. I still thought that they might kill me. Who were these people and why did they do this to me, to us?"

Foster thought quickly. "They're part of a terrorist cell with links to groups in Europe and the Middle East. We thought we'd shut down the whole organization back when I was with the NSA, but we didn't know about these two, apparently. The message they sent me indicated that they came after you as payback for their comrades."

'Lying bastard', Alexis thought to herself as she held him and buried her head in his shoulder.

"I'm just so glad that you're OK," Foster told her earnestly. "Did they hurt you at all?"

"No, they just scared the hell out of me but they never hurt me physically. They seemed very concerned with trying to find some information about you, even forcing me at gunpoint to show them your office and where you work."

Foster cut a quick glance over at Manning and Hanover, and both looked genuinely concerned. All relief at finding Alexis alive had already been replaced by their own selfish self-interests.

"Let's help you up and see if we can't get you cleaned up a bit. Do you need some water, or anything?" Foster was falling all over himself to be helpful, but his inherent lack of compassion and mothering skills were obvious.

"Shouldn't we call the police?" she asked. She knew that the sniveling, lying bastard would never do that, couldn't do that. He was going to get even more wrapped up in his lies, she knew.

The question actually caught Foster a bit off-guard, and it was probably obvious by the blank look on his face. Still, he had always survived and thrived by his quick wits. "No, we can't involve the police in this. I'm going to have to call some people I know at NSA and CIA since this involves terrorism. I'm sorry, but we can't afford for word of this to get out to the general public. God only knows what kind of panic that might cause if people knew that terrorists attacked a civilian right here in suburban DC."

Alexis was pretty smart herself. It was the lie, the response that she had expected. "So what if they had raped me? Or killed me? Would you just let them get away with that, too? You'd let someone do this to your own wife and then you'd try to cover it up so that people wouldn't be worried about terrorism any more than they already are?" She was practically screaming at him by the time she had finished.

Foster did not like being yelled at by anyone, at anytime, but particularly not by his wife in front of his men. He was not about to be emasculated by this emotionally overwrought, hysterical woman. "We'll discuss this later, in private." He said this with his usual air of superiority, his 'my way or the highway' tone of voice. It was a tone that was like nails on a chalkboard for Alexis and most people that were on the receiving end of such treatment, but Foster was too narcissistic to either realize it or care about it. "For now, let's worry about making sure that you're OK. I've had experience with these people before, and if they follow their usual pattern, they've already left Dulles and headed out of the country."

God, she loathed him more with each passing moment. Divorcing this smug bastard and having him out of her life was going to be a truly liberating and pleasurable experience. "Help me upstairs, please. I really need to go lie down." Her tone conveyed her displeasure with him and his handling of the subject.

Foster led her up the stairs, and Manning and Hanover continued to wait in the living room. They were both feeling awkward and uncomfortable, as was to be expected. They'd come to the house expecting to find a dead body but had instead found Alexis alive. Then they'd had to sit through a very uncomfortable and disconcerting verbal exchange between husband and wife, the kind of thing that other people, especially virtual strangers, usually aren't around to see.

It was several minutes before Foster came back down the stairs, and it was obvious that he was seething. The joy of finding his wife alive had been replaced by anger and embarrassment that she had challenged him in front of others. "Why the hell isn't Torres here yet? Let's call him and tell him that we need to check all systems for a security breach." Foster took his own cell phone out and punched in the code for Torres.

The phone rang three times, and then Foster heard "Yeah?"

"Torres? This is Foster."

"Oh, sorry Colonel Foster. This is Eric Torres' personal answering service. I'm sorry that he can't come to the phone right now, but he's a bit indisposed. He's dead. May I help you?" Keith was laying it on thick, intentionally trying to piss Foster off.

Foster was outraged, and it showed in his face. "Goddamn you, Bryant. You have just pushed this too far, do you hear me? I'm going to cut your heart out and feed it to you, I swear to God. Do you hear me?"

Manning and Hanover were catching the drift of what was happening even though they could only hear one side of the conversation. Jesus! How could Bryant have taken out a tough son of a bitch like Torres, and where the hell could it have happened? They were all coming straight here from the office. Seeing Bryant get this close -- first getting into Foster's house, now killing one of their closest associates -- was putting the fear of God into them.

"Screw you, Colonel. I haven't even begun to mess with you yet. You're still walking around at this point, but that won't last forever. I promise you; one way or another, this is going to be over very, very, shortly. Hell, I might even be right outside of your door right now...."

"Now you listen to me..."

"No, asshole, you listen," Keith screamed into the phone, cutting him off. "You're history. It's that simple. And everything you've done, all of the people that you've killed, all of the laws that you've broken, they're all going to be made public. And you're going to die. I hope to be the one to kill you, but if I don't get to you first someone in the government will. As soon as this comes out they're going to want you dead so they can try their best to do the old DC cover-up routine. But it will be too late for you. Game over." With that Keith hung up the phone and dropped it out the window. He smiled at Loren. She just shook her head and smirked.

On the other end, Foster was shaking, partly from fear and partly from anger. He hated losing control, considering it a sign of weakness, but by this point he was in a total rage. As soon as Keith hung up on him he flung the cell phone against the wall, shattering it into a hundred pieces. At the top of the stairs Alexis Foster listened as best she could, a smile crossing her face. She didn't know exactly what Keith and Loren had said, but she knew for sure that it had hit a nerve in a major way. Good for them. She was going to wait a few days to see how this played out before confronting her husband with the evidence of his infidelity. As serious as that was, and as much as it hurt her deep inside, she knew that it was a nit in the whole scheme of things. She would just bide her time.

"Bryant has killed Torres," he said, seething. "We need to be extra careful from this point forward, gentleman. If Bryant has learned my identity and where I live, it's reasonable to assume that he has the same information on you." Foster didn't know for certain that this was true, but he thought that the others should be sharing in his pain and paranoia.

"Let's go to my office and see what kind of snooping they did." Foster led the way down the hall to his study. He immediately noticed that someone had been sitting at his desk, no doubt trying to access his PC, he surmised with a slight smile to himself.

"What about your safe?" Manning asked.

"I'll check to be sure, but I'm not too worried about that. Even Alexis doesn't have the combination, and I don't keep it written down, not anywhere. Dr. Bryant seems to have considerable skills, I'll admit, but I doubt that safecracking is one of them." Still, at this point he couldn't be too certain. He hadn't expected Keith and Loren to live beyond the first few hours of leaving Charlottesville.

"Did he try to hack into your PC?" asked Brad Hanover.

"Yeah, it looks like it. Fortunately, there's no way that he could ever figure out the 64-character string required just to have the computer finish its boot-up sequence. And again, Alexis doesn't know the password, plus I change it virtually every day." Foster sat at the PC and typed in his password, and after another minute or so the sequence was complete and it was up and running. "Since Mr. Torres has been eliminated, I'm going to check the status of our systems back at DCG headquarters to make sure that nothing has been tampered with. I don't think that's possible, by the way, but I'd rather check to be sure." In order to access any of the systems, including Electra, a remote user has to enter still another password into a 'soft-token' application, and this action, if successful, provides a password that must be entered within 30 seconds to make the final entry into the mainframe. Foster made the connection without any problems and spent the next half-hour checking the status of various files for possible breaches.

"Everything appears untouched, as I suspected. There's no way that Bryant, or anybody for that matter, is going to get into our systems. On that point, at least, I feel certain. As he went to logout of his computer, he decided to add one final touch. "Just to be extra safe, I'm going to change my boot password prior to shutting down." Then he added smugly, "Bryant may be a lucky SOB, but even he isn't lucky enough to guess a password of this length. Even if he had a Cray supercomputer he wouldn't be able to break it; by the time the computer figured it out I would have already changed it again." Foster smiled. He was back to his cocky, arrogant, superior self.

On the other side of the country Jeff Anders was viewing everything that Foster was doing in real-time. He called Patrick to let him know. "Patrick? Keith's plan worked perfectly. I think we got the freakin' mother lode."

Chapter 23

KEITH AND LOREN CHECKED INTO the Ritz-Carlton in Tysons Corner, by far the nicest hotel they had stayed at over the past week. They had not planned to stay at such a beautiful, upscale property, but circumstances seemed to dictate it. As usual, virtually every room in every hotel in the DC Metro area was already sold out. Even at the Ritz all of the regular rooms were sold out, but they did have a handful of suites left. What the heck, they thought. They could use a little luxury for a change.

Once in the suite, with sweeping views of Washington, DC in the distance, Keith went straight to his bag to grab the PC to check for e-mails from Jeff and Patrick. Loren headed off to take a shower and get cleaned up for dinner. She was back to her old self, more or less, but Keith was starting to worry about the toll that the continual stress, to say nothing of the constant fear, was going to have on her. For that matter, he was starting to be more than a little concerned about his own mental state. Even he recognized the anger, the coldness, and the ruthlessness that had taken over his life the past few days. Maybe they were both going to need months, if not years, of therapy sessions when this was over. He didn't care for that thought, but he knew that he would do anything and everything to be supportive for Loren and to make sure that they came through this ordeal together. None of this would matter if he didn't still have her when it was all over.

While the PC booted up and made the wireless internet connection, Keith used the hotel phone to call Patrick and Jeff on the next phone number in the sequence. This time Patrick answered on the second ring, and then he quickly conferenced Jeff in. Keith had never heard them so effusive.

"My God, Keith, you cannot believe how well your plan worked out!" Patrick started. "Not only did we get Foster's password to log into his PC, we captured his VPN password information and the commands he uses to access many of his key files. We have Jeff and the entire leadership team taking turns accessing the system and retrieving anything and everything they can and saving it to our servers. We've had access to their system for over three hours at this point."

"I'm confused. If this big, long password that Foster had was actually used to allow the PC to boot up, what good does it do for you to have it? You don't have access to his PC, and even if you have the password for his VPN access you don't know where his PC is connecting to when he accesses it, like the IP address. Am I right?" Keith was pretty computer savvy, but certainly nowhere close to Jeff's level.

"You're right on the money, actually," replied Jeff. "But we found a way around that little problem, and, once again, you presented the solution to the problem. Only this time you probably didn't know it."

Keith thought about it for a minute but then had to confess that he didn't have a clue what Jeff meant. "I'm not sure I follow."

"Alexis. You and Loren did such a great job of bonding with her, of helping her see her husband for the piece of shit that he really is, that she agreed to help us. Once Foster and his crew were out of there we simply called her and walked her through booting up his PC and entering the password string. After that it was a piece of cake." Jeff's admiration for Alexis and her bravery were evident.

"But you're still accessing his PC now, right? Are you guys walking Alexis through all of that, too?" Keith was worried that the strain and tension might be too much for Alexis after what she'd been through today, to say nothing of the risk to her safety if Colonel Foster returned home and caught her on his computer.

"No, that's the beauty of it. I dropped a little program onto his computer that allowed us to take control of it from our end. It's kind of like Microsoft's NetMeeting application but a little bit more robust. Of course, being the paranoid intelligence type that Foster is, he'd disabled and removed any type of native remote access software from his PC. Right now Terrell is banging away from his end and grabbing anything and everything he can find related to 9/11, and the rest of the core team leaders are sifting through it looking for anything of value."

"How much data have you accessed? And isn't it all encrypted?" Keith asked.

"So far we've copied about twenty gigabytes of data, basically just grabbing any file that has a name that looks like it might be germane at this point. We're just now beginning to start sorting and reading through it to see what we've got. Now as far as the encryption, that's not an issue. Accessing the system via Foster's PC gets us around that since his PC is equipped with the same encryption program as his servers back in Reston. If we were doing it from any other PC, then yes, we'd have to take the time to crack the encryption code. Even with a supercomputer that could potentially take days, if not weeks," Jeff explained. "It looks like his encryption program is state of the art, to put it mildly. Not that we'd expect anything less."

"And as far as how much we've accessed, it turns out that that's our only issue at this point," said Patrick. "Foster has a Verizon fiber optic connection to his house for phone, TV, and internet, and it's pretty state of the art. It's probably 5-10 times faster than a typical cable modem, but still, all we can grab is what we can shove down that one communications pipe. If we were able to access their mainframe directly from our end, without routing through his PC, we'd have tons more bandwidth available to do the job. But we've got what we've got. We'll make due with it the best we can and just try to grab everything we can until we're discovered and cut off."

"I expect you'll be discovered tomorrow morning, if not sooner," Keith offered. "Maybe less than that if another crew is working at Foster's bunker tonight and realizes that he's had VPN access up for longer than usual. Right now we don't know how many people work there or what type of shifts they work, but personally I'd be shocked if they didn't have people there 24x7."

Jeff had an idea. "Maybe we should try to make a quick sweep of their system to see if we can identify all personnel that work there and, maybe with a little luck, their work schedules."

"Sounds like a good idea to me," Keith responded. "By the way, one of Foster's operatives, a guy named Eric Torres, was taken out of the picture this afternoon. Maybe you might cross-check his name and work schedule, job title, or whatever with some of the other possible players. That might help to narrow down the employee search that much faster. I'm guessing that there probably aren't more than a dozen people in Foster's inner circle, otherwise he'd have too hard of a time keeping things quiet. Oh, and we have digital pictures of Foster, Torres, and two other guys that we can upload to you in case you run across pictures in any of the personnel or security files."

"That's not a problem. Just send them to us now and we'll check them out," said Jeff.

Patrick had to ask. "What do you mean when you say Eric Torres 'was taken out of the picture'? What happened?"

"I can fill you in on more of the details later, but suffice it to say that he was about to kill Loren near DCG's headquarters late this afternoon but I shot him first. And by the way, yes, I did let Colonel Foster know about it. He seemed to fly into a bit of a snit, to put it mildly. Poor guy seems so moody lately; maybe it's PMS."

They all got a good laugh out of that, but Patrick remained concerned. How much longer could their luck hold out against these people?

"Do you have anything that you could e-mail to me at this point? Loren and I could help with the sifting of the data."

"Sure, we'll grab a few of the files and send them your way. We can use a couple of more pairs of eyes on the data," Patrick said.

"One last thing before I let you guys go," Keith said. "One thing is worrying the heck out of me. What if Foster goes home and finds his PC turned on? Maybe because he just decides to walk in and do some work, or maybe because he gets an alert from someone back in the bunker that someone is in the system posing as him? That could put Alexis in real danger, don't you think?"

"You're right," said Jeff. "But we're way ahead of you there. Once she got us access to the PC and we were sure that we had a stable and reliable connection we had her get the hell out of there. Now that we've got control of the PC Foster can't take that control back even if he's at the house, though he could simply disconnect the broadband or pull the power and battery from the PC and shut us down. Regardless, though, if he finds that PC up and running he's going to know that it was Alexis, and I don't think he'd hesitate to kill her."

"You're right; I wouldn't put anything past him. Did you guys give her some ideas about how to handle herself once she left, like where to go, not to use her credit cards, and so on? She's probably not too experienced at being on the run."

365

"True," said Patrick. "But then again, neither were you and Loren barely a week ago, and look at you now." He said it to add a little bit of humor or to lighten up the moment a bit, but it was also a very heartfelt and sincere complement.

"Thanks. And thanks for watching out for Alexis. I feel much better knowing that she's safely away from there," Keith replied.

The call completed, Keith uploaded the picture of Foster and his team to LTBT. As he was finishing that task Loren emerged from the bathroom after her long shower, and she was wearing one of the luxurious bathrobes provided by the Ritz and had her wet hair up in a towel. Still, she looked incredible, he thought to himself. He filled Loren in on what LTBT had accomplished and how they were going to send information over to them for review.

"Feel like another room service meal?" Keith asked with a smile.

"Ah, you really know how to treat a girl," she replied. "As I've said before, you take me to all of the finest restaurants."

"At least here, when we order room service, we have our own dining room table to eat at instead of trying to eat off of the bed or the computer desk." The suite had all types of amenities, not the least of which was, in fact, a dining room table for six. "And I'm guessing that their room service menu is probably top-notch."

Loren just smiled and picked up the room service menu. Keith was right. The menu had everything from the usual sandwiches and salads all the way to *haute cuisine*. And the prices reflected the Ritz's high opinion of their restaurant and food, she realized. "Yeah, I think we should be able to suffer through this without too many problems," she answered. "I could go for a nice bottle of wine, as well. How about you?"

"That does sound nice, actually. We owe it to ourselves, if you ask me."

Loren called in the dinner order, and Keith called down to the concierge's desk and requested a printer and ream of paper so he could print out anything of special interest. The concierge, being used to all kinds of odd requests from guests at such a high-end property, didn't seem to think that Keith's request was that unusual. Within 15 minutes he was at the door, along with a bellman, with the printer and several reams of paper. They even waited while Keith connected the printer to his PC, made sure that Windows would recognize the new hardware and load the appropriate drivers, and printed out a test page. Keith thanked them both profusely and tipped them $100 for their assistance.

It took almost 45 minutes for dinner to be delivered, and by that time Keith and Loren had looked through dozens of files sent over by Patrick and Jeff. Interesting reading, but no smoking gun, they both realized. Still, nothing was deleted. Even if it wasn't printed out it was saved to the hard drive of Keith's PC as well as a USB thumb-drive. Finally, they stumbled on one file that really caught their attention. It was a personnel file that showed the list of people working for the clandestine division of DCG as well as some of their independent contractors, a nice euphemism for 'hired killers' Keith realized.

"Look, here's a picture of Eric Torres and all of his personnel and security background information. And here's one of the guys we photographed, says his name is Bob Manning. Looks like he's probably Foster's second-in-command. Let's print out this entire file, including the contractors. It will be good to have them all identified and have all of their information available. We may have to pay some of them a little visit," Keith said. He just let the thought hang out there without elaborating. Not that much elaboration was needed.

Keith hit the 'print' icon and had it print out the entire personnel file for each of the people he found. Fortunately, there weren't that many operatives showing in the core group under Foster. In addition to Colonel Foster there was Bob Manning, Brad Hanover, Warren Adams, Les Mattox, and the late Eric Torres. Keith had always suspected that Foster's team would be pretty small, especially once he and LTBT had discovered the massive computer power that Foster had at his fingertips. He could let the supercomputer do all of the heavy lifting and keep a small, closely-knit group of operatives for overseeing operations. All the better to keep a lid on things, he reminded himself. By the time he was finished, Keith had printed out over 70 pages of information, including a dozen or more pages listing the names, military history, and resumes of some of Foster's outside contractors. As he thumbed through the pages he couldn't help but wonder which of these degenerate assholes were responsible for the deaths of Bo and Winston, or David and his family, for that matter. Keith had to admit to himself that, as much he'd like to track all of these bastards down and kill them that probably wasn't going to happen. For one, he'd probably never be able to find them. They were probably out of the country by now, or if not, they at least had the knowledge, skill, and wherewithal to become invisible. Maybe these files would be better off being handed over to the police or FBI. He felt pretty sure that these guys would not be able to escape prosecution for murder and conspiracy if they were caught; they were probably considered expendable by Foster and the rest of the key conspirators. Actually, they might very well find themselves becoming scapegoats for the big players. Keith snapped himself back to reality and the task at hand and immediately fired off an e-mail to one of LTBT's dummy e-mail accounts telling them of the find.

"Finding those personnel files was a really lucky break," said Loren. "That could help law enforcement build a heck of a case against Foster and his people."

"True, though I still don't want to see Foster walk away from this alive. No telling how he might have his ass covered. For all we know he may end up with a presidential medal for all of his work in keeping the truth about 9/11 hidden from the world."

While Keith read through some of the personnel files Loren went back to digging into the other attachments that LTBT had sent over. Most of it was relatively mundane, and then one of them caught her eye. "Hello! I think I may have something here."

"What is it?" Keith asked, setting his own files aside.

"It looked pretty innocuous from just looking at the file name, just like any other Microsoft Word document. It's called 'annual report Newcomb 2001.doc', but I browsed through it and found something that caught my eye: 'Newcomb' is Richard Newcomb, the CEO of Daniels Robotics Corporation."

"That can't be a coincidence. Let's look at that." Keith felt his adrenaline pumping. He could feel it in his gut; this was definitely a link. Could it be a link to a co-conspirator? He pulled his chair up beside Loren's and they read through the file together. What they read literally made their jaws drop. "Holy shit! Are you seeing what I'm seeing?"

"Yes! My God! This file proves that Foster conspired with Newcomb to kill DRC's Chief Financial Officer to keep him from stumbling on the original financing for 9/11 and making it public. This is the holy grail we've been praying for!" Loren's skin was tingling from the excitement. This was going to blow the whole lid off of 9/11.

"And look at this. It even gives an account of how Foster hired the killer to slip poison into the guy's drink at a restaurant over in Arlington. Christ! Newcomb was sitting right there with the guy when he dropped dead of a supposed heart attack! Man, he must be one cold son of a bitch."

Loren printed the file and made sure to save it to both the hard disk and the USB thumb drive. She and Keith spent almost a half hour reviewing it in detail and found it hard to conceal their excitement. After digesting the entire file and feeling 100% certain that they did in fact have ironclad proof of a conspiracy, they sent another e-mail to the leaders of LTBT. "You think this will get them excited?" Keith asked, barely able to contain his excitement.

It didn't take but a few minutes before they had a return message from LTBT. It was short, succinct, and to the point: 'CALL US!' That just made Keith and Loren smile. "I guess we got their attention," Loren laughed.

Keith used the hotel phone and dialed the sequential number for LTBT. Jeff answered on the first ring; in fact, Keith wasn't even sure that he'd heard it ring on his end. "Goddamn! You found proof! Woohooo!" Jeff was way past excited. "Hold on while I get everyone else on the conference bridge; it will just take a minute."

"Glad we were able to make somebody happy," Loren joked. "After all of these days of stress and terror it's nice to finally have something good happen."

Moments later all of the leaders of LTBT were on the line and they were hooting and hollering and celebrating like it was Mardi Gras. Finally Patrick spoke up. "Guys, I don't know what to say. Speaking for myself, I'd say that this has to be one of the greatest days of my life. It's a validation that everything we've worked for has not been in vain, to say nothing of a vindication for all of those that have died or suffered at the hands of these maniacs. Keith, Loren -- I don't know what to say. You guys made this all possible. What you've been through, what you've lost, is simply unimaginable to me. I hope that the fact that you've uncovered the truth behind one of the greatest crimes in history, as well as the fact that you're going to make it possible to bring the guilty to justice, is enough to give you some solace."

"Thanks, Patrick. Loren and I appreciate that, we really do. But not to rain on our parade, but I think we have a lot more work still to do. We've uncovered enough evidence to prove that there was, in fact, a conspiracy around 9/11. We've identified two of the key players in Colonel Ed Foster and Richard Newcomb. Certainly, though, there are others. We need to keep digging, keep searching, and find all of the pieces to this puzzle. Every single one of these conspirators has to be taken down."

"Of course you're right," added Karen Richardson, "but this is an incredibly important first step. Now we know that we're searching in the right place, following the right trail. After years of sorting through various conspiracy theories and ultimately refuting them, it's immensely gratifying to finally uncover the path to The Truth."

"Well, I'm sure that I'm preaching to the choir when I say this, but in all of my research over the years one thing has always rung true when tracking down a conspiracy: *follow the money*. We now know that DRC funneled money to the government and through them to Al Qaeda to carry out the training and operation behind 9/11. Let's follow that money trail and see who else it touches." Keith was finding it hard to contain his excitement, too.

"The good news is that we've been able to download several more gigabytes of data from DCG's computer system," said Terrell Jackson. "That should give us a lot more possible places to look."

"I have an idea on what we might want to search for," said Loren, an idea forming in her mind. "We already confirmed the fact that Foster opened DCG within about a month of 9/11, right? And now, from this file on Richard Newcomb and DRC we know that one of his first tasks after forming DCG was to order a hit on Fred Abraham, the CFO of DRC, to keep him from stumbling on the money transfer. So, if all of this happened so shortly after forming 9/11, isn't it reasonable to assume that Foster was already working on the whole conspiracy prior to forming DCG?"

"You're right!" said Jeff. "And before he left to form DCG, he spent several years at the NSA."

"Exactly. So maybe we should be looking for links to someone, or maybe multiple people, somewhere in the upper echelons of the NSA that had a hand in funneling the money to Al Qaeda. And that someone obviously had to have a pretty close working relationship with Foster." Loren's logic, as always, was well founded and indisputable.

"Excellent," said Patrick. "Loren is right, so let's do all that we can to dig into any files that look like they may have any connection, no matter how tenuous, to the NSA."

"How much more data is out there to retrieve?" Keith asked.

"Tons. Mountains of it, actually," answered Jeff. "Our biggest issue is having enough time to grab it all before we lose our connection. That, and hoping that what we do get is the stuff we need. Once they discover us in their system and cut us off there's no getting back in."

"Actually there's one scenario that's even worse than that," added Keith. "Once they discover the breach they may go in and delete all of the data to keep it from getting into our hands. No matter how valuable they think the data is to their mission, they'll probably still be willing to erase it to keep themselves out of prison. Or worse."

"Uh, oh" said Terrell. "They're on to us." He checked his connections. "We're still up, but they know they have a breach. They're trying to back trace our access path."

"How long before they're able to track us down?" asked Karen.

"I don't know for sure, maybe five or ten minutes at most. They already know that we're accessing via Foster's VPN, so even if they don't care about tracking the breach all the way back to us they know that it all starts at his PC. So what do we want to do? Shut down now to keep them from tracing it back to us, or keep on going as long as possible to grab some more files?" Terrell was ready for whatever the group decided.

"They could pull access from their end by disconnecting their entire system from their network connections, but even that will take a few minutes with all of the circuits they have," offered Karen. "I vote that we keep at it for a few more minutes anyway."

"I agree," said Jeff. "Besides, they already know that any breach has to lead back to Keith and Loren, and, by extension, us. All they'll really be doing is confirming what they already know. Plus, all of their tracing is just going to lead them to a dead-end, spoofed IP connection. Nothing that they'll be able to use against us in the future."

"You forgot the most important thing," said Keith. "These motherfuckers aren't going to *have* a future."

"Oh, God. What are you thinking now?" asked Patrick. "Every time you take that tone it seems that people die, and up until now you've been pretty lucky. We don't want to see your luck run out."

"Neither do I, but we have an opportunity to end this, right here, tonight. We've validated that Foster was part of a larger conspiracy, and God knows what else we **may** already have that we haven't even had a chance to sort through. And now we know where he's heading, him and possibly some of the others, too."

"You're not thinking about going back to Foster's house are you?" asked Jeff. "That could be suicide."

"That's exactly what I'm thinking. We should be able to get there in less than 30 minutes this time of night. We just need you guys to run some interference for us by calling to their community security gate and getting us access. We'll check in with you right before we get there and you can tell us how we're supposed to play it with the security guard."

Nobody from LTBT was happy with the plan, but they knew that there was no sense in trying to dissuade Keith from following through. All they could do was support his efforts as best they can. "You and Loren head on then, and we'll keep on working on the data from this end. If anything interesting comes up we'll let you know. And for God's sake, be careful."

Chapter 24

It was total pandemonium inside the Bunker. Foster had directed Bob Manning to have the entire team come in after they had found out about Torres' death. He did this to make sure that everybody was accounted for and that everyone heard the same plan of action. That plan was simple and straightforward: protect the data, and kill Dr. Keith Bryant and Ms. Loren Davis. After they took care of those two immediate needs, which Foster made clear he expected to be accomplished tonight, they would start putting plans in place to eliminate the core leadership team of LTBT and as many of the associate members as they could identify.

"We need to silence LTBT once and for all. We should have done that earlier and I accept the blame for that. I was more concerned with trying to limit the fallout from Bryant and Davis and contain any repercussions that their death might create. I should have dealt with LTBT immediately. Hell, for that matter, I probably should have dealt with them a year ago." Foster was obviously upset, but he was thinking and acting rationally for a change.

"Colonel, I've traced through about 12 hops that the intruder is routing through. It looks like the link is originating in Silicon Valley. I'm going to try to trace the IP address and see if it's linked to a particular person or company." Les Mattox was working at a feverish pace to try to get this nailed down, but this was far outside of their normal day to day routine. Usually they're tracking individuals that are posting or retrieving information relative to the 9/11 conspiracy theory websites and the people aren't making any attempt to conceal themselves. *'If they even know how to conceal themselves'* he thought.

"Keep looking, but I doubt that it's going to matter. I'm sure it's going to come back as belonging to some fictitious person or dummy corporation. Probably one that's controlled by LTBT, if I had to guess. More importantly, have you been able to determine how in God's name this intruder has managed to enter our system using my credentials?"

Bob Manning spoke. "There can't be but one answer, sir. If you're here with us, and the PC in your office is turned off and disconnected from the network, then somebody has to be accessing your PC at home."

Foster was fighting hard not to fly into a rage. Not just because this was happening, but also because he didn't want anyone pointing the finger at him as the breakdown in security. "Can you explain to me how the hell that is possible? You were right there with me today when I checked my PC, and in fact, I even changed the goddamn password again before shutting it down!"

Manning heard Foster's voice going up again, knowing that he was about to lose it at any second. He tried to keep his own voice calm and matter of fact. "I don't know what to tell you sir, I…."

Foster cut him off abruptly, screaming. "Well somebody for goddamn sure better figure it out, and quickly. Obviously we are going to need to head over to my house to find out what the hell is going on, but in the interim, what the fuck do we do about this intruder, this imposter, that is in our goddamn system?"

Warren Adams spoke up. "Sir, our intrusion detection systems can pinpoint which port the intruder is accessing and we can shut it down right now. Once that's done we can shut down all remote VPN access. That way nobody outside of this Bunker can get access to the system, including us, for that matter."

"Finally, somebody with some goddamn answers," Foster said as sarcastically as possible, "Make it happen, Mr. Adams. Now, who can tell me what our intruder has done since gaining access to our system? Have they dropped in a virus or a worm, or have they simply gone in and stolen a bunch of our data?" Foster was more worried about what they'd accessed than he was about catching and killing the person responsible. The information on their computers could tear this country apart, he knew, to say nothing of sending him and many others to prison. Or worse.

"Whoever it is appears to only be accessing and downloading files, sir. They can't very easily drop any kind of virus or worm into our system, nor can they do anything to block us out and take full control of the system from their end. That would require administrator access, and that's protected by 128-bit encryption. It would take them weeks, at least, to get through that type of protection." Adams felt confident that their system security could stand up to anything anybody, no matter how skilled, could throw at it. The fact that someone got into their system from outside by using Foster's login could only mean one thing: Foster fucked up.

"Alright, then, Mr. Hanover please disconnect our intruder from the system and take the necessary steps to block any and all outside access to the system until further notice. Then take Electra offline completely; I don't want to take any chances unless we're physically here with her. Mr. Adams, I need you to get me a list of every file that has been viewed and/or downloaded and print it out for me. When you two are done with those tasks meet the rest of us at my house, and don't dawdle." Foster was growing impatient. "Bob, you and Mr. Mattox are with me. Let's go."

"You're going to leave the Bunker unmanned and shut Electra down?" Manning asked, almost disbelieving. Since its inception it had only been left unmanned for a few hours, and that was earlier today when they had all rushed out to head to Foster's house. That had resulted in the killing of Eric Torres. And Electra had never, ever, been taken offline. "Our mission is to monitor all relevant searches and postings on the internet related to 9/11, not just those from Bryant and LTBT. There are thousands of hits per day that Electra is tracking, sometimes tens of thousands. Aren't you putting the bigger mission in jeopardy by shutting Electra down?"

You could almost see the steam coming off of Foster's head. This was the second time today that one of his men had questioned his orders, and he did not take kindly to being questioned by anyone. "I don't need to be reminded what our goddamn mission is, damn you! I *created* the goddamn mission! Now do as I tell you to do, and do it *now*." The words came out with as much venom as he could muster.

Manning was at first taken aback, but he quickly recovered. He was pretty much beyond his breaking point, tired of Foster's abuse and condescension. More than anything, though, he was sick of Foster's obsession and the dangerous path it had them on. He had no intention of going down with this ship. He got right up in Foster's face, his finger poking him right in the chest for emphasis. "No, you listen to *me*, you piece of shit. When this is done, *we're* done. After tonight you're on your own. I'm out of here, and, I'm willing to bet, everyone else is out of here with me. You want to go down for your stupid obsession with Bryant? Be my guest, asshole, but none of us care to go down with you." There was fire in Manning's eyes, and the rest of the team was almost frozen in shock. Even when they had gotten pissed at Foster or talked bad about him, Manning had always been the loyal lieutenant, never speaking ill of their leader or allowing them to forget the bigger mission. Now he was in Foster's face, practically coming to blows with the boss that he had been so loyal to.

Foster was frightened but trying hard not to show it. "If that's how you want it, then after tonight you and anyone else that wants to walk away from this mission are free to do so. But I would suggest that you all get your heads out of your asses and start to focus on what's important, namely, making sure that Bryant and the others aren't left walking around to expose us, *all of us*, to prosecution and a firing squad. You think you're through with *me*? Screw you! Screw all of you! *I'm through with you!*"

"Good," screamed Manning, still only inches from Foster's face. "We're on the same wavelength then. Now let's get the hell out of here and get this shit done. *Now!*" Manning poked him in the chest one last time for good measure, and as he turned to head towards the door Les Mattox followed right behind. It was clear that his allegiance was with Bob Manning rather than Foster, and from the looks passed between those two and Hanover and Adams it was clear that they were in the same camp. Foster may still be the ranking member of the group, but he was definitely no longer their leader.

Manning and Mattox drove together to Foster's house, forcing Foster to ride alone. "Watch your back tonight, Les. Don't trust Foster, not for one second. He's unstable and he's totally lost perspective on the situation. He's liable to do anything, especially if it can shift the focus and the blame from himself to others." Mattox didn't need to answer. It was clear from the look on his face that he was already thinking along the same lines.

⌘

WHEN ALEXIS FOSTER HAD GOTTEN the call from Jeff Anders and Patrick Treadwell a few hours ago, warning her to get away from the house as quickly as possible, she had heeded their advice. She had thrown a few things in an overnight bag and headed out within ten minutes, not even taking time to call her kids until she was in the car. Those were very difficult conversations to have, telling her children that she was leaving their father. She didn't mention a word about his involvement in the 9/11 disaster; she couldn't bear to broach that subject with them at this point, figuring that it was best to wait until the situation was closer to resolution. *Whatever 'resolution' might mean in this case,* she reminded herself. Alexis simply told her kids that she was leaving their father because of his infidelity, something that she'd known about and ignored in the past but something she could no longer tolerate or abide after his many promises to never stray again. She knew that even this would be painful for the kids to hear, especially after seeing their parents married for 32 years. Still, she wanted to make sure that the kids took her side and supported her in this action. She didn't want them trying to talk her into going back home, and by playing the 'cheating husband' card she didn't think that they would.

Both kids tried talking her into coming to their homes to stay, but she declined by saying that she just wanted to get away by herself for a few days, be somewhere alone to just relax and consider her options. Of course, what she was really doing is trying to protect them from her husband. She prayed to God that he would never do anything to harm his own children, under any circumstances, but she could no longer count on anything where he was concerned. She no longer knew him, she realized. The man that was responsible for the deaths of over 3,000 Americans on 9/11 was not the same man she had married 32 years ago.

After leaving the house Alexis had gone to the bank and withdrawn as much cash as she could get her hands on. Unfortunately, at least in this situation, most of their assets were tied up in various stocks, mutual funds, IRA's, and CD's. Great for a long-term investment strategy, not so good when she wanted to get hold of cash. She did manage to get her hands on $12,000 in cash, certainly enough to tide her over for a week or two until she could make other arrangements. The rest of the afternoon was spent preparing herself for life on the run, much as Keith and Loren had done the week prior. She prayed that this would all be over quickly. There was no way, she knew, that she had the stomach or the constitution to live this way for long.

Alexis checked into her hotel using an alias and paid cash for the room. It was around 7:30pm as she was getting settled into her hotel room at the Fairview Park Marriott in Falls Church, VA, unpacking only what she knew she would need tonight and in the morning. That was another bit of coaching from Patrick and Jeff: always be prepared to run on a moment's notice, and don't take anything with you on the run that you wouldn't be willing to leave behind, forever, if you had to leave without time to pack. She thought she had done that. Enough clothes for maybe five days. No personal items, no mementos. But as she got to the bottom of her bag she felt a growing panic. Where was it? *'Dear God'*, she whispered to herself, *'please don't let me have forgotten it'*. She searched both bags and finally concluded that she had, in fact, forgotten her insulin and injection kit. A Type 1, insulin-dependent diabetic since early childhood, Alexis routinely checked her blood at least three times per day and usually had to inject herself up to four times. It wasn't pleasant, but she had long ago learned to live with it. It was just part of her reality, and part of that reality was that she could not live, could not even function, without the insulin injections. She fought to quell the growing panic that she felt.

She quickly considered her options. Her doctor's office was obviously closed for the night, and she knew that she didn't have any refills left on her current prescription at her regular pharmacy. She'd just picked up new insulin and supplies last week and the pharmacist had even commented that she would need a new prescription for her next refill. There was no way that she could skip the injections, not even for a short while, without risking a diabetic coma or death. There was a fleeting moment when she considered asking one of her kids to go to the house to fetch her medicine, but she quickly realized that she'd be exposing them to unnecessary risk and danger. No, if it had to be done she had to do it. Yes, it was risky. Yes, she might be caught, maybe even killed. But without the insulin she was as good as dead anyway. And if something should happen to her and she was rushed to a hospital, there's no way that her husband wouldn't find out. Either the hospital would contact him, or he'd have some sort of way of finding out that her name was in the hospital database. Wouldn't he? She wasn't sure what he was tapped into. Some things? Everything? Who the hell knew *what* he was capable of? Of one thing she felt pretty certain, though: he'd probably see to it that she never left the hospital alive.

Finally Alexis made her decision. She would go to the house, check things out to make sure that he wasn't there, then get in and get out as fast as she can. The thought made her almost nauseous with fear, but she knew it was her only chance. She took the elevator down to her car and then headed west back to Ashburn, the trip taking a little over 25 minutes. As she reached the guard house at the entrance to her community, she pulled into the visitor's lane instead of going through the lane reserved for residents. Putting her window down, she spoke to the guard on duty, "Hi, Sam. Do you know if Colonel Foster has come through yet? I have a little surprise for him and I'm hoping that I beat him home."

Sam walked out a couple of steps from the guard house. "Evening, Mrs. Foster. No, I haven't seen the Colonel come through yet, and I've been on duty since 4:00pm. I think your secret is safe." Sam gave her a friendly smile, not just because it was his job, but because he genuinely liked Alexis Foster. She was one of his favorites, always quick with a smile or a wave.

"Thanks, Sam. If he does come through don't tell him that I'm home yet. Have a nice evening." Alexis drove off, wishing that she had thought to tell Sam to call her on one of the cell phones that she had bought earlier today if her husband did show up at the gates. Then she realized that it probably wouldn't do a whole lot of good anyway; by the time Sam could ring her phone Colonel Foster would probably already be pulling onto their street and see her car. Their house was less than a minute from the community entrance.

She approached her street slowly, and as she rolled past the intersection she looked towards her house. Good. No cars there, not in the driveway or on the street. There was no way to know if he'd pulled his car into the garage, but she rationalized that he probably wasn't home since no outside lights were on by the garage doors or the front door. She pulled a u-turn at the next street and slowly rolled back by from the other direction. Satisfied that things appeared to be as quiet and safe as possible, she turned on her street and headed for the house. This time she pulled into the driveway and hit the garage door opener, pulling in quickly and lowering the door behind her. Within seconds she was out of the car and into the house, turning off the security system and turning on lights as she went so she could quickly find her way upstairs. Her heart was beating so hard and so loudly that she thought it would burst from her chest at any minute. Finally reaching the bedroom she turned on the light and quickly made her way to the master bathroom, grabbing her blood sugar test kit and her insulin injection kit. The insulin itself was downstairs in the refrigerator, and she scurried around quickly to find something to carry everything in. She wondered and worried about how she would keep her insulin cold if she had to stay in hiding until this was over. *When* would it be over?

Moving quickly down the steps and to the kitchen, Alexis was grabbing her insulin vials from the refrigerator and stuffing them into a plastic grocery bag when she heard a sound that took her breath away. It was the distinctive beeping sound from the security system indicating that a door or window had just been opened. She had turned the alarm off when she came in, so she knew it wasn't going off or sending a message to the police or monitoring company, instead just giving the sound as an indication to anyone inside that a point of entry had, in fact, been opened. She froze, knowing that it had to be her husband. God! What could she do? What could she say? Does he know about the security breach to his system? Then she heard the front door close and heard Ed talking to others. She tried to quietly set the bag full of insulin vials back in the refrigerator, not knowing how in the world she would explain them if he walked in on her. If he'd even give her a chance to explain, she reminded herself.

"Alexis, I'm home, honey." Colonel Foster tried to call out to her in a normal, everyday voice.

"Hi. I'm in the kitchen. I'll be right there. I didn't expect you home this early," she said, trying to stall for time and collect her thoughts a bit.

'Yeah, I bet you didn't expect me home, bitch' Foster muttered to himself. There was no doubt in his mind that she had betrayed him. "I was worried about you after all that happened today so I didn't want to be too late. I'm sorry I had to be gone even this long, but it was critical, if we're going to have a shot at catching these terrorists, that I work with the NSA and CIA to get the investigation going." He tried to put on his best impression of the concerned husband.

When Alexis walked out he could see that she was nervous and very ill at ease. "Alexis, this is Bob Manning and Les Mattox. I've talked to some of my former contacts in the intelligence community about what happened today, and they've asked these two gentlemen to spearhead the investigation."

"Very nice to meet you both," said Alexis, acting as gracious as she could under the circumstances. "May I offer you a drink, maybe something to eat? I'm sure that you've been kept very busy today."

"Oh, yes ma'am we have," replied Manning. "But we're fine, thank you. We've already had dinner."

Foster spoke up again. "Bob and Les have already made considerable progress in tracking the two people that broke in here today and attacked you. They took off from Dulles, as I expected, and we were able to track them to a small airport just outside of Belize City. We expect to have them in custody by morning, if not before."

"Thank God. I know that I'll sleep better knowing they're in custody," Alexis lied. She wondered how long this charade of a conversation was going to keep up.

"I have to grab some papers from my office that might assist them in their investigation," said Foster. "Would you guys mind waiting here with Alexis while I grab those documents? I'll be back shortly. Honey, maybe a beer or a glass of wine might be nice for our guests, despite their protests to the contrary."

She realized that he was trying to cut off any chance of her making a break for it. There was little doubt in her mind that as soon as he found his computer turned on, along with the video camera, she'd be dead. She had to fight hard to hold back the tears and the urge to scream and run. It wouldn't do any good, she knew. These two men, if they're anything like her husband, would simply kill her without batting an eye. Steeling herself, Alexis vowed to swallow her fears and face what was sure to happen bravely, and she resolved to confront this bastard with evidence of his indiscretions with that....*whore*, the night before. She wanted to make sure that he knew that he hadn't pulled the wool over her eyes, at least not this time, and that his lying and cheating was going to help ensure his own downfall. Killing her wouldn't change that; she'd make sure that he understood that fact in no uncertain terms.

Foster went to his study and immediately saw that his computer was running. Still, he wondered, how the hell could she have gotten past the security? His password had just been changed and it was a random quote from Mark Twain that he had chosen. Nobody could have guessed it. He hadn't written it down. The people that had been in the room with him could not have seen him type the password in. Nobody could have dropped a program onto the computer to record his keystrokes because, in a definite case of '*Catch-22*', they couldn't have gotten logged into the computer in the first place. What was he missing? He walked around the study, thinking about how Alexis could have pulled this off, even with help from outsiders like LTBT. Then something caught his eye, something out of place. Some of the books on the built-in bookshelves were not stacked as neatly and symmetrically as usual, as if someone had rearranged some of the stacks. He went over to the wall and started moving things around and quickly found his answer. There, focused directly on his desk, was their video camera, apparently recording his every move. Tracing the connection he found Alexis' PC connected to the camera and to an internet connection run behind some furniture and behind the books in the bookcase. It was then that he realized that she wasn't recording what he was doing; she was uploading the video feed directly to the internet. Someone, somewhere, was watching a live feed of him at his computer even as he entered passwords, changed passwords, accessed files, everything. Goddamn it! All of his security, all of his safeguards, all of it undermined by this duplicitous bitch aligning herself with Bryant and Davis, to say nothing of those bastards at LTBT. His blood was boiling, knowing that she had conspired with others to spy on him, to ruin his life. *Fucking traitorous whore!*

He was beyond livid. It was bad enough to be betrayed by his own men, having them threaten him physically and then threaten to quit on him. But to be betrayed by his own wife, the mother of his children, that was more than he could take. He stomped down the hall back to the family room where Alexis, Bob, and Les were sitting and then, without even speaking, walked directly to Alexis and grabbed her by the hair and dragged her out of her chair. "*You bitch!*" he hissed. "You dare to fucking betray *me*?"

Alexis screamed in pain as he practically ripped her hair out by the roots. Before she could even say anything he slapped her hard across the face, knocking her to the ground and causing her to see stars. "Stop, God damn you!" she screamed at him.

"Pick her worthless ass up and bring her back here," he commanded Manning and Mattox. The men immediately went to Alexis and helped her to her feet, and then, practically dragging her down the hall, they followed Foster to his office. Alexis was still too groggy from the blow to put up much resistance.

As they entered the study Foster yelled, "Behold! We have the answer to our security breach. My own wife, *this conniving bitch*, betrayed me and our country!" Foster held up the video camera and Alexis' PC. "She obviously worked with Dr. Bryant, Ms. Davis, and those sniveling little shits at LTBT to send a video feed to the web, where I'm sure it was viewed by our friends and enabled them to capture my passwords."

"But even with the passwords they couldn't have gotten into your computer without someone here to turn it on and enter the password for them," suggested Manning.

"That's true, of course," answered Foster. "That's how we know that my dear, sweet Alexis has been even more duplicitous than I first thought. She not only set up the video for them, she stayed behind and got them full access to our systems. After that, LTBT had full control and full access to any and all files they could get out of Electra before we detected them and booted them out. Isn't that right, sweetie?" he said, but before she could speak he hit her with a backhand slap that split her lip and loosened two of her teeth. The only reason she didn't go down was because Manning and Mattox were still holding her up.

Alexis groaned, but she refused to plead or beg. She wasn't about to give him the satisfaction. Gathering herself back up, she just smirked at him and then spit blood all over his face and his shirt. "You're pathetic, you bastard. Killing 3,000 of your own goddamn countrymen, and now you're ready to kill your own wife to hide your dirty little secrets. You're a loser," she said, and then spit blood again.

Manning and Mattox were both uncomfortable, not just at the prospect of seeing this woman beaten like a dog in front of them, but at the inappropriateness of witnessing this kind of meltdown between a husband and wife. Still, if either were to be asked, they'd have to say that they couldn't fathom how this woman endured 30-plus years with an asshole like Colonel Ed Foster in the first place.

"Oh, I'm the loser, huh? Is that it?" Foster hissed. "While I'm out here working my ass off trying to serve my president and my country you're conspiring with a bunch of…of…*domestic terrorists* and radicals that want to bring our country down? I could have you tried and hanged for treason!"

Alexis just looked at him and started laughing, a move that just infuriated him more. "Do you even listen to yourself when you're talking anymore? Are you so sick, so demented and brainwashed, that you're starting to believe your own bullshit?" She just continued laughing derisively at him. "You're pathetic."

Foster's response was quick and brutal, a fist buried hard into the pit of her stomach. Alexis crumbled to the floor, totally falling out of the arms that had been supporting her. She doubled over, coughing and retching. Foster was actually quite pleased with himself. After twice having men get in his face and threaten to beat him today he had finally found someone on which he could take out his frustrations. He was actually taking pleasure in causing her pain.

While she lay on the floor Foster went over to his safe and opened it. Inside he had a large amount of cash and both personal and business documents. More importantly, though, he had several old and totally untraceable handguns. They had been confiscated from criminals long ago by local police departments and slated for meltdown, but he had managed to get his hands on a few by citing 'national security' needs. He removed a .357 pistol from the safe. Crude by today's standards, he thought, but still more than adequate to get the job done.

"Stand her up," ordered Foster.

"Are you sure you want to do this?" Manning asked. He had killed before, many times. Still, the people he had killed were men that had tried to kill him in combat, or had tried to kill him or other innocent people in terrorist attacks. He had no qualms whatsoever about killing people like that. But this woman?

"Yes, I'm very sure that I want to do this, now stand her up!" Foster snapped.

Alexis got to her feet slowly, doing her best to do it under her own power just to prove that she was not going to be beaten so easily. "Don't you even want to know why before you kill me?" she said with a smirk.

"Don't I want to know 'why' what?" Foster asked.

"Why I betrayed you, as you say. Why I believed Keith and Loren and the people at LTBT when they told me about you and the things you've done. Don't you want to know why your wife, the woman who has loved you and been a mother to your children, would turn on you?"

"Do you think it matters to me at this point? What's done is done," Foster replied.

"Then don't you think that Bob and Les here would like to know why I betrayed you? Don't they have a right to know why I turned on you, an act that will probably see them dead or in prison for the rest of their lives? What do you think guys, you want to know why your lives are over?"

"They don't care what you...."

Manning cut Foster off. "No, Colonel, I'd really like to know what caused her to turn on you, to put all of our lives at risk. Like she said, we're all probably as good as dead, if we're lucky. If we're not lucky we'll probably rot in prison for the rest of our lives." Turning to Alexis, he asked, "So what has this asshole done to deserve this? I can think of a hundred reasons to betray him, or even kill him, but I'd like to know what motivated you." Manning was not even trying to mask his own disdain for Colonel Foster at this point.

"Pick up that unmarked red file folder on his desk," Alexis instructed. "I'd left it out for him to see because I wanted him to know that he's not half as smart, half as special, as he thinks he is. Check out the e-mails and the photos."

Manning and Mattox looked at the pictures and read through the e-mail, and it made their blood boil. They both recognized Jennifer from the pictures, and it pissed them off even more as they recalled Foster lecturing them about not mixing their work and personal lives and the need to keep everything compartmentalized. They handed it to Foster, and when he opened the file and saw the pictures taken the night before of him and Jennifer he almost felt faint.

"That's why I betrayed you, you bastard! I'd forgiven you in the past when you cheated on me and you promised me, on your children's lives, that you'd never cheat on me again. But you had to try to make a fool of me. You couldn't keep your dick in your pants, could you?" Her voice was rising, but she was fighting to maintain control. "And now I catch you again with some whore on a night that you swear to me that you're heading up to New York for business meetings. And here's you, Mr. Super Spy, getting followed and photographed by a private detective out of the Yellow Pages." She just sneered at him, not even trying to hide her contempt. "I was planning on showing these e-mails and pictures to you tonight and telling you that I was going to file for divorce, and then out of the blue here comes Keith and Loren telling me about you and the people you've killed, the misery you've caused. So after finding out what a lying, duplicitous bastard you are, I didn't find it hard at all to believe them and agree to help bring you down. In fact, I felt it was *my* duty to *my* country."

"Well, then, I'm glad that you feel that you've done your duty for God and country. It's a shame that you won't be around to see how this all ends." Foster raised the gun and shot his wife right in the chest. Mercifully, she died instantly. Blood spattered the desk, the rug, the chair, and even Manning and Mattox.

"You sick son of a bitch!" Manning yelled, wiping the blood off of his face. "So all of this shit is going downhill and falling apart because you have to fuck around on your wife with a goddamn psychopath killer? Our mission is compromised, to say nothing of the fact that our lives are probably ruined, because you have some goddamn illusion that Jennifer loves you, or is even attracted to you? Are you seriously that delusional?"

"No, I have no delusions whatsoever that Jennifer spends any time with me for any other reason but the obvious: I pay her very well. Last night, for example, I paid $5,000 for the pleasure of her company. Love has nothing to do with it. And as far as my infidelity bringing down the house of cards, need I remind you that it was Dr. Bryant and Ms. Davis that have been the root cause of all of our problems? That's where you need to focus your anger and your efforts."

Mattox wasn't buying any of Foster's rationalization, but at this point he really didn't care either way. All he wanted to do was stay alive and out of prison. "What do we do with your wife's body? Maybe take her somewhere in her car and ditch or torch the thing?"

"Not a bad idea, but I think I have a much better one. Plus, it solves a couple of other problems at the same time. I'll just tell the police that I came home from work and found my wife dead, apparently the victim of a home invasion and robbery. I will even be able to give them the names of the suspects, which should be a real boon for our overworked police and aid them in closing the case quickly."

"But how are you going to hand them Bryant and Davis without compromising our mission? Up until now you've been so worried that having them in police custody would cause us more harm if they started talking." Manning wasn't sure he liked Foster's idea.

"Oh, who said anything about handing them our friends?" As Foster said this he raised the pistol and shot them both practically point blank, the huge .357 bullets ripping through their chest cavities. "I think it's much easier if I just hand them you two as the home invaders." He was quite pleased with his solution. Messy, yes, but better than the inevitable questions about what happened to Alexis Foster if her body was never found. Plus, as an added bonus, it allowed him to have the pleasure of killing Bob Manning personally.

After the way Manning had threatened him, humiliated him, there was no way that he was going to let anyone deprive him of the pleasure of ending his life.

Chapter 25

"We've got all that we're going to get out of their computer system, at least for now," Jeff was explaining to Keith. "They've shut down all ports for incoming VPN traffic, so there's no way that anyone outside of their headquarters can gain access."

Keith was talking on the cell phone as he and Loren were heading west towards Foster's house. "So even Foster and his men can't get access from outside then?"

"That's right. I've gone through every possible route into their system and it's sealed off from the outside. The only way to open those remote pathways back up is to do it from inside their headquarters using the administrator passwords and commands, and I'm sure that I don't have to tell you that we don't have that information nor do we have any practical chance of obtaining it."

Keith thought that through for a second, then replied, "You know, this could actually work to our advantage, at least if we can draw all of their people out into the open and away from that bunker. Unless they've already done something to delete all of those files or done some sort of self-destruct command, all of that data is still there and available. They can't delete it remotely, so basically it's there for the taking, right? Assuming, of course, that we can gain access to their bunker."

"My best guess is that we would have to force Foster or one of his men to get us into the bunker and convince them to share their access codes. Something tells me that these are not the type of men to give that type of information up too easily." Patrick was right, of course. Even if Keith was capable of torturing another human being there was every chance that these battle-hardened professionals would be able to withstand almost any pain that he had the stomach to inflict.

"You're probably right," Keith admitted. "But either way, that's putting the cart before the horse. Do you have a way for us to get access to Foster's neighborhood when we get there?"

"Yeah, we have that wired. You're going to be the expected guests of Mr. and Mrs. Fred England of 410 Highland Springs Crossing." Patrick had made the call to the security gate personally after he and Jeff had first accessed a list of all the neighborhood residents and their addresses.

"OK, got it. Thanks for setting that up. We'll call you back when we get to Foster's house and assess the situation. One last thing before we go, though. Have you guys found anything else useful in Foster's data?"

"No, not since we spoke a little while ago. We have lots and lots of data to sort through, so hopefully we'll find more. For now, though, we know what we know." Patrick wished that he could share more good news, but he didn't see any benefit in sugar-coating the situation.

They hung up as Keith was just passing the exit for Dulles Airport. It was only a few more miles to go before taking off at the exit for Foster's house. Loren asked, "So what's the plan once we get to Foster's? Or are we making this up as we go along again?" She smiled to show that she wasn't being critical, just concerned.

"I don't know for sure. I guess we are kinda making it up as we go." He looked at her and smiled. "We don't even know if he went to his house by himself or if he took the whole crew with him. I guess there's no way for us to know for sure. But if we get there and things don't look right, or we don't think we can do this without getting ourselves killed, we'll back off and live to fight another day. How about that?"

"I guess that's the only thing we can do." Loren noticed that they were approaching the toll booth for the Dulles Greenway, the toll road that ran as an extension from the Dulles airport area out to Leesburg, VA. They'd spent a small fortune on this section of road this week, she realized. "Here's $3 for the toll."

Keith moved into the full-service lane to pay. The attendant at the toll booth certainly didn't seem to be in any real hurry, and he definitely didn't seem to care if the cars and the people that were coming through were in a hurry. He counted the bills twice, then spent time arranging them so that they were all turned the right way. He made sure to count the $.30 in change twice before turning to Keith and then slowly dropping the three dimes one at a time into Keith's outstretched hand. Keith was not always the impatient type, but the tension and stress of the day had him wound pretty tight. It was all he could do not to shoot this guy just on principal. As he pulled out of the lane Keith turned to Loren totally exasperated and said, "Christ, I've applied for mortgages that didn't take as long as dealing with that idiot." She just laughed.

While Keith was stuck in the slower full service toll lane, a black SUV one lane over was making substantially better progress in the Exact Change/EZ-Pass lane. The two men in the SUV were also heading west towards Ashburn, and as chance would have it, the passenger happened to glance in Keith's direction as they crept forward towards the toll gate. "Warren, look! Isn't that Bryant over there in the next lane in the Taurus?" Brad Hanover could barely contain his surprise.

"Let me see," Warren Adams answered. It took a second for him to be able to see Keith's face because of the obstructed view from the toll booth, but then he finally got a clear look as Keith started rolling out of the lane. "Hell, yes. That is definitely him. Let's get them!"

"We will, if we can ever get through this goddamn toll gate." Hanover was ready to end this nightmare once and for all. There was one more car in front of them, an elderly couple in a Buick, and they seemed to be moving none too quickly. "Fuck! And now this asshole in front of us is stopping to fumble with his change and hemming us in! Can you get around him?"

"No, damn it! There's a car behind me, so I can't back up." Adams laid on his horn and started screaming obscenities at the car in front of him, but it did no good. It still took the old man seemingly forever to throw his change into the toll collector basket and start moving. Adams was right on his bumper as he moved through the open gate. "I'm going to follow him, and you call Foster and let him know that we have him in our sights." Adams was excited. He always loved the action, the thrill of the hunt. More than anything, though, he just wanted this whole chapter to be closed and put behind him.

It didn't take but a minute to reach Foster and receive his orders. He told Hanover to dispatch both Bryant and Davis immediately. Foster didn't care how it was done or where it was done, just so it was done. He promised to make arrangements to get both of them out of the country tonight, if necessary, so they didn't even have to worry about making it look like an accident or a random street crime. "I don't care if you have to shoot up the whole goddamn town or kill a dozen innocent bystanders, you just make sure that those two don't escape again. I want them dead, and I want them dead *now*." Foster was starting to sound like a desperate man on the verge of panicking, Hanover thought to himself, but his orders didn't leave a lot of room for misinterpretation.

"Let's take them," Hanover said to Adams. Warren Adams didn't have to be told twice; he hit the gas and quickly started closing the gap between them and Keith's Taurus. Hanover checked his gun to make sure that he had a full clip and several spares at the ready. He also spun a silencer onto the barrel of his Glock.

"Wow, this guy is really flying," Keith said casually to Loren. "It looks like an SUV flying up the outside lane." Just as Loren looked over her shoulder and saw the headlights moving quickly towards them, the rear windshield shattered. Loren screamed as glass flew throughout the car's interior. "Get down!" Keith yelled as he fought to maintain control of the car, having already yanked the wheel too hard to the right and onto the shoulder as he realized they were being attacked. "Are you hit?"

"No!" Loren screamed. She could hear other bullets hitting the car, and seconds later another bullet tore into the rear view mirror and shattered it. Shards of glass were hitting both of them, but they had no time to stop and worry about scratches. They had to fight to stay alive.

"Hold on, I'm going to try to get away from them," Keith yelled. It didn't take but a second for both of them to comprehend the futility of that idea, as the underpowered Taurus rental car was no match for the powerful engine of the big Chevy Tahoe that was pursuing them. "See if you can take my gun and get a shot off at them, maybe back them off some." He handed her the pistol and flicked off the safety. The Taurus was now moving almost 90mph and Keith managed to stay in front of the SUV by cutting them off every time they tried to make a move around him. No way was he going to be able to hold them off for long, not with the huge power and size disadvantage they had versus the Tahoe. They'd either power their way around him or just start ramming them from behind until they'd run him off the road. Other cars on the road were swerving into other lanes or jamming on their brakes and heading for the shoulder, assuming that they were seeing their worst road rage fears realized.

Loren took the pistol and turned around in her seat, the constant jerking motion created by Keith's evasive techniques making it hard to keep her balance and take any kind of aim. The shooter in the Tahoe hadn't fired in a few seconds, she realized, probably because he was popping in a new magazine. Realizing that this could be her only chance, she raised the gun and squeezed off several quick rounds, two of them actually hitting the SUV. She saw them swerve and back off a bit, but that only lasted for a second. Then they were right back at it, quickly closing the gap.

"Try again!" Keith yelled. "Go for the windshield, right at their eye level if you can."

Loren did as Keith said and squeezed off four more shots. This time each shot hit the Tahoe but it seemed to have little effect. "They must have bullet-resistant glass," she yelled, trying to be heard over the wind rushing through the broken glass. "I may as well be shooting a BB-gun at them."

"That's OK, as long as you're firing at them they won't stick their heads out the window to fire at us." Keith continued to swerve back and forth, never letting the SUV pull up alongside of them or get in front of them. To do either would almost certainly get them killed. "There's an exit up here in about another half-mile. I'm going to let them get close to us in the left lane and then make a quick exit on the ramp. You need to hold on when I do. I'll be going way too fast for it to be safe, but I'm hoping that we can put at least a few hundred yards between us and them before they can get back to the exit."

"Then what?" she asked, firing off a two shot burst that took out the passenger side mirror on the Tahoe.

"There are some pretty deep woods right along the area where we're going to exit. As soon as we're clear of the ramp I'm going to ditch the car on the shoulder and we're going to bolt for the woods. We'll each grab one of the H&K's and a set of night vision goggles, and then we'll find a place to set up an ambush for these bastards when they come in after us." The exit was quickly approaching, and Keith started letting off the gas just enough to allow the SUV to start to pull alongside. He swerved at them and bumped right into the passenger side of their vehicle, but other than putting some dents in both cars it didn't really manage to push them aside. He did it a few more times, always with the same result.

"Put down the rear window on your side and let me squeeze off a shot at the passenger," Loren yelled.

Keith did as she asked, and as the window got down to its lowest position Loren raised up and fired two quick shots directly at the passenger side. The Tahoe swerved violently, and Keith used that momentary advantage to jerk his wheel to the right and onto the exit. The SUV couldn't react in time and rolled past the ramp, followed immediately by the sound of tires screeching and the sight of the vehicle fishtailing as the driver slammed on the brakes. Keith was at the end of the ramp as he saw the reverse lights come on as the driver through the Tahoe in reverse. He had to back up nearly 200 feet to reach the ramp, and all the while cars were blaring their horns and swerving to avoid an accident. The driver obviously didn't care; he was hell-bent on continuing the pursuit and killing his prey.

"I think you may have hit and wounded one of them," Keith said. "Whatever it was, it gave us the few seconds we needed. Hold on, I'm going to pull off the road right up here, so get ready to grab your stuff and run. And listen, the woods are going to be pitch black, but once we're set up out there and we put on the night vision goggles you'll be able to see almost as well as during the day. Just be careful, those goggles take some getting used to."

"You think these guys will pursue us rather than wait for help?" she asked.

"I think they'll definitely follow. They can't afford to wait around for the cavalry, and on top of that they're trained soldiers, probably Special Forces like every other asshole we've come up against. That means they're overestimating their own abilities and underestimating ours. We use that to our advantage. They probably have no way of knowing that we have night vision equipment or our silenced H&K carbines. They're expecting us to be lightly armed."

"So do we stick together or split up once we hit the woods?" Loren had no idea what he was planning, but they had to make the decision quickly since Keith was already slowing down and moving towards the shoulder.

"We'll go into the woods together, but then we'll split up once we find a place to set up our ambush. We'll look for trees or some other natural cover and we'll wait until we see these guys approaching and then take them out. Just make sure that you wait until you have a clear, clean, kill shot."

Keith hit the brakes hard and the car skidded to a stop. They both jumped out and headed into the woods, thankful to at least be able to use a flashlight as they started in. Both of them moved quickly, Loren with the flashlight and Keith with the duffel bag. "Quick, take the gun and your night vision gear. Let me help you put it on." Keith flicked off the flashlight as he helped Loren into the gear, and he could already hear the big SUV approaching at a high rate of speed.

Keith adjusted the straps quickly on her headgear and helped her to a large tree about 20 feet away. "OK, this is where we make our stand. You ready?"

Loren nodded, frightened at what she was being asked to do but understanding that this was an 'us or them' situation. Kill or be killed. "I'm ready. Go." She wanted to add 'I love you', just in case, but it was too late. Keith was already moving away.

Keith put on his night vision gear and quickly found a place to set up. The Tahoe was screeching to a halt out on the road, and he heard both car doors slam and the two men yelling to each other. Keith was completely concealed behind two good-sized rocks, and the muzzle of his H&K was pointed right in between them. Which way would these guys approach? Would they stay together and come straight into the woods, or would they split up and try to move in a more serpentine fashion, making it harder for Keith and Loren to target them? Were they even expecting Keith and Loren to be trying to make a stand, or would they assume that they were doing their best to escape -- like most reasonable people would? All of these thoughts kept flooding Keith's mind, and he had to will himself to focus.

Hanover and Adams started moving to the woods, each carrying a large Maglite flashlight, their Glock pistols, and a rifle slung over their shoulder. The rifles were similar to the H&K's that Keith and Loren carried but were AR-15's from a different manufacturer. They even shot the same type of ammo as the H&K's and they had silencers. No matter how you sliced it, there was enough firepower out here in the woods tonight to cause a lot of death and destruction.

Once they were a few yards in, Hanover and Adams started moving apart to cover more area. They stopped every few steps to listen, but other than the sounds of nature the woods were completely silent. They were able to communicate without any problem, both of them using a compact over-the-ear headset and a voice activated microphone that sat low across their throat. "I'm going to move a little further down and to my right," said Adams into his communicator. "It looks like there is a pretty thick stand of trees and some large rocks about 50 yards ahead. Let's kill the flashlights."

"Be careful," admonished Hanover. "We don't know for sure that they're running. They may be set up and waiting on us."

"God, let's hope," Adams answered, his own sense of invincibility and cockiness still very much intact.

Keith and Loren could both see Adams and Hanover clearly, including the fact that their pursuers were carrying rifles slung on their shoulder in addition to the pistols they were carrying. Damn. Keith had hoped that they'd only be armed with pistols since those weren't as useful and accurate at longer ranges. Or at least that's the theory, he reminded himself, since these guys are probably both expert marksmen. Hanover started moving in Keith's general direction, making his way a little bit off to Keith's right. Adams was now within 50 feet of Loren's position and heading straight towards her. That made Keith realize that he had to take action, and quickly.

Taking aim as best he could, Keith prepared to squeeze off a shot at the man closest to him. He hoped that Loren was ready, too, as she would need to take her guy down the second she heard him fire. Even with the silencers, Keith knew, the guns were far from silent. If Loren hesitated after Keith fired his weapon, the man closest to her would have time to react and get off shots of his own. He hoped, even prayed, that that wouldn't be the case. 'Steady, wait for it…' he whispered to himself. He squeezed the trigger and an agonizing scream went up from Brad Hanover.

"Brad!" Adams yelled, and before he could utter another sound a bullet smashed into his face just below the right eye and exited out the top of his head. He crumbled to the ground.

Hanover was screaming in pain, cursing loudly. Keith had intentionally shot him in the knee rather than killing him, hoping that maybe he could be coerced into providing information about Foster and his work. Moving quickly, Keith secured Hanover's weapons and then pointed his gun barrel right between the assassin's eyes. "Lie there and shut up. Another sound out of you and I will pull the trigger. Do you understand?" Hanover just nodded.

"Loren, are you OK?" Keith called. "I'm over here." He heard her moving through the woods toward him.

"Yes, I'm OK. The other one is dead." She kept walking in Keith's direction, able to make out him and the man lying on the ground. When she finally reached him she tore off her goggles and threw her arms around his neck. "I'm glad you're OK. I heard the scream and it scared the hell out of me."

Keith kissed her and held her, never moving his gun from Brad Hanover's forehead. For his part, Hanover just lay there moaning, nearly passed out from the pain. "I decided to just incapacitate our friend here, at least for now." Keith looked back down at Hanover. "Whether or not he lives or dies in the next few minutes will be entirely up to him." His tone was deadly serious, and that fact was not lost on Hanover.

Keith picked up the flashlight that was lying beside the injured man and shone it on his face. "I recognize your face from the personnel files. You're Brad Hanover, right? One of Foster's primary operatives?"

"Yes," Hanover said in a voice shaking from both pain and fear. "I work with Foster."

"So you're familiar with the little taste of hell that Foster has given us this week? Trying to kill us, killing my friends and co-workers, killing my dogs? Were you involved in any of those operations? And let me warn you, if you lie to me I will shoot you in the other knee right now."

"I was aware of them, but I wasn't a part of them. Foster ordered those hits. I just work on the computer system and analyze data from our monitoring."

"You're just an analyst, huh? But you're out here shooting up the highways like this is the Wild West."

Hanover swallowed hard, trying to fight the incredible pain that was wracking his body. "We weren't looking for you, we just happened to stumble on you at the toll plaza. We were on our way to Foster's house to meet him and help find out how you had gotten into our computer system."

"So Foster is at his house then? Who else went with him?"

"Bob Manning and Les Mattox. Then Warren Adams and I were heading over there after shutting down the computer system." He tried moving slightly to ease the pain, but it only exacerbated the agony causing him to moan loudly. "Tonight was going to be it, for all of us. We were all quitting tonight and walking away from Foster and DCG. We'd all had it with that psychotic bastard."

"And did Foster know this?" Keith asked.

"Yeah, he knew it. He and Bob Manning had a major blowup this afternoon, practically came to blows. That was the final straw for Manning, and if he walked out all of the rest of us would have walked right behind him."

Keith and Loren stepped back a few yards and discussed the situation for a few minutes, leaving Hanover alone on the ground, still writhing in agony. Deciding on a possible course of action, Keith approached Hanover again. "One more question: Do you want to live?"

"Yes, I want to live. I have a wife and a kid on the way." Hanover was telling the truth about being married, though Keith didn't know that his wife was pregnant since it wasn't included in his personnel file.

"OK, then here's the deal. This offer is good for one minute and it is 100% non-negotiable. If you don't accept, I'll just kill you now. If you do accept, then you'll be allowed to live so long as you do exactly, and I do mean exactly, as we ask. Got it?"

"Yes, I got it. What do you want me to do?" Hanover knew that his only chance of surviving and seeing his wife again was to do what Keith said.

"You're going to help us take Foster down, including getting us into your underground bunker and getting us every bit of information that is there with regards to 9/11. *Everything*."

"If it will help take that bastard down you don't need to make threats," said Hanover. "I want to see him taken down as much as anyone." He was being truthful and sincere. Working for Foster had always been a miserable existence, but in the past couple of weeks it had become intolerable.

"Good. You help us get what we want and we'll work with the federal prosecutors to request amnesty, or at least leniency, for you. It's much more than you deserve, by the way." Keith was willing to see one of the little fish get away so long as he was able to lead him to all of the big fish.

"I'll do what you ask. But tell me that you're going to get Foster first before going after the data, please." Hanover's dislike for Foster was palpable. "With his money and resources he could disappear forever. Don't let that happen. The data will still be there. Nobody can access it remotely, so until we go back there and physically fire-up the systems again, it's inaccessible."

Keith was OK with that plan, and in fact it fit exactly with what he was thinking. He asked Loren to keep an eye on Hanover while he went over and checked on the other downed man. He knew that Loren didn't want to see that kind of blood and gore, especially since she had been the one to pull the trigger. So far she seemed to be holding up pretty well, at least as much as he could tell here in the dark, but he had no doubt that the reality of killing another human being was going to hit her hard sooner or later. Probably sooner.

There was no doubt that Adam's was dead, Keith saw. There was a ghastly exit wound out of the top of his skull that left way too little to the imagination. He grabbed the weapons that Adams had brought into the woods as well as his car keys, identification, cell phone, and military communications equipment. Keith wanted to make sure that there was no chance that the body could be identified, at least not quickly. As he took a look around he realized that it was fairly unlikely anyway; they were far enough off the road that the body wasn't likely to be discovered for quite a while. That is, as long as the police didn't come this way looking for the cars involved in the shooting back on the toll road.

When he got back to where Loren was standing guard over Brad Hanover, he said, "Can you take all of these weapons and throw them into their SUV? Here are the keys. I'll stay here and keep an eye on our friend."

"You don't want to take our car?" she asked, obviously not yet thinking clearly again.

"No, we don't want to take ours. It will attract too much attention with the missing back window and all of the bullet holes and dents. I'll try to pull it off the road a little further up ahead and hide it in the woods. At least their car has all of its windows intact, even if does look like they've been playing bumper cars with it."

"Maybe we can use the Tahoe to get back over to Dulles Airport and pick up the other rental car that we parked there the other day," she suggested.

"That's what I was thinking as well. We'll just leave their Tahoe in the airport lot." Keith waited while Loren carried the guns to the SUV, and when she got back he had her keep her gun trained on Hanover.

"Alright, here's how we're going to do this," Keith said, addressing Brad Hanover. "I'm going to help you up and help you to the car. Once you're in the car I'm going to bind your hands behind your back and try to take a look at your wound. If you try to make any kind of move I'm going to have Loren shoot you in the other knee? Got it?"

"Yeah, I got it. There's a first aid kit in the SUV; it should have something in there to clean the wound." Hanover was in too much pain to even think about trying something. Even if he managed to overpower Keith -- and he had no doubt that he could kill Bryant even with his injured leg -- he knew that Loren would shoot him before he could make any type of escape. He certainly was in no condition to run away.

"Anything in that first aid kit for the pain?" Keith asked.

"A few syringes of morphine. Enough to take the edge off, at least for a while."

Keith thought that through. "That's probably preferable to dropping you off at a hospital, at least at this point. The ER docs would have to contact the police if you show up with a gunshot wound."

Hanover replied, "That's right. You can't take me to the hospital yet, and besides, you may need my help with Foster. Just give me enough morphine to take away some of the pain but not enough to be incoherent. Once we get Foster I can have you contact a doctor here in the Leesburg area that will take care of my leg, no questions asked. He provides services for lots of military and clandestine missions so we don't have to worry about him going to the police."

Keith realized that this was one tough son of a bitch. Most men would be screaming and crying in pain from this kind of wound. The bullet had shattered his kneecap and essentially blown the whole knee and surrounding tissue to hell. The wound was so bad that Keith doubted that doctors would be able to save the leg, probably requiring amputation above the knee. "Alright. That's how we'll play it. Let's get you up and get you to the car." Keith let Loren hold his weapons and take a few steps back, just in case. He then reached down and pulled Hanover up using the arm and shoulder opposite the injured knee. Hanover gritted his teeth and grimaced from the pain and the exertion, but he did not scream, did not cry out.

It took almost 10 minutes for them to make their way slowly back to the SUV, both men needing to stop several times to rest along the way. Despite the chilly weather they were both covered in sweat by the time they reached the car. It took considerable effort to get the injured man up into the car, and Keith decided that the easiest way to do it, and probably the most comfortable method of transport for Hanover, was to fold down the back seat of the Tahoe and allow him to lay stretched out with his feet facing the rear tailgate. Keith found the first aid kit and looked through it, quickly realizing that this kit was well-stocked enough to practically perform minor surgery. In addition to the five syringes of morphine he found several different types of antibiotics, a surgical needle and thread for stitching up wounds, and all manner of large pads and gauze for taking care of wounds both large and small.

"Where do you want the morphine injection?" Keith asked.

"Let me have the needle and I'll do it myself. I'm a pro," Hanover said with an attempt at humor, even though it didn't come across real well as he bit down on his lip and gritted his teeth in pain. As soon as the morphine hit his system he felt some measure of relief, though it was still far from comfortable. "In the kit there is a vial of broad-spectrum antibiotics. I think it's Amoxicillin. Let me have a few of those, too."

Keith waited while Hanover took the pills, and Loren stayed about 10 feet away. Her attention, or her gun, never wavered for a second. She knew that she didn't want to kill anyone else, especially if this man was going to help them, but she would do what had to be done if he made a move against Keith. Pills taken and morphine injected, Hanover placed his hands behind his back and waited while Keith secured them with duct tape. He sat on the edge of the back cargo area and slowly lowered himself onto his back. Keith went around to the rear passenger door and reached in, grabbing Hanover under the shoulders. 'Hold on, I'm going to pull you all the way in as gently as I can." It took everything Keith had to pull this almost 240 pound man all the way into the car. For his part, Hanover barely allowed a sound to escape his lips, though the pain had to have been excruciating.

"Loren, if his legs are all the way in go ahead and close the tailgate." Keith then fashioned a pillow for the injured man's head using his folded up jacket. Not exactly a room at the Ritz, he realized, but the best that they could fashion out of their current situation. "Why don't you drive," he said to Loren, "and follow me up the road a bit to see if I can find a place to bury the Taurus. We need to hurry up and get out of this area before somebody comes by, especially the police."

They only had to drive about a half-mile before Keith saw a small dirt road off to the right, probably a right-of-way for the utility companies, he reasoned. He turned off and drove the car about a hundred yards off of the highway before turning the wheel and driving as far into the woods as he was able to go before getting stuck. Keith looked quickly around the car and made sure that he had all of their personal belongings out of there; he would simply report the car stolen to Hertz in the coming days. Jogging back to the SUV, he hopped in on the passenger side and Loren headed off towards Dulles Airport.

"Let's take the back roads to the airport. We don't need to go through the toll booth with a car shot to shit and a wounded man in the back," Keith said. What he didn't say, mostly out of fear that he would jinx things, was that he could almost see the end in sight.

Chapter 26

"They came after us right after we hung up with you earlier," Keith was explaining to Patrick and Jeff. "Totally by chance. They just happened to see us as we were stopping to pay a toll."

"What about the local police? I would have expected every person on that road to be dialing 911 as fast as humanly possible," said Patrick.

"Most of them were scrambling for their lives, I imagine. Luckily the traffic wasn't super-heavy like it would have been during rush hour, otherwise some innocent people might have gotten killed. But to your point, I assume that some people did in fact call the police, but fortunately we didn't see any before we got out of the area. We heard some sirens in the distance, but nothing too close, thankfully."

"And you both are OK?" Jeff asked, truly concerned.

"Yeah, we're fine. Just a few scratches from running through the woods, that's about it."

"And what, may I ask, is the latest carnage and body count?" asked Patrick. "I'm almost afraid to ask."

"One bad guy dead, one wounded that will live. Both of them are from the personnel file that you looked at earlier. The dead guy is Warren Adams, and Brad Hanover has a pretty serious injury from where I shot him in the knee, but like I said, he'll live."

"What did you do with them?" A reasonable question from Jeff.

"We left Adams in the woods, took all of his guns and ID. Hanover is here in the car with us." The silence made Keith and Loren smile. They knew that Patrick and Jeff were probably both hyperventilating on the other end.

"Tell me you're kidding, please," said Patrick.

"No, I'm not. In fact, Mr. Hanover has been convinced to assist us in bringing down Colonel Foster. Let's just say that there's not a lot of love for Foster among his once-loyal troops."

"And you think you can trust him?" Jeff asked.

"Not totally, but it's a chance I'm willing to take. He knows that if he crosses us I'll not only kill him but also his pregnant wife," Keith said by way of a bluff for Hanover's sake. "But I don't think we have to worry about him. Right now I'm only worried about getting to Foster while we still can."

"So where are you now?" Patrick wanted to know.

"We just picked up our other rental car from the airport and then dumped their SUV where hopefully no one will find it for a while. We're about 3 miles from Foster's house and heading there now." Keith was anxious to get there, but at the same time he was apprehensive. Not just because of the possibility of more violence, though that possibility was certainly there. He was more apprehensive because he realized that he didn't really have a plan for what they should do when they got to Foster's. How would they get in, or how would they lure him out? How could they avoid a shootout in the middle of the neighborhood, an event that would draw God knows how many police and SWAT units to the scene?

"And the plan is still to try to take Foster alive? As much as I hate to think about all of the blood that has been spilled and all of the people that have been killed because of this mess, you know that it's probably a lot harder to take him alive, right?" This from Patrick.

"Yes, that has crossed my mind. But fortunately, so has this: with Brad Hanover willing to cooperate with us and the authorities, including getting us access to their headquarters and their computer network, we don't really have a need for Colonel Foster. As much as we'd all like to see him stand trial for what he's done we know that we can't take that risk. For all we know he'll be pardoned or someone will manufacture evidence to implicate someone else further down the food chain. Bottom line, I have no problem whatsoever if Foster doesn't survive our little encounter, but I'm not going to take him out from a distance. It's got to be up close and personal. I'm going to talk to him face to face, eye to eye, and make sure he understands what he has cost me, what he's cost this country. I want him to feel something when he dies." He didn't have to add that he'd also make sure that Foster felt a tremendous amount of physical pain before he died. *'He'll be begging to* die' Keith thought to himself.

They talked a few minutes longer, and then Keith hung up as they were approaching the security guard station at Foster's community. The ruse set up by Patrick and Jeff worked perfectly, and they were through the security area in short order. Hanover was in the back seat, his injured leg stuck straight out and his mind barely able to remain conscious after his second hit of morphine.

Keith pulled the car over to the side of the road as they turned onto Foster's street. He turned in his seat to address Hanover. "Hey, wake up. Wake up, damn it!" Keith reached back and shook the injured man's shoulder and he finally opened his eyes, awake but far from fully coherent. "There's a car parked in front of Foster's house. See it? Whose car is it?"

Hanover tried his best to focus. Finally, he said, "Bob Manning's. He and Les Mattox left the same time as Foster."

"And they came to Foster's house to see if his PC was the one logged into your computer systems?"

"Right." Hanover was answering the question but his eyes were once again closed.

Loren asked, "They must have been here for close to two hours. Why would Manning and Mattox still be here? After what happened today with Alexis, then finding out that she obviously betrayed him by setting us up with remote system access, you would expect Foster to be there by himself, wouldn't you?"

"Yeah, I agree," replied Keith. "Add to that the fact that his men were all pissed at him for the security breach and planning to leave his organization, and you have to figure that Foster probably didn't ask them to stay over for high tea."

Keith turned back again to Hanover. "What can you tell me about security at Foster's house? I know that he has an alarm system, but how sophisticated is it?"

"I've never been to his house, but I've heard him talk about it before. Supposedly has cameras focused on the front door, the back door, and the garage doors. Beyond that I don't know."

An idea was starting to form in Keith's mind. "Hanover! Wake up! Look down there at Foster's house. Is that his car in the driveway?"

"Yeah, that's it," was the slightly slurred response.

"What are you thinking?" Loren asked.

"It might be a little bit crazy, but hear me out. We have Hanover call Foster and tell him that he's wounded, tell him that he needs help. That will hopefully draw Foster and the others out, because they'll either want to come save their man, or…"

Loren interrupted, "Or they'll want to come kill him to make sure that he can't talk." She thought about it for a second and smiled up at Keith. "That just might work, if we can keep him coherent enough to pull it off."

"We'll have to try. We'll leave him in the car parked a few houses down from Foster's, then you and I will take up positions on either side of his house. When Foster and the others open the door to leave we'll be waiting in the shadows and force them back into the house at gunpoint, hopefully without having to fire a shot."

Loren nodded her agreement. "Let's see if we can get him to wake up enough to do this. He needs to keep Foster on the phone and hopefully too distracted to check his security monitors."

"Good point, especially since we don't know if his monitors are by the door or located somewhere else in the house." Keith realized that this plan was fraught with danger and uncertainty, but he couldn't think of any other way to get into the house short of storming the place with guns blazing. Having a full-fledged firefight in the middle of a residential neighborhood wasn't a viable alternative, obviously, so he had to rely on some sort of subterfuge. "I'm counting on the fact that Foster is probably going berserk waiting to hear back from Hanover and Adams. It's been well over an hour since they first called him to say that they had spotted us."

"Hanover, you with me? Come on, wake up," Keith said as he tried jostling the big man in the back seat. "I need you to call Foster. Tell him that Adams is dead and you're wounded and need help." Keith could see that he was still groggy. "Loren, hand me that bottle of water, please. We've got to wake his ass up and get him thinking straight."

Keith splashed some water on Hanover's face and practically forced him to drink some in an attempt to wake him up. When those efforts weren't enough he resorted to the one thing that he knew would overcome his grogginess: pain. Keith reached down and squeezed Hanover's leg just inches above his knee. Hanover's eyes flew wide open and practically burst from his head. He started to let out a loud, guttural scream but Keith managed to get his hand across the man's mouth. Even with the windows rolled up the scream probably would have been heard a couple of houses away if Keith hadn't stifled it. "I'm sorry that I had to do that, but I need you to wake up and stay awake. Got it?"

Hanover was almost whimpering as he cursed under his breath. The curses weren't so much directed at Keith as directed at the pain. "Yes, goddamn it, I got it. What do I need to do?"

"Call Foster and keep him talking. You need to draw him out of the house. Tell him you're wounded and Adams is dead, tell him Loren and I are dead, too. He needs to come get you because the police are crawling all over the area. You can fill in the details however you want, just keep him talking and distracted and draw him, Manning, and Mattox out of the house. You with me?"

"Maybe pretend like your passing out, incoherent. He'll want you to stay conscious so that you can lead him to you. That should keep him on the phone, hopefully, even as he leaves the house." Loren made this suggestion, and as she looked over at Keith he nodded his agreement.

"OK, I can do that," Hanover said, still struggling to form the words but, at least, seemingly more awake. "Take the flashlight, and when you're in position and ready for me to make the call, flash me a couple of times. I'll reach up and turn the interior light on for a quick second so you'll know that I got your signal."

Keith liked Hanover's suggestion, and he realized that it was something that he wouldn't have thought of. He would have been standing down by Foster's house, risking detection, and would have had no way to know if and when Hanover made the call. Obviously, the man was experienced in field craft. Keith reached behind Hanover and removed the tape bindings from his hands. "Alright. Here's your phone. You need anything else before Loren and I head on?"

"No. I'll be OK. Just watch Foster. He's a tricky bastard." Hanover wanted to tell Keith that Manning and Mattox were decent guys that would gladly turn against Foster and testify about his operation, but he decided against it. That was partly because he figured that it would just fall on deaf ears at this point; Keith was obviously out for blood and revenge. The second reason, though, was more selfish. He was prepared to cut a deal to save his own ass.

If others looked to make the same deal then his value was diminished, to say nothing of the risk that others might try to place blame on him to save themselves. No, at this point, it was every man for himself, he realized. Even if those that went down in flames were friends.

Keith and Loren grabbed the duffel bag with the two H&K carbines and extra ammunition and made their way down the street. They only had to walk past a few houses to reach their destinations, but they both felt completely naked and exposed. "Let's head over here in the shadows of these trees," Keith whispered as they reached Foster's house. "Sure wish these 'McMansions' had more than three-quarter acre lots so the houses wouldn't be so close together."

Loren agreed. With houses practically on top of each other they had to worry even more about being seen by a neighbor or having a dog start barking as they moved around the houses. "I'll take up a position here behind these bushes and wait for your signal," she said, lifting one of the rifles from the bag and clicking off the safety. "If you go to the other side of the house you should be able to get a line of sight for Hanover to see your signal." She reached up and gave him a quick hug. "I love you," she whispered.

"I love you, too. Be careful, and if things get too bad and you need to get out of here, go. Do whatever you've got to do to stay alive." He kissed her quickly and was gone. He quietly made his way around the back of Foster's house, being careful to keep to the shadows. That was made all the more difficult because, like so many newer communities across America, this one was built on former farm land with very few trees. What passed for trees in most of these yards wouldn't provide cover for an anorexic thirteen year old, much less him. He was able to see that there were lights on throughout Foster's house, but the curtains were pulled in every room. That was actually to his advantage, since even though he couldn't see in, it was more important at this point that they not be able to see out as he made his way into position. Once he reached the far side of the house he took a minute to survey the situation. The house next door was less than 50 feet away, but at least there were a dozen or more tall Leland Cypress trees that either Foster or the neighbor had planted as a privacy barrier that provided him with some shielding. He had never been so happy to see shrubbery in his life.

Stepping up to the corner of Foster's house, he aimed his flashlight back down the street and pressed the button twice, quickly. He prayed that Hanover would still be conscious and acknowledge the signal. A couple of seconds later Keith saw the return signal, a quick flash, not even a second long, from the overhead light from the rental car. *'Thank God'* he whispered to himself. He set down the flashlight and then slowly, quietly, lifted the H&K rifle from the bag. He clicked off the safety and tried to steel himself for what he might be facing when Foster and the others, all trained military and certainly armed, came out that door.

It was less than a minute later when he could hear Foster yelling. He couldn't make out what he was saying, but he was sure it sounded as if Foster was yelling into the phone at Hanover, probably trying to keep him conscious and talking. Foster's voice was getting closer to the front of the house, and Keith guessed that he was moving towards the front door. Taking a chance, particularly with the amount of light flooding out of the front windows and from the front porch lights, he started slowly inching his way towards the door. Then he froze as he heard the distinct sound of the deadbolt on the front door being unlocked, and he knew that in any second the door was going to open. Foster was still talking, practically yelling into the cell phone. Suddenly the door flew open and the Colonel stepped out. Keith didn't waste any time or any motion. It took only a second to close the gap between them, and before Foster had even seen him Keith hit him a vicious blow to the back of the head with his rifle stock. Before Foster even hit the ground Keith had turned his gun towards the house and was bursting through the door, ready to shoot anyone and anything that moved. But then he was shocked, almost frozen. The room was empty. Where he had expected to confront Manning and Mattox there was no one there. He stayed low, his eyes scanning the room for any movement, his ears attuned for the slightest noise from anywhere in the house.

Loren was in the door only a couple of steps behind him, her gun also at the ready. Thinking quickly, she told Keith, "I'll cover you from here. Get Foster back in the house and close the door before someone sees what's going on!"

"Stay down, they could still be anywhere in the house." Keith moved quickly, turning off the lights on the front porch and then grabbing Foster under the arms and dragging him back into the house. He grabbed Foster's cell phone from the front porch and then quickly ducked back into the house, closing and locking the door behind him. Picking up the cell phone, he said quickly, "Hanover, you there?"

"Yeah, Rambo, I'm here. I saw you clock that cocksucker a good one."

"You did good work, too, obviously. Thanks. You sit tight there in the car and we'll be back out as soon as we can. No sign of Manning or Mattox yet, by the way. Maybe they're still in the house somewhere waiting to ambush us."

"More likely they're already dead," Hanover said. "Foster knew they were going to quit on him, maybe he just decided to eliminate them a little sooner. I never trusted the bastard, personally."

That didn't make sense as far as Keith was concerned. Foster wasn't stupid. He needed all of the help that he could get until this was over. What would he gain by killing them now? "We'll be back to you in a bit." Keith hung up the call and turned to Loren and said, "Keep an eye on him. I'm going to check out the rest of the house."

Loren nodded her head, but she was so frightened that she was shaking. She had hoped that the adrenaline would make her brave, but all it did was keep her alert and moving forward. Hopefully that was enough.

Keith moved forward, still trying to keep low and using whatever was available for cover. A chair here, a sofa there. He wondered if pieces of furniture would really offer him any protection if and when the bullets started flying. He doubted it; real life isn't like they portray it on TV. He peered around the corner to the hallway leading back towards Foster's office. From there he could see into the kitchen and towards the family room. All clear. He slowly made his way down the hall, then reaching the doorway, swung his rifle quickly into the room while crouching low. What he saw made him gasp, completely startled by the unexpected sight. There, lying on the floor not 10 feet away, were the bloody corpses of Bob Manning, Les Mattox, and, most shockingly, Alexis Foster. He moved quickly to check the bodies to see if they were all, in fact, dead, but with the amount of blood on the bodies and on the floors he knew that they had to be. Still, mindful of the little ruse that he and Loren had staged with Alexis just a few hours ago, he checked anyway. Dear God, what was Alexis doing here? Patrick and Jeff had told her to leave, to run and not come back. Surely she had listened, right? Why in the name of God would she have risked coming back here?

Keith headed back to the living room and told Loren what he had found. She was stunned, questioning, as he did, why Alexis was even at the house. Her eyes started to tear, both shocked and saddened at the thought of Alexis, this smart, lovely, brave woman, being brutally murdered by her own husband in her own home. Even though they hadn't met Alexis before today both Keith and Loren felt a special connection and bond with her. Maybe it was the fact that they had a common enemy, or that they found themselves reluctant combatants in a battle that they had not sought to fight.

Keith brought them back to reality. "I'm going to pull this dining room chair over here and sit him there, and then we'll tie him up and have a little talk."

Loren was apprehensive about how far Keith might go in his 'little talk' with Foster, but she didn't say anything. The hatred that she felt for the man lying on the floor burned every bit as hot in her as it did in Keith.

It took Keith only a few minutes to drag Foster over and set him in the chair. He was smaller than Keith had imagined, certainly a lot smaller than all of the members of his team and the killers that he had sent on their trail. Probably a man with a serious Napoleon complex, he thought to himself. Blood ran down the Colonel's head from a nasty gash where Keith had struck him, the kind of gash that would probably require almost 20 stitches to close. Too bad for Foster that he would never live to see the inside of a hospital. Checking him quickly for weapons, Keith found one large semi-automatic pistol in a shoulder holster and a smaller pistol in an ankle holster strapped to his right leg. Once again using duct tape, Keith quickly secured Foster's arms and legs to the chair, and, planning ahead, he tore off a piece to place over Foster's mouth to keep him from screaming loud enough for the neighbors to hear. And Keith knew that he was going to make Foster scream.

"Loren, will you run upstairs and see if you can maybe find some alcohol, like rubbing alcohol, in their bathroom and bring it back down here? If you can't find that, maybe see if they have a bottle of bourbon or vodka or something." As Loren moved upstairs Keith went to the kitchen and his eyes quickly found the knife block sitting on one corner of the granite countertop. He considered his options and decided on a 6" boning knife. Long, thin, and razor sharp, there was no doubt that it would serve his purpose.

As he walked back into the living room Loren started down the steps, holding up a bottle of isopropyl alcohol in her hand. Seeing the knife in

Keith's hands startled her; she knew for sure that he hadn't brought that in to cut the tape binding Foster's arms and legs. He also had a large glass of water with him, and presumably that wasn't because he was feeling humane toward Foster and wanted to offer him a drink. More likely Keith wanted to make sure that he could splash some water on him to keep him conscious. This was not going to be pretty, she thought to herself.

Keith walked up to Foster and shook his shoulder, urging him physically and verbally to wake up. Foster didn't move. Keith slapped him a couple of times across the face, not hard enough to hurt him but enough to start to bring him around. Foster slowly started coming around. As his eyes opened and started to focus, the rage and the hatred were evident. As he started to scream Keith simply put the piece of tape over his mouth, further infuriating Foster but delighting Keith. "Hello, Colonel. We're finally meeting face to face, just like I told you we would." Reaching out to grab the bottle of alcohol, Keith slowly opened the bottle before Foster's eyes, then stepped behind him and poured a good amount on the deep gash on his head. Foster let out a loud, guttural scream and fought against his bindings, the tape covering his mouth barely able to suppress the scream. Keith looked him straight in the eye and just smiled. "You think that hurts, you bastard? We haven't even *begun* to show you what pain is." The look of rage and hatred in Foster's eyes was being replaced by another look. Fear.

"Let me tell you how this is going to work," Keith began in the same slow, calm, menacing tone that Foster had used on him. "You're going to die tonight, as I'm sure you already realize. How much pain you go through before I let you die is going to be totally up to you. You tell us what we want to know without jerking us around, making shit up, or wasting a lot of our time, and I'll let you die pretty quickly and painlessly. Just one quick bullet to the head." Foster started squirming and trying to scream again, the rage returning.

"But you're not going to do that, are you? You're just going to try my patience and try to prove that you're a tough little bastard, aren't you? I was sorta hoping that you would." Keith took the knife and made a quick gash in Foster's left thigh. Foster screamed, and the blood immediately started soaking through his pants. Just to make his point, Keith smiled at Foster, and then slowly started pouring alcohol on the wound. That caused the Colonel to scream and squirm even more, tears involuntarily starting to show at each of his eyes.

Loren walked closer to this monster that she hated more than she'd ever hated anyone in her life. "And you know the best part, Ed?" she said derisively, not even showing him the respect of using his military rank to address him. "There's no one to come to your rescue. No one. You killed Manning and Mattox, and we took care of Adams and Torres ourselves."

"Maybe he thinks Hanover will come be his savior," Keith said sarcastically.

Loren got down close to Foster's face. "Is that what you think, Ed? You think Hanover is going to run in here, guns blazing, to save your sorry ass? Wrong! He's waiting in the car for us, injured but alive. And he's begging for the opportunity to tell the world about you, to help take down everyone involved with 9/11." Foster's look of hatred and anger was unmistakable.

"So let's get started with our little conversation, then, Colonel, since we know that we won't be having any interruptions." Keith just sneered at him, showing his own contempt for the man. "I'm going to ask you some questions, and every time you lie to me or give me an answer that I don't like, I'm going to cut you. It's that simple. If that means that I only cut you once, that's fine. If I have to cut you 100 times and watch you sit there and bleed and cry and beg, that's OK, too. We've got all night." Keith knew that that last line was a lie. Hanover desperately needed to get to a doctor, and it couldn't wait forever. It's not that he was feeling any compassion for the man, it was simply a practicality. If Hanover was going to help them he had to be kept alive.

"OK, first question: who else did you conspire with to pull off the terrorist attacks on 9/11?" Keith reached up and slowly, almost gently, pulled the tape back from Foster's mouth.

Foster looked at Keith and Loren with nothing but contempt and practically spat out the words. "Fuck you, I'm not telling you anything! Do what you want to me, there's nothing you can do to make me talk. You fucking civilian!"

Keith just smiled. "God, I was hoping you'd say something like that." Foster had just given Keith the reason he was looking for to inflict even more pain. He took the knife and slowly cut him across both forearms, then made two or three fast slashes on each leg. Foster screamed and cursed, and Loren put the tape back over his mouth. Loren looked at Keith questioningly, wondering how far he was prepared to take this. His reply was simple and to the point. "I lied. One cut at a time just doesn't give that warm, satisfied feeling I was looking for."

As he looked down at Foster he saw blood soaking through his clothes in numerous places, and more blood starting to drip onto the floor. The look of rage and hatred had once again been replaced by a look of fear, this time coupled with a look of pain. "Let me try my question one more time. Who did you conspire with on the terrorist attacks of 9/11, other than Richard Newcomb, of course? We already know about him and he'll be dead by morning." A bluff, but Foster didn't know that. The look of shock on Foster's face, realizing that Keith had been able to identify one of the main co-conspirators, was obvious. It also had the added effect that Keith was hoping for: it knocked some of the confidence and bravado right out of the Colonel.

Foster still tried to put on a brave front, but Keith could already see a crack in the tough façade. This man was a soldier only by technicality. He wasn't a trained fighter like the men that he was giving orders to. He was nothing but a desk jockey who pretended to be tough. Even the toughest of men can be broken, Keith knew, so it shouldn't take too long or too much pain to see this asshole collapse in a heap. When Foster continued shaking his head 'no', refusing to talk, Keith didn't even bother to remove the tape. He simply took the knife and cut Foster slowly on both side of his face, each gash being nearly four inches long. Foster screamed with each cut, and blood poured from the wounds. Loren finally had to turn away, almost sickened by the sight and the screams of pain. As tears welled in Foster's eyes, Keith grabbed him by the hair and yanked his head to one side while pouring alcohol on the cut, then slammed his head the other direction and poured the liquid on that gash as well. The sounds coming from Foster were almost primal, the pain at such a level that he was almost on the verge of passing out.

"Don't you pass out on me, goddamn it!" Keith said as he slapped him back to his senses. "Let's try this again, for the *third* goddamn time. Who did you conspire with on the 9/11 terrorist attacks?" Keith reached up and ripped the tape off his mouth, not being the least bit gentle about it this time.

Foster was whimpering and sniffling, barely able to speak. He was obviously beaten, defeated, but still trying to hold on to some shred of dignity and resistance. "I'll tell you this much. In addition to me and Newcomb there were only a few others. Admiral Colbert, the head of NSA, was one, as was Bill McKenzie, the former White House National Security Advisor. Everybody else only knew their small part in the plan, but nobody else knew the whole plot." His head hung down, blood pouring from all parts of his body as if he'd been in a massive car accident.

Loren was writing down the names as Foster spoke them. Keith demanded the rest of the names of the other conspirators that, according to the Colonel, didn't know everything. He got them with only token resistance. That's one reason that Keith didn't believe that this was all of them, or at least not all of the 'big fish'. Foster was too willing to throw them under the bus. Keith looked at him and just smiled. Then he took the knife and made a quick slash across his chest, putting a gash that was every bit of twelve inches right across his pectoral muscles. Foster cried out in pain, his eyes bulging to the point of almost bursting out of his head. Keith grabbed him by the hair and screamed at him, practically nose to nose. "Do *not* fuck with me on this, Colonel, or I swear to God I am going to cut your goddamn eyes right out of your head! Now you tell me, *right this second*, who was running this operation and who authorized it or you are going to feel more pain than you ever thought possible. Do you hear me?"

Loren almost wanted to run over to Keith and pull him off, tell him that he was going too far. His level of anger, and the resulting violence, was every bit as bad as what Foster and his men had brought on them. Were they becoming as bad as the very people they were trying to stop? Did it matter at this point? She finally decided that she had to let Keith do whatever needed to be done, regardless of how bad this was going to get. They had to get the information that they needed, especially if there was any chance that what Foster knew wasn't stored on DCG's computer systems.

Foster looked up at Keith, the look in his eyes one of pure terror. Thoughts of resistance were quickly fading. "Bill McKenzie was the chief architect of the operation, I swear. He recruited Admiral Colbert, and he brought me in."

"And what about Newcomb. How did he fit in?"

"He was a major campaign contributor, and he'd worked in the past with this administration, and others, to get weapons or cash into the hands of our allies when conventional routes couldn't be used."

"You mean when you were breaking the goddamn law and couldn't risk Congress or the public finding out about it, right?"

"Yes. He's a rich man, and a loyal American who has done what his country's leaders have asked him to do in times of crisis."

"And what kind of fucking crisis did you have in 2001?" Keith was almost screaming again. "What the fuck did you have going on anywhere, what threats to our country, that would have Newcomb and the rest of you willing to kill 3,000 of your own people?"

"The rise of Islamic fundamentalism and terrorism around the world, you goddamn fool! While you and the rest of the idiots in this country ignored what was happening and kept your heads buried in the sand as the threat was growing, some of us were chosen to take action to save our country and our way of life. You should thank me, you pompous ass, not condemn me, for keeping you and the rest of the unwashed masses safe, safe to go about your mundane little lives with your SUV's and your affordable gasoline. Without us this country would probably already be in ruins, or at the very least you'd be paying $5-$10 for a gallon of gas and watching our country's economy go down the toilet." Foster was sitting up straighter, talking louder and prouder, convinced of the correctness, the necessity, of the mission he had taken on. Collateral damage be damned; that was the price that must be paid for the freedoms that we enjoy.

"And how did the President fit into this plan? Did he give the orders to carry out this plan?" Keith knew what had to be true, but could Foster admit to the truth? Did he even know the truth himself?

"The President had nothing to do with this, you fool! Had he known he would have surely tried to stop it." Foster was not the least bit convincing on this point.

Keith jumped up and put the knife right in the crease of Foster's right eyelid and once again grabbed a handful of his hair and pulled his head back. He was using just enough pressure on the knife to cut into the skin and cause it to start bleeding. Foster was about to scream from the pain and the pressure on the vertebrae in his neck, but Loren stepped in and once again put the tape over his mouth. "I told you not to lie to me, didn't I?" Keith threatened. "Do I have to start cutting your eye out, or are you going to tell me the truth?" He started moving the knife along the crease of the eyelid, drawing blood as he went.

Foster started trying to nod his head to show that he would tell Keith what he wanted to know. He was screaming that he would talk, but the tape muffled the words almost completely. Backing off of the pressure on the knife, Keith once again ripped off the tape. "Talk. And one lie, one hesitation, and this knife is going right into your eye."

"Please. I'll tell you," he said, choking back tears. "The President didn't know about the plan, I swear. He wanted something done, anything, to give him a reason to prosecute the war on terrorism. He'd run on a platform of 'tough on terror' and had criticized the lack of resolve and results that Clinton and the Democrats had before he came to office. He wanted to do better, but he needed a reason to go after the terrorists."

"And he assumed that the American people wouldn't support him simply invading a sovereign nation like Afghanistan or some other Muslim country without some catastrophe to rally around?"

"Of course. The American people don't have the guts or the goddamn attention span to take on something as nebulous as the war on terrorism. They needed something to prove that Al Qaeda and the Muslims wanted to kill all Americans and try to change our way of life." Foster practically spat these words out, his contempt for the very Americans that he claimed to be protecting evident. "It was left to people like me to help develop a reason to go after the terrorists and take this war to them, not the other way around. It had to be something to shake every American's sense of safety and normalcy. And we had to do it without the President's involvement."

"So basically, he wanted the reason to start the war but he wanted to maintain plausible deniability should the shit ever hit the fan," Loren said. "Typical chickenshit behavior for a politician. Give the orders without *really* giving the orders, let your minions do the dirty work, and then throw our men and women in uniform into the fight to go die for a cause that's a lie. There's a special place in Hell for assholes like you."

"I did what had to be done to keep our country safe, damn you! Don't you presume to judge me for carrying out the wishes of my Commander-in-Chief. Because of great men like him, and the men that I worked with on this project, our country is a safer place! There has not been another attack on American soil since we've stepped in to fight this war on terrorism!"

"Right. And yet you've managed to kill and maim thousands of our military and probably a hundred thousand or more Afghanis and Iraqis since this whole war on terror started, and the whole goddamn rationale for the war was a lie. The whole tragedy of 9/11 was a lie! You set up and planned the operation, then paid Al Qaeda to do the dirty work. And all so Bush could get an oil pipeline built across Afghanistan and so he could go after Saddam Hussein for trying to kill his father." Keith was livid.

"That oil pipeline that you are so quick to dismiss will help to guarantee affordable energy prices in the future for you and the rest of America. Especially at a time when the entire Middle East is a powder-keg and the robber barons of OPEC are constantly threatening to cut output and raise prices in a bid to blackmail the US or force us into poverty. You ungrateful bastard! You should be down on your knees kissing my ass for defending you and your way of life!" Foster actually believed his own bullshit.

"And I guess we should also thank you and your friends for giving Bush what he wanted since he started his run for the presidency, an excuse to start a war with Iraq and Saddam. The man comes to office with a personal ax to grind, and after six years it has cost all of those lives and all of those billions of dollars, and for what? To destabilize the entire region? To foster even more hatred of America and breed even more terrorists than we had before? You must be the stupidest group of white men to ever hold power in Washington." Keith reached out and, just because Foster had pissed him off, slashed him twice across the stomach.

Foster barely screamed this time, just hung his head and whimpered.

"Last question. Your organization is still together, monitoring internet chatter and websites about the 9/11 conspiracy. Why? Why so much time spent and money spent on this if you're so well positioned with the government bigwigs? Surely they could cover up anything that was discovered, or provide you with pardons if the shit ever came down." Keith was staring straight at Foster, but he had not yet reopened his eyes.

Finally the Colonel looked at Keith. "We couldn't afford for anyone, not Americans and certainly not our enemies, to figure out how this attack was carried out and planned. It would destroy the public's confidence in our President and our government, for starters. But if the rest of the world found out they would never trust America again. We'd become a pariah not just to the Muslim world but to the entire world. Even to our traditional allies."

Keith looked at Loren and said, "I think he's telling us the truth." He turned back and looked Foster in the eye, so close that their noses were almost touching. "At least part of it".

Keith stood up and pulled the tape back over the Colonel's mouth. Foster looked at him and pleaded, begged. "You're not telling me everything, goddamn you. Apparently just cutting you isn't getting your attention any longer. Let me try this." With that, Keith stuck the knife deep into the Colonel's left arm right where the shoulder and arm meet, a place where there are a bundle of muscles and tendons and nerves that can cause unbearable pain. As he stuck the knife in and dug and twisted it around, Keith hissed at Foster, "This is for killing Lowell Westbrook and David Ward and his wife and son, you piece of shit." Foster was practically howling under the tape, tears flowing and his breath coming in short gasps. He was on the verge of passing out once again.

Loren was shocked at the viciousness that Keith was displaying, but she knew that they had to continue. The end was near, or at least she prayed it was.

"Last chance, Colonel, or you're going to lose that eye, maybe even something more valuable to you." Keith touched the knife tip to his crotch, and Foster quickly got the picture.

Foster held his head down once again, crying almost uncontrollably beneath the tape. He was broken. Any further resistance was futile and he knew it. He welcomed death, would give anything right now if he could have a gun to take his own life. He just needed the pain to stop. Keith removed the tape from his mouth, and he slowly tried to look up through the tears and the blood. "We kept my team going out of necessity."

"What kind of necessity?" Keith asked.

"The necessity of having to plan for our next attack on America," Foster said, whimpering.

Keith and Loren were shocked into silence. They looked at each other, totally disbelieving. Whatever they had expected to hear from Foster, this was certainly not it. "Tell us about it."

"We have been planning another 9/11 attack for next year on the seventh anniversary. It was going to be even bigger, more audacious, than the first 9/11 attack."

"Why in the name of God would you do another attack on Americans? Haven't you already gotten what you wanted, the so-called War on Terror? What the fuck else could you possibly want to accomplish that requires more people, more Americans, to die in another terrorist attack?" Keith was incredulous, to say the least.

"Because the American people have short memories, that's why. They still remember 9/11, or so they claim, but they've already forgotten the bigger lessons of that day. Now all they do is bitch about the lines at the airports, the inconveniences, or the civil rights of terrorists and enemy combatants. They've forgotten what's important, namely, keeping America safe from Muslim extremists. We're planning to send America another wake-up call." Foster managed to give his smug, arrogant smirk even through the blood and the pain.

"You sick, demented fucks. And why next year on 9/11? Why not this year, or the year after? Or any other day, for that matter?" Keith thought he already knew the answer, but he wanted to hear it from Foster.

"We could do it any day, but 9/11 already holds a special place in America's memory. This will just reinforce those memories and ensure that it becomes a national day of focus for keeping America free from terrorism for years to come. As far as why next year, that's pretty simple, actually. That will be just a couple of months before the next presidential elections, and our actions will ensure that the electorate stays focused on the most important issue in this election and every election, namely, keeping our country safe. They'll clamor for more and tougher laws from our President and the conservative members of Congress, and we'll oblige. All you liberal, pansy-assed people that would have voted Democrat for president and members of Congress will get slaughtered when the majority of Americans get out and vote for a truly conservative ticket. Congress will go back to a Republican majority, and the White House will stay Republican. 'The way God intended', as I like to say."

"You're insane, totally certifiable," Keith said, almost disbelieving what he'd just heard. But in his heart, he knew that what Foster was telling him was true. Christ! "So what was the plan? How were you going to top 9/11/2001?"

"It was easy, really. I'd say much easier than the first one, in fact. The lawmakers in this country are so stupid, so concerned with civil rights and the cost of securing our nation and our borders that they still let virtually 100% of the cargo that goes on commercial planes get loaded onboard without inspection. We were going to have packages containing military grade plastic explosives placed on 25 planes from American, European, and Asian airlines and then have them detonated within hours of each other all over the globe. Regardless of where the plane was traveling to or from, there would be 150-200 or more passengers on each plane, most of them Americans."

"And I suppose these planes would have been blown up out over the ocean where there would be no chance of finding survivors or any significant evidence, just like the Muslim terrorists planned last year when they tried to smuggle on liquid explosives?" Loren asked.

Foster gave a bloody smile. "That's where you're wrong, little lady." He seemed almost pleased with himself. "We wanted people all over the world to be able to see these planes get blown up right before their eyes, not just on TV but even right there in front of them at the airports. Every one of the planes would have been destroyed when they were within 100 feet of touching down at their destination airport, and with a little bit of advance warning to the media, having live camera feeds in place was not going to be an issue."

Keith and Loren again looked at each other, just totally stunned by the coldness and callousness of Foster and the other conspirators. Blowing up all of those planes, killing all of those people, and all broadcast live like it were a reality show. The loss of life, and the damage to the American psyche from such an event, was unimaginable. For that matter, the financial impact on the airlines and the economies of America and, conceivably, other countries around the world, was immeasurable. Keith didn't even want to get into that debate with Foster. He knew that, if asked, Foster would simply write it off to 'the price that must be paid for freedom' or some other meaningless platitude.

"Watching you die is going to be a pleasure," Keith said to Foster in a calm, low voice. "It's going to be an even bigger pleasure when we take down everyone involved in this plot with you, from the President all the way down to the lowest operative we can find. The Congress, to say nothing of the media and the American people, are going to have a field day with this." Keith took a breath to calm himself, and then slowly reached over and put the tape back over Foster's mouth. "Before I let you die, though, I have one more thing for you." Foster's eyes again showed terror, and Keith just smiled at him. Then, reaching back, he plunged the knife as hard as he could into the Colonel's right thigh, all the way to the hilt. He then twisted the knife back and forth as hard as he could, slashing and ripping and tearing flesh and muscle all of the way through the leg. Foster was screaming beneath the tape, his eyes pleading, and his body thrashing harder than ever. For a minute Keith wasn't sure that the chair was going to stand up to the violent motion. "This is for killing my dogs, you cocksucker." He twisted the knife some more, doing everything he could to cause as much pain as was humanly possible. "You go after my house or my boat or other possessions, I might eventually get over that. They can all be replaced. But you go after my friends, my family, the people I love, they can't be replaced. And my dogs were a part of my family. You killed them, along with six other dogs belonging to other families that are out there grieving right now for the loss of a pet, a family member, that they loved and lost because of your psychotic madness." Keith pulled the knife from Foster's leg, blood running off of the knife and out of the wound on his leg. "I should cut your eyes out, just leave you here to die and rot like that. It's better than you deserve, better than you did for them."

Keith stepped away and turned to Loren. She was crying, partly from the stress and what it had done to them both, but mostly for the loss of their beloved dogs and the memories that were coming flooding back. Keith held her and had to fight hard to hold back the tears himself. "I'm done," he said quietly to Loren. "I can't do this anymore. I've got to end this. Now."

"I know," she said. "We need this to be over."

Keith sat back down across from Foster and pulled the tape off. "We're done here, Colonel. I told you that when we were done you were going to die, and I meant it. If we just sit here long enough you'll die from loss of blood, but to be honest with you, I think there are better ways to die." Keith's voice was low and calm; all earlier signs of rage and hatred were gone. Now he was simply negotiating a contract, a contract in which one of the parties could choose how to die. "You tell me how you want it. Consider it a dying man's last request."

"Please, just shoot me and get it over with. A bullet would be welcome at this point." Foster could not wait to escape the pain.

"I have a better idea. I'll give you one of your pistols with a single bullet in the chamber, then I'll free your right hand and let you end life on your own terms. Is that acceptable to you?"

"Yes." Colonel Ed Foster could not think of anything more to say or anything more that needed to be said.

Keith put one bullet into the small pistol that Foster had earlier carried in an ankle holster. Before handing the pistol to Foster, he turned to Loren and said, "You might want to step around the corner a bit, just in case he decides to take one last shot at us." He didn't expect that to happen, not for even one second. He just wanted to spare her from having to see a man end his life this way. Why it should matter now, after all of the death she'd seen in the last week, to say nothing of the torture she'd witnessed tonight, wasn't really clear. Keith just wanted to do something to protect her, to shield her. He wanted her healing to start now. His would have to wait.

Reaching down with the knife, Keith cut the duct tape holding Foster's right wrist and then handed him the small pistol. Stepping back out of the way a few steps, Keith kept his eyes on Foster as he slowly brought the gun up towards his right temple. Foster kept his eyes closed, then Keith heard him whisper slightly, "God forgive me," and then he pulled the trigger. The bullet shattered his skull and tore through his brain, shredding tissue and nerves and blood vessels as it went. Death was instantaneous and, Keith was sure, a welcome relief for Colonel Foster. Keith felt almost as much relief himself.

Loren came back into the room and looked down on the bloody, dead corpse that was Colonel Foster. "May God *not* have mercy on his soul."

"We should head on out of here. It's time to start to blow the top off of this conspiracy and put all of this behind us." Keith took her hand and headed for the door. They turned and looked back one last time at the house that had seen four brutal deaths in one day, hoping to God that it would be the last brutal death they would ever have to witness in their lives.

Back in the car, they checked on Hanover. He'd actually slept since talking on the phone to Keith earlier, but now that he was awake the pain was back. Loren offered him another one of the morphine syringes. "It's all over," she told Hanover. "Foster is dead, and so are Manning, Mattox, and Alexis Foster. Just like you predicted."

"Let's get you to that doctor and get that leg taken care of," Keith said. "We need to get you healthy. There's a lot of work still to be done."

As Keith started the car he picked up the cell phone and called Patrick and Jeff. Patrick answered. "It's over," Keith said simply. "Foster's dead, so are all of his people. And we have the whole story, past, present, and future, from him. Hopefully we can find the documents to corroborate what he said, but either way, we're ready to blow this thing wide open."

"Thank God," said Patrick. "Listen, I'm on my way to you now. I'm just boarding a charter jet in Charleston and I should be there in a little over an hour. I have a surgeon friend with me if we need to transport Mr. Hanover out of there and to somewhere safe. Regardless, let him know that I will be his attorney and he is not to speak to anyone, got it?"

"Yes, I got it. That's a great idea, by the way. He's providing us with the name, phone number, and address of a doctor in the area that does work for a lot of the spy agencies, so we're going to take him there to get checked out before you get here. His leg is in pretty bad shape, and we can't afford to have anything happen to him. We'll plan to meet you when your plane lands and then take your doctor to check on him as well, then he can decide if Hanover needs to be admitted here or flown somewhere else with you."

"Sounds like a good plan. By the way, Jeff and the rest of the core team are on their way to DC as well. We're going to want to plan an announcement about what we've uncovered, hopefully get it posted on our website tomorrow. The sooner we get this information out there the better for everyone, the less chance they have to try to stage a cover up. To say nothing of making your lives safer once this is out there in the public domain."

"That sounds like a good start, but I think we may want to engage the mainstream press in this as well. Let them get this out on the front page of the *Washington Post*, get this information out there and let it start shaking things up."

"Don't worry, Keith. All of the leaders of LTBT agree with that 100%. We've always pledged that we don't care where the truth comes from or who gets credit for it; the important thing is that it *is* found and it's shared with the world. Thanks to you and Loren we now have something to share, and we intend to live up to our commitment."

"Just wait until you guys all get here and we get to fill you in on some of the details that Foster gave us. It will probably curl your toes," Keith said with a smile, the first smile he'd had in quite a while.

"I can't wait," said Patrick. "Meet me at the charter terminal at Dulles when we land. I'll call you as we're coming in. We'll figure out what to do with Mr. Hanover and then we'll start putting our heads together on a communications plan. The other core leaders will be arriving at different times throughout the night, but we can at least get started on a plan. I have to tell you, I'm so excited and nervous my stomach has butterflies. I've been waiting for this day since we founded LTBT."

"I can imagine," said Keith. "It's time, thankfully, to share the truth with the whole world. Let's hope the world learns its lesson and we never see such events again."

"Amen to that."

Epilogue

THE STORY OF THE CONSPIRACY of 9/11 was published on the Let the Truth Be Told website the next day, though the story was far from complete at that point. The photos that Keith had taken on the York River and Chesapeake Bay, when he and Loren had been attacked by Foster's men in both boats and helicopters, were downloaded thousands of times over the ensuing days. There were still thousands of documents and tens of thousands of man hours of research still to be done before all the facts would be known, as LTBT was sure to point out with each new posting. By unanimous agreement of the core leaders of LTBT, as well as Keith and Loren, a reporter from the *Washington Post* was picked to have the exclusive story for the mainstream media. It was, unquestionably, the biggest story since Watergate. In fact, Watergate paled in comparison. The Post started with a ten part series, and as more and more information came out it was expanded five-fold. There were more pages dedicated to this story, and more money spent on reporter research, than any single story in the history of the venerable newspaper.

As the story first came to light the public outcry was deafening. The new Democrat-controlled Congress immediately called for hearings, with every committee jockeying for position and media coverage as they explained why they should be the ones to right this grievous wrong. The Republicans tried their best to head off any talk of hearings or, God forbid, impeachment, but as the story continued to unfold it became clear from the vitriolic response from the American people that any politician that stood against bringing down anybody and everybody involved in this scandal would pay with their political life. Even in the traditionally 'red' states there was a roar from the people demanding the heads of those involved with the 9/11 plot, many dyed in the wool neo-cons finally realizing that the end didn't always justify the means when it came to the practices of 'their' President and administration.

The reaction around the world was almost as swift. World markets took a major short-term hit as fears of war, or at the very least an increase in the frequency and severity of terrorists attacks, shook the financial world. America's enemies pointed to these revelations as just one more example of how the Great Satan shows their hatred and disrespect of the Muslim world and our desperate need to continue the 'crusades' to crush Islam. Even our staunchest allies condemned us, justifiably. There were even threats of sanctions against the US from Britain, France, Germany, and other members of the European Union and countries from the Asia-Pac region because the attacks of 9/11 had killed many of their own citizens. There were demands for the accused to stand trial at The Hague for war crimes and crimes against humanity. Those same allies made no secret that they wanted the President to be standing in the gallows along with the other defendants.

Perhaps most ironic was the impact on the leadership of Al Qaeda and other terrorist organizations. There was a leadership purge as the members of these organizations rose up against their leaders upon discovering that they had been hired, unknowingly, by the very Americans that they were trying to destroy. They had been used to do the American government's dirty work in order to bring the American military into a fight to kill their Muslim brothers. The leadership of Al Qaeda, including Osama Bin Laden, were either killed or kidnapped and delivered to Western forces in exchange for the sizable rewards that the US had established. The American administration tried to deflect growing criticism of their role in the 9/11 conspiracy, as well as a growing cry for their collective heads, by pointing to the fact that Bin Laden and his deputies had been killed, captured, or replaced by more moderate elements. The new leaders of Al Qaeda showed just how moderate they were just a few days after having millions of dollars in reward money wire transferred to their accounts: they conducted near-simultaneous attacks on the American embassies in Pakistan, Indonesia, Saudi Arabia, and Egypt. More than 500 Americans lost their lives in the attacks. The new leader for Al Qaeda, Muhammad Al Salah, promised more attacks saying, "The American war on terrorism is dead. It is now *our* war on America. Thank you, Mr. President, for helping the Muslim people focus their anger and their calls for *jihad* on their true enemies: Americans, Jews, and all infidels, but Americans before all others."

Brad Hanover recovered from his wounds but had to have his leg amputated just above the knee. He was grateful beyond words to still be alive, and he never wavered in his commitment to help with the investigation into 9/11. His wife gave birth to his first child, a son, just days after being released from the hospital. In the coming months doctors plan to fit him with a titanium prosthetic limb to replace the lost leg. As Keith had promised, he fought tooth and nail with a reluctant federal prosecutor to get Hanover full immunity from prosecution. The prosecutor finally escalated the request all the way to the US Attorney General, and, as expected, the AG tried to sit on it or find every reason to deny it. He knew that the information that Brad Hanover was going to uncover was going to implicate a lot of people in this administration. He, thankfully, was not one of them, but he felt an incredible sense of loyalty to the President and his people. Keith expected as much. When he saw that things were being stalled, he fed that information to the *Washington Post* reporter that was leading the paper's investigative team and, *voila!*, it was front page news in the next morning's edition. Public outcry and congressional pressure from both sides of the aisle were heaped on the AG's office, so by the next day Hanover had his full pardon and immunity signed, sealed, and delivered.

Congress rushed through legislation mandating that the inner workings of Destiny Communications Group and any and all relationships between Colonel Ed Foster and other members of the 9/11 conspiracy group be thoroughly investigated and the results made public. Of course, they preferred that they be made public in front of one or more congressional committees and in front of the television cameras. After all, they were the ones stepping in to see that justice was done and that America was put back on the right course. Or, at least, that was their spin on things. The legislation passed through the House and the Senate without a single dissenting vote; any vote against it would have been political suicide. Millions of dollars was appropriated for the investigation, and Dr. Keith Bryant was announced as the unanimous choice to lead the investigation on behalf of the American people.

Keith and Loren took leave from UVA for the rest of the semester to help guide the initial investigation, and the core leaders of LTBT made their first public appearances and acknowledgment of their role in the investigation.

They also stepped away from their own jobs to help lead the investigation in partnership with Keith and Loren. While new discoveries were being made almost daily, they all realized that an investigation of this magnitude would take at least six months, if not more. They all arranged sabbaticals to last from January until at least mid-summer. This was a once in a lifetime experience, a higher calling. It couldn't be ignored, not only for their own insatiable curiosity or because they felt it was their duty, but because they truly believed that they were the ones best equipped to bring The Truth to the people.

⌘

December 28, 2007 Charleston, SC

KEITH AND LOREN STROLLED DOWN the lovely downtown area of Charleston, SC in the early evening. Even this time of year, with the cold weather, Charleston was a gorgeous town. Of course, it didn't hurt that the Christmas decorations were still in place and there were still a lot of tourists around, giving the place a nice, festive air. As they walked hand in hand down the street, enjoying the weather, the ambience, and finally having a semblance of normalcy back in their lives, they spotted their destination.

"There's Magnolia's. I haven't eaten there in years, but from what I remember it's one of the best restaurants in Charleston." Keith led Loren by the hand, and then held the door for her as she entered and approached the hostess stand.

"Hi, we're with the Treadwell party. Party of seven," Loren told the lovely young hostess.

"Yes, of course. The rest of your party is already here, if you'd like to follow me, please." The hostess led them to a round table in a private section near the rear of the restaurant.

Patrick Treadwell was the first to see them and stand to greet them, and then the rest of the group, Jeff Anders, Karen Richardson, Tony Winchester, and Terrell Jackson, stood as one. There were handshakes and hugs all around. This group of exceptional people had bonded closely in the short time since their paths first crossed. Sometimes tragic circumstances have that affect.

"So Keith, Loren, we're so glad that you guys could make it down here to God's country to join in a little bit of post-Christmas celebration," Patrick announced. He poured them each a glass of wine and then topped off the glasses of everyone at the table.

"A toast, if I may," announced Jeff Anders, standing up from the table and raising his glass. He had everyone's attention. "Here's to Dr. Keith Bryant and the lovely and talented Ms. Loren Davis. Without the two of you the secrets of 9/11 may well have remained hidden forever, and those responsible would have continued to live their lives as free men while 3,000 of their fellow Americans lay dead and their families grieve. It has been a pleasure and an honor - though at times scary as hell- to work by your sides."

Everyone got a laugh out of Jeff's last line, but they all clinked glasses with a rousing, "Here, here!" from all.

"And one more thing, while we're toasting," said Patrick. "The leaders of LTBT have talked amongst ourselves and we have come to a unanimous decision. We would like to invite the two of you to do us the honor of serving on the leadership team of Let the Truth Be Told along with us. You have both proven yourselves to be not only incredibly resourceful in the field but also incredibly brilliant in your thinking and your situational analysis."

"We all agree that you will both make a fantastic addition to our team. Please say that you'll join us," implored Karen Richardson.

Keith and Loren were pretty stunned. "And you're unanimous on this? No hesitation or reservations on anyone's part?" Keith asked.

"Absolutely positive," said Terrell. "Until we met you guys we never had any plans to expand LTBT, nor did we think there would ever be cause to. But after working with you we see how much value you bring, and, quite frankly, we're much better with you than without you."

"Yes, I agree," said Tony. "You complete me," he said, pretending to wipe away a tear as he did his best imitation of Tom Cruise's character from *Jerry McGuire*. That cracked everyone up.

"Of course, we'd love it if you could manage to get through at least some period of time without shooting anybody," Patrick said as he laughed. Everyone else laughed with him.

Keith and Loren looked at each other and nodded their agreement. "I guess if you want us both, you got us!" Loren said. "We really love you guys, and it means a lot to us that you want us to join your team."

"This is really neat," joked Keith. "It's like getting invited to sit with the cool, popular kids at the lunch table." The laughter continued.

As the laughter died down, Keith spoke up again. "One question, though, on a slightly more serious note. Now that we've cracked the code on 9/11, what are your plans? After all, LTBT was founded to ferret out the truth behind 9/11. With that done, now what?"

Jeff smiled. "A reasonable question, we admit. But we've been looking around at all of the possibilities for our research after we wrap up 9/11, hopefully this summer. The way we see it, there are plenty of conspiracies to investigate, especially since this administration came into office. We're thinking about looking into some of those. Maybe none of them are as big as 9/11, but on the other hand, maybe without the other conspiracies the road to 9/11 would have never happened."

"Such as?" Loren questioned.

Tony responded. "Well for starters, the whole election debacle of 2000 and how that got settled. Or, more recently, when the new touch-screen voting terminals were brought online but, mysteriously, were built without leaving a paper trail of the votes. And of course, my favorite part, when the votes get challenged in court the ruling comes down on the side of the voting machine manufacturers who just happen to be major contributors to the Republican Party. The courts, Republican controlled, of course, rule that the computer source code is a proprietary trade secret and the manufacturers can't be compelled to share it."

"Or, how about the whole intelligence snafu that was used as a basis for leading us into the Iraqi war? Remember how we were told that there would be WMD and how the Iraqis were trying to acquire the necessary components for nuclear weapons? Karen added.

"Or, as a scientist, my personal favorite," said Terrell. "The constant and consistent twisting of science in the name of this Administration's 'beliefs'. Whether or not those beliefs were true or just their pandering to the Christian right is still to be determined, but look at the constant stream of scientific fact that they have disavowed, if not outright lied about or changed in official reports. Like their stance on global warming and climate change, or their stance on Creationism when they tried to disguise it as 'Intelligent Design'. They have set the cause of science, to say nothing of the concept of separation of church and state, back a hundred years. Cretins."

Keith held up his hands in surrender. "OK, OK, I got your point. LTBT is not out of a job." Everyone laughed, not just at what Keith had said but at the passion and fervor that they all had for uncovering the truth and exposing people, especially people in power and positions of trust, for liars and frauds and cheats. "Loren and I would be honored to join you. Thank you for having faith and trust in us, but most of all, thank you for your friendship." Keith hoisted his glass in a solute to the team.

"Here, here!" they all shouted again.

"Just one more thing," Keith added with a smile, knowing that those words usually sent a chill down the spines of Patrick and Jeff since it usually meant that he was on to some other dangerous, possibly reckless, adventure. 'We'd like you all to keep the date of Saturday, June 14th open on your calendars for a little celebration up our way in Charlottesville."

"What's the occasion?" asked Tony, being clueless in a way that only a man could be. Karen Richardson looked over at him and rolled her eyes.

Loren held out her left hand, showing the beautiful diamond and platinum engagement ring that Keith had surprised her with on Christmas morning. "We're getting married!" she practically squealed with excitement.

"And we'd like you all to be there," Keith added. "It will be the most special day of my life, I don't mind telling you, and for such a special day we have to surround ourselves with special people."

"I think this calls for a huge celebration!" Patrick said enthusiastically. He signaled for the waitress. "Three bottles of Cristal, the best in the house! Our friends are getting married!"

The group stayed until closing time, and by that time they'd had plenty of wine and champagne. Keith and Loren took a carriage ride back to their hotel, the Ansonborough Inn, and for the first time in more than a month they slept without the nightmares that had plagued them both since the night at Colonel Ed Foster's house. Maybe they were past it for good, maybe not. All they knew is that they would get through it together and learn to live with what they'd done and the things that they'd seen. If that meant seeking professional help, so be it. If it meant begging God for forgiveness, they would do that as well. They had come to believe the old saying *there are no atheists in a foxhole*. What Dr. Keith Bryant and Loren Davis, soon to be Mrs. Loren Davis-Bryant, had learned took that one step further: *There are no atheists once they survive the foxhole, either.*

LaVergne, TN USA
08 October 2009

160189LV00001B/124/P